Praise for *Last Flight for W.*

This book is a real winner. I read it until 1:00 last night—couldn't put it down.
—US attorney (name withheld due to regulations)

Bartholomew has created something very special here. It will keep you wondering until the end.
—Major Patrick Collins, US Army, retired

My only question as I finished the manuscript was, "Who is going to play the lead role? This has movie written all over it!"
—Professor Philip Hoffsten, MD, MACP

Absolutely brilliant!
—Robert Allison, MD, MACP

The complexity is phenomenal, but the writing is so good you don't get lost.
—Phil Meyer, MD, FACP

I just have one question. What are you doing still playing doctor?
—Jim Peitz, professional stunt pilot and FBO owner

Last Flight *for* Whiskey Mike

A Novel

KENNETH BARTHOLOMEW

PAGE PUBLISHING, INC.
Conneaut Lake, PA

First originally published by Page Publishing 2019

ISBN 978-1-64628-414-6 (pbk)
ISBN 978-1-64628-415-3 (digital)

Printed in the United States of America

Prologue

He wedged his torso firmly against the rock, then his legs and arms. Now he would have to sleep. It would be difficult, but his body needed it. The temperature was 90 degrees Fahrenheit and would climb steadily for the next eight hours. He did not know how long he could take it, but what he did know was that he had to stay out of the August sun or he would bake like the rocks a few feet from his face. His bones would rebel in less than an hour, but he would deal with that later. For now, he needed sleep.

How had he come to this? How had he gotten here from his perfectly safe life, now seemingly an eternity away? And how did the president of the United States come to be in the predicament he was in?

Suddenly, movement above his head startled him. He craned his eyes upward. Just within his peripheral vision, he caught the unmistakable shape of a rattler slithering down the rock toward him. He could lie perfectly still, and it would pass by, unalarmed. Still, his hand reached down and retrieved his knife, opening the blade deftly with a flick of his thumbnail. He waited until it passed just below him. Then slowly hefting a large rock in his left hand, he brought it down, pinning the snake to the earth as he severed its head. It wasn't that he was afraid of the snake; he just needed the protein. He quickly skinned and filleted the still-writhing reptile then draped the pieces carefully across a south-facing rock. By nightfall, it would be baked to perfection.

Chapter 1

The Call

Thursday, 10:00 p.m. EDT, Virginia airspace

Scott already regretted his decision to come to DC as he applied slight right rudder and rolled the aircraft gently to intercept the glideslope, raindrops the size of cherry tomatoes hammering the windscreen relentlessly. He had promised Rachael he would quit, and here he was again. Every time Gary called, Scott caved in. It was no wonder she was mad. He powered back and began his descent through the clouds to the Leesburg airport.

"Potomac Center, November 6-8-7 *Whiskey Mike* established on the ILS," he said as he keyed his push-to-talk switch on the yoke.

"6-8-7-*Whiskey Mike*, Potomac Center, you are cleared to land runway 1-2, Leesburg."

"6-8-7-*Whiskey Mike*, cleared for 1-2 Leesburg," Scott confirmed the instructions along with his aircraft's tail number then switched off the intercom music. Although Beethoven's Ninth was his favorite, the stormy night had begged for the Sixth.

Outrunning the low that had built all the way from Idaho, he could see nothing but white wingtips against white clouds. Centering the needles on the Instrument Landing System glideslope indicator, Scott brought the aircraft down in a controlled approach that would allow him to break out of the clouds 800 yards from the runway with only 200 feet of safety between him and the unforgiving earth.

Correcting his heading two degrees and easing back on the power, he glanced out the window but saw nothing but white in the glare of the landing light. He corrected his heading with subtle pressure on the rudder pedal, tracking 120 degrees to line up with runway 12. He double-checked that his landing gear was down and locked, the three green lights reassuring. Suddenly, almost magically, flashing approach lights appeared through the dense overcast, and the runway lights were centered in his windshield.

Chopping the power, Scott floated *Whiskey Mike* gently onto the runway, the rubber barely complaining as it kissed the pavement. Taxiing to the tie-down area, he powered down as a tall, lean man in a black suit under an oversized black umbrella walked to the wing's edge. Scott opened the clamshell door, and the steps fell open automatically.

"Dr. Piquard, I'm Sam Davies, Secret Service. President Brady asked me to escort you to the White House. I'll take your bags."

"Thanks." Scott swung down his duffel and his flight bag, then exited, and quickly locked the door. "And thanks for the umbrella. This rain is going to be with us for a couple of days."

"Roger that. I've been watching the forecasts," Davies said as they hustled to the door of the fixed-base operator. "It's one of those systems that we only see once or twice a year. It will cover the country from here to the Rockies. Good thing you got out of Idaho when you did."

Scott stepped into the doorway and held it open as Davies collapsed the umbrella and slipped inside. "Definitely. I had to pack and get out of there quickly after Gary called, and my wife is none too happy about it. You married?"

"Eighteen years. Three kids."

"Then you understand."

"Oh yeah!"

Scott walked to the counter and handed his keys to the night-duty lineman. "November 6-8-7 *Whiskey Mike*. Top off all tanks and check the landing light. It seemed to flicker when I was taxiing." He signed the work order as the attendant tagged the keys and placed them in a drawer with a dozen other sets.

Sam Davies started toward the exit. "There's a driver waiting, but I'll have to wipe down your bags for traces of explosives. Routine, you know."

"Knock yourself out, but the only thing about to explode after five hours in that cockpit is my bladder." Scott laughed as he headed to the men's room. Upon his return, he saw a frown on Davies's face as Sam fingered a microphone on his lapel. "I have a level one trace at Leesburg. Davies out."

"I'm sorry, Doctor Piquard, but I have a positive nitrate swab on your duffel. Probably a false positive, but we'll have to keep these bags for further inspection."

"Of course, and it's probably not a false positive. I load my own shells, and I use this duffel a lot. It could have traces of 4350 or Blue Dot. Sorry, I wasn't thinking. I left on such short notice."

They walked to the stretched Town Car waiting at the edge of the canopy as Davies fingered his mic. "ETA thirty minutes. Davies out."

"This leg room is great," Scott said as they started toward the city. They were more than forty miles from the White House since Scott had been required to land across the Potomac in Virginia due to the no-fly rules established after September 11, 2001.

"So you're Mr. Brady's best friend and personal adviser," Davies said. "Must be pretty heady stuff to have 'the man' call you to hang out."

"He's just Gary to us." Scott shrugged as the Lincoln sped toward the lights of the city, the newly repaired Washington Monument a white beacon in the glow of its floodlights.

"I suppose it's different, growing up together, going to school, serving in the army together."

"Exactly. We had planned to go to law school together, but I didn't like what I saw in my international relations major and applied to med school instead."

"Do you miss city life?"

"Not for a minute. That's why I chose the family medicine residency and moved back home. Doctors are sorely needed in small towns, and the further from the crowds and the traffic, the better."

"What brings you here tonight?" Sam asked.

"Sorry. Doctor-patient confidentiality, you know?" Scott laughed, but it was forced—the hazel eyes suddenly narrowed, the powerful jaw suddenly set.

The late hour had thinned the traffic, and soon the limo was crossing the Potomac at Theodore Roosevelt Island, the Lincoln Memorial on their right, the Jefferson Memorial just barely visible through the mist, artfully situated on the south side of the Tidal Basin. They cruised down Constitution Avenue and, minutes later, were pulling into the private White House entrance. Scott could see the armed soldiers pacing the roof in the rain, the silhouette of the surface-to-air rocket launchers on their shoulders unmistakable against the eerie skyline.

"I'll just keep these bags for now," Sam said as they entered the security office inside the private visitor's entrance flanked by armed soldiers on all sides. "Empty your pockets completely, remove your shoes, and step through the whole-body scanner, arms out, and we'll clear you through."

Scott stepped into the millimeter-wave full-body scanner, spread his limbs, and stood motionless for a second. Then he slipped on his shoes and followed Sam between the busts of James Madison and George Washington up the ornate marble staircase to the first family's private quarters. Gary Brady, older looking each time Scott saw him, was standing in his private den silhouetted against the large picture window, gazing out over the rain-drenched grounds toward the Jefferson Memorial. With the handsome jaw, the perfect nose, the magnetic blue eyes, the subtle wave in his hair—not unlike Jack Kennedy windblown on a sailboat—Brady was perpetually camera ready. *Born for politics*, Scott often thought. But the sag of the shoulders, the furrows in his forehead, and the gray rapidly overtaking the temples betrayed the toll the office took on each inhabitant.

The shuffling footsteps brought Brady's attention back inside the room, and the pondering frown changed to the photogenic smile when he saw his friend. "Scott!" he nearly shouted, his pleasure obvious. "God, it's good to see you." He grabbed his hand and hugged him. Davies, satisfied, backed out and closed the door.

"You look great!" Brady said. "Solid as a rock," he added, gripping his bicep. "Still doing your early morning workouts, I see. Christ! Don't you ever age?"

"One day at a time," Scott answered, sensing the president's body language. A smile was what he saw; tension was what he felt.

"You made good time."

"Sixty-knot tailwind. A pilot's dream. But I'll probably pay on the way back."

"Sorry about the short notice."

"That's life. You should have seen the look on my new nurse's face when your call came. I was doing a vasectomy, and she just stood there with her mouth open and then walked back to the phone, muttering to the receptionist, 'The president of the United States calls, and he tells him he'll have to call back!'"

Brady chuckled. "Janet went to bed since we didn't expect you until later. Big day tomorrow with the Central America press conference. Can I get you a drink?"

"Crown-Seven sounds great."

Scott walked to the window and gazed out over the grounds, the rain still pelting the window and the flowers sagging under the oversized drops. "Rachael's not too happy with me splitting on such short notice. I promised to go to Coeur d'Alene with them for some school shopping, and the kids and I haven't been on the river since June. It's been crazy at the hospital, and until we get another partner, I don't see things changing. I'm beginning to think I'm the worst father in the world, and Rachael would probably agree this week. The kids were pretty disappointed until I promised them a Redskins game this fall. So this is going to cost you four tickets, and they'd better be good."

"Fifty-yard line, row ten?"

"That just might do. And speaking of fifty-yard line, what's new in Central America? Are we watching from the sidelines, or are we getting into this war?"

"There's chaos in Mexico and Central America. Their retreat is turning into a disaster, and we could have millions of people on our borders in the weeks ahead. We already have so many children coming across unescorted that we're running out of places to board them, and we can't deport them—it would be murder. And if the retreat collapses completely, those countries will default on billions in loans, which puts us right in the middle whether we like it or not."

"Then the rumors are true. The fighting is going that badly?"

"It's getting worse by the hour, and I have too many generals itching to jump in. You'd think they would have learned something after that never-ending debacle in Iraq and Afghanistan."

"Dobermans don't retrieve!"

Gary laughed. "That's why I call you. My advisers would have given me a fifteen-minute diatribe on the vagaries of decision-making in the face of multivariate analyses. You sum it up in three words." He looked at Scott. "Thanks again for coming. With you, I can say anything and not worry about leaks, political posturing, or insider games. I can't get that here. And be assured, I *will* call Rachael tomorrow and take compete responsibility for the short notice."

"Good! She never could say no to you."

Gary finished pouring the drinks and joined Scott at the window. "Cheers!" The clinking glasses were reminiscent of college days too long forgotten.

Brady looked out the window. "The last time we talked, I told you about the behind-the-scenes maneuvering in the conflict. When the northern countries formed their alliance and declared themselves the United Nations of Central America, their main goal was, ostensibly, independence from the outside influences that had kept them poor and backward for so long. But the constant conflict with Colombia and the increasing drug flow threatened the stability of the UNCA. The expanded canal has given Panama bargaining power, and she wanted Colombia out of her borders."

"I remember, but what brought Peru and Brazil into this?"

"Nobody saw that coming. When the skirmishing began, they thought it would be a short fight. No one saw Peru and Brazil jumping into the fray alongside their old enemies Colombia, Venezuela,

Ecuador, and Guyana. The raw manpower of Brazil alone was enough to stop the northerners."

"I thought you met with them?"

"I almost headed this off. I offered huge financial aid, which would also help buffer the Chinese and Russian influences, which prior administrations permitted to slink into our hemisphere without even a pip. This could have solidified the six northern countries and either forced Panama to cooperate or leave her isolated with no support on either side. I also floated a not-so-idle threat of our helping Nicaragua attain its long-sought dream of their own canal through Lake Nicaragua with locks big enough to possibly handle super-max ships. That project alone could lift Nicaragua out of its poverty position and put her eventually on a par with Panama."

"What happened?"

"Human nature happened. The northern alliance wasn't patient enough to wait, so confident were they in President Ambrosio's prediction of quick victory over Colombia. Ambrosio had stirred up such hatred of the Colombians inside of Mexico and the other countries that they all began to see it as their God-given duty to cleanse the area of the drug lords who run Colombia and control influence in southern Panama with money and fear. With Colombia neutralized, the unification of Central America could be realized. But when Mexico overextended herself and took a shellacking in the mountains of Colombia, things started to unravel."

"Go on."

"The leaders of Peru and Brazil were likewise made promises, and they knew that if Colombia won, the drug lords would target them for reprisal. They were in a bind, but they could use the continental issue in their own defense. Using the Monroe Doctrine philosophy and claiming sovereign domain of South American soil, they denigrated the northerners as land grabbers. Once Peru and Brazil joined the fray, the ill-equipped and even more ill-disciplined Mexican army, the bulk of the northern vanguard, began to crumble. Now they are taking heavy casualties, and the retreat is in danger of becoming an all-out panic."

"And they want Uncle Sam to fix it," Scott said as he paced around the room.

"Once the coalition began to crumble, the economic consequences emerged full scale. All the northern countries are on the verge of economic collapse. Default after default, like so many dominoes falling, will put many lenders at risk. It could mean bankruptcy for some very large banks, and not just Stateside. Many lender countries are very nervous."

"And all are pressuring you."

"You cannot imagine."

Scott walked back to the large picture window where Gary stood looking out over the grounds at the storm oozing from the west. They stood silently. In earlier years, alone in the mountains, they could sit for hours, watching the campfire, and say little, as secure in their quietude as they were in varied discussion.

Gary swirled his drink and took a sip. "When the fighting started going badly, there was a lot of pressure coming from inside the US to help the alliance financially. But worse than that, I have just learned that someone in our military—someone high up in our military—offered arms and aid if the fighting went badly for Mexico. They apparently promised someone, probably in their military as well as their administration, that the United States would never let her closest neighbor lose control of her own destiny. In actuality, the economic concerns were there all along. It was the military developments that surprised me."

"Are you sure they can be separated?" Scott asked.

"Explain."

"Maybe someone engineered it to fail. Maybe promises were made, but assets never provided for their success. Could someone engineer a disaster that you were forced to rectify? Do you let several huge banks fail, or do you put in the fix? If they fail, millions of people suffer. If you step in, the military solution binds Mexico, Belize, Guatemala, Honduras, and possibly El Salvador. Then how can Nicaragua and Costa Rica afford to stay out of the new alliance? And military control would essentially push out the Chinese, who have been stealthily taking over a major influence role with their billions in investments." Scott started to take a sip, then stopped short, and spun toward Brady. "Maybe that is why they strung themselves out so thin. What if they were waiting for help that never came?"

Gary looked at Scott and shook his head up then down. "Why didn't you accept that post I offered you? Then we could do this routinely."

"I would have lasted about twenty minutes in politics, and you know it. We've had this discussion before, Gary. You do it so well because you have exactly what I don't have. You have the ability to listen to all sides and carve out a middle ground that works. You are a master at that. I would not, could not, survive in Washington. I switched to medicine because I'm so concrete. When I diagnose a disease, I try to find a way to outsmart it. In my world, there's only one set of rules—the laws of nature. In your world, there are no rules. What works with one group of people doesn't work with the next. In medicine, you do what is right. In law, you do what works."

"Ouch!" Gary took a long sip of his whiskey. "So what do I do now? Do I give in to the pressures? We're practically broke, still recovering from our years in the Middle East and the housing and banking debacles."

"Who's pressuring you?" Scott asked.

"That's the million-dollar question. It seems like everyone wants us to get into the fracas, and yet no one wants to say it. Certainly, the banks are looking for a fix. The repercussions are staggering if those nations default, and if one defaults, the others will likely follow suit. But yesterday, CIA picked up a snippet of radio transmission that used the words 'Manifest Destiny' and 'Central America.' The only people who have used the words 'Manifest Destiny' are a few ultra-right, ultra-Christian congressmen."

"Maybe it's just all theoretical."

"It doesn't feel theoretical. The Army, Air Force, and Navy have necessarily stepped up maneuvers, virtually encircling the area with troops on land, sea, and air. Critics say that the numbers moved into position are far greater than the numbers needed to prevent a mass exodus of refugees across our borders, but we felt the numbers were justified. In the past three weeks, a number of comments by military advisers have hinted at how quickly we could be in control of the entire region down to the southern tip of Panama. No mention was made in that meeting of going on into Colombia—no comments about the moral objective of curtailing the drug trade—just hints about how simple it would be to stabilize the area now that there is chaos. Vice President King and members of congress, particularly the southerners, are all for it. They see this as the perfect chance to make a historic change in the course of the western hemisphere, like Teddy Roosevelt did when he helped engineer the war with Spain so we could take Hawaii and the Philippines and free Cuba. Some of my advisers whisper in my ear, tantalizing me, reminding me that all the great presidents took great positions and fought for them. They say I could be remembered as one of the greats if I could unify the hemisphere."

"You do know there is no room left on Mount Rushmore, don't you?"

"Very amusing," Gary said as he took another sip. "Now I have to figure out what is best. Engagement will cost thousands of lives and billions of dollars that the taxpayers will have to ante up. But the chaos that is about to erupt—is erupting—in Central America right now will probably cost billions of dollars and possibly millions of lives by the time the dust settles around the bankruptcies and the famine and potential civil wars. Hundreds of thousands of people will be flocking to our borders, so in the final analysis, it is our problem after all. Congress wouldn't build that wall. Now it will cost us twice as much to secure the border. Do we let them starve? Do we turn them back? Do we shoot them if they cross? Will it be less expensive in the long run to take the aggressive action? Will it work? Will I go down in history as a hero or a fool?"

"War and conquest and the greatness of a nation sound good in history books but ring hollow to a dead soldier's parents. How would you feel if it were Jeremy or David dying?" Scott walked over to the bookcases and ran his hand down a long row of books. "How many innocent lives have to be sacrificed? And for what? Will the financial losses really be that great?"

"They will be enormous, and the repercussions are expected to reach down to small, private investors, some of them retirees who are depending on this government to protect their life savings." Gary turned toward Scott. "Do we allow tens of thousands of people to be ruined when we have the power to prevent it?"

"Have you ever paid for a war?"

"No."

"Would it really be any cheaper to fight a war than to reorganize some bank loans?"

"I don't know."

"We spent a billion dollars a day to rid Iraq of Saddam Hussein, and all it bought us was years and years of war. Are you that anxious for a fight? Remember the lessons of Vietnam? Communism wasn't defeated with a gun. It was defeated with an idea. It decayed from within. That is what brought down the Iron Curtain, not eighteen-year-olds running through the jungles with M16s. Spend those billions on education. Then you'll have something!"

"Point made."

Scott stared deep into Gary Brady's eyes. "And you have to ask yourself just how much you are being tempted by history. If you take military action and it works, you could be hailed as one of the greatest presidents that ever lived. How much of that is weighing on your subconscious, Mr. President?"

The room was suddenly so quiet all they could hear was the roar of history echoing through the halls of the White House.

Brady's unblinking eyes stared up at him, and Scott realized from the silence exactly how close to the mark he must have hit.

Gary shook his head very slowly. "God, you make me mad!"

Scott took a long drink. "What's the vice president's opinion on this? He's a Southern boy."

"The South believes that if we don't stop the panic, they will be overrun with refugees, creating an economic burden they can't handle. They're already inflamed about the illegals flocking across the borders every night as it is. King walks the party walk and talks the party talk, but privately he is very aggressive. He has ambition to spare, and the right move at the right time would guarantee him the nomination in three years.

"The biggest problem with Marshall King is that he will tell one group one thing and the next group another, depending on the political winds. He is the penultimate politician. I suspected as much years ago, but we needed the South, and he delivered. I compromised to win the election. Now I have to deal with it."

"Politics," Scott said, shaking his head, unable to hide the sneer that usually accompanied that word.

Just then, the door burst open, and Jeremy and David Brady charged into the room, bypassing their father and swarming Scott, pumping his hand and pelting him with questions in an alternating staccato. "How's Chad? How's Stephanie? Did you run the Middle Fork this summer? Tell us about the time that wave pushed you straight up the wall in Rattlesnake Rapids. How's Chad's football team this year? Can we go chukar hunting this fall?" They both turned to their dad. "Please?"

"Whoa! Slow down. One question at a time," Scott said as he shook their hands and gave them each a hug. "David, you've grown another four inches, I swear. You are catching up to big brother. Watch out, Jeremy, what goes around comes around." He reached over and grabbed David's right bicep. "Been lifting too, haven't you?"

The fifteen-year-old smiled sheepishly and answered, "A little."

Jeremy, two years older but no longer a head taller, retorted, "A little, my butt. He lifts all the time. But I have to admit it has helped his soccer game a lot. He doesn't get pushed around like he used to. He was such a wimp." Jeremy grinned and punched David on the arm.

"Just remember, Jeremy," Scott said, "David is two years younger, and he always had to play against older kids. You pay the price for a while, but it makes you stronger in the end."

"Yeah, I know. He got tired of getting beat all the time. Now he's starting to make up for it. Kind of like Stephanie playing basketball against Chad and his friends. Man! She handles the ball like a guy. And both hands too."

"Yes, she is pretty good, I must admit," Scott said.

"Good?" David responded. "She could make our boys' team. And she's so fast."

"Geez, Davey, why don't you just write her a love letter and get it over with? You talk about her all the time."

"Yeah, well, you think she walks on water. Everyone knows you have her picture on your dresser," the retort was delivered quickly but not quick enough to hide the blush creeping up his neck.

Scott turned toward Gary and spoke quietly. "Testosterone on the rise, I see. They're definitely growing up."

"You flew your own plane out here, right?" asked Jeremy. "That is so cool."

"Way cool," added David. "And Chad has his private license already because *his* dad isn't worried he'll hurt himself."

"Hey, your dad has a lot to worry about—things you won't even understand until you are older. Besides, your dad gets to fly in big jets, while I just have a little prop job."

"Yeah, but you fly yourself, not sit in back and have someone else do it. And you kayak your own rivers and climb your own mountains and shoot your own bears. I wish we could live in Idaho."

"Maybe you can, when this job is over." Scott was talking to David but looking at his friend. He could sense that the barbs had hurt. "Maybe your dad and mom will have had enough of the city by then."

"We'll be in college by then," Jeremy added, "at Boise State, with Chad and that awesome football program."

"They are pretty set on going to college out west. They've had all they want of private schools," Gary said. "Okay, boys! Scott's had a long day. You can visit with him tomorrow." Brady ushered the boys out of the room.

Scott looked at Brady and said, "You are keeping something from me, Gary. I can sense it. We haven't really covered that much new ground. Why did you really call?"

Brady shook his head as he walked to the bar and splashed a half shot of whiskey over his ice. He took a sip and turned back to Scott. "I haven't told Janet. I don't want her to worry, but I need a fresh perspective and a totally confidential one. My life may be at risk, Scott.

Intel picked up some tidbits, but the pieces don't fit. You need some sleep, and I don't want to start into this tonight, but I want to run some things by you in the morning. The press conference is at noon. How about breakfast at seven thirty, right after morning briefing?"

"Sounds good. I'd like to go for a run before breakfast, but they kept my bags in security. I wear running shoes in the plane, but I need some running clothes."

Gary slipped into his bedroom and returned with a gray T-shirt, shorts, a pair of athletic socks, and light warm-ups. "You'll sleep in the Lincoln Room as before. That bed fits you. See you in the morning. And thanks again for coming on such short notice."

"Not a problem. With the rain coming, we should get a lot done since we won't be able to go anywhere or do anything exciting."

Chapter 2

Going for a Run

Friday, 6:00 a.m. EDT, the White House

Perpetually an early riser, Scott dressed and laced his shoes in front of the elegant Victorian drapes. The city lights glistened through the Chesapeake mist as it merged with the rainclouds in the dawning sky. The rain had steadily increased its tempo during the night. He slipped into the hallway and ran into Gary, who was preparing for his early morning briefing.

"You aren't running outside, are you?" Gary asked.

"I don't mind. It's warmer here than in the mountains."

"I would prefer you stay inside. There is going to be a lot of activity because of the press conference. Besides, I don't want Rachael mad because you came home with pneumonia."

"Where should I run?"

"Exercise room, basement level."

"How do I get in?"

"Take the elevator at your end of the hall to B level, and—Oh! You'll need an access card. Look, I'm running late. I'm not supposed to do this, but I'll give you this card to use for now," he said, reaching into his pocket and handing Scott a bright-red card key. "I'll get you your own card after breakfast. B level, to the left. See you later."

Scott stretched as he stepped into the elevator at the far end of the hallway, inserted Gary's card, and looked at the vertical line of buttons. His hand reached for the button with the big *B* as his eye scanned the column of buttons below the *B*. His hand wavered.

In grade school, two older bullies had terrorized the younger students with stories of a foul stench oozing from the dead bodies that littered a cave a few miles from town. They told of a wolf man who lurked near the mouth of the cave hungry for his favorite meal, unwary children. Most of the children had run home, cringing at every shadow, but young Scott had looked at young Gary, and without a word, they knew where they would be going that weekend. They knew the mountains around town like the backs of their hands, and they knew of the little cave. They had been there before but had only gone in as far as the ambient light would allow. Returning home Saturday evening, they reported that their candles showed the cave narrowing to a dead end a few feet past the first turn, the only bones those of a few dead bats. The older bullies slipped away in disgrace, their credibility dimmed by the new light shed on the Bat Cave.

Scott's index finger floated down, as if by a curious will of its own, to the button labeled "Security One." He was about to move his hand back up when his finger, unbidden, brushed the button. His ears popped as the elevator hurtled deep below the White House and came to a quick stop several stories down as the doors opened. Scott knew he shouldn't be here, should only take a quick look outside the door, and then go back up just as quickly as he had come, but because the curious kid in him had never left, he looked down the long hallways that stretched out of sight in both directions, took a breath, then stepped out. The door closed behind him, and the absolute silence engulfed him. He looked at the card in his hand and at the elevator door but turned, instead, into the long hallway filled with nothing but gray concrete and pipes.

His rubber soles made no sound as he stretched and walked down the empty tunnel, the dull fluorescents giving off ample light to see wire conduits and pipes of all sizes running to and fro the length of the endless hallway. The tunnels had been built as secure escape routes for people of rank and had grown under Washington like a giant spider web. The web branched in several places, but Scott stayed to the main tunnel so he could find his way back. He was about to do just that when he heard voices coming from a darkened doorway on his left, the signage declaring "Pump Room."

Unconsciously, the hunter in him emerged. Rolling his foot softly, he took a dozen silent steps and peered down a darkened hallway toward the muffled voices. The lights were out in this narrow shaft, and Scott froze when he heard the words "President Brady." Breathing silently, he stole a few steps until he felt the wall give off to the left, then slipped behind a vertical run of pipes, hoping that his pounding heart did not betray him.

As a child, Scott had never fully understood the saying, "My blood ran cold," but three times in his life he had experienced something like it: first, when his single engine aircraft threw a rod and died in flight; second, when he thought he had accidentally cut into a patient's vitreous humor during surgery; and this morning, when he heard the words "when Brady is finally dead."

Instinct urged him to bolt; instead he inched closer. It was difficult to make out the whispered words. He strained his ear as a basso profundo voice spoke.

"When King is president, everything will move forward as planned. He doesn't suspect anything. That way he isn't compromised. It's enough that we know how to handle him."

Another voice, quieter, spoke. "He is the perfect tool. He has already said privately that he would take the bold road, as he called it. I know him. He wants to make history as one of the great presidents with a larger vision that expands the greatness of this country, as God has intended. He will act, and the time is ripe. We can't wait for the next election."

A third voice, quieter still, now joined the conversation, but it was so muffled Scott could only catch fragments. "King will definitely…in history…Mexico…promised Molina…assured…our military…"

What are they saying? What was Molina assured? What would the military do? Scott leaned forward. The ambient hum of fans and water pumps muffled their voices. It was the perfect meeting place.

With the lights out, a camera system would be blind, and with the background noise, listening devices would be hampered as well. But why risk meeting here? Then it dawned on him. They were supposed to be here!

"The recruit is convinced that Brady is the Antichrist. His indoctrination could not be more complete. He is so committed that he is willing to die for this, which will be very handy. He believes that his reward will be in heaven. All we have to do is get him close enough. The gun is in place."

"I'll get him into the press conference with Campanelli's security pass. You will stand directly behind him and kill him the minute he kills Brady. Your friendship with King over the years, coupled with your hero status for killing the assassin, will assure the next stage. After that, there will be no stopping the cause."

"And the Lord shall crown his righteous warriors with glory!"

Scott clutched a pipe as a wave of vertigo spun his head. *Why?* An almost imperceptible sweat moistened his flesh as the vertigo passed. *Gary Brady is one of the most decent men this country has ever produced. Who would want to kill him?*

"The Americas will be one when our movement is finished. The greatest empire this world has ever known will be united under the one true God. Brady is not only too weak to take action, but his refusal to embrace Christ borders on heresy. He lets in the Jews and Muslims like there is a revolving door. That will come to a halt soon enough. King will close the borders."

"And the people will demand it when the FBI finds the Muslim literature we have used to decorate the recruit's apartment. There will be no question in anyone's mind that this is just another extension of al-Qaeda's many tentacles. They breed like rabbits and then want our wheat to feed the offspring of Hell. Let them eat their oil. When we cut off exports of food to non-Christian countries the scriptures will come true. 'Behold, I am sending on them sword, famine, and pestilence!'"

"Amen!"

"For the Brigade!"

"For the Brotherhood!"

"For the country!"

The three voices alternated and then intoned as one. "For the Lord!"

"Everything is in place. Turn the power back on three minutes after we leave. Our time is running out here, but our country's greatest time is just beginning. Unless the press conference is cancelled, the green light is on. We have the recruit sequestered in the major's uniform. He looks so much like Major Campanelli that security won't give him a second look. He'll walk right up to Brady like he is supposed to be here. You are permitted to carry, and you'll shoot him immediately unless the Secret Service beats you to it. Dead men tell no tales."

The third voice now spoke, again too quietly for Scott to hear clearly. "Our…boy…homecoming…marshal…parade in September."

Scott had not thought about his exit, so transfixed was he by what he was hearing. Now he had insinuated himself too deeply. He was crouching behind the pipes when the lights suddenly flashed on. The man facing his direction caught the movement. Scott's eyes met his momentarily, and as his eyes adjusted, he could see that all three wore high-ranking stripes and two were carrying guns. He did the only thing that came naturally. He ran.

A shot rang out. Concrete shattered from the corner and showered down on him as he flew out the door uninjured. He turned back the way he had come and bolted down the long hallway. His only thought was to warn Gary, but when another burst of shots rang out, he knew he was an easy target going straight away from the shooters. Sprinting to the next juncture, Scott turned left. He raced down this hallway, waiting for the shot that would take him down. Three shots echoed in a short burst, and he heard the high-pitched whine of bullets passing within inches of his ear. He came to another junction and turned right, hoping that he was not putting himself into a dead-end trap.

Suddenly, alarms were going off in all directions. He raced headlong down the next hallway expecting shots at any second, but just as he heard footsteps turning the corner behind him, he saw a door opening on his left. A Capitol Police sergeant stepped out, gun in hand, and turned toward the sounds. Scott didn't have time to think. As the man raised his weapon, Scott lowered his shoulder and slammed him into the wall with his full momentum.

The guard crumpled to the floor, grunting to catch his breath. His gun flew several feet down the hall, but his two-way radio fell next to the doorway. Instinctively, Scott grabbed the radio and launched himself through the doorway as two bullets struck the door. He bounded up the concrete staircase.

Scott's long legs took the stairs two at a time. Three, four, five flights up and still no exit. Finally, after several long flights, he saw a doorway. He also sensed his pursuers falling behind; they couldn't handle the stairs. *Thank God for those early morning workouts*, he thought as he bolted through the door.

As he turned east again, a plan of sorts began to form in his head. If he allowed himself to be caught by someone other than the three chasing him, they would take him for questioning, President Brady would vouch for him, and he would expose the plot. As these thoughts gelled in his head, the security guard's radio crackled to life. "Assassin in tunnel system, heading east from central core. Armed and dangerous. Explosives on body. Shoot for the head. Shoot to kill. *Do not approach!* Repeat! *Do not approach!* Explosives strapped to body. Shoot for the head! Shoot to kill!"

They were one step ahead of him. Even if it didn't kill, a head wound could render him harmless. Scott continued to run, and as he turned into the next corridor, he finally saw what he was looking for. An elevator. The alarms continued to wail as he slid to a stop in front of the door, his hand clutching Gary's access card. As he jammed it into the opening and pressed the up button, he knew he could wait only a few precious seconds. Enemy footsteps clattered down the adjoining hallway as his hard-earned lead dwindled on a hope. As the footfalls slowed to make the last corner, he prepared to run again just as the elevator door opened, welcoming him to momentary safety.

Friday, 6:09 a.m. EDT, White House

Although Scott Piquard was running for his life, the urgency he felt was for Gary Brady. Unknown to him, the chain of events he had set in motion had done more to secure the president's safety than he could have guessed. The assassins' plot could work in a relaxed environment of "business as usual," but the instant the alarms sounded in the tunnels below the White House, "business as usual" did not exist.

Secret Service agent Sam Davies was preparing himself for a monotonous day when the alarms jolted him into overdrive. Ninety-nine percent of an agent's life was ritual boredom. Watching, waiting, waiting, watching, hoping nothing happened on your shift yet secretly wishing it did. Every agent secretly dreamed of being the one to save the president in a daring shootout.

Sam sprinted down the hall to the private quarters of the first family and burst into the room, hoping that Mrs. Brady was clothed but unable to wait for a knock. It was part of the training for both the agents and the presidential family. The near-total loss of personal privacy when one decided to go for the top offices in the country could not be explained; it had to be experienced.

President Brady, expecting another drill, was startled when he saw Sam perform a visual sweep of the room over the .40-caliber bore of his Glock 22. Once he ascertained the immediate safety of President Brady and the first lady, Sam backed against the president, his gun pointed toward the door. "Stay exactly where you are, sir. The team will be here in about ten seconds. Mrs. Brady, please stand directly behind your husband."

As Janet Brady hugged her husband, they could hear agents in the hallways, doors slamming and shouts of "Clear!" echoing one by one as they worked their way methodically down the corridor. Two agents raced into the living quarters, repeating the gun sweep and then turning to face the other doors. As the rest of the team completed their room-by-room sweep, they converged on the first couple. A double circle of lethally trained men and women quickly surrounded President Brady and Mrs. Brady.

Sam Davies's strong voice carried easily over the din. "Mrs. Brady, team 2 will escort you and the boys to your safe rooms. Mr. President, please come with us to the elevator. Stay in the middle of the circle and move as quickly as possible until we get to the command center. There has been a breach of security, and gunshots have been fired." The circle of people moved quickly, and as they reached the elevator, Sam pushed his card into the slot and pressed the lowest button. The car shot into the depths.

The elevator that Brady had told Scott to use was accessible to multiple levels of personnel—it had been built for redundancy. This elevator, however, was for use only by the president and the very highest-level security personnel. It was twice as fast as the other elevator and emptied into a bunker area that was surrounded by enough concrete and structural steel to withstand a direct hit by an atomic device. The circle of people exited the elevator and fanned out, allowing the president to walk with Davies through a short hallway to the stainless-steel vault door. Sam entered his code and placed his hand on the palm print identifier, and when Brady did the same, the twenty-thousand-pound door swung slowly open. If Scott Piquard had known any of this, he might have relaxed just a little, for the president of the United States was now standing in arguably the safest place in the entire world.

Sam entered the room with the president. The guard snapped a salute to the commander in chief and barked an abrupt "Attention!"

"At ease, gentlemen," Brady responded.

"Mr. President, let me bring you up to date on the situation," Major Brinkman, the shift officer, said. "We have had an intruder in Security One. Shots have been fired. Condition red exists. The perpetrator has not been apprehended. No knowledge exists of how he breached security. However, we are only a few minutes into condition red. It is just a matter of time. There are thousands of people converging on this area as we speak. He is probably hiding in a storeroom somewhere if he is not already in custody. We are now preparing for closed-circuit playback. If you will step up to these screens here, you can see what we know so far."

The end of the room was a partial octagon with computer screens, radar monitors, speakers, and video outputs filling every square inch of wall space. There were stations manned by the Army, Navy, Air Force, FBI, CIA, Secret Service, Coast Guard, and National Security Council. There was layer upon layer of overlapping security, with feedback from every imaginable source of information.

"Roll the films, Captain Ellis."

"Yes, sir! We'll begin with the four screens in the center. These will show the main, long hallways on Security One. In a few seconds, a middle-aged Caucasian male will come walking down the central hallway on monitor number 3. We do not know how he got there. None of the exits were breached, and the exit cameras are devoid of activity. He just showed up out of nowhere. However, several of our cameras are black—some kind of power problem that we are still working on." The video screens looked like still pictures. "About now you will see him." Down a stretch of hallway, they could see a white male walking slowly toward the camera. "He appears to be proceeding with caution, making sure he is not seen. We heard a report over the radios that he is armed and possibly has a bomb strapped to his body, but when he gets closer here, it is hard to tell where he would be hiding anything. He is wearing a jogging suit, and I see no bulges." Captain Ellis pointed to the pocket areas of the jogging suit as the figure came closer to the camera. But neither Gary Brady nor Sam Davies noticed any of that; their eyes were riveted to the face on the screen.

"That's—" Davies began. Then he felt President Brady's hand methodically jabbing his ribcage. "Amazing!" He cleared his throat and looked at the president, but all he saw was a little shake of the head that said, "Not now!"

"As he goes down this hallway, we lose him. We lost the cameras in the northeast sector several minutes before this. We had just called for crews to sweep the lines when all hell broke loose. We'll get those disks and analyze them, but there must be a power problem. Five cameras don't malfunction at once. We're in the process of changing over to high-def, and there is a lot of equipment hacked together right now as we make the switch."

A navy lieutenant spoke next. "He must have an accomplice on the inside who cut the power. They were probably off on their timing, or we wouldn't have this much."

Ellis continued. "From here on, this is as new to us as it is to you, sir. We will just have to roll the video and see where we pick him up again. Levels A, B, and C all report no intruders, and we saw nothing on the live monitors from those levels except hundreds of our guys infiltrating downward after initiation of Red.

"One more thing," Brinkman added. "Someone has issued a shoot-to-kill order because of the alleged bomb. It went out on all frequencies. By the time we see this guy again, he'll probably be riddled with bullet holes."

"Absolutely *not!*" President Brady sprang forward. "We must talk to this man. Cancel that shoot-to-kill immediately. That is an executive order! I want that broadcast on all frequencies. We *must* be able to question him. This man is to be brought in alive no matter what! And I want him unharmed."

Sam Davies watched as the president's outrage was spent. His upper lip was sweaty, and his face had gone pale. He now had his composure again, Sam realized, but why was he being so coy? They both knew that the person on the video was Dr. Piquard. Why wasn't he identifying his friend?

Friday, 6:10 a.m. EDT, Homeland Security Command Center

Lieutenant Colonel Floyd Curtis had reported for duty early, as always, his insulated mug of black coffee in one hand, a leather-bound copy of Ulysses in the other, ready for another monotonous day in the Homeland Security Command Center. Although things were more interesting since he had transferred to Homeland from the Army base, the days still crept. Curtis had two years until full retirement, and he was looking ahead. It wasn't that he disliked his job or his location; he couldn't ask for better. He was just tired of the daily routine of absolute boredom. A communications expert testing near the genius level and applying himself rigorously to every job, he had made grade on schedule. As life became routine, he turned more and more to history and literature, devouring books like a machine and losing himself for days in a good read. Today promised to be one of those days, he told himself as he started for the coffee room.

"Sir, we have a report of activity in the White House tunnel complex. There has been a breach of security. White male. Fifties. Pictures on the way shortly. Shots fired. No knowledge of how many perps involved or who fired shots."

"Thank you, Lieutenant Block. Activate Homeland Security alert level red. Scramble ground units to condition red locations. Be sure the airport and bridge units secure their areas ASAP. Zimmer, get Navy and Coast Guard units into the water and have the Navy pilots stand by—condition red status."

Curtis turned toward another console of desks and barked orders across the room. "Wainright, notify Andrews Air Force Base. I want pilots in the cockpits. Kesselhoff, contact FAA and ground all aircraft into and out of Washington Class B airspace, and tell them that we *will* shoot down anyone that enters Area P56 without authorization. Dugan, activate all backup personnel. I want them at their posts in less than thirty minutes. I want every bridge, major building, and landmark posted, and I want every airport, train station, and bus depot secured. Relay condition red alert to every military base. Now everybody move!"

Many officers would have consulted the manual for the situation and gone down the checklist systematically to avoid the repercussions that follow mistakes in military careers. But Curtis saved valuable minutes by taking action, a trait not lost on his superiors. He studied scenarios and cemented them into long-term memory. When minutes counted, Curtis had them.

"Smolik, get me White House Command. I'll take it at the head console."

"White House Command Center on 1, sir!"

"White House Command, this is Lt. Colonel Curtis at Homeland Security Command Center. We have activated security condition red in accordance with title 6, sections 111, 201, and 202. Do you have any new information for us?"

"Sir, this is Major Brinkman at White House Command. All we know is that shots have been fired and the president is secure. Condition red has been activated from this end as well. Let us know as soon as any of your ground troops gather any new information. Brinkman over."

"I am in constant contact with Andrews Air Force Base, Major. We are contacting Navy and Coast Guard units, and they will have additional units in the water shortly. Army units are on the move. Curtis over."

"We'll keep this line open for directs to you. You'll have coordination from there, and if this heats up, you will be augmented by ranking personnel."

"Affirmative, Major. Curtis out."

Friday, 6:12 a.m. EDT, White House Command Center

The massive door of the bunker swung open and Greg Stroud, the head of the Secret Service, and General Gus Taylor from the Joint Task Force on Terrorism entered at full stride. General Taylor, an old friend of Brady's from their army days, never did anything at half stride. "Hello, Gus. Good to see you." President Brady gave a salute as he spoke, even though he was the highest-ranking person in the room. Having made it to the rank of lieutenant in his brief stint in the Army, Gary instinctively saluted rank. "Good morning, Greg."

"What do we know so far?" Stroud was slightly out of breath from matching Gus Taylor's stride.

"Please replay the video for these gentlemen."

"Yes, Mr. President," Brinkman said.

Secret Service Director Stroud turned and spoke directly to Sam. "Davies, did everything go by the book or is there anything you need to brief me on?"

"By the book, sir. Total time from red to command center couldn't be much over four minutes."

"So where's the breach? Any clues?"

"No, sir. Tall, middle-aged, Caucasian male in a jogging suit just shows up out of nowhere. No breaches at the upper levels. No breaches at the emergency exits. No breaches at the stairwells. None at the elevators. However, there is a major power grid problem in northeast with several cameras black. Those disks might help, but we cannot access them right now. The guy disappears in the northeast tunnels, and there we lose him. He is probably hiding somewhere. There is absolutely no way he can get out unless one of the buried emergency doors was propped open with the alarm disabled and the camera spooled on a repeating loop."

"That's a good idea," Ellis interjected. "Whoever got this deep has to be an insider, and there could be more than one—likely, in fact, as sophisticated as their security avoidance has been. If it hadn't been for someone spotting him, God knows what might have happened."

Stroud thought for a minute. "Have the buried emergency exits been covered?"

"Yes, sir," Brinkman replied. "I was about to issue that order when someone confirmed all clear. That was when we heard he had a bomb, and the shoot-to-kill order went out. It must have been whoever spotted him. It's pretty chaotic right now, with every available man and woman in uniform closing in on him. Once we go red, all elevators go maximum security, all exits are double locked, and the stairwells were flooded with our people within seconds. Assuming it is an assassination attempt, he was trying to get *in*, toward the president. We have that covered. And there is no way he can get *out*."

Friday, 6:12 a.m. EDT, Tunnel Complex

Scott jammed the red card into the elevator control slot and pressed the top button. The door closed quickly as his pursuers rounded the last corner. As he had hoped, the president, in an emergency, would be able to go anywhere, anytime; no matter who else was left to use the stairs in a crisis, he was free to go where he wanted as long as he had Brady's card.

The upper levels had been steadily flooding with Capitol Police, soldiers, and agents of every stripe. The elevator system had gone to level red the instant the alarms sounded; the agents and officers filtering into the tunnel system were methodically penetrating the lower levels via the stairwells. As a force of heavily armed and lethally trained warriors descended into the depths below the capital city, one lone person ascended through them. The only thing that Scott knew at this point was that they were looking for him in the tunnels, so he had pushed the top button and collapsed against the wall to catch his breath.

I have to get to Gary, he thought. *I have to warn him somehow.*

The elevator came to a stop, and with every nerve on edge, he stepped out into the hallway. There were no alarms sounding here, but red lights blinking at both ends of the corridor told Scott that the alert was on in this building as well. When he saw the office of the secretary of the treasury, he knew he had crossed under East Executive Avenue and was in the Treasury Building. The maximum-security elevator had landed him behind the usual lines of security, where a cabinet member could quickly descend to safety. He hurried to the stairwell and started down, knowing that each entrance was guarded around the clock. There was no way he was going to casually walk out the door.

Walk out the door? No! Do the unexpected. The best defense is a good offense. Scott took a deep breath, pulled a fire alarm handle, and then burst around the corner, down the stairs, and sprinted toward the pair of armed guards at the door. "There's a man up there. He's crazy. Five-eight, 180, dark skin, black hair, thick accent. Clear the building immediately! That's an order!" He flew past the perplexed guards. They were trained to stop people coming in, not going out. The metal detectors and X-ray units lined the entrance aisle; the exit aisle was wide open. The guards turned back toward the staircase and assumed a defensive position as they called for backup.

Scott bolted out of the building and turned north. Slowing to a steady jog, he turned the two-way radio off and slipped it into the pocket of his jogging suit. Jogging across Lafayette Square, he picked up his pace as he passed Decatur House and started up Seventeenth Street. Umbrellas were everywhere, but joggers are joggers and there were many of them out despite the rain. He was Joe Citizen again, just like four million others in this city—male, middle aged, and running for his life.

Jogging past Farragut Square, Scott ran for a few blocks to get his thoughts together. The further he was from the White House, the less likely he was to be stopped. Finally, he flagged down a vacant taxi. He hopped in and slammed the door, but as he settled into the seat, three realities struck him. He did not have a clue where he was going, he had no identification, and he did not have a single penny to his name. *Helpless* had just taken on a new meaning for Doctor Scott Piquard.

Friday, 6:21 a.m. EDT, White House Command Center

President Brady listened as General Gus Taylor barked orders. "We will need to debrief everyone when we've caught him. We need to figure out who spotted him and how he got so deep. I don't want him dead." When Gus Taylor spoke, everyone heard him. At six feet, six inches, he was 255 pounds of lank and muscle and had a jaw as massive as his frame. When Brady was in the Army, he had picked up Taylor to play center for his basketball team. Between Brady's outside shooting and Taylor's put-backs, they had won many a tournament along with many a side bet. They had been a good team then, and when Brady won the election, Gus was one of the men he knew he could count on to give him straight advice. He had always joked that Gus was too tall to kiss anybody's ass.

"I issued an executive order that he was not to be injured just before you got here, Gus. We need him alive."

Anne Lema had been with the Secret Service for nine years. With an exemplary record and a father and grandfather in lifelong military service, she had quickly earned top-level clearance. She was turned toward Brady, trying to catch every word, and she jumped when her speaker crackled to life. "Command One, this is Northeast Seven. We have a report from the Treasury Building. Someone came flying out of there, scared as hell—says there was an armed intruder with a bomb, about five-eight, one-eighty, dark hair, accent. We have two platoons from the Third Infantry en route to that area, and the Capitol Police have the area surrounded. They are starting a room-to-room search, and extra marksmen have been deployed to the roofs."

"Copy, Northeast Seven. Affirm that all entry and exit points have double guards, and that complete lockdown is in effect. Command One over." Agent Lema had regained her professional posture immediately after being startled, and she hoped that no one had noticed her little lapse.

"Cannot confirm lockdown—personnel still moving into position—Capital Police have the perimeter surrounded at one hundred yards. Northeast Seven over."

Ellis sighed with exasperation. "That doesn't fit this guy's description, but with the cameras down in that sector, we can't get a look."

The president turned toward Stroud. "How long are we going to be down here, Greg? I've got things to finish upstairs."

"I'm sorry, sir, but we may be down here for a very long time. If they catch him, they'll still need to interrogate him. He may have accomplices. There may be bombs or poisonous gas. The air down here is piped in and triple filtered. We cannot allow you to leave this area until we have made a complete sweep. It will be all of a day, if not two. We can bring down your papers, but you cannot leave. The vice president is being sequestered according to protocol, as are the speaker and the chief justice.

"Understood. I would like to have the private quarters to myself for a few minutes to call Janet. Sam, come with me, please." He led the way to the opposite end of the room where a door opened into a set of inner rooms. Beyond the center rooms were sleeping quarters for approximately two dozen people, and beyond that were the private quarters for the president. Brady walked to the private phone and rang the White House operator. "Connect me to the first lady's safe room, please."

"Hello," Janet Brady answered on the first ring, the fear in her voice obvious.

"I'm safe, Janet. Are you and the boys okay?"

"Yes, we're fine. What's happening, Gary?"

"There has been an intruder in the tunnel system, and everyone is on high alert. It could take a couple of days to be sure there are no bombs or poisonous gases, so we have to stay put. Tell the boys that

I love them, and we'll all have a good laugh about this when it is all over."

"Do you know where Scott ended up?"

Brady glanced at Sam Davies. "Scott went running. I'll talk to you later. Love you."

"I love you too. Be careful."

"Always." He hung up the phone and turned to Davies. "Sam, you know why I wanted you back here, don't you?"

"I think so, sir, but I hate assumptions, so why don't you tell me?"

"First, tell me what you are thinking."

"Well, sir," Sam began, "I think we both know that the person in the tunnel was Dr. Piquard or a man who looked exactly like him and was his exact height and build."

"Agreed. Go on."

"I have a hunch on how he got into and out of Security One without being detected. You may have a theory on that yourself. And I also know that you don't want anyone else to know quite yet, or you would have spoken up immediately. You know him best. Why did he run? If he wanted to kill you, he could have done it a hundred times. We both know that. So why did he run when all he had to do was go through the motions and wait to be ID'd? That's what has me puzzled. Running makes him look guilty, so why aren't you stepping up to vouch for him?"

"Something is wrong, and I'm playing my cards close to my chest until I know what it is," Brady said. "Something doesn't fit. Scott Piquard wouldn't be running unless he had a reason. There were several shots fired down here this morning, Sam, and my bet is that Scott knew every one of those shots was meant for him. Once we find out who fired those shots, we may learn why they fired them. And someone issued a shoot-to-kill order too damn quickly. All I am asking is that you play dumb with me for a while until we have time to figure out who was shooting and why. We'll keep silent and let them make the first mistake. If we don't find any other intruders in the system, it can only mean one thing, right?"

Sam looked at the president and then slowly shook his head. "Whoever else was down here had clearance to be down here!"

"Bingo!"

"It's probably just some overzealous Capitol Police officer apprehending an intruder. Once Dr. Piquard turns himself in, this whole thing will reveal itself."

"It might not be that simple, Sam. What I am about to tell you goes nowhere outside of this room. Understood? I don't know whom I can trust and whom I can't, and until I know more, I don't want anyone to know what I'm thinking. I have to include you now because I need your cooperation. The longer it takes to identify him, the more time there will be for someone to make a mistake. Time we need.

"Sam, I have been worried about my safety for some time now. There have been little hints here and there but nothing concrete. We have networks of informers with little tastes here and there, nothing firm, but occasional comments like 'after the change' or 'when the new guys take over' make you worry. Then one of my friends at CIA picked up a clue that could be nothing or could be something very important. Now this. Scott is running for a reason, and we need time to figure out why and from whom. Will you help me?"

"My oath is to protect the office of the president of the United States, sir, and I have never taken anything more seriously in my life. I will do whatever you ask."

"Thank you, Sam."

They turned and walked toward the door. "If you have any advice, Sam, I'm all ears. I don't have a clue what to do next."

"I like your idea, sir. Play dumb and let everyone else do the talking. It's easier to think when your mouth's not moving."

"Agreed."

Sam opened the door, and they stepped out into the command center where the large door was just closing behind new arrivals.

"Mr. President," Gus Taylor said, "I think you know General Curt Nearman, Air Force representative for the White House Command Center, and Commander Matt Karber, US Navy. General Anthony Shaffer, Marine representative, is several miles away yet.

Your national security adviser is on his way. That makes up the core of the emergency command group. If the need arises, the joint chiefs will join us by telecommunications link."

Greg Stroud turned to Sam Davies. "Davies, I think we have enough redundancy down here. Why don't you sign out and give us a little more elbow room?"

Sam looked at the president, his eyebrows raised in the universal question mark.

"Actually, Greg," Brady cut in, "I would prefer it if Sam stayed. In fact, I asked him personally to do just that. He knows me, and I know him, and there is some comfort in that. You don't mind?"

Friday, 6:30 a.m. EDT, Washington, DC

The cab pulled away slowly, the driver in no hurry to get any-where. He drove a half block before he looked languidly into the mirror, his raised eyebrows asking the obvious question. This cabby had been around the block so many times with so many people that nothing surprised him. Scott's mind was racing. *Where do I go? How do I get a message to Gary?*

"Take me to the *Washington Post*," he blurted.

"You got it."

The driver accelerated up Seventeenth then turned east on L Street as Scott sat back and tried to tame his thoughts. If he could get inside the Post building and talk to a reporter, he could get the story out. Most reporters would betray their own mothers for this story, but would they believe him? Unshaven and with no identification, Scott was questioning his impromptu plan as the taxi turned onto Fifteenth Street northwest. Ahead, he could see the *Post* building, and stationed in front were two armed officers checking IDs.

Press control! They're ahead of me. He had no clue what to do next. He couldn't think fast enough. His mind felt like thick glue. "Take a left up there," he said as he pointed toward the next intersec-tion. "I just remembered I need something for a meeting."

"You going back to your hotel?"

"No. Leesburg Executive Airport. I left my attaché in my airplane."

The driver turned his head toward Scott for the first time. "That's a long ways, buddy. You got cash?"

"Of course, I've got cash."

"Let's see it."

"Actually, that's part of the problem. It's in my attaché, and I can't pay you until I get it."

"Of course it is. Look, I want my money now." The cab began gliding toward the curb.

Scott considered running as soon as the car slowed, but where would he go? Uniformed personnel throughout the city were looking for him already, and if he ran, the cabby could provide them with a description and a last known location. "Look, Aaron," he said, reading the name on the dash card, "I flew here to finalize a multi-million-dollar deal. I went for a run to clear my head. A few bucks in cab fare is the least of my worries." Scott pulled up the sleeve of his jogging suit and pulled off his watch. "Here! This diving watch is worth a grand. You can hold it for me until I get your cash." He held it forward, dangling the beautiful Luminox Nighthawk by the band.

The cab driver took the bait. He hung the watch on his gearshift handle and pulled away again. The clouds hung low over the Potomac as they weaved westward through the building traffic.

What will happen at the bridge? Could they have roadblocks this soon? He wanted to turn on the two-way radio, but that would be too suspicious with the storyline he had just handed the cabdriver. *I should have said I was working undercover.* It had been difficult to think up a story on the spot. Effective lying takes practice. *I've got to be ready*, he told himself. *I may need a sack of lies before this day is over.*

As they worked their way through the traffic, the driver leaned forward and turned up the radio. The talk show host was interrupting the program with a breaking bulletin. "DC Police are searching the Capitol Hill area for a male suspect believed to be armed and dangerous. He is a white male, six feet two inches tall, dark hair, and wearing gray clothing. Anyone with information should call their local police department or 911. Do not try to apprehend this man.

He is considered armed and dangerous and is reported to have a bomb."

"Man, this city is full of crazies," Scott said too loudly. "It seems like every time I come here, there is some weirdo killing his family or abducting little girls." Scott hoped that his voice sounded normal to the driver, because it seemed terribly forced to him. He looked at his clothing, thankful that the rain had darkened the gray toward black. "Wasn't it around here that those snipers did those random killings a few years back?"

"That was over in Maryland, but close enough to make everyone edgy. You never knew where they were going to hit next, murderin' bastards! I could pull the switch on that older one myself, but he'll sit in jail for twenty years before they have the guts to kill him, and they'll spend a hundred grand a year keeping him alive."

"Amen to that!" Scott agreed. "I guess that's why I don't come here very often."

"What field you in?"

Scott's mind searched frantically for a story line. A voice in his brain said, *Stick to what you know.* Scott knew medicine. "I'm a doctor. I do research on lasers. I've developed a new ultrahigh-frequency YAG laser that can vaporize cancer tissue down to one fifth of a millimeter. It leaves the healthy tissue unburned, which has great applicability for skin cancers. I have the patent. Now if I can get my FDA approval, I can begin manufacturing." He couldn't help smiling at his lie. He might get good at this.

"That sounds awesome," Aaron said and then paused. "Hey, mind if I have you look at a spot on my ear when we get a chance?"

"No problem. Which ear?"

"The top of my right ear, right here," he answered, pointing to the sun-exposed area on the very top.

Scott leaned forward and examined the dry, flaky spot with the small central redness. "Does it ever ooze or bleed?"

"No. Just gets flaky and peels off, but never really heals."

Scott palpated the tip of his ear. "It's not hard or raised, so I think you're okay for the short run." He had just entered the taxi driver's personal space, and most people would allow that only if they trusted you. "What you have is an actinic keratosis from repetitive sun damage. You can have your doctor freeze that with liquid nitrogen. If it keeps coming back after a couple of treatments, then you should have it biopsied, but you don't need to go to that expense right now. Hand me that pen and paper, and I will write it down for you. Take this note to your family doctor, but don't go to a dermatologist yet—he will charge you four times as much as your family doctor and do the same thing."

"Thanks, Doc. That's really nice of you. Hey, I'm sorry I talked disrespectful-like back there, but like you said, we get so many crazies that we just gotta be careful. Here! Here's your watch back. You probably just saved me a couple hundred bucks anyways." He slid the watch off the gearshift handle and passed it back to Scott.

"No problem, Aaron," Scott replied. He slipped the watch on and peered out the windshield. The bridge to Arlington was just ahead, and he could see trouble looming. Outbound cars were backed up several deep, and uniformed officers were jumping out of a truck and starting to check outbound vehicles. A cold sweat chilled his skin, and his head began racing, panic imminent. He didn't know how to deal with this. It was too foreign. A heart attack victim, or white-water rapids, or life and death in the operating room—that he could handle. But armed guards hunting for him—this was too outside his realm.

The cab inched up to the checkpoint. Aaron cracked the window, keeping the rain at bay. The officer looked inside. "Have you picked up any fares acting strangely or seen anything out of the ordinary?"

"No, sir! Just the routine."

"Who's your fare?"

"He's my doctor. Brilliant. Inventor too! Lasers." He winked knowingly.

"Carry on, gentlemen," the officer said as he waved them through.

Scott melted into the seat. Cold sweat covered his body. His palms were clammy, and his pulse was 130. He had to get over this panic to think clearly.

The cab sped over the bridge and eased into the flow of 66 West. As they left the city proper and wound their way onto Highway 7, Scott pondered his next move. *I'll get inside the FBO, use a phone, call the* Post, *get this story out in the open, and this nightmare will be over.*

The forty-minute drive to the airport seemed to take forever, but soon Scott was stepping onto the sidewalk in front of the fixed-base operator. "I'll be back in a couple of minutes. I promise you will be paid, Aaron."

"I know you're good for it, Doc," he replied as he reached over and paused the meter. He turned up the radio and lit a cigarette.

The lobby was empty, but Scott could hear voices coming from the back office. He started back to the pilot's room to use the phone when he saw flashing red lights racing toward the airport from the northeast. He bolted to the door for a better view. There were three military vehicles, and they were racing toward the security gate. *Of course! They would secure the airports! I'm trapped.* Then it struck him. *The airplane radios.* Scott slipped behind the counter and opened the key drawer. He grabbed the brightly colored tag he had placed on his key ring and clicked on the guard's two-way radio as he raced through the east door. The flashing lights were to his left, but the security gate was still closed, and *Whiskey Mike* was down the line to the right. He slithered through the shadows of the building to the tie-down area, unlocked the aircraft door, jumped in, and scurried forward.

He crouched low in his seat, flipped up the red master switches, and slipped on his headset. His radio was still set to 126.1. Scott keyed his mic. "Potomac Approach, I have a request."

"Who is calling Approach?"

"Potomac Approach, this is an emergency."

"Who is calling Approach Control?" A strong male voice asked the question. "All flights are grounded. What is your position?"

"I am on the ground at Leesburg. I need you to get a message to the White House."

"What is your name, and where are you ramped?"

Something wasn't right. Scott keyed his mic again. "Potomac Approach, I am declaring an emergency."

"What is your name, and where are you ramped?"

Just then a second male voice fairly screamed over the airwaves, "Step on that frequency. Now!" Instantly a squelching static filled Scott's headphones as someone keyed their mic switch and held it, blocking any further communication.

Sometimes hostility could be sensed better than heard. Once again, Scott's instincts took control as he jumped out of the plane, released the tie-downs, then climbed back in, and latched the door behind him. He pushed the key into the panel, turned on the magnetos and fuel pump, pushed the mixture full rich, and cranked the starter on the left engine. It responded quickly, and he repeated the process on the right side. Looking back across the tarmac, he saw soldiers rounding the corner of the building. He could not wait for the engines to warm up. Taxiing between the parked planes, he steered for the southeast end of the airport, away from the soldiers.

Instinct had told him to run. His conversation with the voice on the radio had been all wrong. The terminology was wrong. The tone was wrong. A controller had never asked him his name—ever. It was superfluous. They needed to know tail number, make, model, position, and airspeed. More importantly, if a pilot declared an emergency, the controller gave him his full and undivided attention. The voice on the other end was no controller, and Scott had naively betrayed his own location as Leesburg Airport. Now he was taxiing without authority, and he knew before thinking about it that he was about to take off into instrument meteorological conditions without FAA clearance. For the first time in his life, he was about to intentionally break a federal law. If he had time for second thoughts, the security guard's radio put an end to them as it crackled to life.

His taxiing aircraft had been reported, and a second, eerily familiar voice now came over the two-way. "All personnel at Leesburg. All flights are grounded. Stop all aircraft. Use of deadly force authorized!"

Taxiing parallel to runway 1-7, Scott could see two vehicles racing for the runway. One had already made it to the middle of the runway, and a second was barreling down the runway to get into a blocking position at his end as well. A soldier jumped into the third vehicle and started toward the taxiway.

If there was any singular concept that Scott hammered into the medical students he taught, it was that assumptions lead to gross mistakes. The soldiers had assumed that he needed a runway to take off and they had blocked it effectively. Jamming the right brake pedal and thrusting full power on the left engine, he spun *Whiskey Mike* around in a sharp 180. "These taxiways are bigger than our runways back home, you bozos." Slamming his feet hard into the toe brakes, Scott poured full fuel to both engines, and when the brakes would no longer hold back the surging power plants, he released the brakes and shot down the taxiway.

By the time the soldiers realized what he was doing, it was too late. Even fully loaded, a Navajo was capable of climbing well over a thousand feet per minute. Empty, save for Scott, it accelerated toward the third vehicle and shot off the concrete with room to spare, soaring upward at over two thousand feet per minute and accelerating still more as he raised the gear. He saw several muzzle flashes before the low overcast shrouded the plane in mist. Normally a pilot's worst enemy, the early morning frontal fog and low clouds closed around the cream-colored airplane, blending white with white and shrouding him from the deadly hail of bullets.

Reaching one thousand AGL, one thousand feet above ground level, Scott settled into a gradual five-hundred-feet-per-minute climb, trading lift for speed as he lowered the nose and dumped the flaps. Knowing that any overflights into P56, the Washington National Airport Prohibited Area, created an immediate target for military fighters, he turned *Whiskey Mike* toward the west. Scott Piquard did not know where he was going or what he was going to do, but whatever it was, he knew it would not be in Washington, DC.

Chapter 3

Navajo West

L t. Colonel Floyd Curtis paced impatiently as information trickled in. Platoons were deploying around the entire city. They were not all housed at the bases as in previous years but spread throughout the metropolitan area, cutting arrival times by 80 percent. The noose was tightening around the capitol when an urgent transmission came from the tactical operations center of the First Battalion, Third Infantry—'The Old Guard'.

"Homeland Command, this is Lieutenant Osterholt."

"Osterholt, Homeland Command, Lt. Colonel Curtis here. Over."

"Sir, we have secured the airfield at Leesburg Executive Airport but have had a confrontation with an unknown person or persons. He taxied out in a twin and refused to acknowledge radio contact and refused to stop. We blocked the runway, but he had power to spare and took off right over us from the taxiway. Shots were fired— no hits confirmed. The ceiling is low, and he was out of sight within seconds. Over."

"Do you have a description? Over."

"Negative, sir. We couldn't even make out his tail number in the rain. Osterholt out."

"Wainright, get me the open line to NEADS and HQ." The Northeast Air Defense Sector, headquarters, and the command center were linked by a hotline, and these three decided if fighters would be launched. They had worked the bugs out since 2004, when Kentucky Governor Ernie Fletcher's plane had entered the Washington airspace FRZ—Flight Restricted Zone, or 'Freez'—on his way to President Reagan's funeral and was nearly shot down when radio contact was lost. Luckily for Fletcher, no one knew who was supposed to give the order.

"Brigadier General Proctor at NEADS is on the open line, sir."

"Hello, General Proctor. Lt. Colonel Floyd Curtis at Homeland Security Command Center. Please stand by for headquarters. Over."

"General Marrington at headquarters. With you, Hotline. Over."

"Good morning, General Marrington. We're live with General Proctor from NEADS. This is not a drill, gentlemen. I repeat—*this is not a drill!* We have an unauthorized flight that originated in the Washington ADIZ. However, he is heading away from the Freez, not toward it. Nonetheless, I want conjoint authorization to launch fighters to intercept. There has been an incident in the tunnels at the White House, and shots have been fired. We do not know if these two occurrences are related, but we must be prepared for any eventuality. I am not asking for authorization for deadly force unless he turns back toward the Freez—merely recon at this point. Curtis over."

"Headquarters affirms launch. Marrington over."

"NEADS affirms launch as well. And, Curtis, make sure the DEN is awake. Proctor over."

"Thank you, General Proctor, that was next on my list. Gentlemen, I am authorizing launch of F-35s from Andrews Air Force Base. Andrews Ops, are you copying this transmission? Over."

"Homeland Command, Andrews Ops. We have copy loud and clear. Does NEADS concur? Over."

"NEADS concurs. Proctor out."

"Does headquarters concur?"

"Headquarters concurs. Marrington out."

"Homeland Command, Andrews Ops. That is affirmative. We are scrambling the fighters. Once airborne, they will be closing at six hundred knots. We are talking to Potomac Approach Control, and we are both tracking a lone target proceeding due west at 192 knots ground speed out of Leesburg. We had him pegged at 9,500 on his Mode-C transponder, but we just lost that signal. Either his transponder malfunctioned or he shut it off. We have not lost sight of him since he went airborne out of Leesburg. I have two controllers whose sole duty is tracking the unauthorized flight. He can't get away. Andrews over."

Floyd Curtis looked at his radar screen. The target was easy to pick out. Normally, an aircraft with a filed flight plan will have its N number displayed on the radar screen above a changing field that flashes its destination identifier and its aircraft type, alternating with its altitude and airspeed. Since Potomac Approach had no flight plan filed, and since this aircraft had taken off without clearance inside an ADIZ (or Air Defense Identification Zone), this aircraft was designated VIOLATR, the designator block being limited to seven characters and unable to hold the entire word *violator*.

"Andrews, is there any other way you can identify that airplane. Curtis over."

"No, sir. The only way we can be one hundred percent is with a visual ID, and conditions are zero-zero up there. Andrews over."

"Affirmative. Curtis out."

"Andrews out."

Curtis turned to his Air Force man. "Kesselhoff, brief all DEN sites." He was referring to the Domestic Events Network, a vast web of radar and communications networks across America that has been perfected and consolidated from multiple units since Homeland was created; prior to that, it was difficult for one branch of the military to get information quickly from another branch. "I don't know how far our friend intends to fly, but we will need help tracking him."

Just then, Lt. Block handed Curtis a quickly scrawled note.

"Block! Patch me live to White House Command!"

Friday, 7:12 a.m. EDT, White House Command Center

White House Chief of Staff Todd Pederson lugged down a satchel full of papers, and he and President Brady retired to a desk in the private quarters. The pandemonium was subsiding as people began to relax and establish a new routine. The Air Force captain spoke from his post. "We have Homeland Security Command Center live on overhead."

"White House Command, this is Lt. Colonel Floyd Curtis at Homeland Command. There has been an incident at Leesburg Executive Airport, an unauthorized takeoff, westbound, shots fired, visibility poor, no tail number on the plane. It is heading away from the Capitol, so it would not appear to be a suicide mission. It is proceeding due west. Fighters from Andrews Air Force Base are scrambling for intercept, and just now an unknown source has issued a radio order for them to shoot it down. Group Commander is asking for clarification on that order, General Nearman."

Curt Nearman had worked his way through the ranks by earning every step the hard way. He had never been reprimanded in nearly three decades in the Air Force, and this was not going to be the day to start. He walked briskly to the console and grabbed the headset as President Brady reentered the main room. "Nearman here. Who else is on frequency?"

"I have both operations HQ at the base and Andrews Tower on this frequency, sir," Curtis replied.

"Operations, this is General Nearman at White House Command Center, code name Blue North. Be advised that the president has issued an *executive order* that no shots are to be fired. Your orders are to intercept and track only. Has there been any radio communication?"

"White House Command, this is operations at Andrews Air Force Base. Army personnel entered the control tower at Potomac Approach Control in accordance with Homeland Security directive alpha. The pilot refused to identify himself. All he would say was that there had been a mistake. They have repeated the order several times, but there has been radio silence since then."

"Operations, Nearman. Do you still have him on radar?"

"Affirmative, sir. We have one target westbound at 190 knots."

"Keep us informed of any communications."

"White House Command, this is Curtis at Homeland. We have activated force protection condition delta. We are contacting FAA, but currently, Homeland Security directive alpha is in effect."

Nearman keyed his microphone. "Nearman here! No shots are to be fired per executive order. However, if that aircraft turns around or heads for any critical targets, arm those missiles. If he enters the Washington no-fly-zone, prohibited area P56, and refuses intercept instructions, you will have no choice but to shoot him down. Nearman out."

"Affirmative, General. Ops out."

"Affirmative. Homeland out."

Friday, 7:15 a.m. EDT, Homeland Security Command Center

Floyd Curtis thought for only a second, and then keyed the frequency for the Leesburg Airport army platoon. "Osterholt, find out how many fixed-base operators there are over there. Check with every FBO and see if anyone saw anything. Also, check their logs for all arrivals, departures, and fuel sales. Intel will be there shortly. Curtis out."

"Block, get an intel team over to Leesburg Exec. Make sure it's a Homeland team. They can get through red tape ten times faster than an Army crew."

"Colonel Curtis, I have Osterholt at Leesburg again."

Curtis took the mic and turned the speakers live. "Curtis here."

"Sir, we found a cab driver waiting curbside at the FBO. He says he was waiting for a fare, but he's getting pretty upset now because the guy hasn't shown up, and he hasn't been paid. The time frame fits our suspect. Also, sir, he picked him up just a few blocks from the Treasury Building. Osterholt over."

"Good work, Lieutenant. What did he look like? Over."

"Caucasian, six feet two inches, two hundred pounds, good-looking, brown hair, graying at the temples. Over."

"What else did he tell you? Over."

"He said the guy told him he was a doctor and invented lasers and did cancer surgery. Thought he was from LA. Said he left his briefcase in his private plane and needed some papers for an important meeting this morning. Offered the cab driver an expensive watch for collateral, but he trusted the guy—he told a good story. Over."

"Good work. Hold him there for intel. Curtis out."

"Colonel, there is one odd thing."

Curtis's head jerked up. "What is that, Osterholt?" He loved odd things. Odd things were like candy for his brain.

"Well, sir, it's kind of strange. He said he was a doctor, but he also wrote a diagnosis and treatment on a piece of paper for the cab driver to give to his own doctor, and it sure looks like medical stuff. I can't read it. It's Latin or something. Over."

"Very good, Osterholt. Our first piece of hard evidence. Don't let that out of your sight. And don't handle it! Intel will want print and handwriting analysis. Any word on which plane is missing? Over."

"Sergeant Ripley is inside the FBO talking with their personnel. We'll get back to you as soon as we know more. Osterholt over."

"Curtis out."

Curtis turned back toward the other people in the room. "Well, well, it may be nothing, but a professional would never leave a paper trail—certainly not in his own handwriting—and a pro would never pay with a credit card, but maybe he filled out a fuel ticket, and we can match the handwriting with that from the cab driver's note. Hopefully, we will have a tail number on him within the hour. They are much easier to track than an automobile registration—tighter record keeping at the FAA and far fewer of them." Floyd Curtis felt that things were under control as he finally went to get the fresh cup of coffee that had been evading him half the morning.

Friday, 7:20 a.m. EDT, White House Command Center

President Brady had vacated his desk and stared into the flickering monitors. *If it is Scott, why isn't he talking to anyone? Why doesn't he just tell them what happened and come in for debriefing?* Then he answered his own question. *Because they keep shooting at him. Now someone has issued an order for an F-35 to shoot him down. Someone wants him very dead.*

Gus Taylor stepped to the Army's desk and called for the ops dispatcher at Army headquarters. "Ops, this is General Gus Taylor, code name Red Sierra. I want direct communication with what you know when you know it. Taylor out." He turned back to the group. "It would appear that we have one not-so-smart pilot in a gas-burner trying to outrun fighter jets. Now the only thing left is to wait until he lands, then pick him up and see what's on his mind."

Friday, 7:40 a.m. EDT, November 687 Whiskey Mike

The drone of the twin Lycomings was Scott Piquard's only company on this flight. Never had he felt so absolutely alone. Flying through clouds, pelted by rain, and hunted by the United States Armed Forces, he did not know where he was going or what he was going to do when he got there. Someone was trying to kill his best friend, and he had no clue where to turn for help.

Shortly after takeoff, he had reached over and shut down the transponder that was sending air traffic control a constant readout of his location and altitude. He had ignored the repeated commands to identify himself until he had time to think. Instinct told him that confusion worked for his purposes. Singularity of purpose created strength; confusion diffused it. As long as they were confused, he could buy time, and by heading west, he was a diminishing threat with each mile.

Scott throttled back to 65 percent power, buying fuel efficiency at the cost of a few knots. Having taken his flight bag to the White House, he was flying without current maps and charts. Several years previous, however, bad weather had forced him into unfamiliar territory, and it had nearly proven disastrous. Since then, he always kept a set of used WAC maps and instrument charts in his seat pocket for backup. Not as detailed as sectional charts, the scale on World Aeronautical Charts was 1:1,000,000. A dozen maps covered the continental US and northern Mexico. Without radio frequencies and map data, he would be flying lost. Scott fished CG-21 from the pouch in his seatback and opened to the DC area.

Familiar with the area from yesterday's flight, he quickly located the Linden VOR and dialed 114.3. Centering the VOR needle, he steered 255 degrees, just south of due west. Over the Linden transmitter, he merged his flight path with Victor Airway 128 westbound. Locking in the autopilot, he could track Victor 128 to the next VOR transmitter in West Virginia.

Instrument flight rules dictate that IFR flights cruise on the 1,000-foot marks, while visual flight rules set VFR flights at the 500 marks. IFR flights are thus performed at 3,000, 4,000, 5,000 feet, etc., and VFR flights at 3,500, 4,500, 5,500 feet, etc. This system helps avoid deadly midair collisions, although if the visibility is good enough to fly VFR, all pilots are bound by regulation to "see and avoid." With today's weather, Scott could be assured that he would have no company at the 500s. He set his altitude hold for 9,500 feet, sat back, and took his first deep breath in over two hours.

The mountains of West Virginia lay imbedded in the mist ahead. The highest peaks reach 4,880 feet, what they called "hills" in the Rockies. He continued to monitor Center traffic to get updates on barometric pressure changes, a small bit of trivia that will kill if not understood. An altimeter is nothing more than a pressure chamber with a dial that moves when changes in atmospheric pressure move the diaphragm in and out. Without a reference point, however, moving from one weather system to another could move the dial 500 to a 1,000 feet in a short time. A 1-inch change in barometric pressure moves the dial approximately 900 feet. If Scott lost his reference point, he could be flying into the "cumulous granitarius" on the Allegheny ridge ahead.

The mountain ridge was eighty miles west, and Scott would traverse that in less than 30 minutes. Beyond the mountains, the great Midwest plains stretched for hundreds of miles like a pilot's dream, less than 2,000 feet above sea level and, except for the Ozarks and the Black Hills, were dotted with small hills that created no significant obstructions to flight. In the Midwest, pilots often did "scud runs" or sneaked under very low clouds, although occasionally one paid the ultimate price for the gamble. Once over the Alleghenies, he could turn south toward clear air. Beyond the mountains, he would be free from natural dangers; man-made dangers, he was certain, were in the air already. They would either intercept him or shoot him down. Hopefully, the president could keep the guns quiet.

Can I influence those pilots? Scott asked himself as he adjusted the vertical trim. *It is easy to fire on an unknown combatant, a mere objective, but it becomes much more personal the minute you look into his eyes or talk to him. Can I talk to them?* The problem was the frequencies. Military aircraft use different frequencies than civilian traffic, for obvious reasons. Civilian aircraft use VHF frequencies, 118.00 to 135.97, while military aircraft use UHF frequencies, 225 and above. *Do they have VHF now?* In years past, they did not, but he knew that since 9/11, they were intercepting civilian aircraft on a routine basis. He had nothing to lose.

Scott keyed his microphone. "Any military aircraft on this frequency, do you copy this transmission?"

Friday, 7:42 a.m. EDT, Homeland Security Command Center

Savoring his second cup of coffee, Floyd Curtis had another idea. "Block! See if you can get me Dr. Dan Townsend over at the Ft. Myer Clinic." Floyd had known Dan for several years, both as a doctor and a friend. They had met at the Officer's Club and had meshed intellectually, and their small group met at the club once a month for poker. Lieutenant Block transferred the call to Curtis.

"Dr. Dan, I need a favor."

"How can I help, Floyd?"

"We have a situation over at Leesburg Executive Airport. There is a handwritten note there that I would like you to look at. It was supposedly written by a doctor, and my man either can't read it or can't interpret it. If you could read the note, interview the cab driver who provided it, and call me with your report, I would owe you big time."

"Does that mean you'll let me win next week?" Townsend chided.

"Hey! This is only a national emergency. You're talking poker."

"Yeah, what was I thinking? I'm on my way, Floyd. I'll radio you as soon as I get there."

"I'll let them know you're coming. Thanks, Doc."

Curtis turned to Lieutenant Block. "Block, call our intel crew and tell them that Dr. Dan Townsend is en route to give them a technical assist. Make sure they know he is one of ours."

"Yes, sir."

Floyd Curtis turned back to his monitors, focusing on the large radar screens on the huge wall. He could see the F-35s closing on their target. Soon they would be making large oval holding patterns around it, the trio dancing their way west until the weather cleared and they could get a visual ID. It seemed that things had barely begun, and yet there they were, miles to the west. In no time, they would be crossing the Allegheny ridge. The DEN would help him manage radar coordination from sites to the west. He would still run the recon from here, but soon his radar coverage would fade, and they would digitalize live coverage from on top of the ridge then from west of the ridge. His specialty was coordinating these communications efforts to make it seamless, but he had the knack of getting intelligence quickly, coordinating it, organizing it, and helping to interpret it, all in real time.

"Dugan, they will be coming up on the Evers MOA in a few more minutes. Make sure there aren't any operations going on over there, although I would doubt it with this weather."

MOAs (military operations areas) are scattered across the country and are designated as restricted areas to civilian aircraft. Commercial airplanes usually fly above the restricted areas, but private flights often go through the MOAs, and it is the pilot's responsibility to obtain clearance for MOA flights. It took several minutes and six calls but finally Dugan reported back to Curtis that there were no scheduled maneuvers in Evers MOA that day.

Curtis sipped on his coffee as he stared at the radar screen. The total number of blips was slowly decreasing as the FAA grounded flight after flight, but he was watching the three blips on the screen moving steadily westward. Curtis had a handle on the technical situation, but what he really wanted was the human side of this equation. He had made friends at the Bureau and the agency, as well as inside Homeland. He had a fantastic network, and his goal was to be first with the information. *So what do we have up there?* he thought to himself. *Who is this guy? If he was the perp at the White House, if he was smart enough to crack security over there, why was he dumb enough to try to outrun military jets in a prop job? And why would he leave handwriting samples behind? Was it medical terminology or smokescreen? Moreover, why would he stiff a cabby for his fare? Talk about drawing attention to yourself! Something doesn't fit.*

Floyd Curtis sat against his console and began to take another sip. *Who is that guy?* he wondered. Then he nearly spilled his coffee down Captain Block's back as he saw a fourth target appear on the screen. A fourth target that was not supposed to be there—a fourth target that was heading straight for VIOLATR, a fourth target that was moving far, far too fast.

Friday, 7:42 a.m. EDT, November 687 Whiskey Mike

Scott keyed his microphone. "Any military aircraft on this frequency, do you copy this transmission?"

There was a long silence on center frequency, and then finally his radio crackled. "Aircraft calling military—ident and say position."

"Military aircraft monitoring this frequency. Do you read?"

Again, his headset sputtered. "This is military flight Foxtrot Alpha 1. Say position and direction of flight."

"Foxtrot Alpha 1, you must relay a message to President Brady. There is a plot on his life. Can you relay that message to him?"

"Identify and say position and direction of flight."

"Alpha 1. Can you relay that message for me? This is an emergency."

"Identify and say position and direction of flight. That is an order!"

"Alpha 1. You know my position. There is a plot on President Brady's life. You must get this message to the president."

"Our orders are to verify your identity and then escort you to a military airbase."

Scott sat silent for a minute as he conjured a new tack. If he could think of a code that only Brady would recognize, Gary would know this was no hoax. Scott only had to think for a second. There was one phrase only the president would recognize. As he keyed his mic, the last thing he remembered was the intense pain in the center of his head as his whole world turned white, then black.

Chapter 4

Unexplained Explosion

Friday, 7:43 a.m. EDT, Homeland Security Command Center

"What the hell was that?" Lt. Colonel Floyd Curtis shouted, the flying coffee barely missing Captain Block as he lurched toward the radar screen. He knew instinctively, the very second he had seen the speed of the fourth target, what it was. But from where? Who? How? He hadn't followed it more than ten seconds when the radar screen showed a large starburst echo that disappeared almost as quickly as it had emerged. Then the screen faded back to the soft green glow of two F-35s still closing and VIOLATR losing altitude at an alarming rate. The fourth echo was gone, vanished like a puff of smoke.

Curtis stood and stared at the screen as he digested what he had just seen, a few dots on a greenish-black screen. He watched the alternating printouts below VIOLATR flash back and forth and watched as every few seconds it flashed 095, 093, 091, down, down, down. Every few seconds, the radar screen counted down the altitude in hundreds from safety to danger. He watched the numbers in disbelief until the signal weakened then finally disappeared altogether. Now there were only two echoes left, racing west at 600 knots, closing on—nothing.

"Heaven have mercy on his soul," he whispered.

"Wainright, get me back to White House Command. Now!"

"White House Command is live, sir." Wainright passed him the handset.

"White House Command, this is Curtis at Homeland again. We have had an incident. I repeat. We have had an incident. Do you copy?" He had to be sure they understood every single word he said.

"Homeland Center, this is General Nearman at White House Command. We read you loud and clear. What is your report?"

"White House Command, we acquired a fourth target on radar. We have witnessed it intercept the target of interest at speeds capable only of an AIM-120, AIM-9 or AIM-7, or something in their league. It did not come from either of the fighters. It came from the vicinity of the Evers MOA. We have witnessed a detonation echo in the vicinity of the target of interest, and then our target rapidly lost altitude. We have now lost radar acquisition of VIOLATR. Homeland over."

"Curtis, this is Nearman. Who else is out there? We need more information!"

"General, I am as puzzled as you are. We were assured there were no maneuvers in Evers today. We have no other echoes. You know what we know. Curtis out."

He turned back toward the group of faces that stood spellbound behind him, watching and listening as the drama unfolded. "Gentlemen, we have some work to do." They took their places at their consoles while Curtis barked his orders.

"Wainright, call every Air Force installation within two hundred miles of here and find out if they had anyone—and I mean anyone—in that MOA today. I want every man, woman, child, vehicle, ordnance, and scrap of butt wipe accounted for. No one comes or goes without authorization. I want total accountability."

"Block, ditto that for the Army. Zimmer, Navy, and Marines. Smolik, Coast Guard. Get on those phones. Now!"

He turned back toward his screens. *What in the name of God is going on?*

Friday, 7:44 a.m. EDT, White House Command Center

President Brady was reviewing documents with Chief of Staff Todd Pederson, but at the words "detonation echo," he flew from his chair and into the control room. Gaining the front of the room next to General Nearman, he stared at the remote radar screen. Their radar viewing capability was limited by space, and they had to rely on the feeds from their primary locations. He and Nearman stared at the two blips coursing west. His heart fell as he looked at the nearly empty screen.

"What is going on, General? And don't tell me what I think you are going to tell me."

"Mr. President, there has apparently been a missile fired from an unknown combatant. Our target of interest lost altitude rapidly and has now been lost from radar contact. We must assume that he was fatally disabled by that missile."

"I gave explicit orders! Explicit orders! No force was to be used! Explicit orders! I wanted him alive!" He paced back and forth in front of the electronic wall, and as he turned, he sent an empty water bottle flying against the adjoining wall with a sweeping blow of his right hand. "I want to know who fired that shot. I want to know everything about everything that happened today. I want a thousand-man search and rescue mission sent to that crash vicinity. I want every military base locked down until I have answers. I want every person accounted for. And when you find the person who fired that missile, I want him here, in front of me. Do you understand?" The rage in his voice was unmistakable, but Agent Lema was struck more by the plethora of his face. She was afraid he was going to have a stroke.

"Mr. President," her quivering voice broke the silence, "losing radar contact does not necessarily mean that the aircraft has crashed. It could mean that he has only passed below effective acquisition azimuth."

Brady turned toward Lema. "And just what the hell does that mean?"

Anne Lema had never faced the most powerful person in the world before. She had always thought it would be too daunting for her, a simple third-generation government employee, but here she was, carrying on a conversation with her president, trying to calm him down. "Well, sir, our radar is only effective down to a certain altitude and out to a certain range. And that is not as far as you might expect. Most of our radar is twenty-year-old technology coupled with twenty-year-old equipment, but everyone thinks it's good enough for what we do on a routine basis."

The quiet that settled over the room made her realize that every eye in the room was on her and that she was instructing the president of the United States—unsolicited instruction at that. Try as she might, she could not halt the crimson blush creeping up her neck. "Of course, I am not a radar specialist, Mr. President. I am sure Captain Ellis can explain much better than I can." She turned to her console to avoid his glare, but not before she saw him relax just a little and turn toward Ellis.

"Explain!"

"She's right, sir. We have been asking for newer-generation radar for years, but the cost has been too great. Mostly we use the GPN020 surveillance radar, but that fades at about sixty miles. The IFF system is better, but it relies on transponder information for 'identification, friend or foe." If a transponder is inoperative, we are still left to guess. But it is more complicated than that. Radar has its limitations, even with the best of equipment. It picks up metallic echoes best, but multiple echoes, such as trees near a target, can confuse it. It is not as foolproof as people think, sir."

"So you are telling me that that airplane could still be airborne?"

"Theoretically, yes, sir."

"Theoretically?"

"Yes, sir. Theoretically."

"Likely?"

"No, sir. Not likely. Theoretically."

"Thank you, Captain." He turned to the group again. "I want the contingent at Leesburg Executive doubled, quadrupled, whatever it takes to speed up identification of that missing aircraft. And I want a status report on the search in the tunnels. God, we are helpless down here, aren't we?" President Brady walked slowly out of the command center, motioning silently for Sam Davies to follow.

"Sam, get my wife on the line." Neither a command nor a request—it was more like a statement of defeat.

Janet Brady answered on the first ring. "Gary?"

"One minute, Mrs. Brady." Sam handed the telephone to President Brady and retreated to the corner of the room, leaving them as alone as a first couple could be in a crisis.

"Honey, we think Scott might be dead."

"Oh god! How? What is happening, Gary?"

"We don't know. We just know bits and pieces. About an hour after this all began, a twin-engine Piper took off from Leesburg. Janet, Scott landed at Leesburg. And we saw him in the security tunnels on videotape. Security thinks he is an assassin. Shots were fired. There are too many coincidences. But worst of all, I think he was down there because I broke protocol. I gave him my security card to make things easier for him. Janet, I think I just helped kill the one person in this world who really means anything to me besides you and the boys."

"Oh, Gary! There has to be some mistake." Her voice broke.

"We can only hope, dear. We can only hope. We have to run a check on a missing plane over at Leesburg, and that is going to take some time. If his plane is there, then we have hope. I have to go. I love you. Tell the boys I love them. Don't tell them anything else until I say so. Don't tell *anyone* anything. And for God's sake, don't call Rachael. Okay?"

"Of course. Of course, I won't. I love you."

As they hung up, they both realized that all the glamour, all the headiness, all the intrigue of Washington melted away in their tears for Scott Piquard, the one friend they could always count on.

Chapter 5

The Sparrow

Friday, 7:40 a.m. EDT, Evers Military Operations Area

The Apache helicopter skimmed the treetops slowly enough that, even with the reduced visibility, Captain Ray Lang could navigate to his holding area safely while staying below radar minimums. Although practiced for emergencies, piloting the Apache solo was highly irregular. Irregular, but so important that his promotion to major was assured if he did exactly as he was ordered.

The orders arrived in the secret code that he had been allowed the privilege of learning. There could be no mistake. His beloved country had been in decline for decades, and finally someone was doing something about it. The Brotherhood would be the vanguard for taking the country back from the vermin who had infiltrated every niche of government. Only a select few had been chosen for membership, and his loyalty to the basic principles of their founding fathers had earned him his invitation. All full members were on constant lookout for new members, but only those demonstrating a lifelong pattern of proper ideals could be invited inside. It was the only way to save this country.

With the massive low-pressure system that was drenching the country, Lang had not dreamed he would see action today. The First Battalion, 210th Special Operations Aviation Regiment had been in the field for ten days, practicing unconventional attack and live-fire exercises. When he received the coded message, he could hardly believe his luck. A terrorist had stolen an airplane and was in his sector. The airplane carried a bomb and must be destroyed. His mission was to take it out and return to the assembly area—undetected. It was risky, but he had flown in worse. He had flown under overcast as low as fifty feet; the three hundred he had today was child's play. It was the time limitation that would challenge his skills. There had been no warning. Minutes were of the essence. If he could not complete his mission before the aircraft was out of range, he would lose his best chance yet at a below the zone promotion to major.

His takeoff from the assembly area had been extremely hurried, but his practice runs now paid their dues. Following instrument flight rules, he flew quickly to his holding area and then cancelled his flight plan with Potomac Approach. However, once below radar, he flew several more miles to his rendezvous point using visual cues and GPS. Potomac thought he was still on the ground.

His bird was still settling onto the ground when he saw a four-wheeler with two riders slipping out of the trees with a heavy load. No words were spoken—everyone knew their jobs. The black-clad men expertly lifted the standard army-issue Hellfire missile from the bottom left pod and replaced it with an adapted hanger and electronic harness from the oversized duffle on the back of the four-wheeler. They lifted an AIM-7 Sparrow into position on the hanger, connected the electronics harness, and then gave Lang the go sign.

As the engine spooled up to liftoff RPM, he called his superior for an updated position report using the secure frequency. The news was good. The airplane was coursing east to west across his effective range tangent, cruising at 190 knots, level at 9,500 feet. Captain Lang lifted off to a low hover and turned the attack helicopter southwest. The newer D-model AH-64 Apache carried the Longbow MMW radar mounted above the rotor head. This made acquisition simple, and once he confirmed speed, altitude, and absence of competing traffic, he knew he had the right target. Low and slow, it was easy to distinguish from the F-35s. The rest was simple. Lock, fire, and vacate.

The plan was beautiful. By using the AIM-7, he did not actually need to hit the target. His orders were explicit: bring the aircraft down without a direct hit. His superiors did not want that kind of evidence at the scene. The Muslims would think that their pilot had crashed in the storm. The older model-7 air interception missile, the Sparrow, was perfect for the job. New technology had armed the Sparrow with a "smart fuse" that gave it proximity capability. It no longer had to impact the target to detonate. When transitioned to proximity mode, it needed only to sense enough metallic signal in its immediate environment to explode. And as the Sparrows were phased out for newer versions, it had been easy to declare one defunct and secret it away for a mission just like this.

Operating an Apache solo was not that difficult for a skilled pilot, although it was against regulations under normal circumstances. Sitting in the command pilot's seat, behind the gunner's seat, Lang had access to the weaponry. He could fly and fire from here. After he launched the Sparrow, he waited only long enough to confirm detonation and witness the rapid rate of descent of the target. Once he was sure of a hit, he descended.

Setting his bird gently on the ground again, he watched as the two men slipped into position, removed the used hanger and harness, and replaced the unused Hellfire missile.

"Excellent execution, Major Lang," the taller man hollered through the open window.

"I'm Captain Lang," he responded, correcting the man but feeling his heart jump at the sound of "Major Lang."

"Not much longer, sir. Good work out there! Can you confirm a hit?"

"Hit confirmed. He went down like a rock."

"You may now return to the battalion assembly area. You saw nothing. You heard nothing. Your armament count is correct. You will have no problem when you check in with your full ammunition count. Fly below radar to your original IFR descent point, land, and then call control and tell them you are returning to the assembly area. They saw you go below radar several miles to the north. They will see you pop up in the same location and return IFR. Just another practice mission—you sat there awaiting further instructions and then returned to the assembly area. Understood?"

"Totally, sir," Lang replied. "Who do I say gave me authorization for a solo recon?"

"Tell them you were scrambled for ongoing practice for Operation Eagle Thunder. There are three others out as well as you. It will look like business as usual, Major."

Ray Lang grinned again at the salutation he had worked so hard to earn. The terrorist bastard had come right to him, and now his future was certain.

Chapter 6

Weight and Balance

here…am…I? the thought came gradually, hesitantly. Some distant sense told a part of his brain that he was talking to himself, but he couldn't remember the context. *Am I sleeping? Where's Rachael? I must have been dreaming, but the ringing in my ears…* What little he could remember was so surreal, but the pain in his head was too real to ignore. *I've…got…to…wake…up.*

Scott forced his eyes open and pushed himself into a sitting position. The movement helped to awaken him further. Only then did he realize that he had been slumped forward, his weight on the control yoke, forcing his airplane into a steep dive. He grabbed the yoke and pulled back, but it would only move a few inches. Something was binding. He pulled harder, and still it would not travel correctly. Bracing both feet hard against the foot pedals, he pulled with all his strength. Finally, he felt a popping sensation, and the yoke came back against his chest. The surge of positive Gs felt like a weighted pendulum inside his throbbing head as the aircraft leveled off. He glanced at the altimeter: 4900 MSL.

The number seemed familiar. In the haze that he was recognizing as his own consciousness, the number 4,900 seemed important, but he couldn't focus. He couldn't think clearly. Then, slowly, steadily, it came to him. He was heading west, and some of the peaks in this area were 4,800 feet above sea level. He pulled back still harder on the yoke as he scanned the panel. What was the matter? Was he still dreaming? The panel was entirely black.

Peering through the windshield, he could make out the shapes of trees below. He was breaking in and out of the overcast, but he only had a few hundred feet of ceiling and less than 500 yards of forward visibility. At least he could tell that the upslope was to his left, valley floor to the right. He pushed right rudder and banked slightly until he had *Whiskey Mike* centered over the valley floor, but he had to hold hard backpressure or he immediately began to descend. Something was wrong with the elevator. He needed to figure it out. He needed to think, but his head wasn't working right.

Trim! Give her more trim, he heard himself say. He hit the electric trim button. Nothing. He pressed it harder—still nothing. *Manual*, he told himself as he reached with his right hand and began dialing back the elevator trim wheel. The forward pressure of the yoke was nearly too much for one hand. He dialed as fast as he could, and ever so slowly, he could feel the pressure begin to subside. When the trim wheel was fully deflected, he was at last able to hold the yoke with one strong hand. *What next?*

Scott's head swam. The ringing in his ears had lessened but the headache was still overpowering as it came in waves of crescendo-de-crescendo pulsations. There was a memory flickering there, too, but he had trouble grasping it. One second, two seconds, then it came.

Synchronize.

He looked at his panel. All the electrical instruments were black. Scott eased back on the right throttle knob, evening out the engine power. Engines that were out of sync resonated unevenly, making a loud, undulating sound. As the rpm's merged, the pulsating noise lessened appreciably.

What's next? First, fly the airplane. Then think.

He peered ahead. The valley was becoming more narrow and shallow as he neared the crest. He still had one hundred feet of ceiling, but that was precious little at this speed. He concentrated on the valley floor. There, at the base, he could just make out a jeep trail. It was darker than the surrounding terrain and gave him something to focus on. Jeep trails usually crossed a ridge at the saddle, the lowest point. If he could keep it in sight, he just might negotiate the ridge. There was no possibility of making a survivable landing here.

Pelting rain and wisps of cloud did nothing to aid his slant vision, but seconds later, he could make out the crest and the downslope terrain on the west side. The aircraft drifted up into the clouds slightly as he instinctively pulled away from the deadly ridge. Only when his visibility approached zero did he realize he was pulling up. Easing off on the yoke, he let the plane drift back below the clouds. As the ground fell away into the next valley, he was able to relax a little, having acquired nearly three hundred feet of vertical clearance. Relative to the fifty he had just negotiated, three hundred seemed surplus.

Things were starting to come back to him now. The ringing was still there, the throbbing was unforgiving, but at least he was starting to figure out what had happened. He remembered the flash of light and the intense pain in his head before he had blacked out. He must have had a concussion from whatever exploded. That would explain everything from the loss of consciousness to the pain and tinnitus, as well as his dead panel. A few seconds more and he would have been dead.

What to do next? His resources were frightfully limited. His electrical panel was fried. The simple mechanical instruments were all he had to work with. Scott was now flying on a par with the pilots of the 1940s—stick and ball, compass and altimeter. The directional gyro also seemed to be working, drawing its kinetic energy from a vacuum pump connected directly to the engine block and not from an electrical source. Other than that, he was on his own. In good weather, no problem, but in this soup, he couldn't navigate. He could fly straight and level until he ran out of fuel, but he didn't know where he was going. He was flying blind.

Most urgently, he needed to climb. Altitude was paramount; he would die trying to negotiate mountainous terrain in these conditions. And he couldn't turn back, or they would shoot him down.

Shoot me down? His head was clearing. *Shoot me down. Of course.*

Now it all fit—the flash, the explosion, the concussion, the damaged elevator, the fried instruments. *Those bastards tried to shoot me down. They want me dead, and they have the resources to do it.*

Scott knew he must keep going west at least until he cleared the mountains. But how could he navigate? His old Loran, obsolete since invention of the GPS, was out. Both VORs were out, and his GPS was black. Even the antiquated automatic direction finder was dead. There was not a single electrical instrument on the panel that was worth a damn. Then slowly, like a light gradually brightening in the distance, it came to him.

Somewhere in the back of the aircraft was his old flight bag, and somewhere in that was his old handheld GPS receiver, along with a few other things that he had stashed there for an emergency, hoping never to use them. How could he get to them? His autopilot was out, and without constant backpressure, the damaged elevator nosed his plane downward. Scott slackened his grip and immediately sensed the craft nosing forward. He watched the altimeter drifting downward. How could he risk leaving his station even for a few seconds? Even if the GPS was there, the batteries were probably dead. He always intended to charge them periodically, but out of sight, out of mind. Now he would pay for his laxity.

Slowly, another idea formed. Scott reached across the copilot's seat and grabbed the right seat belt. Looping it around the yoke column, centering the pressure, he clipped it into the buckle. It barely reached, but he was able to secure it and pull out the slack. Again, he reduced backpressure. Just a small amount of down drift. He tightened the seat belt further. *Close.* A little tighter and his drift seemed to be neutralized. Now, to make a dash for it.

Unfastening his belt, he crawled out of his seat, made one last scan to make sure his attitude was okay, then lurched down the narrow center aisle. *Please be there*, he said to himself as he searched under the back, right seat.

"Yes!" he shouted as his hand grasped the familiar shape. He pulled, but it caught on something. He pulled again. Still it resisted. He reached his hand under the seat and untangled a strap from the upright, pulling it free. Clutching his prize, he sprinted forward and folded himself back into his seat. He looked out the windshield but all he saw was white. He was back in the clouds, and he was in deep trouble.

Scan.

His eyes automatically went to the artificial horizon, but that was inoperative. *Turn and bank indicator*, he somehow managed to tell himself. Rarely used these days, it was still a fundamental backup when primary instruments failed. Slight left bank. He leveled the wings. Next, he scanned to the Directional Gyro—260. He had drifted a little to the left. Next, altimeter—5,120 and climbing. But the climb was actually leveling itself off. Why?

"You idiot!" he groaned aloud as he solved the riddle. When he trimmed the airplane with the copilot's seat belt, he had trimmed it for the weight and balance as it was. His weight was up front—fore of the center of gravity. When he went to the back of the plane, his weight was aft of CG. That was over a four-hundred-pound difference in torque. He had climbed nearly three hundred feet into the clouds, and, once he was back in his seat, *Whiskey Mike* had readjusted herself to the original straight and level attitude.

Now he dared not descend. As reassuring as eye contact with the ground might be, he could not be assured he was still in the valley. Trying to find clear air now would likely prove fatal. The mountaintops were shrouded in clouds, and he could easily hit one before he broke out. He had dealt his cards, now he had to play the hand. Scott pulled back on the yoke and climbed to temporary safety.

Alternately scanning his partial panel and struggling with the flight bag, he finally unzipped the top and found the GPS receiver inside. Easing it out like a delicate crystal, he cautioned himself not to drop it. It might be the last thing between him and the ground. Scanning again, he corrected his left drift. Unconsciously holding his breath, he placed the GPS antenna in the front window and turned the power knob to the right. He felt the click as it traversed the stop. His eyes squinted at the tiny screen. Blackness. He scanned his panel, then looked back at the GPS screen. Still nothing. The batteries were drained.

Slumping back in his seat, he felt a wave of despair as he realized just how much trouble he was in. He could easily climb over the mountains and cruise into the flatlands of the Midwest, but eventually he would have to descend, and where he broke out would be a matter of chance. Would it be a beautifully flat field, or a hardwood forest or a rugged river valley?

As Scott was beginning to think that this was, after all, his day to die, he again had a remnant of an idea. It was maddening to be in this condition, this haze fogging his brain, throbbing with each heartbeat. He couldn't think quickly enough. His brain seemed to be operating on partial power. Then the picture in his mind completed itself.

The little GPS had an auxiliary power cord!

Fishing in the bottom of the bag, he felt the shape of an electric cable. Pulling it free, he attached it to the top of the unit. He scanned his panel—another slight correction to the right. He grasped the twelve-volt adapter, reached across the panel, and plugged it into the cigarette lighter; being a direct feed from the airplane batteries, it was powered by a simple loop of two wires, not an advanced electronic circuit. Hopefully, the explosion hadn't fried it as well.

Nothing appeared on the screen. He returned to his scan. Left drift—corrected. Altitude—6,100 and climbing. Turn and bank indicator—centered. His eyes drifted back to the GPS. Still nothing. He checked all his gauges and the few instruments he had, then, satisfied that he had done all he could do, he allowed himself one more look at the GPS screen. It was black, and his despair deepened as he sunk back into his seat.

Why had he left Rachael on a negative note? They had promised never to do that. Why was he such an obstinate fool? What would his family do if he died? How would they manage? Did he have enough life insurance, or would they slowly become destitute? His despair now complete, he glanced one last time at the GPS screen on his lap. It was black, but then ever so faintly, he thought he saw a faint glow. Was he imagining this? He squinted harder. Gradually, the glow took on more definition as the depleted batteries sucked life from the airplane battery. He found himself hoping and simultaneously warning himself against hope. He scanned again, and then looked back down to the GPS display. There, in the upper corner, something was barely discernible on the screen, and as he looked closer, he could just make out two faint words.

"Acquiring satellite."

Chapter 7

Organizing a Trap

Friday, 8:00 a.m. EDT, Homeland Security Command Center

"Andrews Control, Foxtrot Alpha 1," the F-35 pilot said as he keyed his microphone button.

"This is Andrews Control, Alpha 1."

"Andrews, Alpha 1. I have acquired a single target on radar, proceeding due west at approximately 185 knots. Do you confirm?"

"That is a negative, Alpha 1. We have no target. Track and report. Andrews over."

Floyd Curtis jumped to his feet as he heard the transmissions from the F-35 pilot. His eyes bored into the screens as he scanned for a third target. *How far west?* He felt his heart pounding with excitement. Was this VIOLATR or a new entrée? The chase might still be on.

Potomac Control normally handled arriving and departing traffic in the DC sector, but when this became a military operation, Andrews Headquarters Control took charge of the military aircraft. Not located in the tower, which only controlled traffic out to seven miles, the headquarters was located in a far more secure location and operated by remote radar in conjunction with Potomac Control TRACON. A tower could be neutralized with a simple grenade, but

74

headquarters could withstand a direct hit by a conventional bomb. Its location was known only by those who needed to know.

Curtis stared at the screens. Gradually, an inconsistent blip several miles to the west flickered on his screen near the F-35s. Thirty seconds later, that blip became constant. Almost simultaneously, he heard Andrews call.

"Alpha 1, Andrews Control. We have radar contact with your target. Heading 2-6-0, speed 185, altitude 6,000 and climbing. Your instructions are to follow, but do not engage. Maintain 10,000. Maintain radar contact with target at all times."

"Ten thousand. Maintain radar contact. Control, did you copy that air-to-air transmission earlier?"

"Negative, we only got a fragment of that. Andrews over."

"The caller said there was a plot on the president's life, and we were to relay a message to the president. That is when we had the explosion and lost communications. Nothing after that. Alpha 1 out."

"We copy, Alpha 1. Andrews out."

And I copy, too, thought Curtis. *This is getting better by the minute.*

Friday, 8:00 a.m. EDT, White House Command Center

President Gary Brady stood transfixed as he listened to the live transmissions. He could feel his shirt moving rhythmically to the pulsations of his heart, and he hoped no one else noticed.

Curt Nearman spoke first. "That must be the guy who took off from Leesburg."

"Very likely, General." Brady said it quietly and without emphasis, trying to hide his emotions. "What is the word on the tunnel search? Any solid info yet?"

"No, sir. The search is still underway. All the major tunnel structures have been cleared, and every building connected to the tunnel system is being searched. It will be some time before every broom closet is cleared, but I assure you, Mr. President, every broom closet will be cleared."

"Thank you, General." Brady tried to hide his elation as he turned back to his private quarters and his unfinished business.

As Nearman walked to the front of the command center, the air was abuzz. "So, Curt, what do you think about all this?" Matt Karber asked. He and Gus Taylor had been conversing. "Do you believe that line about a plot on the president's life, or do you think it was a decoy to buy some time?"

"It does make you wonder, doesn't it?"

Gus Taylor rolled his eyes. "Come on, Curt. You don't buy that conspiracy crap, do you? There's a new one every month, but none of them ever pan out. Why, we haven't had a really good conspiracy theory since Kennedy was shot. That was half a century ago, and that one never amounted to anything either."

"Well, Gus, I hope you're right. The president doesn't need another major distraction right now. He has enough to worry about down south."

"That's for sure. I don't envy the guy one bit, and I'm eternally grateful that I don't have to make those decisions." Taylor turned toward Karber. "What do you think, Matt? Do you think he'll send in the troops? We have nearly half a million around the southern perimeter right now, and we have another half million ready to move within days. Do you think he will do it?"

"I don't know." Karber was nearly whispering, glancing over his shoulder like a child talking in the library. "I think he and the joint chiefs will have to go for it. What else can they do? There is already chaos in the isthmus, and if the Colombians get across the Sierra Madre del Sur, there will be pure panic. We probably should have done it while it was contained in the isthmus. At that point, we could have at least controlled the flanks with the Navy. By allowing their northward advance, we have forfeited that advantage. The Navy could have been more effective if we had acted sooner. I don't know what we are waiting for. We either stop them down south, or we have to stop them up north. The American taxpayers are not going to set-tle for wholesale border crossings. It's already bad enough."

"I know what you mean, but what can we do?" Nearman was now more animated. "Three to four million a year come across as it is, and we do nothing but token border control. If we don't do something, the Minuteman groups are going to open fire."

Gus Taylor studied the two men for a second. "I've known Gary Brady for over thirty years. He'll find a way out of this, believe me. He found his way out of pure shit when he was deployed, and he'll find a way to navigate this creek, too. Mark my words. There has to be a middle ground somewhere. We have to trust him to put it all together. He has access to information we don't, and Brady is one of the smartest men I've ever known."

"You're probably right. You know him better than any of us," Karber whispered a little louder. "It's just that this might already be over if we had done something a few weeks ago. Do either of you think for one minute that those greasy little bastards would have moved an inch if there had been a couple of American battalions in front of them?"

"Whoa! I didn't mean to ruffle any feathers. I was just asking questions," Taylor said as he took a step back. "Sometimes I don't know what to think."

"Well, I know what to think," Karber replied. "If we don't do a little now, we'll have to do a lot later. Always been that way—always will."

"I guess you're right. I just wish it was easier to see what's going to happen," Taylor said as he turned back toward the control area, indicating with his body language that the discussion was over. He insinuated himself between Tim Ellis and Major Brinkman. "Were there any maneuvers today?"

"Negative," Brinkman answered. "There were some helicopter maneuvers this morning, but it was local, low level stuff—foul weather practice. They will all take a complete inventory, but that will take time."

"Yeah, it takes forever to get information. That guy will be a thousand miles from here before we know anything. Then we will corroborate and verify for another month. Then the politicians will form a commission and study data for two years. Then they will release a four-thousand-page report telling us that security was breached, a missile was fired by an unknown person at an unknown target, but we can't be certain of anything else." Taylor spat out the invective like a bite of rotten food.

"I couldn't agree with you more, sir," Brinkman added. "We joined the military because we like to get things done, but we find ourselves mired down in paperwork until we get so sick of it we retire. It's only in battle that we can really do anything."

Friday, 8:00 a.m. EDT, Homeland Security Command Center

Floyd Curtis turned to Captain Block. "Any word from Leesburg yet?"

"No, sir."

"Get me the First Platoon again."

Curtis turned back to the wall of displays and watched his target. Control had now labeled this westbound aircraft WHO in their ID block since VIOLATR had already been assigned. It could be the same aircraft, or it could be whoever fired the shot. It could also be a new flight altogether, although that was unlikely—the speed, direction, and altitude had VIOLATR written all over them. *I am going to find out who you are, my friend, and when you land, we will have an F-35 on each end of the runway before you have time to refuel. You are mine.*

"First platoon, sir," Block said, handing Curtis the radio. "Lieutenant Osterholt."

"Osterholt, this is Lt. Colonel Floyd Curtis at Homeland again. Do you have any tail numbers for me yet? Curtis over."

"Colonel, this is Osterholt. We are just completing our inventory of ramped planes, but most of the hangars are locked. We will have to finish our count when they get the hangers open. We are assuming that the plane in question took off from the tarmac. We are going through the logbooks at the FBO, cross-referencing fuel and work tickets. We do have a list of all the planes that pay long-term ramp fees, and we are crosschecking tail numbers. Still, it will take a while before we can tell you what you want to know. Osterholt over."

"Force the locks on those hangars if you have to. Finish that inventory. I can accept no assumptions. Is the intel team there yet? Curtis over."

"No, sir, traffic is the usual morning mess. I'll let you know when they arrive. And I will authorize forcing the locks on your order. Osterholt over."

"Thanks, Lieutenant. Did your men compare the plane they saw with the pictures at the FBO office?"

"Yes, sir. We all agree it looked like a Piper Twin. They call it a PA-31."

"Thanks. Curtis out."

"Wainright, I need to know how long this guy can keep going. What's the range of a PA-31?"

"I think it's about a thousand miles, Colonel."

"I think it's about a thousand miles, too, but we have a life-and-death situation here, and 'think' isn't good enough, now is it? Now get me data! I want to know which cornfield he is going down in when he runs out of fuel."

Wainright turned and walked sheepishly to his computer. He knew he was lucky that Curtis was on duty today. Any other officer would have chewed his ass for a guess like that, but then most officers would not be as meticulous as Curtis. "Details, details, details. It's all in the details," he had told them a thousand times.

In less than two minutes, Wainright had the answer. "Sir, I have that range data for you. Depending on how it is configured, a PA-31 has a range of 1,210 to 1,400 nautical miles at best efficiency cruise power. But if they mistook it for a PA-30, that would give a range of only 892 nautical miles."

"Good. Now give us near, middle, and far marks on that wall map."

Curtis turned to the next bank of consoles. "Kesselhoff, get me HQ at Tinker Air Force Base. And Dugan, get me NEADS on the line again. I don't know how far west he plans to go, but I plan to have a reception party waiting for him."

Thirty seconds later, Dugan motioned to Curtis. "NEADS on your line 3, sir."

Curtis picked up line 3. "Hello, NEADS command? This is Lt. Colonel Floyd Curtis at Homeland Security Headquarters, Washington, DC."

"Good morning, Colonel. This is Major Tony Brannen at NEADS. The general is in conference. What can we do for you?"

"Good morning, Major. We have a situation out of the DC sector, and I need some help coordinating a tracking mission." Curtis briefed him quickly. "We have two F-35s following a PA-31 west across the Appalachians. They are halfway to Kentucky already. I need to coordinate a handoff, and I need a pre-auth in case they get into the Western Area Defense Sector. My 35s will have to turn back eventually. They have the speed, but they don't have the range. I am asking you to contact WADS for me and pre-authorize a hand-off. In addition, I want NEADS to okay this coordination for as long as the target is still in the northeast sector. We might as well give SEADS a heads-up too in case he turns south. We don't know where he is headed or how far he plans to go, so I am asking for carte blanche on what I need, when I need it."

"That shouldn't be a problem, sir. There is nothing going on today. I'll update the general and make sure the brass gets you top-level cooperation."

"I'm calling Tinker to request further help out west, and I want a fighter escort until he lands. We also want ground units on standby to mobilize to that point, but we have no idea where to send them right now."

"Thanks for the info," Brannen said. "I'll get right back to you."

"Thanks, Major. Talk to you later."

As Curtis was hanging up, he saw Kesselhoff waving at him. "Oklahoma on line 2, Colonel."

He picked up two. "Lieutenant Colonel Floyd Curtis, Homeland Security Command Center. Good morning."

"Good morning, sir. This is Colonel Wes Alvine at Tinker Headquarters. What can I do for you today?"

Curtis went through his story again. "Can you launch an E-3 for me? My 35s do not have the range. We'll have to hand him off until he lands, and although I want a fighter escort at all times, I cannot risk losing him. This is absolutely top priority."

"I'm sure the commander will allow that, given the circumstances," Alvine said, obviously interested. "We are a little shorthanded right now, though, due to the concentration of operations on the southern border. I'll call you back the minute I contact the general."

"Thanks, Colonel. We'll be in touch."

Curtis cradled the phone and looked at the screens on the wall. His target droned on to the west. It seemed so slow compared to the jet traffic he was accustomed to monitoring, yet the three blips were steadily crossing the Appalachian range and would soon be into the flatlands. At least he had the semblance of a plan. The idea to use AWACS surveillance had been his own little gem.

The Airborne Warning And Control System developed by the Air Force utilized incredibly powerful radar units mounted on the fuselage of Boeing 707 frames. The "flying saucer" atop the aircraft gave the E-3 Sentry one of the most distinct silhouettes in all of aviation. The E-3 was often called an AWACS plane, people mistakenly calling it by the name of the program that gave birth to it instead of the name given it by Boeing. Fitted with long-range fuel tanks, it had an endurance of over eleven hours, and the radar generators were so strong that the walls of the aircraft were lined to shield the men inside. In fact, Curtis was aware of the inside rumor that AWACS men only conceived male infants.

Between the E-3 and the F-35s, the rogue aircraft could not escape. The F-35 was one of the most capable fighters in the history of flight, but what it could carry in armament, it gave up in fuel load. Its effective operational radius was only about five hundred nautical miles, but they did not have to fly out five hundred and back five hundred. They could follow until they were near another base. Then they could hand off, refuel, and return to Andrews. That put an extra one to two hours at his disposal. Curtis would have the trap set, but he needed help springing it, because he had no idea where they would attain convergence.

Chapter 8

Mapping a Plan

Friday, 8:45 a.m. EDT, West Virginia airspace

T he pounding in his head was easing and the vertigo had waxed, but the tinnitus was still horrific. Scott feared he had suffered permanent cochlear damage. It was hard to concentrate on his maps. The fog in his head was almost worse than that in his windshield. He oriented his maps and used the GPS to figure his coordinates. It was essential that he avoid major population centers, or it would give them another excuse to shoot him down. The Ohio border was ahead, and Cincinnati was the next large target to avoid. He turned ten degrees south. This would also take him south of Indianapolis. Beyond there, no major obstacles loomed for the next two to three hours. He would track north of St. Louis and stay clear of Kansas City airspace. Other than that, he had fairly clear sailing into Kansas and the first part of his hastily conceived plan. He would stay in the safety of the clouds until his hand was forced. After that, he would take one step at a time.

As he tried to shake the heaviness from his head, he had a brief vision of another time that his life had hung in the balance with Gary's. How long ago? That was in another life. But there was no time to think of that now. *Fly the airplane first. Everything else is secondary.* How many pilots had died because they had not heeded that basic principle? How many had augered it in because they were so concerned about their heading and destination that they forgot to control airspeed and attitude, either stalling and crashing by getting too slow or breaking up in flight due to excessive airspeed in a graveyard spiral? *Fly the airplane first!*

One thing did remain constant, now and in that previous life. Pain became a secondary cortical signal if the primary signal was strong enough. While he was concentrating on his maps and his readouts, his head throbbed less, and the ringing faded. To control his pain, he concentrated on otherness. He had one problem to solve; he had another problem to tolerate. The best way to repress a problem was to work on its solution.

"I know I am being followed," he thought aloud, the better to understand the words in his thoughts. "They can outfly me, they can outmaneuver me, and they can outgun me, but if they can't see me, then I have one advantage. Sometimes one advantage is all you need—like the halfback who knows which way he is cutting before the defender knows. Therein lies his tiny edge. And I have something else they don't have." He chuckled to himself as he thought about his next move.

Chapter 9

Expanding the Trap

"Tinker Air Force Base on line 2, Colonel," Kesselhoff said as he motioned to Curtis to pick up. "Commanding Officer."

"Good morning, sir. This is Lieutenant Colonel Floyd Curtis at Homeland Security Headquarters."

"Good morning, Curtis. This is General Verne Kinney, commanding officer at Tinker Air Base. Colonel Alvine said you've been having an interesting morning out there. What can I do for you?"

"Well, sir, I was hoping you might have an E-3 that you could loan us. We have a tracking job of the utmost priority. There has been an intrusion into a secure area of the White House and a threat made on the president's life. Shortly after that, a PA-31—or at least what we believe is a PA-31—took off on an unauthorized flight despite explicit military warning, and he is now heading toward your backyard. I am requesting an E-3 launch to monitor until he is in custody. We have a pair of F-35s following him, but AWACS capability would greatly help us."

"Isn't a Sentry a little bit of overkill for a PA-31, Colonel?"

"Well, yes and no. It depends on how important the objective is. And we think this one is very important. Any threat on the president's life is serious, and they seem connected—the timing is too coincidental."

"Colonel, ordinarily I would jump at the chance to help, but right now we are down to one E-3 on the field. They've pulled most of our base south. We are flying recon sorties over the Isthmus of Panama around the clock. I don't think this sounds like the best use of resources. Hell, if a group of F-35s with onboard radar can't keep him in sight, they had better get some better pilots."

"I realize that, sir, but we have zero-zero conditions out here, and according to the weather maps, your conditions are no better. Since my boys can't use their eyes, I thought you might let us borrow some of yours. The radar on a 35 is pretty good for hard targets in flight, but when he lands, we run the risk of losing acquisition. With a set of AWACS eyes, we can tell which half of the runway he is landing on. Besides, it would look good on your report if you help nab him."

"Why not just shoot the bastard down?"

"I do understand your position, sir, but no shots are to be fired. That is a direct order from President Brady. Actually, I have a hot line to the White House situation room. Would you like me to patch you through to the president? It would only take me a few seconds." Curtis turned toward Kesselhoff, Block, and Dugan, a smirk just beginning to form on his lips. "Check," he whispered, covering the mouthpiece with his left hand.

"No. That's okay. My boys can always use some practice. We'll launch within the half hour. Alvine will call you for a position update when they are ready to roll. You boys have fun, you hear?" Kinney added as he hung up.

Curtis turned to his men and grinned. "Mate."

"Nice job, sir," Dugan said. "But couldn't you have just invoked Homeland priority?"

"Lieutenant colonels don't pull rank on generals, son. If I had tried that, he might have gotten his hackles up and cost me more time. I got what I wanted, and he didn't lose face. You get more bees with honey than you do with vinegar."

Dugan's line lit up again. "Major Brannen from NEADS, sir."

Curtis picked up the dedicated Triad line. "Major Brannen, Curtis here. Sorry to bother you again, but I need to alert all northeast and western bases that I would like helo crews on alert to intercept."

"Excellent idea, Curtis. I'll make those calls for you. I'll tell McChord to expect to hear from you within the next, what, one to three hours?"

"He has about four more hours of fuel. I have already talked to Tinker and have an E-3 authorized, but I would like to alert Peoria, Grissom, Springfield, Ft. Wayne, Hulman, and Mansfield, at least. Farther west, we can alert Des Moines and Lincoln, plus Forbes in Kansas. That is about the limit of his fuel, so we'll have him by then. If he turns south, we replot our possibilities."

"Sounds good to me, Curtis. I'll let them know. I'll also make sure the army boys have their pants on when this turns into a ground operation. They will have the helicopters ready for the final intercept."

Curtis turned back to his monitors. He had that feeling of satisfaction that a well-planned mission afforded a methodical person. Still, he had that sense of gnawing unease that he knew too little. Who fired that missile, and why? What was he missing?

Friday, 10:45 a.m. EDT, White House Command Center

President Brady strode from the inner room, stretching. "Any news?" He was dying to ask about the airplane but remained circumspect. "What do we know, and when can we get out of here?"

"Nothing yet, sir," Greg Stroud answered. "But it takes time, and your safety is my priority."

"What about Leesburg?"

"There's a team over there looking at all arrivals and departures for the past few days, but they don't have anything concrete yet. There is a battalion on their way to where we thought VIOLATR had crashed earlier, but we don't expect them to find anything. We think it must be the same guy who climbed out of the mountain valley several miles to the west. The only other airports in that area are on the other side of the ridge. In this weather, no one else would be tooling around in those mountains, especially no one with that kind of airspeed, but they need to complete the search just the same."

"How long until they're done at Leesburg? I want something concrete."

"Good question, Mr. President. We thought they would be done by now. Ernie Knoll is our FBI liaison over there, and they tell me he's good, but there's no tower there so all the records are at Warrenton, and half of them are probably in a trash can. They keep everything on tape for a couple of weeks, but that will take days to parse." Stroud shrugged his shoulders, palms up.

"That aircraft—is it still airborne?" Brady asked nonchalantly.

"Yes, sir," Air Force General Curt Nearman answered. "It has been airborne about three hours and is several miles north of St. Louis, still west bound and almost to the Missouri border. It had been heading straight toward our B-2 installation at Whiteman Air Force Base but then turned several miles north. Those B-2s cost $2.2 billion a pop, and there is a strict no-fly policy there. His turn was intentional." Nearman took Brady to the bank of screens on the wall and pointed at three blips moving steadily westward. "The Homeland Security Command Center is coordinating reconnaissance. A lieutenant colonel named Floyd Curtis is running the show over there—seems to know what he's doing. His commanding officer is Major General George Kidner. He was at his country home two hours south, and traffic is slower than usual with the storm. This Curtis sounds like the workhorse over there, though. Everything has been coordinated seamlessly."

"How much farther can he fly?" Brady asked, knowing that Scott had only refueled once to come nearly two thousand miles.

"We think he has one to two more hours of fuel, sir, unless he has had special tanks installed."

"How far can he fly if he has special tanks installed?"

"That depends on their size. *Air Force One* can stay aloft for eleven hours and cover half the globe on one refill, but it is unlikely that a civilian aircraft has more than tip tanks. Another hour or two would be my guess."

"Good! When they corner him, I want him flown here immediately for questioning."

"Can we do that, sir?" Taylor asked. "I mean, extradition takes time."

"This is federal. I want him in Washington before that governor even knows he was there."

Friday, 10:45 a.m. EDT, Homeland Security Command Center

Floyd Curtis keyed the frequency for the First Platoon. "Osterholt, I need information. Why isn't that ramp search completed yet? Over."

"Sorry, sir, but there's a lot of planes out here and scanty records on their comings and goings. We have accounted for all the planes that are here year round, and no aircraft were missing from the hangars. We found fuel tickets for seventeen planes that landed here within the past week that we cannot confirm whereabouts on, but only three of those were in the last four days. We are trying to call the numbers they listed on their flight plans or on the fuel ticket but aren't having a lot of luck. So far, we have only located four of those pilots, so we still have thirteen to account for. And I have one very pissed off guy with a broken hangar lock. I gave him your name. He quieted down after I said you were in charge of Homeland Security. Hope you don't mind, sir, but I had to get him out of my face. Osterholt over."

"No problem, Osterholt. Now listen! I want you to fax me that list of tail numbers with those three most recent ones underlined. I know a guy at FAA in Oklahoma City. All US aircraft are registered there and are logged in their computers. They can find ownership information in a few minutes." Curtis gave him the fax number and signed off. "Block, find the number for FAA Headquarters in Oklahoma City. See if Mickey O'Loughlin is working today and get him on the line. If not, get me whoever is in charge." One of the things that made Curtis so good at what he did was the network of friends he had established over the years. His staff was repeatedly amazed at his recall of names, but he quietly reminded them that an information specialist should have information.

Grabbing a fresh cup, Curtis sat down for the first time in nearly four hours and thought about his next steps. He would soon have helicopters ready to intercept the suspect aircraft, and when it landed, they would close rapidly. But if this person had someone waiting for him, they could be gone in minutes. They could lose him regardless of how quickly the choppers got there. So what he needed was a name—a person he could run to ground.

"Oklahoma on three, Colonel," Block said from his console.

"Lt. Colonel Curtis, Homeland Security Command Center."

"Hello, Floyd. This is Mickey. How you doing?"

"Good. Real good. How's life been treating you?"

"Good. Family's healthy. Amy is starting college, so that will wipe out the raise I got and then some. Fishing's been good, so when are you coming out this way?"

"Soon, I promise, but right now I need you to run some planes for me. I want to fax you a list and have you run down ownership names, addresses, and phone numbers—everything you've got. The list I'm sending you has three tail numbers underlined. Give those three top priority, and call me back ASAP."

"Will do, Floyd."

Curtis turned to Block. "Tap into the FAA database. Find me a list of all fixed-base operators in the United States and a list of all US airports, airport managers, and their phone numbers."

"Yes, sir." Block turned to his console and went to work.

Curtis picked up his two-way radio again. "Osterholt, Curtis again, over."

"Osterholt here, over."

"Osterholt, have you seen Dr. Dan Townsend yet? He's the doctor from Ft. Meyer. Over."

"Yes, sir. He's been asking that cab driver a lot of questions and has been talking with the FBI guys. You want to talk to him? Over."

"Yes. Have him call me on a landline. You have my number?"

"Yes, sir. Osterholt out."

One minute later Curtis' phone came to life again, and he recognized the voice.

"What have you got, Doctor Dan? Does that note look real?"

"Sure does. The terminology is correct. The spelling is correct. The diagnosis matches the treatment. Whoever wrote this knows some medicine."

"You think he's a doctor?"

"Could be. The cab driver is pretty convinced. The guy even examined the spot on his ear, palpated it for texture, and didn't hesitate one second when he explained the diagnosis and treatment. He is either a very smooth operator, or he was just doing what came naturally. Only someone who knows medicine could have written this note. He might not be a doctor, but he's at least a tech or higher."

"Thanks, Dan. If you come up with anything else, call me back. I'll be here until this thing is over. I owe you one!"

"No problem, Floyd. Talk to you later."

"Before you hang up, is there a guy named Ernie Knoll from FBI over there?"

"He's right here. You want to talk to him?"

"Yes."

Another pause. "Knoll here."

"Hello, this is Lieutenant Colonel Floyd Curtis at Homeland Security Command Center. How is your morning going?"

"Interesting, to say the least. What can I do for you?"

"I'm just wondering if you know any more than what Osterholt and Doctor Townsend have already told me." Curtis explained what he knew so far.

"Not really," Knoll said. "The two staff people on night duty were in a back room and didn't see a thing. There's nothing missing at the desk area. We don't know if he hot-wired a plane or had his own keys. If we get any leads on those tail numbers, we can try to match the handwriting on the cab driver's note with whatever we get from FAA, but that could take days."

"I have a friend at FAA headquarters in Oklahoma City, a guy I served with back in the day. He is already working on the list. Let's work together and share our information. Time is of the essence. We can run parallel searches. I can get military access quicker than you can, and you can get a lot of civilian information faster than I can, so let's augment one another. Okay?"

"Sounds good, Curtis. I've got your direct number from Osterholt along with your fax. I'll give you my cell number since I'll be on the move. By the way, where is he now?"

"He's north of St. Louis, still heading west. He held the same heading for a long time, but then he turned northwest. He had been heading straight toward Scott Air Force Base at St. Louis, and we made a hand-off there. Now he is going to pass quite a few miles north of Whiteman Air Base at Sedalia, Missouri. They have a group of stealth bombers there, and if he kept going, we were going to have to take him out. This is no suicide mission—he's passed up dozens of good targets already."

"Thanks for the info, Curtis. I'll get my guys cracking and get back to you when I know something."

Chapter 10

Running Low Near Kansas

Friday, 11:45 a.m. CDT, Missouri airspace

S cott watched his fuel indicator needles relentlessly tilting to the left. Burning off his tip tanks first kept the weight inboard but burning them completely dry was something he had never done before. Today was a different day; today required a different plan. To maximize range, he waited to switch tanks until he lost rpm's, assuring that he had drained all useable fuel from the tanks. Waiting for the rpm drop was mind wracking. If his timing was off one second, he could aspirate air and kill the engines.

His shoulders ached, and his head throbbed with each heartbeat. All he wanted to do was go to sleep, but thankfully, it would be over soon. He could only hope his hastily conceived plan would work. He would travel as far west as *Whiskey Mike* would take him and then turn himself over to local authorities. The truth would come out in the investigation. After all, he had the president of the United States for his defense attorney.

The headwinds had slowed his progress, but certain now that his fuel would take him into Kansas, he felt oddly reassured. No one in Kansas would care about what went on in DC this morning. They would go through their paces methodically. They would be dubious.

They would make some calls. But they wouldn't shoot at him, and that was a start.

Poring over his maps the past three hours, he struggled to select his landing site. The final choice depended on his fuel, but now he was convinced he could make it. The chosen spot had all the ingredients he needed to buy the one thing he needed most. Time.

Once clear of the congested Kansas City airspace, Scott turned 30 degrees south. Heading—2-4-0 degrees. Altitude—descending to 4,000. Speed—180 knots. Fuel—1/8 of a tank. Not much, but enough. Cruising until his bearing to the Manhattan, Kansas, airport was 210 degrees, he turned to a heading of 2-1-0. Now he should be lined up directly with runway 2-1. Slowly, he descended to 3,000. Those watching would see that he was lining up for an approach to Manhattan. Air traffic control would notice that the "no radio aircraft" was descending, and they would clear the corridor for him. Now all Scott could do was pray that he had enough ceiling for an approach. With no radios, he had no weather updates or visibility reports, and his fatigue was beginning to play on his nerves. He realized he was crazy for trying this, but it was too late to turn back. He had no fuel. If conditions at Manhattan were zero-zero, he would probably die.

Friday, 12:45 p.m. EDT, Homeland Security Command Center

"Tinker Headquarters on three, Colonel." Wainright was motioning Curtis back to his desk.

"Curtis, Homeland Security."

"This is Alvine at Tinker, Colonel. General Kinney wants to inform you that your Sentry is airborne."

"Thank you, Colonel Alvine. What are their orders?"

"They are cruising due north until intercept, then they will slow her down, cruise at twenty thousand, and keep an eye on your man. From that vantage point, there is no place we can't see him—unless he flies into a tunnel."

"Perfect! Fort Leonard Wood has two choppers with fourteen-man crews airborne, and Fort Riley in Kansas has two more preparing for a handoff. Thanks for your help, Alvine, and if you ever get out to Andrews, the drinks are on me."

As Curtis turned back to his work, Kesselhoff whispered to Block, "Why is he always buying the drinks? Seems like he's the one doing all the work."

Block returned Kesselhoff's whisper. "You haven't been here long, but you'll learn that the colonel has a huge network. If he ever needs help, he has dozens—make that hundreds—of people he can call, and they will go out of their way. They all feel like they owe him a favor. Watch and learn, son. You are working with the master."

"Yeah, whenever we go out, I've noticed he's always buying the first round."

"And he always will. He is the main reason people re-up for this stint. You couldn't find a better job if you tried. If we get a captain or a major in here who is one of those ego types, the colonel will weed him out of here, pronto. Says it's the worst morale killer there is. And the general will pretty much do whatever the colonel asks because he makes his life so easy. Hell, Kidner can golf six days a week because he knows all the *t*'s are crossed and all the *i*'s are dotted."

Kesselhoff was getting that "I see" look on his face. "No wonder the general's never here. I just thought it was part of the operation."

"Not only that," Block continued. "I think the colonel prefers him to be golfing. The guy just slows him down. Curtis has to stop and explain any new technical stuff to him. You watch sometime. Watch his eyes. I don't think he knows we know, so don't say anything, okay?"

"Okay. Thanks, sir." Kesselhoff was starting to feel like he belonged.

Back at his desk, Curtis grabbed his notebook and dialed a number.

"Knoll, here."

"Ernie, Curtis at Homeland again. I don't want to be a pest, but this has gone out on the Teletype, hasn't it?"

"Oh yeah. At least an hour ago, I'd say."

"Do you guys still do corridor calls?"

"Yes. That should be underway already. The message went out to every city police and county sheriff's office in the United States. I called headquarters with your update, and they were starting the calling chain. They will call all law enforcement offices within a two-hundred-mile radius of the last known path of travel to make sure they didn't miss the message. It's pretty automatic."

"Thanks, Ernie. Just checking. Talk to you later."

They hung up, and Curtis looked back at his men. "Anything else?"

"Nothing I can think of," Block said. "Maybe the general will have some ideas. He just walked in. Attention!"

"At ease, gentlemen," Kidner said as he breezed into the control room. "Sorry you got stuck with all this, Curtis. Traffic was a bear. What do you have so far?"

Curtis spent the next ten minutes reviewing the situation with the general. "And when he lands, the choppers will drop a thirty-soldier perimeter around him. He can't take off again because he's out of fuel, and there will be an F-35 on each end of the runway within minutes of touchdown. He either surrenders or he dies."

"Well done, Curtis. Well planned and well orchestrated. I'll be in my office. Send for me if there's any action. I want to see this thing finished up cleanly."

"Absolutely, sir, and we'd appreciate any ideas you have. There is always some little thing you don't think about until you see it unfolding."

"I'll let you know if I think of anything." Kidner started toward his office, a large glassed enclosure that allowed him a panoramic view of the entire situation room. Pausing, he turned back. "You know, I have a friend over at the FBI. They should know about this too. It's not just a military operation, you know."

"Good idea, sir. Let me know if he has any leads." Curtis turned toward his desk, his eyes rolling momentarily before he closed them and gave his head a subtle shake. The whole thing took less than a half second, but Kesselhoff had been watching. A thin smile crossed his lips as he glanced at Block and winked.

"I wish I could be there when he lands," Curtis said as he looked at the radar screens and then looked closer still. Was that what he thought it was? Yes. The blip was changing directions. It was turning southwest. "Manhattan, Kansas. He turned straight for Manhattan, Kansas. He must be about out of fuel, but good Lord, doesn't he know he's heading straight for an army base?"

Chapter 11

Phone Call West

Brigadier General Allen Carpenter exited the Pentagon parking lot, turning south on Jefferson Davis Highway. He came this way frequently, often meeting friends in the Crystal City underground mall for lunch. To stay in shape, he usually parked in a public lot and walked, but today, time mattered. The valet parking at the Crown Plaza would save him ten minutes. If he missed contact, money was superfluous.

Carpenter handed the valet a five and walked through the electric doors. A bank of telephones and computers were artfully nestled in the corner of the lobby, but that was far too public despite the ambient spacing. Bounding up the stairs two at a time, Carpenter glided past the second-floor restaurant and slipped down the hall to a single-stall phone kiosk. He could not use his cell phone for this call. He pulled a handful of quarters from his coat pocket and placed them on the tiny shelf then quickly dialed the number that for so long had been committed to memory. On cue, he put in several quarters. It rang once. He hung up. Exactly sixty seconds later, he dialed again and reinserted his coins. The phone was answered on the first ring.

"Brian's Flowers. How may we help you today?"

"Do you have any gold and pink chrysanthemums?"

"No, sir. We only deal in purple chrysanthemums during this phase of the moon."

"What phase is that?" Carpenter looked over his shoulder. The hallway was still empty.

"What phase do you want it to be?"

"Blue moon phase."

"How can I help you?"

"Do we have a man in Kansas—Fort Riley?" He could hear a keyboard clicking in the background during the long pause.

"Yes, we do."

"There will be a chopper mission within the hour. Get him on it."

"We will try, sir."

"He *must* be on that mission. There is no room for failure here. Pull out all the stops. Assure him we have his back."

"Yes, sir. We will do our best. What are his orders?"

"Operation Ammo Count. There is a lone male in the aircraft they will be intercepting. He is low on fuel and will be landing soon. Our man is to take the shot when he has it. You can guarantee him this will mean immediate advancement."

"Yes, sir. Consider it done."

Chapter 12

Manhattan Two-One

Friday, 1:00 p.m. CDT, Manhattan, Kansas

T here is a sense of four-dimensional thinking, a sense of space in three dimensions changing over time, which some people possessed naturally and others never would. It couldn't be taught. Tom Wolfe called it the "right stuff" for a reason. It was what culled the weak from the survivors. Scott had survived many close calls, but he had never pushed his skills this far beyond the envelope. Today would be the ultimate test. He had created several approaches into small towns using GPS only since small towns generally had no nav aids, but he was always able to test them in good weather. Today, he did not have that option. He was preparing to run an instrument approach with a fried instrument panel, empty fuel tanks, and no weather report. Failure equaled death.

Friday, 2:00 p.m. EDT, Homeland Security Command Center

"Colonel, Kansas City Center is reporting a "no radio aircraft" making an approach to Manhattan Regional Airport, Manhattan, Kansas."

"Thanks, Dugan." Curtis hit the speaker button so his team could hear. "Kansas Center, this is Lt. Colonel Floyd Curtis at Homeland Security Command Center. What is your report?"

"Colonel, we are tracking the aircraft designated WHO. Several minutes ago, he turned southwest—directly toward Manhattan Regional Airport. He is aligned with runway 2-1. That is the larger of the two runways, 7,000 feet long, 150 wide. There has been no radio contact, but he obviously has the ability to navigate. He is pretty close to centerline, six minutes out."

"Roger that, Kansas. The choppers from Fort Riley are deploying three dozen soldiers around his perimeter. I want you to clear those 35s to land as soon as he exits the runway. They will then block the runway until he is in custody."

"We understand, Colonel. The team leader is holding at four thousand, and the other is holding at five until we clear them down."

"Can't they just follow him in?" Curtis asked.

"Negative, sir. If he misses his approach, he will have to climb out and try again. Regulations require three miles lateral and a thousand feet vertical separation in weather like this. I'll clear them to land when able."

"Thanks, Kansas. We'll stay live with you."

Curtis watched the blips approaching Manhattan in a long final approach to the runway. *Why would he pick Manhattan out of all the places he could have landed? Did he just fly as far as his fuel would take him, or does he live in Manhattan?*

"Dugan, get me Mickey O'Loughlin in Oklahoma City again." Curtis turned. "Smolik, call Manhattan Regional and tell them to get their fire and maintenance personnel to pull out all their big equipment and block all the taxiways as soon as he lands. We don't need a repeat of Leesburg."

Less than a minute passed when Dugan spoke. "O'Loughlin on line one, sir."

"Curtis, here. Mickey, have you got anything for me yet? Are any of those pilots from Kansas?"

"I was just about to fax you the first sheets. I have the three priority aircraft ID'd and the first four from the secondary group.

The three at the top come from Connecticut, Idaho, and Texas. The one from Connecticut is a 182—not even close to the description or airspeed. The one from Texas is a Seneca, and the one from Idaho is a Navajo. Either of those could be the configuration your men saw in the mist. But we still have several other craft to ID. I'll get you more as soon as I can. Enjoy!"

"Thanks, Mickey. Talk to you later." Curtis hung up and turned to Wainright. "What's the range on a Piper Seneca, Wainright?"

"I'll get it for you in a minute, sir. I know just where to look," he said as he gave a little salute and hung his head.

As soon as Curtis heard the whir of the fax machine, he grabbed the papers from Mickey and dialed Ernie Knoll's cell number. It rang twice. "Knoll here."

"Ernie, this is Curtis at Homeland. Do you have a pen and paper handy?"

"Let me pull over. I'm in traffic right now."

"No rush. I have a couple of names for you to run for me."

"Okay. What do you have?"

"I need you to find out whatever you can about a Russell Jameson from Bridgeport, Texas, and a Scott Piquard from Granger, Idaho. If they have an alibi for today, fine. If not, I want to know their current and last known whereabouts, what they do, where they go, whom they associate with, what their politics are, and what color of shorts they wear."

"That's all?"

"Get me that much, and I'll be a happy soldier."

"Talk to you when I can."

"Thanks, Ernie," Curtis said as he hung up.

"Well, boys," Curtis intoned to the men in the room, "it's been fun, but he's flying right into our hands. I can't figure it though. Why would he take off over a military roadblock, fly for almost six hours, and then land right next door to a military base? Maybe it's not the same guy. We have been assuming that the plane that climbed out of that Appalachian valley is the same one that went down after that explosion. Suppose it's a different one?" His voice trailed off as he pondered.

All eyes were on the radar screens as the aircraft approached the northeast end of the runway. Kansas Center came over the speakers again. "This is Kansas Center. Our aircraft is drifting right of centerline. He is down to eight hundred—the ceiling is about six right now—but he's definitely right of centerline, and he doesn't appear to be correcting." There was a pause, and then the voice resumed. "He is down to seven and further right. Six-fifty. Six hundred. He's almost a half mile to the right now. He's not going to make it."

Friday, 1:30 p.m. CDT, Manhattan, Kansas

Six miles out, Scott had descended to two thousand, still nearly a thousand feet above Manhattan's 1,056 feet above sea level. He coordinated his altimeter with his GPS altitude. Three miles out, certain that he was now clear of the large radio towers to the northeast, he began a steady, controlled descent. He kept his GPS indicator centered until he was one mile from the runway. Here, Scott purposefully drifted right, away from the control tower that loomed left of the runway. His shoulders ached and sweat coated his palms as he gripped the yoke too tightly. His heart pounded frantically. *Will there be enough ceiling, or is this my day to die?* His GPS told him he should be near the threshold, but still he could see nothing. Scott inched the plane lower. He had no other choice. Whiteout conditions still persisted as he let *Whiskey Mike* drift lower still. He sensed a growing tremor in his muscles as he searched frantically for the ground. At last, he could make out the dark shadow of the earth below him, brown through white mist. Seconds later, he broke out under the overcast exactly as planned—one half mile right of course and heading slightly away from the runway. He had a ceiling of nearly 600. Plenty of room.

Scott set his altimeter to 1600 as he skimmed the bottom of the clouds. Now he had a solid reference point. The next approach would be much easier. *That will give them something to think about*, he said to himself as he climbed into the mists and began a banking right turn, back to the northeast.

He climbed to two thousand and cruised outbound six miles. Turning 180 degrees, he again aligned *Whiskey Mike* with runway 2-1. Again he waited until he was within the three-mile mark, and again he began his descent. Much more relaxed, he could now anticipate breakout.

Friday, 2:37 p.m. EDT, Homeland Security Command Center

Kansas Center had been narrating the play by play. "Now he is beyond the threshold. He should be breaking out any time, but I doubt he can save this approach. Five-fifty. Negative! He is climbing and turning back to the north. Missed approach!"

"So," Curtis said aloud, "I guess he's not that good after all. He never did try to correct. Maybe his radios aren't the only things that aren't working?"

They all stood motionless, watching the blips moving. "Does that happen very often, sir, a missed approach?" Dugan asked.

"I don't know," Curtis replied. "I'm not a pilot, but I would imagine it does. It would be hard to do all those things at once. I've read that over half of the people who start pilot training never make it through, and it is much harder for instrument training."

On their small screen, they could not see the kind of detail that Center enjoyed on their expanded radar, so they welcomed the play-by-play. "I'll bet you a beer he makes it this time, Colonel." Kesselhoff was smiling and holding up one finger.

"No bet. I think he will too."

Kansas Center came back live with the next approach. "He's down to seven hundred, but he's starting to drift right again. Six hundred, five-fifty, five hundred, four-fifty, four hundred, three-fifty, three hundred—he's not correcting! He needs to pull up!"

Everyone watched as the aircraft continued to drift to the right, losing altitude rapidly, and then disappeared from their screens. "Looks like he might have augered it in, Colonel. Radar contact lost. Kansas Center, out."

Chapter 13

Clay Center, Kansas

Friday, 1:40 p.m. CDT, Kansas airspace

Scott could feel the adrenaline ramping up. He always had this sense of intensity when making an instrument approach. Maybe that was what kept him alive. Maybe, without a healthy sense of fear, he would already be dead like thousands of pilots who let complacency take the place of compulsiveness. But compared to being shot at, this was like a sip of decaf.

On the first approach, he had been extremely nervous; on the second, he was ready for his gambit. Rock beats scissors. Knowledge beats fear. With two hundred feet of ceiling, he would have been forced to land; with six hundred, he had room to spare. As he made his final approach, he drifted further to the right, and when he broke out, he dove the plane to the west. He had to avoid the Flint Hills, but his calculations had been flawless, and after a few miles of barreling across the hilltops, he could see the reservoir and the Republican River. He dove into the river valley.

Friday, 2:44 p.m. EDT, Homeland Security Command Center

Lt. Colonel Floyd Curtis flew to his phone bank. "Kansas Center, do you have radio contact with an E-3 Sentry that we launched for AWACS capability?"

"Not yet, sir. We can try to raise them for you."

"See if they have a look yet. And see if the fighters have radar acquisition."

Almost simultaneously, they could hear the chatter from Center as the group leader came back live. "Kansas Center, this is Red Dog Three Three Charlie. We still have a weak signal—target is proceeding at low altitude west of the airport. We will maintain altitude and follow."

"3-3, Charlie Kansas Center. Released from hold. Maintain four thousand. 4-7 Delta, released from hold. Maintain five thousand. Keep us informed." Both fighter pilots acknowledged and broke to the west.

"Sentry 8-7, Kansas City Center."

"Kansas City Center, Sentry 8-7."

"Sentry 8-7, do you have acquisition of targets in the Manhattan, Kansas, area?"

"Affirmative, Kansas. We are still a hundred south but do have targets in your area. We have two targets bearing west from Manhattan Regional Airport following a third target that is bearing north-northwest at low altitude, approximately 50 to 100 AGL. That signal is weak, but he's still there. He's hugging the ground so you can't see him, but he can't hide from us. 8-7 over."

"Kansas Center copies. Do you copy that, Homeland?"

"Affirmative, Kansas Center. Curtis over." Curtis picked up another phone. "Fort Riley, this is Curtis at Homeland. Get those choppers reloaded and airborne."

Friday, 2:00 p.m. CDT, Kansas airspace

The rain pelted his windscreen incessantly, but compared to the last five hours, this was easy flying. After hours of intense instrument flying, visual flying was like driving a car. The eyes and the cerebellum did it automatically.

Scott slowed to maneuvering speed as he sliced his way through the river valley to the northwest, at times just clearing the top of the water. He peered ahead for towers on the hilltops that would signal power lines crossing the river. If there were any lines, he would go under them. He pushed the "Nearest" button twice on his GPS, then highlighted CYW on the screen and pressed Enter. The Course Deviation Indicator centered immediately. *Six miles. Two minutes.* Three fuel gauges were sitting on empty. The fourth was in the red.

A smile had involuntarily crossed his lips earlier when he realized he had something the F-35's didn't—he could land where they could not. He had been heading for a seven-thousand-foot runway before he made his little move, but now the game had changed.

The river turned hard west, but CYW—Clay Center, Kansas— was due north. It was do or die time. He pulled back on the yoke and climbed out of the river valley, his prop wash blasting the treetops. Keeping the needle centered, he steered north, cutting power and slowing as he peered into the mist for trees and power poles. He double-checked his maps, and finally, after a minute that seemed like an hour, he could see structure straight ahead. Out of the mist a pitted runway appeared, the old white numerals badly faded—runway 3-5.

Friday, 3:10 p.m. EDT, Homeland Security Command Center

Lieutenant Colonel Floyd Curtis was livid. "Major Syverson, this is Curtis at Homeland. How long before those choppers are airborne again? That son of a bitch just faked us out!"

"The platoon on the ground at Regional is reloading. We had him surrounded. It will be just a few more minutes before they actually depart Manhattan. A backup platoon is being readied."

"Okay. AWACS radar will give you coordinates as soon as he lands. You are in charge of tactical decisions. Remember that there is an executive order that this man is to be brought in alive. No shots are to be fired."

"Yes, sir. My men have their orders."

"Thanks, Major." Curtis hung up and turned toward Block, a little smile betraying his emotion. "That Bastard can fly!"

Friday, 2:15 p.m. CDT, Clay Center, Kansas

Scott throttled back, added a notch of flaps, and dropped his gear. He felt three distinct clunks as his wheels locked, but the gear-confirmation lights—"three in the green"—had burned out with the rest of his panel. Not that it mattered. He had to land with or without confirmation. Empty fuel tanks limit one's options. Adding full flaps, he allowed *Whiskey Mike* to settle toward the ground over the threshold. She touched down gently, just beyond the numbers, and he let her roll out until she slowed enough to make a U-turn. As in most small towns, there was no parallel taxiway here. At the entrance taxiway, he turned west onto the ramp and pulled close to the fuel tanks in a wide U-turn to the north.

Scott shut down the left engine, but then, out of curiosity, hit the starter switch. To his surprise, it cranked, screeching the Bendix against the gear wheel. He hadn't known if that system had been fried also, but it is a simple loop system built for dependability, not an intricate electronic system with micro circuitry. He shut down the right engine, reset the altimeter to 1208, and clicked off his GPS.

Friday, 3:20 p.m. EDT, Homeland Security Command Center

"Sentry 8-7 reporting. WHO is no longer airborne. His velocity slowed consistent with landing, and then we lost signal. Last known coordinates: 39 degrees 23.23 minutes North—97 degrees 9.43 minutes West. That fix is Clay Center, Kansas, Municipal Airport, runway length 4,199 feet, width 35 feet, elevation 1208 MSL, identifier CYW."

"Good work, Eight Seven! Homeland Command, do you copy?"

"Homeland copies. Kansas Center, can our F-35s land on that runway and block him in? Homeland over."

"That is a negative, Homeland. This is Air Force Control on frequency. That runway has no nav aids. They cannot shoot a safe approach. In addition, it is only thirty-five feet wide and probably does not have a mat thick enough to support our weight. We cannot risk a twenty-million-dollar aircraft on an unknown surface. We will continue to circle and monitor as fuel permits. Sorry, sir. Over."

"Understood. Homeland out."

Curtis grabbed his open line to Fort Riley. "Syverson, did you get all that?"

"We got it, Colonel. Relaying coordinates now. Choppers will be there in another ten minutes."

"Major, we don't want this guy running again. What are your plans?"

"I propose we drop a perimeter of men out of audible range. A mile in this weather should do it. If he doesn't hear the rotors, he might think he gave us the slip. This will give us a perimeter in case he tries to escape on foot. My men can then move in on his position quietly. As soon as the soldiers are deployed, the Blackhawks can block the runway. Hopefully, we can have that all done before he has time to refuel. I am also calling the county sheriff to have the access road to the airport blocked in case there is someone waiting for him with a vehicle. If you have any better suggestions, tell me now."

"That sounds workable to me, Major, but is there time for that? Shouldn't we just drop out of the mist onto his position?"

"We understand he is armed, possibly carrying a bomb. My orders are to not endanger my men or my aircraft."

"Understood, Major. We'll go with your plan—quick and quiet."

"Will do, sir. I'll talk to you when we have our man."

Friday, 2:25 p.m. CDT, Clay Center, Kansas

Climbing out of the seat, Scott felt old. His legs rebelled against straightening, as did his back. He limped down the aisle to the door. Opening like a clamshell, half going up and half going down, the door has steps hinged inside the lower portion. They clanged open automatically as the door banged against its cables. The rain felt good on Scott's face as he stepped down and stretched skyward.

A man in rain gear emerged from the hangar, carrying an umbrella. "Good afternoon." The older man walked up to Scott and handed him the umbrella. "Didn't hear you call. Top her off?"

"Yes, please. One hundred low lead. Both mains and both tip tanks. She's dry." Scott didn't know how he was going to pay for the fuel, but that was the least of his worries.

"You got it." The man attended to work as Scott walked to the tail of the aircraft to get a look at his damage. Any black residue had long been washed clean, but his elevator problem was apparent immediately. The explosion had sent a piece of shrapnel into the trim tab on the elevator, bending it awkwardly downward. That was catching air and pushing the tail up. He grabbed it with one hand and tried to bend it back. It gave a little. He set the umbrella down and grabbed with both hands. Made from thin aluminum, it yielded to Scott's efforts.

"Trouble?" the man shouted from in front of the wing.

"Yeah, I hit some birds. Thank God, they missed my wind-shield. That could have been deadly."

"Yep. Happened around here a few years ago. Goose came right in through the pilot's windshield and killed him instantly. Lucky they had a copilot, or they'd have all been dead."

"I'm going inside—haven't peed in six hours."

"Make yourself at home. There's coffee on. Help yourself."

"Thanks." Coffee sounded good. Anything sounded good.

After relieving himself and washing his face and hands, Scott walked back to the lobby. He poured dark coffee into a foam cup. It was two hours old, but he didn't care. It tasted heavenly. Eyeing the honor bar on the far counter, he grabbed a granola bar and gulped it down, feeling guilty. *I just ordered five hundred dollars' worth of fuel I can't pay for. What's one more dollar?* He stuffed two more into his pocket.

Scott walked around the lobby, stretching his legs and limbering his upper body. It was an old hangar, run by a couple who had lived there for years. They hung on more out of love for flying than good financial sense. As flying became more expensive, the fraternity of flyboys grew smaller and smaller, and the Saturday morning hangar club hadn't met in months. The days of pilots coming out on weekends just to fly around and share stories were over, probably for good.

Walking back to pour another cup of coffee, he noticed a dozen water bottles behind the honor bar. They weren't chilled, but he was too thirsty to care. He unscrewed the top and guzzled sixteen ounces with barely a breath between gulps. The hollow pit that was his stomach began to feel normal again.

As he saw the owner approaching, Scott tensed. The man had been friendly, but how friendly would he be when he found that Scott had no way to pay him? The owner walked in, shaking the rain from his body as he closed the door. "What brings you to Kansas on a day like this?"

"I need to talk to the police. May I please use your phone?"

Friday, 2:25 p.m. CDT, Kansas airspace

Captain Peter Norton loved the new helmets with their built-in communication systems. It left both hands free for fighting. He barked his orders into the mouthpiece. "Clay Center is one mile north, begin deployment now." He tapped the pilot on the shoulder and gave him the go sign.

"Roger that," the pilot confirmed. His bird circled west while the other circled east, the soldiers rappelling one by one in a circle around the Clay Center airport.

Lieutenant Shane Larrington had huddled next to the large exit-door of the Blackhawk, his excitement level higher than he could ever remember. Larrington had joined the Army ten years earlier. He wanted to do something different, something important. If everything went well today, his future was bright. He was now a member of the elite, and today he would have the chance to prove it. He had longed for a battle op, but he missed out on his request for transfer to the isthmus. Fearing that he would spend four more landlocked years before he saw real action, he could hardly contain himself when this mission had been handed to him. It was providence. His orders were explicit, and he knew he could carry them out. He would show his worth.

Larrington made sure he was the first man off Norton's chopper. No one was going to beat him to his prize. He landed on his feet, slid off his descender in one swift move and sprinted north; he was in excellent condition and would be in position before the northern sector was even secured. Larrington had been to Clay Center before and he knew the layout of the field. The hangars were on the south end of the field, so he was not only the first one off but also the closest. As he sprinted north, he had a feeling this was going to be his day.

Friday, 2:26 p.m. CDT, Clay Center, Kansas

"What did you say?"

"I need to talk to the police. May I please use your phone?"

"Trouble?" the man asked, concerned.

Scott thought briefly about telling him the truth, but he already owed him several hundred for fuel, and the man was going to be very unhappy when he learned that Scott had no cash or credit cards with him. If he started talking about a plot against the president of the United States, things would likely go downhill. Scott decided that a slight bending of the facts would be appropriate here.

"I witnessed an attempted murder this morning. I had to take off so I didn't get shot myself."

The man dialed a number and handed Scott the phone.

"Clay Center Police. How may I help you?" The dispatcher had a friendly voice with that slight southern inflection that begins in Kansas.

"Could I speak to your police chief or sheriff, please?"

"I'm sorry, but the chief is out. You can call 5601 for the sheriff's office, sir."

"Is there a deputy there?"

"I'm sorry, but he is out on patrol. Is this an emergency?"

"Time is of the essence," he replied. "Could you radio one of them and have them come to the Clay Center Municipal Airport? I want to report an attempted murder. If they can pick me up at the airport, I will come to the station and file the report."

"Yes, sir. I will relay your message. Please stay right where you are until they get there."

"Yes, ma'am. I will be waiting in the main hangar. Please tell them to hurry." Scott reached across the counter and hung up the phone.

"Is there anything else you need," the owner asked, "or would you like to take care of the bill before you go to town?"

Scott felt a slight sense of panic. He needed more time. "Could you just check the oil for me? Make sure I'm not a quart low on either side."

"Sure. Synthetic?"

"Yes. Aero 15-50."

"Got it," he said as he grabbed two quarts and a funnel and headed out to the ramp. The man raised the hood on his raincoat and walked to the left engine. The oil level was normal, and he walked around to the right side. This side was full, too, but as he was closing the tiny maintenance door, he noticed the fuselage. Looking closer, he realized that it wasn't mud on the wing and fuselage. There were bare metal marks up and down the side of the plane.

That was no bird he ran into. These look like shrapnel marks. I wonder what this guy's hauling? He walked to the door of the aircraft and started up the steps. One quick look couldn't hurt anything.

Inside the hangar, Scott saw a flashing light through the south window. He wiped the condensation off the old single-pane window, but it was filthy and the smearing only made it worse. He unlocked the catch on the double-hung window and lifted. At the end of the airport access road, at its junction with Highway 24, a police car was pulling into a blocking position, lights flashing.

If they are already here, why did she tell me to wait? he asked himself. It was a rhetorical question; he knew the answer. *Because they already know I'm here. They're just waiting for backup.* Then he heard the sound. Even with the mild ringing still hovering in his ears, the *thud, thud, thud* of large rotors was impossible to miss. A mile, despite the muffling of the rain, was not enough to hide their footprint—not from someone who was accustomed to hearing them. And Scott had heard enough of them.

I guess my little feint didn't work so well after all, he said to himself as he walked back to the large plate glass window. *Now what is he doing?* he wondered as he saw the hangar owner starting up the steps into *Whiskey Mike.*

Friday, 2:30 p.m. CDT, south of Clay Center airport

Lieutenant Shane Larrington was a good officer. He prided himself on being not only the fastest in the platoon but also the best conditioned. When everyone else hit the showers, he ran an extra three miles a day. His high school best in the 1600 had been a respectable 4:25, so he was confident that he was the first one in position. He could see the twin-engine airplane as he took his position against a small tree and caught his breath.

Each of the Bushwhackers from Bravo Company's Second Platoon had been issued a "basic load" for their M-4s—seven 30-round clips of standard 5.56 loads. The shorter barrel and collapsible stock on the carbine model of the M-16 made this weapon much easier to pack into small places, but it was still accurate to at least six-hundred meters, depending on the shooter. Larrington had earned a sniper scope from the marksmanship sergeant for all his practice; he was accurate out to a thousand. He leaned against a tree while he caught his breath. The other soldiers carried 210 bullets, but Shane had brought 1 extra per his special orders for Operation Ammo Count. Fishing inside his pocket, he found bullet number 211, a hot, full-metal-jacket, armor-piercing hand load. He removed his clip, inserting the FMJ into the chamber. He did not bother to replace the clip. He only had one chance. His instructions were clear: when the pilot attempted to reenter the aircraft, he was to take him out. He only had one bullet to spare. He must return with full armament.

Looking through his scope, Larrington could see a man walking around the aircraft. But who was it? The only way he could be sure it was the pilot was if he climbed inside. A lineman wouldn't do that. He peered through the scope. They had a description, and this looked like the guy. Six feet, two hundred, Caucasian. Everything fit. When he saw him walk to the aft portside, he clicked off the safety. When he saw him approach the steps, he inhaled deeply. When he saw him mount the steps to climb inside, he squeezed. Everything felt perfect. Sometimes you just knew—the exhale smooth, the hold dead-on, the squeeze perfectly soft, no hint of a jerk—still he took one last look to see the man fall before he slammed his clip back into the gun, picked up his spent shell, and ran south as fast as he could.

Larrington had run nearly three quarters of a mile. His chest was burning when he saw a large badger hole. He stopped and flung the empty cartridge deep inside, kicking dirt into the hole. He ran another hundred yards. Next, he carefully turned his left ankle underneath himself and put all his weight on it. The pain was intense. He was certain he had done it hard enough to cause swelling. Hopefully it would discolor as well. Now all he had to do was wait until they picked him up. He was injured. He had never made it to the perimeter. He had a swollen ankle to confirm his story, and he had all 210 bullets issued to him this morning. He had thought of everything. He was not just faster, stronger, and more dedicated than anyone in his platoon—he was also smarter.

Friday, 2:36 p.m. CDT, north of Clay Center airport

"Hold your fire! Hold your fire!" Captain Peter Norton was screaming into his microphone. He was the last man off, and he had barely rappelled from the chopper when he heard a single report to his south. He had no idea what was going on. "Who fired that shot? Report immediately."

No one was talking. He headed south at a sprint that he knew he could not sustain. He screamed into his microphone again.

"Choppers proceed directly to the runway. Block it off. All personnel converge immediately on target. Watch for anyone on foot. Do not let anyone between you." Norton now wished he had two platoons. Suddenly, he realized what a flimsy perimeter he held, but there had been so little time to prepare. "Double time it to the hangars!" he yelled into his mouthpiece. "No further shots unless fired upon."

Friday, 2:36 p.m. CDT, Clay Center airport

Scott heard the report of the rifle at the same time as he saw the lineman clutch his chest and fall forward onto the airplane steps. It was like a slow-motion video as he took it all in. *They are going to kill me. No matter what I do, they are going to silence me.* It was the lone thought that occupied his mind at the moment. All his planning and dodging had amounted to nothing. Not his getting a thousand miles away. Not his fake approach to Manhattan, which he thought might throw them off for an hour or two. It hadn't fazed them. They had gotten the word out ahead of him. They were going to kill him, and they had the resources.

"Well, screw you! See if I sit here and wait for a bullet!" Scott was talking aloud, anger replacing resignation. He stepped around the counter, stashed four bottles of water into his pockets, grabbed two more in each hand, and sprinted for the aircraft. Throwing the water bottles inside, he grabbed the dead man's legs and dragged the body onto the tarmac. Scrambling inside, he latched the door and scurried forward. Slamming the mixture full rich, he hit the starter as he settled into his seat. To his relief, the left engine cranked and started immediately, followed by the right. He half expected them to flood, as hot engines often did, but old reliable *Whiskey Mike* was rolling before he knew it.

Approaching the runway, he saw the first helicopter sliding in from the north. Scott jammed the throttles forward further still, accelerating almost too much to make the turn. He arrived at the runway in a dead heat with the Blackhawk, slamming his left brake as hard as he could while he applied full power to the right engine. The surging right engine and the clamped left brake swung him hard left, skidding on the wet pavement. Still sliding, he slammed both throttles ahead full and accelerated down runway 35. The Blackhawk had never gotten into position.

Barreling down the runway, Scott saw the misty shape of the second helicopter. It was cruising ten feet above the ground at the far end of the runway, gliding to its intended blocking position at midfield, aiming straight at him. He expected to see bursts of gunfire erupting in his face, but nothing happened. As he closed, he realized that it had no machine guns. A red cross was painted on the nose. He was staring down a medical helicopter. It was unarmed.

The only way he can stop me now is to crash into me, but I'll wager that he doesn't want to die today. And I have nothing to lose. He accelerated directly toward the Blackhawk.

*****

Captain Billy Bohnenkamp couldn't believe what he was seeing. The guy wasn't slowing down. He had a fully fueled, twin-engine bomb heading his way, and Billy had no way of stopping it short of killing his copilot and himself. His orders were very simple—block the runway and allow no one on or off. *Easier said than done.*

"He won't stop, Captain," he called into his mic. He saw the airplane hurtling toward him, now less than four hundred feet away and gaining speed, but all he could think of was his beautiful wife and three babies.

"Hold your position, BeeBee! He'll stop. He's just playing chicken with you."

"No, he's not!" Bohnenkamp hollered. To himself, he said, *And I'm not going to sit here and piss myself in a bloody fireball for some crackpot. Besides, they said not to endanger our birds. Let the rest of the United States Army be all* they *can be. We'll find him later.* With the Piper bearing down on the last hundred feet of mist separating them, BeeBee pulled as hard as could on the collective and swung up and left. The twin shot beneath him, and by the time he turned around, all he could make out was the tail of the Piper disappearing into the clouds.

"He's gone, Captain! Shot right past me and took off into the clouds. There was nothing I could do," he said as he glanced at his copilot. "I couldn't get into position in time." His copilot gave him a double thumbs-up. He knew only too well that Bohnenkamp did have one other choice.

*****

"All personnel meet at the hangars. Both helicopters proceed to the tarmac." Norton called as he ran south. His lungs were searing, and he had the taste of blood in his mouth. This had sounded like an easy adventure, so he decided to take the lead himself. Now he wished he had let his second lieutenant play platoon leader, just like it says in the manual.

The thought had barely crossed his mind when his earpiece crackled to life. "Man down on the tarmac. He's not moving. Halverson, over."

"Be careful, Halverson. Make sure he's not armed." Norton called back.

"He's not armed, sir. He's lying in a pool of blood. He's dead!"

"Don't touch a thing until I get there. Out."

The platoon converged on the tarmac, slowing like a stream of mourners as they approached the body. They formed a quiet circle around the dead man. Norton did a quick count—one man missing. He activated his microphone. "Larrington, do you copy?"

"Yes, sir. I copy."

"What is your position?"

"I'm just a little north of my drop point. I'll need a pick up. I think I broke my ankle. Sorry, sir."

"What is your position?"

"Due south, sir."

"Affirmative. Light up and we'll pick you up on the way back." He switched frequencies as he turned back toward the dead man. "Norton to base. Tell the major that whatever Washington wanted that guy for, they can now add murder to the list."

Chapter 14

Whiskey Mike West

Friday, 2:50 p.m. CDT, Kansas airspace

The tail of a Navajo rises just over thirteen feet in the air, and when BeeBee Bohnenkamp pulled his craft's nose up, the counter-rotational forces pushed his tail momentarily downward. Scott could see the angled tail-wheel at eye level. He forced his yoke forward, smashing the nose wheel onto the runway as the helicopter lifted away. Then when he was practically off the end of the pavement, he pulled full back on the yoke and was catapulted into the air. Once more the clouds wrapped their protective arms around *Whiskey Mike.*

After five hours of fighting a bent elevator trim tab, the upward propulsion shocked him. "Reset the trim!" he hollered at himself. Having straightened the bent trim tab, the full deflection of his trim wheel now shot him into a dangerously steep climb, the kind that sometimes ended in a stall and spin for inexperienced pilots. He leaned his torso onto the yoke as he frantically rolled the trim wheel forward. Slowly, his ascent moderated until he was in a safe thousand-feet-per-minute climb.

He banked left and headed the only way he knew. West. As he rolled out to straight and level, he noticed he did not have his seat belt on. *As if it really matters.* Still, he put the lap belt on since turbulent

117

weather can throw a pilot around. He had no way of knowing how long he would have steady rain before the backside of the powerful system gave him trouble. His cloud cover couldn't last forever. Then they could see and shoot at will. He needed a new plan, and the seeds of an idea from somewhere over Illinois, from half a lifetime ago, floated into his consciousness. His little ruse at Manhattan hadn't done much to throw them off track. Whatever radar they were using was too good for that. However, something he saw at the hangar in Clay Center meshed with a thought from earlier in the morning. *It just might work.* And if it didn't? Well, he was dead anyway.

At ten thousand feet AGL, Scott grabbed the roll of duct tape from the pouch in the back of the copilot's seat and scurried aft. He could hear air hissing through the bullet hole opposite the doorway, and he knew it would severely hamper his ability to pressurize his cabin. Scott pulled off a small piece of the gray tape, wadded it into a ball, and stuffed it into the hole. He darted forward, checked his heading, and returned aft. He packed tape into the hole until he could force no more inside. Shuttling back and forth, doing his best to keep *Whiskey Mike* straight and level, he then covered the hole with several overlapping layers of tape until he was sure he had done all he could to seal it. *Duct tape—never leave home without it.*

Climbing into his seat, he felt a lump in his pocket. Removing the four water bottles and two granola bars, he tossed them on the right seat. Four more bottles of water lay scattered on the floor in back. This comprised the sum total of his nutritional assets—precious little for the plan he was formulating. Pressurizing, he climbed to eighteen thousand, hurtling through the clouds and rain to the west.

Friday, 3:50 p.m. EDT, White House Command Center

"Mr. President, we have a new development with that rogue aircraft," General Curt Nearman said. "The pilot landed, refueled, killed the airport manager, and took off again. We had an army platoon and two helicopters surrounding him. He must have gotten wind that we were converging on him because he shot the guy and took off. He is heading west again. We still do not have an ID on him, but Homeland and FBI are working on it. Of the planes that have been in and out of Leesburg Executive in the past month, they have the unaccounted ones narrowed down to a handful, and of those in and out the last four days, they think they have it down to two. And you won't believe this, sir, but one of them is from your old stomping grounds, or so they think. The FAA has one of them listed as leaving Idaho just yesterday morning."

"Really?" Brady said, surprise written on his face. "Whom did he kill?"

"Some guy who owns the fixed-base operator and manages the airport. Early sixties, married, lives with his wife there at the airport. This wasn't his lucky day."

"Any description of the killer? Any witnesses?" Brady asked.

"No. Too hazy. No one knows what happened for sure. The army platoon was still closing in when the guy was shot. That's all we know."

"I want a full report when you know more."

"Yes, sir!" Nearman left, closing the door behind him.

President Brady asked Todd Pederson to take a break and leave him alone for a few minutes. He motioned for Sam Davies to stay. "Poor Scott. Why in the hell did I ever ask him to come? I don't know how he got into the middle of this or how I can get him out, but I do know that Scott Piquard never killed an innocent man in Kansas."

"Are you positive, sir? People can surprise you. Are you absolutely sure he is the kind of person you think he is?"

"Beyond a doubt! Scott has spent his life helping others. He chose to live in a small town where he could make a difference instead of earning the big bucks in the city. He is the kind of doctor who will take care of anyone, no matter how poor they are. And he is the kind of person who would take a bullet rather than kill an innocent man."

"How can you be so sure, sir?"

"I'm sure, Sam. We grew up together. We went to the army together. Scott saved my life… Now all of a sudden, he wants to kill me? I don't think so! And those gunshots in the tunnel this morning? I am now more sure than ever that those bullets were meant for me."

Chapter 15

Reinforcements

F loyd Curtis could not believe what he was hearing. His day had started curiously and was going steadily downhill. "We have an E3, two F-35s, two Blackhawks, and thirty-two armed soldiers surrounding him, and this guy lands, refuels, kills a man, takes off again, and we can't stop him? Thank God for our airborne radar, or we would have lost him completely. This is embarrassing. What next?"

"For starters, we are going to get reinforcements," General Kidner said loudly as he stormed out of his office and into the control room. "I want General Pat Collins down here. Now! He can cut through red tape faster than a paper shredder. We are going to pull units from the southern command, and wherever this guy lands next, we are not going to piss around with a mere platoon to surround him. We will greet him with a battalion. He is not going to embarrass the United States Army."

This was exactly what Curtis did not want. Call it turf protection, call it ego, but he had wanted this mission for himself. It had looked straightforward, and he thought it would easily be over before change of shift. Now the guy probably had six or seven more hours of fuel. He didn't know where he would land next, but he doubted it would be next door to an army base. At least Curtis knew Brigadier General Collins, a nice guy who hadn't let the one star go to his head. Extremely knowledgeable, he would be a definite asset. It wasn't that Curtis disliked Kidner; it was just that the general was slowing down, wasn't keeping up on technology, and would rather be golfing. On the positive side, two generals brought a higher level of authority that would fast-track orders—things that Curtis would have to dance for like he had for the AWACS help. Still he was disappointed that he couldn't finish it solo. It just wasn't the same.

Kidner was still talking. "I want open lines to the major commands in the southwest sector. Get those bases on my line and get the general officers in their situation rooms. I want command structure—general to general. And I want Gus Taylor at the White House to get me full authorization from the Pentagon to do what we have to do short of shooting this asshole down. I don't want someone out there questioning our every move. They need to know this is coming from the top, and if they even think of countermanding any of our orders, make sure they remember that shit runs downhill. Now make those calls. Curtis, I want you here at my side all day. You know all this technical crap."

"Yes, sir. Actually, I'm looking forward to it. This guy has pissed me off, and I want to see it through to the end."

"Yeah, I knew you would." Kidner smiled as he said it, letting Curtis know that he wasn't angry with him, just the situation. "Who would have guessed that so many troops would miss their chance in Kansas? With so many assets pulled south, they couldn't mobilize any more, so don't feel guilty. Still, nobody expected him to be able to fly like that. How in the hell do you land without nav aids in fog and rain? I'm not a pilot, but I know that can't be easy. Hell, there have been plenty of people killed at well-equipped airports with runways three times that big."

"Exactly, sir. This guy intrigues me increasingly by the minute."

"Attention!" They heard someone's call to attention and turned to see General Collins entering with an aide.

"As you were," Collins said as he walked up to Kidner and extended his hand. "Hello, George. What's brewing?"

"Thanks for coming down so quickly, Pat. I know you have work upstairs, but you are a pro at moving men and machines. Floyd can brief you. He's been here from the start."

Curtis spent the next several minutes reviewing the morning's activities from the time of the gunshots in the tunnels to the report of the shooting at Clay Center, Kansas. "So unless we find someone hiding in the complex, we have to assume that this is the same man. However, it's likely that we have multiple perpetrators, given the depth of the security breach." Curtis turned his hands palm up. "Sorry, but that's all we've got."

"I have General Taylor on the White House line, sir." Captain Block held the phone toward General Kidner.

"Gus, I need some authorizations, preferably from the commander in chief. I want the Pentagon to give us carte blanche on any troops we need to move. I want top-priority. I have General Pat Collins here, and he understands about as well as anyone where our resources are and how to move them. The next time this guy lands, I want him so surrounded he'll think he's on a goddamn military base."

"Unless you hear otherwise, consider it done. I am down in the bunker with the president. You do know that Brady is adamant that this guy isn't hurt, don't you?"

"Yes. So who the hell fired at him?" Kidner asked. "It could have been a Sparrow with proximity detonation. The speed was right, but nobody is reporting ordnance in that area today so where was it launched? A shoulder shot maybe?"

"That's some of the speculation here, George, but how did they know where to be? I mean, they would have practically had to know his flight plan and have a man waiting for him. Radar showed no other aircraft in the area, so it must have come from the ground. Now suppose we find no military ordnance missing. That leaves a nonmilitary origin. Who knows where to be and when to be there?"

"You've got my interest," Kidner replied.

"The same group that planned it. It's a double cross. They send this guy in to kill the president, and they know his escape route. They were waiting for him. It wasn't punishment for failing—they were planning to erase the evidence all along. And who has that kind of loyalty to their soldiers? Al-Qaeda or one of their fringe groups. If we catch him alive, we might break the case wide open. But you know these guys. They will die before they let themselves be taken alive."

"Thanks, Gus," Kidner said.

"I'll talk to you later, George. Goodbye."

The three of them stood looking at one other. Collins was the first to speak. "That is as plausible an explanation as any. Everything seems to fit, especially the part about them knowing where he was going to be. And there was no one airborne in that area this morning. That leaves us with a ground launch."

"Well, sir, there were actually four helicopters airborne on maneuvers this morning. None of them were in the immediate area of the missile launch, but neither were they identifiable. They were reported to be on the ground at that time," Curtis said.

"What are you getting at, Colonel?" asked Collins.

"Lack of proof that they were there does not constitute proof that they were not there."

"What the hell did you just say?" Kidner was looking at him quizzically.

"Just because we didn't see something on radar doesn't prove that something wasn't there. Remember, gentlemen, we even lost the aircraft for a while. General Collins, what do you have in mind?"

"First of all, do we have any idea where he is heading?"

"No. We are only now getting a presumptive ID. We think he might be from Idaho. FBI is working that, but it's all nebulous so far."

"Give me a few minutes to check with Scott Air Force Base and the Army's western command," Collins went on. "I need to see what resources we have at our disposal. Scott Air Force Base monitors all flights of Air Force craft around the world. Army Airborne will have the men we need if we can move quickly enough. You say this guy probably has five or more hours of fuel, right? A ground operation is out of the question since we have no idea where he is going. So we have to arrange a mobile welcoming party for him with troop carriers. The minute he lands, we drop a thousand paratroopers around him. That leaves us fully mobile. The helicopters have neither the range nor the speed to keep up with him, and he can obviously land where an F-35 can't, so that is not a good option."

"Very good, sir. You make your calls while I do the same. You can use this desk next to mine." Curtis turned to his desk and dialed Ernie Knoll.

"Agent Knoll," Ernie answered after one ring.

"Curtis, Homeland Command. How are you coming?"

"I have some preliminary information, but nothing is firm."

"Understood. Go ahead."

"We have located the pilot from Texas. He has been home for three days. The pilot from Idaho is from a small town. Our nearest field office is three hours away, but I have instructed them to dispatch two men immediately. Our Boise office staff has made contact with the chief of police there. The chief is new to the area but says he knows the owner of that aircraft. His name is Scott Piquard. He is one of the local doctors—well thought of, solid citizen, midfifties, tall, athletic, intelligent, workaholic type. Doesn't seem terribly political but leans definitely left by what the police chief has heard about him. He takes care of poor people for free and is into conservation and a lot of tree-hugging shit. He has a wife and two kids, but the police can't locate any family members. The house is dark. Neighbors think they went to the city for the weekend. Maybe the four of them left town and someone stole their plane? Makes about as much sense as anything else today."

"Good work, Ernie." Curtis was logging the permutations. "Anything else?"

"Yeah, I had one of my guys at headquarters run a family check on him. You said the plane's been heading west since takeoff, right? Well, this Piquard has a brother in California, a little place north of Bakersfield. Criminals usually seek out family when they are on the run. I have two teams on their way to the brother's place. We'll watch, and we'll tap his phone, but we will not show our presence."

"You work fast, Ernie. Nice job."

"Thanks, but I couldn't have done it without that head start you gave me."

"Let me know if you find anything else. I'll have Mickey O'Loughlin fax you the rest of the info as soon as he runs it down."

"Okay. Send it to the headquarters' fax, but if possible, have him e-mail the file to me as well. I can print it right here in my car."

"You guys get all the toys." Curtis jotted down the address then walked to his large wall map. The current flight path was indeed pointing a few degrees north of Bakersfield. He walked back to the generals and smiled. "Gentlemen, we may have a name and a destination."

Chapter 16

Plan B

Two hours to the west, Scott knew he was steadily leaving the forgiving terrain of the Great Plains behind. The land below him now would be the foothills territory, a few thousand feet higher than central Kansas. With the Colorado Rockies looming ahead, there were few places to land, and the clouds would be shrouding the mountains in zero-zero conditions—zero ceiling, zero visibility.

His shoulders ached, his trapezius muscles pulsated up his neck into the base of his skull, and his arms felt like sandbags. He was disgusted with himself for not coming up with a better plan. Why hadn't he just stayed in DC and looked for a safe place to tell his story? Why had he gone to the airport? In retrospect, it seemed obvious. He should have known they would cover the small airports as well as the commercial ones. How could he have been so stupid? Harbors, trains, bus stations—they would all have been monitored. He now realized that, by running, he brought more attention to himself than if he had just stayed incognito in Washington. Ah, what clarity, the retrospectoscope. But now his hand was dealt, and he must play it.

And what was that hand? Every time he turned around someone tried to kill him. Why they didn't fire another rocket and end

126

his misery, he wasn't sure. With two Blackhawks full of soldiers, they could have easily immobilized his plane in Kansas and grounded him. Instead, there was a single shot through the chest of a man who vaguely fit his description. How many others would die? They wouldn't rest, couldn't rest, until he was dead.

Plan A was a bust, and for two hours he had been wracking his brain, working on alternatives. *If I can't give myself up in the middle of Kansas, is there a safe place anywhere? I have no way to communicate. I can't call home, even if I had my phone. They will be watching the house and tapping the phone. How can I get a message to Gary? How can I send him a code that only he will understand, so only he knows what to do? Think! There has to be a way*, he told himself as *Whiskey Mike* droned on over the first peaks of the Colorado Rockies.

Scott looked around the cabin, taking note of each resource he had. For one thing, he had an intact body, and there was no greater asset than that. He had a smattering of food and water, some maps, and a small knife from the flight bag. There should even be some old hardtack candies in the bag. He had kept some in every backpack and flight bag since the night he spent trapped on the side of a mountain.

As long as you are alive, there is a chance. He thought out the permutations as he adjusted his bearing. *Do I have enough fuel to take me that far against this westerly wind? It's worth a try. The worst that can happen is that I die trying, and that's better than some people get. My cup might not be half full, but it is far from empty.*

Chapter 17

Battalion Calls

Friday, 6:00 p.m. EDT, Homeland Security Command Center

G eneral Pat Collins was a treat to work with. Unlike those who used a coworker's back for their next stepping stone, Collins was cast more like Curtis. He had gotten where he was by intellect, efficiency, and hard work. Four combat tours had accelerated his career in his twenties, and the Purple Heart and Silver Star spoke of his mettle.

Within two hours, he had been on the phone to thirteen major commands, had learned where the bulk of troops were bivouacked in case of action at the border, and amazingly, had arranged for an entire battalion from the Eighty-Second Airborne to be at his disposal. Half of them were already in the air.

"Maybe I can be king for a day sometime," Curtis said jokingly. "When you give orders, people move."

"The situation creates the power. Plus, our friend is now going from an area of low concentration of resources to an area of high concentration. Where do you find eight hundred paratroopers in the middle of Kansas? With the massing of tens of thousands of troops in the southwest, borrowing a few was no big deal. You had a partially gutted medical unit at your disposal. What were you supposed to do, wrap him in gauze?"

"Thanks, but you just pulled an entire battalion in two hours and have them airborne. In another hour, they will be alongside our friend. I'm impressed."

"Okay. Let's review," said Collins, loud enough for everyone to hear. "We handed off to two fresh fighters in Kansas. They will hand off to the two we scrambled from Hill in Ogden, Utah. We have the boys in Las Vegas shooting craps at Nellis to see who gets the mission there. They currently have a large training contingent and are offering to send up six just for the practice. Imagine the look on that guy's face when he finally breaks out into blue and finds six F-35s and four transports riding shotgun."

"I'd pay to be there," added Kidner, who was quietly making calls of his own.

"We have choppers on readiness from six directions in case he varies, and if he lands, they will converge as quickly as possible. This time, though, we *will* drop right on top of him—no subtle demarche for round two," Collins added.

"Agreed," Curtis said. He was still smarting from his decision to let Fort Riley override his instincts and deploy quietly.

"Beyond that, I don't know what else we can do. We've pretty well got it covered."

Just then Block picked up a flashing line and turned to Curtis. "It's for you, sir. Captain Norton from Fort Riley."

Curtis punched the speakerphone button. "Hello. Curtis here."

"Hello, Colonel, this is Captain Peter Norton at Fort Riley. First off, I want to apologize for losing your man today. I take full responsibility, but I have just spent the last two hours questioning everyone around here, and there is something curious."

Curtis came to attention. There was that tingle in his brain again. "How curious?" he asked.

"Well, I questioned the deputy who had blocked off the entrance to the airport. He said he was almost there when his dispatcher called him. She had received a call from someone at the airport who wanted to talk to the police. He said he had witnessed an attempted murder. He wanted someone to come to the airport and pick him up, but the deputy had orders to block the access road instead of going in.

So assuming there was only one person out there, if the guy wants to steal gas and commit murder, why does he call the police? Something doesn't fit, sir. I thought you might want to know."

"You bet I do, Captain. Thank you very much. Anything else?" added Curtis.

"Not really. Well, there is one little thing, but I'm sure it's nothing."

"There are no little things, Captain, just different-sized pieces of a puzzle. Tell me everything you know."

"The deputy was parked on the south end of the airport road where it meets the highway. He heard the gunshot. He couldn't tell where it was coming from because it was raining and he had his windows up, but he said that he snapped his head around to the south the instant he heard it. Later, he figured that he must have gotten an echo from the hangars. The fact that his head snapped to the south caught my attention because I think our brains do that automatically. When I questioned each soldier, some of them thought it came from the south, and some thought it came from the east. Those metal hangars cause weird echoes, so we don't really know for sure. Oh! One last thing, Colonel. Is this guy military?"

"We don't know, Captain. Why?"

"When I heard the shot, it sounded like an M-16 or M-4. Of course, it could have been a high-powered pistol, and we could have been mistaken with the rainy weather. Just thought I'd pass it along. Sorry if I bothered you."

"Not at all, Captain. Not at all. You have been a great help. By the way, you did inventory your men's basic loads to make sure no rounds were missing, didn't you?"

"Yes, sir. Each soldier has a full basic load accounted for, no more, no less. We counted them out, and we counted them in."

"Very good, Captain. Also, I want you to order the autopsy on the dead man immediately, not tomorrow. Call us when you have the preliminary report."

"Will do. Good day, sir."

Curtis turned to Collins. "I so want to talk to this guy. Earlier today, I was wondering if we were following a case of mistaken identity—someone not at all involved with what went on at the White House. The more we learn, the more convoluted it gets. Was it our man who called the Clay Center Police? If not him, then who? And if he wanted to talk to the police, why would he shoot a man in cold blood? Nothing makes sense, and my bet is that only this guy can clear it up. No wonder the president wants him alive. If he dies, this mystery will die with him."

Chapter 18

Descent

H our four had passed with Scott as lost in thought as he was in IMC. He didn't much like his plan, but then he didn't much like his alternatives. Tussling with maps while trying to hand fly in instrument meteorological conditions was challenging enough when the instruments actually worked. He remembered too well the years before he could afford a twin. His light single would barely clear the mountain peaks, and he was forever wet-palming his navigation through mountainous terrain with scant vertical margins. At least with the twin, he could climb above the peaks and relax.

Today, however, he could not relax. With lost communications, he had not been able to reset the Kollsman window on his altimeter since he had been on the ground at Kansas. He was, however, flying toward better weather. The weather system that had provided his cover until now would be blowing itself east, making way for the inevitable high-pressure system that pushes out a big low. "High to low, look out below," was the pilot's mnemonic. At least he was going "Low to high, you're high as the sky." Unless this weather system was very convoluted, he would actually be higher than his indicated altitude of eighteen thousand feet.

The downside, of course, was constantly on his mind. Flying toward improving weather meant clear skies, and that meant exposure. His biggest asset so far, practically his only asset, had been the whiteout conditions. With clearing skies ahead, concealment would be impossible.

Throughout the last hour, he had rigged and fine-tuned his new "autopilot." *Whisky Mike* wanted to drift left, and it was draining Scott's energy. Using duct tape, he strapped the yoke stem to its guide and the yoke handles to the dash. Sequentially adding tape, he now had *Whiskey Mike* remarkably straight and level. Analyzing his heading, he was pleased with his work.

Although Alaska boasts the top sixteen peaks in the United States, Colorado lays claim to twenty-three of the top fifty. Mount Elbert, the tallest mountain in Colorado at 14,433 feet, was now safely behind him, along with the fifty-three other "14-ers" in Colorado. Having cleared the highest peaks of the southern Rockies, he was comfortable moving around in the cabin in short intervals. He knew he was now over the relatively lower terrain of southern Nevada.

Scott made three waypoint entries into the memory of his GPS using lat-long data he had carefully gleaned from his map. He double-checked and triple-checked and quadruple-checked his coordinates. He could not be wrong; wrong meant dead. He labeled the first point 001 on his user waypoint list, a personal collection of points in the memory separate from the thousands of aeronautical waypoints already in the GPS database. The second point he labeled 002, the third 003. These he entered sequentially into a flight plan and pressed enter.

He looked again at the line on his map. From 001 to beyond 003, the line extended a few miles north of Bakersfield—precisely where *Whiskey Mike* was pointed. Scott rolled the trim wheel slightly forward. It was time to descend.

Chapter 19

Final Approach

P resident Gary Brady, Lieutenant Colonel Floyd Curtis, and the combined occupants of both command centers stared in disbelief at the radar screens. An oppressive silence descended on both rooms as they watched WHO inexorably descending toward the master peak of the Sierra Nevada. Mount Whitney, 14,491 feet above sea level and the tallest peak in the Lower 48 states, has snared its share of pilots. It appears on every map as a dominating presence. Even L-5, the low-level en-route IFR map that shows airways but not terrain, displays its prominence. That map is dominated by a huge white area around Mount Whitney—there are no low-level routes there. The people in both rooms watched as one, mesmerized. No one had expected a descent until the Sierras were cleared.

Paratroopers were prepared to jump at Lone Pine airport, the only airport in the vicinity, but all eyes watched in disbelief as the little dot flew beyond the last level outpost on the eastern slope of the range.

"Out of fuel?" Captain Ellis said quietly, half question, half statement.

"Airspeed's still high—nearly two hundred. That's consistent with a powered descent," Air Force General Curt Nearman replied just as quietly. "I think he has fuel but has lost orientation. He was heading straight toward Bakersfield but began his descent too early. He probably thinks he is west of the ridge. It kills pilots all the time. If he doesn't turn back toward Lone Pine now, he only has about ten miles to the face of the mountain. That's only three minutes, and now he's below fourteen thousand."

President Gary Brady stood in the center of the group, his jaw clenched so tightly that his mandible throbbed, but he never uttered a word. Instead, he spoke to Scott inside his head. *Turn, Scott. Please turn, Buddy. Check your coordinates. Figure out your maps. Time is running out. Turn! God, please turn!*

Three minutes could seem like a lifetime—did seem like a lifetime—and yet they sped by so quickly it seemed like three seconds. One pass of the radar sweep and the little green dot was there; the next pass and it was gone. No one could speak for several seconds, and then Nearman, the pilot, broke the silence. "Flew right into her," he said matter-of-factly. "At least it was painless. At that speed, he never felt a thing."

"We have an ELT signal," Captain Turner said as he listened to his feed from the AWACS unit. An emergency locator transponder is installed on all licensed aircraft as standard equipment. Upon significant impact, momentum throws a weighted switch, which activates a radio signal. Search planes can home in on the signal, and the newer satellite systems can pinpoint a crash within meters.

"Could he have activated it manually?" Brady was grasping.

"Yes, sir, they can be activated manually," Captain Ellis replied. "Sailors and climbers carry them all the time for emergencies."

Brady relaxed momentarily until Nearman spoke again. "Not in a Navajo, I'm afraid. The ELT in a Navajo is inside a compartment in the tail. It can only be accessed by a ground crew from the outside."

President Brady's hopes fell as quickly as they had risen. He turned to Sam Davies and Greg Stroud. "How much longer do I have to stay cooped up down here? I have to get out of here. I need to talk to my family. I have things to do. What's the status of the search up top? What's the status of the air and radiation testing? Why in the hell haven't they found anything yet?" He was animated like few had seen him since the Middle East talks had swirled down the toilet right before his eyes.

"The fact that they haven't found anything yet is good news, sir. It probably means that there is nothing to find. But you cannot go up until tomorrow morning at the earliest. We have to follow protocol," Stroud said apologetically, "for your safety and the security of the country, sir." He could tell that his statement had not affected the president's demeanor, so he added the one thing that might. "It's actually safer for your family this way, sir, until we are sure everything is safe."

Brady paused. "Okay. But call upstairs and tell them that *no one* goes home until this search is over. Have food brought in, but no one leaves the security perimeter until the search is completed." Brady turned and stormed into the inner room.

Friday, 8:30 p.m. EDT, Homeland Security Command Center

Lieutenant Floyd Curtis, Brigadier General Pat Collins, and Major General George Kidner stared at the blank screen. "He just flew right into the mountain!" Collins said in disbelief. "After all the fancy flying he did today, evading us across the whole country, he loses his orientation and descends before he clears the ridge. Incredible."

"Now we will never know what the hell happened today—or why," Kidner added, shaking his head dejectedly.

Curtis was already making alternate plans. "Let's divert the chase planes to Armitage Field at China Lake and ready a ground crew to go to the crash site and climb up. We can't assume the weather will clear enough to use the choppers in the morning."

"Good idea, Curtis," Collins replied.

"But that is one big mountain. The ninety road miles will be the easy part. Once those men are on foot, it could take another day or two to get to the crash site, especially if things are wet and slippery or, worse, snowy. Who knows what the mountain gods have in store for us?"

"We'll see what dawn brings." Collins turned to Kidner. "The E-3 can return to Tinker unless you think otherwise. We'll need the helicopters, but once we've confirmed that there are no survivors, the others can be released to their prior command."

"Agreed," Kidner said. "I think I will go to my apartment at Fort Myer for the night. Do you have a place close by, Collins?"

"I'm just a few minutes from here." Collins turned to Curtis. "You?"

"I'm here for the duration, sir. I'm set up to sleep in my office. Besides, I won't be able to sleep much until this is over."

"I heard that about you. We need more men with your commitment. It's been a pleasure. I'll see you in the morning."

Curtis turned to his men. "I am asking for volunteers to work twelves with me and alternate with the night crew. If you have priors, I'll understand. I'm not leaving until we have this thing wrapped up, and the fewer shift changes the better. If we don't find anything in the tunnel search, we'll have to assume that this pilot was the intruder. In that case, we have lost our ability to connect this guy to whoever launched that Sparrow. From there it will have to be an intel operation."

He picked up his phone and dialed Ernie Knoll's cell number.

"Knoll, here."

"Knoll, this is Curtis at Homeland. Our pilot friend just crashed into the side of Mount Whitney."

"Holy shit. He's having a bad day, isn't he?"

"I'm afraid so. Do you have anything new?"

"No. My men are on their way to Granger. The sheriff still hasn't located the family of this Piquard guy. The neighbors said they went to Coeur d'Alene. I have people searching the hotels for reservations, but nothing yet."

"With this guy dead, we'll probably never know what happened today. I hate unfinished business."

"Hey, I hear you. Let me know when they get a positive ID at the crash site."

"Will do, Ernie. I'll call you later." Curtis hung up, feeling empty and frustrated. It was going to be a long night.

Chapter 20

Intel

President Gary Brady was up long before dawn; he had showered and shaved before most in the command center were stirring. He accepted the cup of coffee from Sam Davies but hardly needed the caffeine. His catecholamine level could have powered a small town. The claustrophobia and helplessness of being locked in, impotent to help Scott, were gnawing at him. If he slept two hours, he was lucky.

"I'm going up!" he said.

"I think they will let you go up this morning, sir," Davies said. "Nothing has been found anywhere in the capitol complex. No accomplices, no gases, no radiation, no unauthorized persons. Just as important, they also did not find anyone who will take credit for the shots fired yesterday morning. Whoever the hero was, whoever found the intruder and drove him off, does not want your thanks. And the fact that he—or they—could slip through four thousand armed militia and dozens of metal detectors appears to confirm what you said yesterday, Mr. President."

"Whoever fired those shots had clearance to carry."

"Yes, sir. The fact that our jogger got out is incredible enough, but the fact that one or more unauthorized armed men or women

138

also slipped out without being detected forces credulity. Ergo, they were not detected because they were supposed to be here."

"I need to talk to my wife, and then I need to talk to Rachael Piquard. It was late when they located her hotel in Coeur d'Alene, and I did not want to awaken her. I thought she could use one last good night's sleep before I put this burden on her. I trust our people in Idaho got my orders not to disturb her."

"Yes, sir. FBI Director Meyer issued the order personally. 'Surveillance only.' However, the FBI and practically every other law enforcement agency in the country now knows Piquard's name as the name registered with the missing airplane out of Leesburg. It will soon be public knowledge that you know him."

"I know, but I need time. I need to talk to Rachael Piquard first. God knows what I'll tell her. Any news on the crash site?"

"No, sir. The search crews made the base around sunset. Some of them started up, but when they hit snow, their commander ordered them to bivouac until dawn. I don't have to tell you, sir, that no one could have survived that impact. AWACS tracked him at full speed right into the side of the mountain. He never slowed down a bit. He never realized his mistake. At least it was painless."

"You know that I am not going to believe Scott Piquard is dead until I see the actual evidence, don't you, Sam? We don't know for sure he was even in that plane."

"Yes, sir, I understand. I am only trying to be objective."

"I know Scott Piquard. However high the incongruity, I will not believe he's dead until I have proof. It might not have been him in that airplane. He might be lying low in the city somewhere. You don't know Scott. He doesn't make mistakes like that!"

"I hope you are right, sir. I hope you are right."

"Now I want to go upstairs to my family," Brady intoned loudly as he opened the inner door and walked out to the control room. Greg Stroud and Gus Taylor were waiting expectantly.

"Good morning, gentlemen," Brady said. "May I please see my family?"

The senior guard looked to Stroud, who was on the phone. "Sir?"

139

Stroud talked briefly with someone and then hung up. "The lockdown has been lifted, sir. You may go up."

"About time," President Brady said as he nodded his head at the guard and then at the door, his body language screaming, "Open the damn thing!"

"Call my wife. Have her proceed immediately to our quarters with the boys," he called over his shoulder as he headed down the hallway, Stroud and Davies following closely. Striding impatiently to the elevator, Brady nearly gave himself away. He didn't have his access card. Thinking quickly, he stopped short to tie his shoe while Sam Davies smoothly slid his own card into the opening.

"I will want Sam with me again, today, Greg. The family is comfortable with him. Any other detail is to be approved by Sam. I don't know whom to trust right now. I would appreciate it if you would go to your office and work on that while I talk to my family."

Sam's next job was to cover the tracks of their missing guest. As instructed by the president, he went to the Lincoln Room, placed all of Scott's belongings into his overnighter and took that and the flight bag to the presidential quarters. He rapped once. The door opened quickly. Sam passed the bags inside and just as quickly closed the door. He then walked down to the guest entrance and told the guards to remove Dr. Piquard's name from the guest list. He informed them that the doctor had gone to the Library of Congress early the previous morning but, with all the activity, had not returned to the White House.

Saturday, 5:00 a.m. EDT, Homeland Security Command Center

Lieutenant Colonel Floyd Curtis rolled off his Murphy bed, stretched briefly, and walked to the coffee room. Floyd was tired. He never slept well when his brain was in overdrive. Savoring the aroma, he poured himself a large cup of black Columbian. Ambling out to the control room, he knew that the sun would just be rising "up top," but he would have to wait three agonizing hours before dawn aided the search in California.

"Good morning," Curtis greeted his night shift as he entered the control room. "Any news?"

"Nothing here, but Agent Knoll from the FBI called a few minutes ago, sir," Captain Wahl said. "He said not to wake you, but you were to call him as soon as you were up."

"Thanks, Natasha." Curtis turned to his phones and began dialing.

"Ernie Knoll."

"This is Curtis at Homeland. Hope I didn't wake you."

"That's okay. I've been up all night." The gravelly fatigue in his voice confirmed his statement.

"So what's on your mind at five in the morning, Ernie?"

"Who did you guys send up to Idaho last evening?" The irritation in his voice suddenly replaced the tiredness.

"No one. Why?"

"Some bird colonel dropped in out of Hill Air Force Base in a Blackhawk with an IFR clearance and beat my man, Klugiewicz, up there. He's been all over town, asking questions, and won't give my guy the time of day—won't even talk to him. 'Need to know,' is all he'll say. Worse, he commandeered the sheriff to drive him around town—two guys in full dress are pretty intimidating—and then he tells everyone this is top secret and they are to talk to no one else until cleared to do so by the military. He has the locals so intimidated Klugiewicz can't find out the price of gas. This is bullshit, Curtis. You said we were going to share intel. I took you at your word."

"Honest to God, Ernie, no one told us about this. We did not send him from here, that's for sure. I'll call Utah and see what the hell is going on. A full colonel has me outranked, but I can get my generals to order him to cooperate. And technically speaking, Homeland regulations make me his superior in an emergency. I'm sorry, Ernie. I truly did not know anything about this."

"Well, you sounded like a straight shooter, so I'll give you the benefit of the doubt, but this lone-ranger crap hampers the group. Klugiewicz is young and didn't stand up for himself very well. Good thing I wasn't there, or your bird colonel would have a broken beak."

"Did Klugiewicz get anything useful?" Curtis asked, softening the tone of the conversation.

"Yeah. He did. He got to one of the hospital nurses before the colonel did. She had nothing but praise for this Piquard. Nicest guy she's ever worked with. Polite, teaching all the time, academic type, reads constantly, likes to hunt, goes camping with his kids—sounds like a regular guy. But one thing didn't fit with that sheriff's report. He said the guy was a liberal. She says he's conservative as hell. How does that work?"

"It's hard to tell a man's politics," Curtis replied, curious.

"Or maybe he's leading a double life," Knoll added, the inflection in his voice making it more a question than a statement. "Now are you wide awake, Curtis?"

"Yeah, why?" Curtis answered, suddenly very wide awake from the change in tone.

"I'm going to share this with you because I believe you're a team player and because I refuse to become guilty of what I was just bitching about. What you do with it is up to you. By the way, any positive ID on that airplane yet?"

"No. The climbers are having a tough time—snow. Why?"

"Well, I'm curious as hell to know who is in that plane. This will make more sense if the plane is stolen. If it's this Piquard guy, there's going to be a lot of unanswered questions. It turns out that one Dr. Scott Piquard went to school with one President Gary Brady. And one Dr. Scott Piquard left Idaho in a twin-engine Piper Navajo on Thursday to go to Washington, DC. Now no one knows where one Dr. Scott Piquard can be found. We have been up all night, searching hotel logs in the DC area for a reservation in his name. Nothing. We extended our search out to all the suburbs. Nothing. Then we extended it to a fifty-mile radius. Still nothing. No reservation for Thursday or Friday. That tells me he's not staying under his own name, which raises red flags all over the place."

"Whew!" was all Curtis could muster at the moment.

"He could be staying with a friend in a private home, but we can't contact the wife for information. It's frustrating as hell."

"I know the feeling. I have to sit down here and wait for people to feed me information, and half the time, it's shoddy and not thought through."

"There's more."

"Give it to me."

"When I was questioning people at Leesburg Executive again late last night, I asked them if they were absolutely positive they had all fuel and work tickets accounted for. That was when one of the mechanics found an order for a landing light repair on a twin Piper, November 6-8-7 *Whiskey Mike*, registered to one Dr. Scott Piquard, same address as your buddy at FAA gave us yesterday. And November 6-8-7 *Whiskey Mike* is missing."

"Nice work, Ernie."

"There's more."

"Come on, quit tantalizing me. Let's hear it!"

"They make pilots sign a work ticket authorizing repairs. The signature on the ticket is Scott Piquard. I had Klugiewicz fax me a signature from the hospital in Idaho. Perfect match! I had my hand-writing expert compare some faxed samples with the note from the cab driver. She says that she is 99.99 percent certain that they came from the same hand. I think we have our guy, but it raises more questions than it answers. I don't know what the hell to do with this until we can talk to his wife, but the order not to disturb her came from Director Meyer himself. He wants her unaware so we can see whom she sees, trace her calls, hear whom she talks to."

"You said it would make more sense if the plane was stolen. If the cab driver's note is from Piquard, then he's in that airplane."

"And, Curtis, there is one more thing."

"Just one more?"

"Just a little tidbit I thought you might find interesting." He paused for effect. "One Scott Piquard from Granger, Idaho, served in the army with one Gary Brady from Granger, Idaho. Now, ain't that a co-inky-dink?"

Floyd Curtis let out a long decrescendo whistle. His head was spinning with possibilities. "Who else knows this?"

"Just a few of us in the Bureau. I've been working this all night. I tried to look up records on Piquard and guess what? I was locked out. A top-level, eyes-only freeze was placed on his file sometime yesterday, I think by Director Meyer himself. However, I know a guy down at archives who owes me a couple of favors, so I slipped down there about two this morning and opened some outdated back-up files. I found out what I needed and slipped out quietly. This is a gift for you to use judiciously, but you don't know the source, understood?"

"Understood!"

"I would love to go over to the White House and talk to Brady myself."

"Access is impossible. They've been in lockdown since yesterday morning, but I know one of the Air Force guys in the White House Command Center. I'll feel him out."

"Call me when you know something."

"Will do. Talk to you later, Ernie. I owe you."

"Ciao."

Curtis sat against the edge of his desk, his coffee forgotten. *What in the name of God is going on?* he said to himself as his mind raced through the permutations. He picked up his direct line to the White House Command Center. "Good morning, this is Lieutenant Colonel Floyd Curtis at Homeland Command. Is General Curt Nearman still down there?"

"Yes, he is, sir. Just one moment."

"Nearman here," a voice answered a few seconds later.

"Good morning, General Nearman. Floyd Curtis from Homeland. Sorry to bother you so early in the morning, but something came up in Idaho."

"What can I help you with, Curtis?"

"I am coordinating operations on the aircraft search as well as intel out west. I received a disturbing phone call from our Washington FBI liaison this morning. He tells me that one of your full colonels from Utah has been all over Granger, Idaho, asking questions, intimidating people, and telling them to talk to no one. The FBI agent in Granger has gotten virtually nowhere because of that, and to add insult, the colonel won't even talk to him. Same old politics as before

Homeland was developed. So I'm asking you if you know of anyone who has given an order, not transmitted to me, for the Air Force to gather information independently in Idaho and, if so, why they are not sharing intel and why they think they supersede Homeland title 6 sections 111, 123, 201, and 202 and title 49 section 114?"

"Curtis, I can say without reservation that I have no knowledge whatsoever of anything remotely resembling that. And I can also tell you that the Air Force has tried its damnedest to prohibit that kind of behavior. We take pride in being the best. I will personally find out what I can about this."

"Thank you, General. I knew you would. And when you talk to your colonel, you might want to remind him of section 111, which gives Homeland discretionary authority over operations involving national security, especially if any kind of terrorism is suspected. If he has willfully violated 111, he could be brought in front of a review board. That is a report I do not want to write. He is probably just trying to help, but he only has a couple of hours to think things over. I am now going to call the FBI operative and authorize him to call on your colonel. Unless he cooperates and tells him everything he knows, I will have no choice. Believe me, General, I don't want to do that. It's work for me that I don't need, and it's trouble for him that he doesn't want."

"I couldn't agree with you more, Curtis. I'll get back to you."

"Thank you, sir. By the way, I'll be here throughout this ordeal, sort of married to the job as it were. Would you be so kind as to call me directly if you have any news, day or night? I do not like important information being relayed through underlings. Too many things get lost in translation."

"Will do, Curtis. I'll be here too. And thanks for the direct communication. A lot of guys would have fired a shot across the bow, and that only hampers cooperation. I'll be in touch."

"Oh, one last thing, General," Curtis added, an afterthought by the tone of his voice. "Did anyone down there recognize the perp in the video?"

"No. No ID so far. Bureau guys are working on it."

"What was the president's reaction—verbal, facial, or otherwise?" Curtis asked, trying to sound curious but not too curious.

"Can't really say—never thought about it. Same as the rest of us, I suppose. Why?"

"Oh, nothing. Just curious what it's like to be down there with *the man*. It's got to be more interesting than sitting down here with a bunch of techno types all day. I mean, you are right there in the seat of power when he's down there. I was just wondering how he reacted."

"Guess I can't tell you much, Curtis. He's always pretty cool, you know. He was outraged when that missile was fired though. I've never seen him that angry. He has a couple of bases in lockdown, but if their inventories check out, we'll have to assume a ground launch. He was adamant that this guy was to be brought in alive, but with him plowing into Mount Whitney, that's not going to happen. After that, he just got real quiet and went into his private quarters."

"Thanks, General. Call me when you know something."

Curtis hung up and dialed the Idaho number Ernie Knoll had given him.

"Klugiewicz here," a very sleepy voice responded on the second ring.

Curtis identified himself and let Klugiewicz know that he had been talking to Knoll, but he did not tell him everything Knoll had said. "So what you did find out about Piquard?"

"The people I've talked to say he's the nicest guy you ever met. Works long hours. Straight shooter. Honest. Generous. If someone comes in who can't pay, he won't turn them away—all the nurses and clerical people agree on that. But as to politics, I can't get a good picture. He seems a little schizo on that. Some people say he's very conservative and believes in the death penalty, low taxes, minimal government intrusion. Others say he is quite liberal, does free care for the poor, donates to environmental groups, belongs to Greenpeace, but hunts and fishes and eats what he kills. Some of that seems like an odd fit to me. Maybe he doesn't know what he believes. But one thing seems certain, Curtis. He's not a politician. Thinks most of them are parasites. Maybe that's his motive. Maybe he has a grudge against the president. By the way, did you know that they graduated from high school together?" he ended triumphantly, hoping to impress Curtis with this last tidbit.

"You don't say?" Curtis responded.

"Yeah, they went to school together, but nothing negative from this end. Seems they were friends, but I can't find out much more because of the colonel's hush order. So what we've got is a middle-aged, overworked country doctor with no priors who may have gone over the edge. Who knows why these guys do that? In my hometown, this guy killed his wife and kids with a .44 Magnum during the middle of the night and then shot himself in the head. No warning, but something made him crack. Maybe that's what we've got here."

"Maybe," Curtis answered. "Maybe. Who knows? Call me if you find anything else interesting, okay? You may use my name and the Department of Homeland Security as your trump card. Don't let that guy push you around. You are Knoll's direct line to Idaho, and Knoll is my direct line to the Bureau. I will not have anyone interfering with those lines, understood?"

"Yes, sir, I understand, but I don't think our Air Force friend does."

"Well, he will before the sun is up. One of my generals is going to be talking to him and setting him straight." Curtis hung up not knowing that, by dawn, their mystery man would no longer be in Idaho.

Chapter 21

Camp David

"No! Gary. No! No! No! It can't be," Janet Brady blurted through her tears as she collapsed into her husband's arms. The news he had just delivered had crumbled her normally strong veneer like wet tissue. "Scott can't be dead! He just can't be! There must be some mistake," she sobbed against his chest.

"I hope you're right. We won't know for sure until the climbers reach the aircraft, but all evidence points the wrong way. It was definitely Scott on the video cameras down in Security One, and the only reason he was down there was that I had given him my access card like the idiot I am. I may be responsible for the death of my best friend, and the irony of it all is that, if I hadn't given him my card, I might be dead myself. Just before the explosion, an unidentified pilot talked to one of the military pilots. I heard the replay, Janet. It sounded like Scott's voice." He hugged her harder, pressing her cheek to his chest, and then continued, "The pilot would not identify himself, but he told the F-35 pilot to relay a message that there was a plot on my life. That was all he said before the missile exploded."

"So this airplane—Scott's airplane—crashed into the mountains out west for no apparent reason? Maybe there was another missile."

"No. A missile is easy to spot on radar, and we had both ground and airborne radar locked on that plane. There was no communication after the explosion. That tells us that the explosion probably knocked out his radios. His guidance systems were working in Kansas, but maybe they failed later, which would explain the early descent. Just as likely, he may have been injured in the explosion and became incapacitated toward the end. His flight path was taking him straight toward Bakersfield, where Keith lives. Maybe he was disoriented and descended too soon, or maybe he was unconscious and the plane descended on its own. Either way, the end was painless. There are worse ways to die."

She shuddered. "Poor Rachael. What is she going to do? I have to go to her."

"Not yet. She knows nothing. Besides, until the climbers reach it, we don't know who is in that plane. Maybe Scott will show up here." Brady spoke confidently, as if saying it could make it so.

"When will the climbers get there?"

"We don't know. It's still dark out west, and the climbing is slow." He pushed away a little and looked her straight in the eyes. "Even then, we may not know for sure. Whoever is in that plane will be unrecognizable. We will likely have to wait for dental and DNA confirmation."

Janet had given no thought to what the crash site might look like. Now the mental picture of it made her shiver and collapse back into her husband's arms, sobbing until her spasms shook his body as well. Finally, Gary could hold it in no longer. The emotional roller coaster he had been riding was ignited by her grief, and he felt the tears starting down his cheeks as he began to sob with her.

They cried together until the sobs wore themselves out. Then Gary washed his eyes with cold water and rang the Secret Service office.

"Greg Stroud."

"Greg, please come to my quarters. Alone."

"Yes, Mr. President, right away."

Stroud was soon at the door. He knocked, and Sam Davies let him in. "Sam, the president said he wanted to see me alone."

"Come in, both of you. Lock the door behind you." One look at the president's expression told Stroud there was no confusion in that order.

Brady walked to the stereo and started Dvorak's Fourth Symphony, skipping to the third movement, Allegro Feroce—lively and with ferocity. The set of nine symphonies had been a birthday gift from Scott and Rachael years earlier, and he had come to love the Czechoslovakian's power and diversity. He turned the volume up. The booming music assured him that no random ears would hear what he had to say.

"Greg, you need to know what Sam and I know, and you need to operate inside of that knowledge base. What I have to tell you, you will repeat to no one."

Greg Stroud had worked his way to the top with the combination of hard work and wary intelligence which advanced people to his level of authority. Very little surprised him, but the president's demeanor galvanized his full attention.

"The intruder in the tunnel was my best friend, Dr. Scott Piquard."

Stroud's eyes were nearly bulging, implication after implication flooding his quick brain.

"I ordered Sam not to speak up, so don't look at him that way. He was doing exactly what I told him to do."

"But—"

"And the pilot's voice on the FAA recording? Despite the static, I think it was Scott Piquard's voice, which means that the overwhelming odds are that my best friend is dead. And that means that, unless someone finds out who fired those shots, heads are going to roll. By the way, any word on the ordnance inventory at the military bases?"

"No, that could take another day or two. But what was he doing down there? Of course, he's going to be treated like an intruder." Stroud was speaking, but his voice no longer carried its usual certainty.

"We don't know what he was doing down there. Knowing Scott, his curiosity got the best of him, but curiosity should not get you shot! Think about it, Greg. If you saw a stranger wandering around down there, would you just pull your gun and start firing? And the missile? Who wants him dead? You heard that FAA transmission as clearly as I did. He said there was a plot on my life. Coming from a total stranger—a fugitive in your eyes—that could be easily dismissed as a crackpot comment. But coming from my best friend, it means that there *is* a plot on my life."

"How did he get that deep into security?" Stroud asked.

"It doesn't matter, does it, Greg? That's just extraneous detail."

"It matters if he's part of the plot!"

"For Christ's sake, he slept right down the hall from me Thursday night! Don't waste any more of my time on comments like that." The tempo of his voice was escalating with his agitation.

Brady continued, "I would trade places with him this instant if I could, but I can't. And he taught me a long time ago to deal with the things that I can deal with and put aside the things I cannot change. I cannot change the fact that someone wants to assassinate me, and I cannot change the fact that they almost did it right under the noses of the Secret Service. But I can try to find out who is behind this. And I can move my family somewhere safe because I sure as hell don't feel safe right here, right now!"

"But, Mr. President, this is the safest place for you right now," Stroud countered, pleading.

"Somehow the events of the last twenty-four hours contradict that claim. Now, call for *Marine One*. I am taking my family to Camp David, and no one is to know except you and Todd Pederson. Maybe I'll feel safer surrounded by Navy people," he said, alluding to the fact that Camp David was a naval site.

"I'm sorry, Mr. President, but I can't allow that. We have security beefed up here to a factor of a hundredfold, and Camp David has only a basic crew right now. Besides, if they had one Sparrow, they could have another. You would be a sitting duck in *Marine One* if someone wanted to take a shot at you."

"They won't if they don't know where I am. That is why I am ordering you to maintain secrecy. Absolute secrecy. Sam and I have thought this through."

Stroud countered, "I don't like the idea of you leaving here, Mr. President. The safe room at Camp David is pretty good, but it's not as strong as the one here."

"Greg, I am not worried about a safe room that protects me from a megaton explosion," Brady countered. "What I am worried about is a single bullet to the head by a person I don't even know is out to get me and who has the credentials to get close enough to pull the trigger."

"This is not safe—"

"It will be at least as safe as yesterday morning. Now quit arguing and start augmenting. We are leaving as soon as Janet and the boys are ready. Now get *Marine One* moving. And remember, not a word to anyone except Todd Pederson!"

"Yes, sir. But I must go on record as objecting to this breach of protocol."

"And I must go on record as objecting to yesterday's breach of protocol, but that and fifty cents won't buy me a cup of coffee in this town. Now get to work!" The frustration exploded in his voice, and Stroud knew he could say nothing more to change his boss's mind. He left quickly as Jeremy and David Brady charged into the room and ran to their father.

"What's going on, Dad? Is everybody safe? What happened yesterday morning? Was anyone killed?" When he had quieted the boys, he told them that they were going to Aspen Lodge, the presidential cabin in the Catoctin Mountains, and they were to tell absolutely no one.

"Where is Scott?"

"He headed west in his plane." He saw the look of disappointment on their faces, but he was not prepared to tell them the whole story. "But even if I can't leave here, you and Mom are probably going to Idaho in a few days." It was only half true, and he knew it, but half-truths had become his life.

Two hours later, the first family descended to the lower level, where they donned their raingear. Stroud and Davies were waiting by the door that led to *Marine One*. Brady handed two envelopes to Stroud. "Greg, I need you to take this larger envelope and put it on my desk in the Oval Office. Then take the smaller one and put it on my dining room table upstairs. Go now. I will be talking to you in a little while." He shook Stroud's hand and ushered him to the hallway. "Thanks, Greg." Brady walked back to his family, putting on his sunglasses and pulling up the hood on his raincoat.

As Stroud walked briskly to the Oval Office, he glanced out a window and could see four figures hustling through the drizzle and climbing into the large Sikorsky. Two minutes later, he heard the *whump, whump, whump* of the huge rotors as *Marine One* and two identical decoy helicopters lifted off. Stroud put the larger envelope on the desk in the Oval Office, as directed, then walked back to the staircase and bounded up to the presidential living quarters. He entered the dining room and was starting for the table when a voice came from behind him.

"Hello, Greg."

Stroud jumped and whirled. President Brady and Sam Davies were standing in the room. "Mr. President? Who—"

"That was a double. Sam set it up," Brady said with a grin. "I need to be here taking care of business, but I want everyone to think I am at Camp David."

Stroud finally relaxed enough to smile. "Well done. You had me faked out."

"I will be up here the next couple of days. You, Sam, and Todd will bring work up the back way. No one else is to know I am here. I want no staff. I don't require much food—nothing beats a hot dog with extra mustard. I will do my briefings by phone. They can all think I'm at the camp. We have a lot to do, but right now, I have a very important call to make. Give me a few minutes." Stroud left with Sam as Brady picked up his secure line and dialed.

"Hello," a sleepy Rachael Piquard answered on the second ring. "Scott?"

"No, this is his college roommate. Do not use names. Just answer my questions."

"What's wrong?"

"I need you to listen very closely, as I only have a minute. There has been some trouble. Your husband headed west in his airplane.

153

You need to take your kids and go straight home. Do not talk to anyone. Do not stop except for gas. Do not let anyone into the house, military or otherwise, unless you know them personally. Your life may be in danger. I am dispatching four agents to watch your home, but it will take them several hours to get there."

"What is going on?" The sleepiness had completely disappeared from her voice.

"There has been an attempt on my life. We think your husband stumbled onto the perpetrators. If they discover his identity, you may also be in danger. Be careful what you say on the phone. Your home phone might be tapped, and your cell won't be safe either. If he calls, tell him to lie low, keep calls very short, and *not* to come home until I give the all-clear. Okay?"

"Okay. I think." She was as puzzled as she was frightened.

"We love you. I have to go. Goodbye."

Gary could hear the worry in Rachael's voice, but he felt powerless to help her.

Chapter 22

Heading Home

Saturday, 6:00 a.m. PDT, Northern Idaho

Rachael Piquard drove like she had never driven before. Her eyes were on the rearview mirror more than they were on the winding roads that led to her home—her home that, until two hours ago, had been her haven, her sanctuary. Now it would be watched and wiretapped and videotaped twenty-four hours a day.

On his second call, Gary told her that a team had been assigned to her but she was to go with no one. "And don't trust their ID. They are too easy to falsify. Make them arrest you if you must. Call their bluff. Do not go with anyone unless you are at imminent risk of physical harm. Promise me." She had.

Chad and Stephanie had been up late, watching a movie, but they had little trouble waking when she broke the news. "Someone tried to kill Gary. Dad's on his way home. Pack up. We're going home."

Looking in the mirrors, she imagined every car carried a spy. Every change of position was a subterfuge. Her once-safe world was in danger of collapsing, and her anchor was adrift somewhere for the first time. She worried about Scott's safety every time he flew, but she had always managed to subdue it. Now she had to face it. Why had she let him go without reaffirming their love? Why had she been so selfish? He had given her everything. Now he was in danger, and the stark reality left an ache deep inside.

Rachael slid around the junction onto Highway 95 too fast, her tires skidding as she negotiated the turn. She tapped the brakes and coasted, forcing the cars behind her to pass. Her eyes were glued to the mirror as she watched the first three cars speed by her, but the fourth car, a plain black Ford sedan, slowed behind her. She coasted to the shoulder, forcing the car to go around. The lone white male, well-dressed and in his midthirties, pulled slowly past her, shaking his head as if to say "Crazy woman driver" and proceeded south on 95.

Rachael was trembling. "Do you want me to drive for a while, Mom?" Chad asked. "You need a break anyway."

"Yeah, I guess I do."

"If they were going to stop us, they would have done it by now. All we have to do is go home and act naturally. Dad's probably there already. Besides, Gary wouldn't let anything happen to us."

She walked around to the passenger's door, stretching. "Okay, Double-O Piquard, let's go." It was the first time she had laughed all day.

Chad accelerated smoothly, but two miles down the road, he noticed the plain black Ford sedan pulled over on the shoulder. Chad slowed despite his mother's protests. He passed the car and then accelerated again.

"Just wanted to get a look at his face," he said as he smiled at his mother.

So much like his dad, she thought.

The Ford pulled out onto the road and began following at a distance. Ten miles from town, Chad turned onto a dirt road that wound into the mountains.

"Where are you going?" Rachael demanded.

"Back way. I don't like being followed."

"Chad!" She started to protest, but it was too late. He started up the hill and accelerated the Tahoe. A mile further, he made the crest, shifted into four-wheel drive, and started down a steep incline, his wheels expertly balanced on the ridges of the eroded, single-lane trail as the ruts grew deeper and deeper. At the bottom, a deep washout required a forty-five-degree approach as he gunned the Tahoe and drug the skidpans across the dried mud. Looking back, they could see the sedan was stopped halfway down the hill and trying to back up. *So much like his dad.* There was comfort in the thought.

From the hilltop, Agent Renner cursed as he watched them pull away. "Idiot," he said out loud as he called Klugiewicz on his sat phone. "Yeah, it's Renner. I lost them, and I might need a tow to get out of here. I'll call you back."

As Chad pulled into the empty garage, the total quiet that greeted them was all too obvious. Their disappointment went unacknowledged as they made quick work of unpacking and putting things away. Then Stephanie and Chad changed into their running gear. They had been running five miles a day, but when they came down the stairs and began stretching, Rachael nearly hit the roof.

"Absolutely not!" Her voice had that mother's inflection that every child knew. "Gary said to stay home, trust no one, and go nowhere."

"Come on, Mom." Now it was Stephanie's turn to speak up. "We can't be prisoners in our own home. This is America. What are they going to do? Shoot us?"

"They just might!" Rachael snapped. "I don't know what is going on any more than you do, but I'm scared. Gary has never called like that before. Never! I felt the emotion in his voice. This is not kid's stuff. Until your father gets home, until we have more answers, we are not leaving this property."

"What about football Monday morning? I can't miss that. Coach will have a cow. Besides, if they wanted us dead, we'd already be dead."

"We'll see about Monday on Monday. For today, we are staying home." Rachael felt badly. She knew how committed they had been to their workouts. "I'll make you a deal. You can go outside if you don't leave the backyard. Stay inside the fence, don't talk to any strangers, and come in immediately if you see anyone you don't recognize. Agreed?"

"Why not?" Stephanie said, looking at Chad. "We need speed work anyway."

The Piquards had purchased the property on the upper edge of town, leveled the small horse pasture, put up a chain-link fence, and replanted it to grass. The large yard gave them plenty of room for wind sprints. Rachael stood in the kitchen and watched them sprinting down the length of the property. The large bay window above the sink gave her a perfect view of the yard and the mountains beyond. If she was going to spend the largest percentage of her time in this room, she reasoned, why not have the best view? The same thought went into putting her utility room upstairs with an oversized window framing the beautiful Nez Perce Wilderness to the south.

"Why put your workroom in the basement? People pay hundreds of dollars a night at resorts for a view like this," she had told the architect when Scott had purchased the land and allowed her free reign with the plans.

God, I love that man. Why was I such a fool? The knowledge that she hadn't heard from him left a dead feeling in her chest, a heaviness that could not be ignored. She stood there for several minutes, finding solace in watching the children race up and back, Stephanie never quite able to keep up with her big brother and trying all the harder for it.

Two hundred yards away, someone else was watching the runners. He picked up his phone. "Yeah, it's Klugiewicz. The three of them are home. No one has come or gone. The kids are outside, doing wind sprints back and forth in this huge backyard. I can see the front door and the garage entrance from here, so I should be able to see if anyone comes or goes, but when you get here, you need to cover the side opposite the garage. Someone could walk up the back deck without being seen from here. We have the bugs in the house and on the phones, so we'll know if he calls. How are you coming?"

"I'm almost to town," Renner reported. "I can't wait to get back to DC or someplace where real shit happens. What did I ever do to get stuck out here?"

"It grows on you. Remember, drugs, murder, and rape are not the norm for everyone. Did it ever occur to you that some people choose to live out here for those very reasons? People who live here are self-sufficient. I've seen it blizzard for four days, and they are happy to stay home, split wood, stoke the fire, and read a good book. You won't hear them crying for help from the government. They want the government out of their lives. Live here for a couple of years, and you'll see what I mean."

"Yeah, maybe, but I doubt it. Talk to you later."

From the trees at the foot of the mountain, another set of optics shared a similar focal point in the backyard. The thoughts behind that eyepiece were of a different shade. *What perfect legs. Not an ounce of fat on her. The brother looks solid, though. He could be a problem, but ten of Valium will take the fight out of him. Unfortunately, they said no fun on this one.* He sighed. *Yet!*

Chapter 23

Operation Darien

Saturday, 1:00 p.m. EDT, White House

Todd Pederson had run the stairs several times that day after dismissing most of the staff. He was panting as he entered Brady's private study. "More bad news, sir. The Mexicans have started their retreat, and the Joint Chiefs want a meeting. Panic is about to set in down there, and they want authorization to move before it becomes a massacre."

"We have more than enough troops to fortify our own borders, and I will not send our boys south to fight someone else's war. Do I have to tell them that again?"

"Sir, the Mexican papers are crying foul. This morning's issue of *La Jornada* is claiming that we promised military help and then reneged at the critical moment. This could make us look very bad in the eyes of the world press."

"In the end, all we got was criticism and more enemies for fighting al-Qaeda and not much better for trying to stop that bloodbath in Pakistan. They take our money and spit in our face. The world press can go to hell!"

Pederson had seen his boss mad, and he did not want to provoke him. He took a long breath before he went on.

160

"The Joint Chiefs want to be given the opportunity to explain the urgency of today's developments. They want to make sure you know that it will be easier to stop the Southern Alliance now than to drive them back later."

"Who's pushing the hardest?"

"Army and Air Force, less from Navy and Marines."

"I want to know who says what and exactly how they say it. Todd, I need to know where the pressure is coming from. I think someone promised the Northern Alliance military aid, thinking I wouldn't dare let them flounder once the kettle boiled. Whoever is most anxious to lend aid is most likely to have made promises behind my back. Find out who is pushing this agenda."

"What do I tell them about a meeting?"

"Tell them we will have a conference call in one hour and hint that I am ready to give them authorization to implement Operation Darien. President Arias has been warned that if the Colombians cross the Panamanian border, we will hit their advance line. Just in case he doesn't believe me, I want sorties to begin flying off the ships in the Gulf of Darien and the Gulf of Panama."

"Yes, sir. Also, sir, the rumor is out that you're at the camp. Everyone knows *Marine One* headed that way when it left here."

"Good. By the way, any news from Mount Whitney?"

"Only that they might reach the plane before nightfall if the weather keeps improving."

"Let me know the minute you hear something."

"Yes, sir."

For the next hour, Brady busied himself with the latest Security Council brief on Central America until he had it nearly memorized. He dialed the number for the Joint Chiefs' situation room. His secure line had no caller ID tag.

"This is President Brady. Admiral Winslow, please."

Lon Winslow was one of the most competent officers Brady knew, was about his age, and both men and their wives had similar interests; a modest friendship bloomed shortly after they met. He was one of the men Brady thought he could trust. "Winslow here."

"Lon, this is President Gary Brady. The password for today is Highlander."

"Thank you for calling, Mr. President. We have a lot to cover today. The Mexican lines are starting to crack. We are unanimously asking for authorization to shore up their defenses to prevent a massacre."

"They started that war. They can end it. Lon, put me on overhead."

There was a slight pause and a quick series of clicks. Brady could hear the background noise in the room. "Gentlemen, I have made my decision. I am not sacrificing American soldiers to bolster the egos and poor judgment of our neighbors to the south. They don't listen to us when we give them millions in aid, but they want us to bail them out in the name of national security. I do not believe our national security is at risk at this point. However, we will initiate Operation Darien from the carriers in the gulf waters as discussed Wednesday. President Arias and his generals need to know we mean business. Our pilots are to fly the border, but they are not to enter Colombian airspace. We will make an obvious presence, and if we have confirmed intel that says the Colombians are crossing the border, we will lob a few live rounds, but you will not shoot to kill. I will be talking to Arias shortly. Do you understand all this?"

"Yes, sir," Winslow replied, "but the general staff is getting worried. There has never been a better time to solidify our relationship with Mexico and Panama and everyone in between."

"Oh god, Lonnie, do we have to go into that again? Look what the Panamanians did to us when the lease ran out. Now they suddenly love us? Look at how much the Mexicans listen to us. They wouldn't give us the time of day when the Chinese money was flowing in, but after the Asian market collapse and that flow dried up, they suddenly wanted to be best friends. As for the rest of them, all they want is a decent meal a couple times a day."

"They may not love us, sir, but at least they won't hate us if we help them now. There is a difference, and the political assets are incalculable."

"The difference is that they would not listen to me months ago, and now they must live with their decision. Good day, gentlemen."

Brady cradled the phone, his thoughts suddenly turning to his sons. Should he tell them now? Should he tell them the whole truth or try to hide it for a while longer? And what was the truth? Did he even know the truth? Just what did he know, after all? Did he know for sure who was in that aircraft? Did he know who was dead and who was alive? Did he know who was trying to protect him and who was trying to kill him? Did he know who wanted to take military action in South America or exactly why? What did he really know? He could not justify lying to his sons—the family creed was honesty above all else—but he could justify protecting them a little while longer.

Chapter 24

No One Home

It had been first a maddening, then a frustrating, and finally a boring day for Lieutenant Colonel Floyd Curtis. Klugiewicz called that morning, informing him that the mysterious visitor from Hill Air Force Base had departed during the night as quietly as he had arrived. Klugiewicz had coaxed a name, Colonel Robert Hedges, out of the sheriff, but that was about all. Curtis had then spent the better part of the day trying to run him down at Hill Air Force Base, only to learn that he had deplaned the Blackhawk and immediately boarded a transport, leaving Utah for an undisclosed location near the Mexican border. He was incommunicado and was expected to be so for at least two weeks.

The next several hours were spent trying to learn details about the life and times of Colonel Robert Hedges. Robert Hedges led an extremely dull life. Other than the basics, his file was about as empty as that of an airman first class reporting for his first assignment. No commendations, no special tour medals, no disciplinaries, no notations, nothing. *He advances all the way to full colonel without so much as a comment on his record from a superior officer yet has access to Blackhawks and transports overnight?* Curtis knew better. His record had been cleansed.

He spent the rest of the day waiting by the phone, reviewing information, and hoping for a call. Then an hour past sunset Pacific time, he received a call from China Lake. Of all the possible calls, of all the possible scenarios, this was the least likely piece of information he would have anticipated.

"Curtis here," he said as the call was routed to his desk.

"Hello, Colonel, this is Commander Horstmeyer at China Lake Naval Weapons Center. The climbing team has just reached the aircraft. It's just a compressed pile of metal, but they were able to make out some of the tail number. It looks like it is November 6-8-7 *Whiskey Mike*. The GPS coordinates match. There is no question that they have the right location, but something's missing, sir."

"Well, after an impact like that, I'm not surprised. What's the problem? Can't find any ID?"

"No, sir. They can't find any pilot."

The ensuing pause was interminable. Curtis could find no words to respond.

"Did you hear me, Colonel? I am reporting that there are zero souls on board November 6-8-7 *Whiskey Mike*!"

Chapter 25

Down and Out

Friday, 5:30 p.m. PDT, California airspace

D r. Scott Piquard looked down at his feet. It was all the far-ther he could see—dark shoes against white fog. He hoped he would be able to handle the landing. It had been a long time. He watched for his opening as he thought back over the last few hours and how he had gotten to this place in time, his life hang-ing by a thread.

After rigging his duct-tape autopilot, he had been able to move around the cabin. Dumping the contents from the old flight bag, he took inventory. He gathered his eight bottles of water and the two breakfast bars, placing them in the flight bag. *I should have grabbed more water*, he thought to himself, not for the last time. He leaned forward and checked his compass and attitude—slight drift left—and added a piece of duct tape to the right yoke, tightening it until he was getting a distinct rightward drift.

He found the miniature Swiss Army knife that had been rele-gated to the old flight bag after the Leatherman had replaced it in the new. Nine pieces of hardtack candy went into the side pocket with the knife. *I wonder how old those are*, he said to himself. *No matter. Sugar is sugar.* The plastic flight calculator was tossed aside, as was a dried-out pen. The pencil, ageless, stayed. Stuffed in the corner, long

166

neglected, was his ragged woolen stocking cap. That old gray cap, bought for a dollar at the Army Surplus Store in college, had seen thousands of miles of trek; it would see a few more. In a true emergency, the simple things mattered.

Again, he checked his drift—definitely to the right—just what he wanted. Lying at the back of the seat, he spied the final prize. Scott picked up the faded Bic lighter and shook it. Although only a tiny amount of butane sloshed in the bottom, it was definitely worth taking. Over the years, he had stashed these lighters in every glove compartment and backpack, replacing the matches. Once a match got old or wet, the sulfur crumbled and would not spark; a lighter could be dried and reused.

Reaching into the wall pocket by the pilot's seat, he found a small flashlight. He always carried at least one spare where he could reach it in flight. Lastly, he put three WAC charts in the bag and closed it tightly. He tossed it down by the door and turned back to his GPS. He had passed waypoint 001 and was only a few miles from 002. Reassuring himself that his heading was stable, he depressurized the cabin and again slipped to the back of the plane. Scott tucked his jacket tightly inside his pants then stuffed the flight bag inside his jacket. Finally, he reached for his old friend in the back.

For several years, ever since he quit stunt flying, his parachute had been abandoned to the cargo rack. Periodically, he had taken it to the local jumpmaster and had it checked and refolded, but it had been a while. Now, he had no choice but to trust it. He slipped it on and fastened it snugly then pulled up and cinched the thigh straps. Scott unlatched the door and kicked open the lower half of the clamshell then rushed forward. The drag of the open door would pull *Whiskey Mike* strongly to the left, and he compensated by rolling the horizontal trim fully right and slightly retarding the right engine. Checking his heading, he still needed more help combating the left drift. Using the remaining duct tape to draw down the right yoke handle, he forced the plane into a slight right-wing low attitude, a poor man's sideslip. The dirty configuration would cause the plane to slow and lose altitude. He hoped the rightward forces were enough to balance the drag of the open door. Out of time, it would have to do.

A last check showed he was past 002. One mile from 003, Scott shut off the GPS and stuffed it into his pant pocket, returning to the door as he counted down from twenty. At ten, he positioned himself in the doorway. At five, he crouched. At zero, he launched himself through the small opening, arching his back and spreading his limbs as he heard *Whiskey Mike* disappear into the west for the last time. He would miss her. She had taken better care of him than he had of her.

Exiting at fourteen thousand, he had ample altitude. Scott pulled his ripcord and felt the reassuring pop and the tug at his armpits. He looked up and made sure his lines were not twisted. "Full canopy." He looked down at his feet. It was all the farther he could see. *Will there be enough ceiling? Will I have time to react? Will they quit looking for me when they think I'm dead?* He floated weightlessly through a layer. Now he could see thirty feet past his feet to the next puff of cloud. A minute later, he could see layers in the overcast. Then suddenly, like a thrown switch, white cloud dissipated, and he burst into clear air.

Scott oriented himself to the terrain below. His calculations had been perfect. The plateau stretched directly below him, and he could see highways to the south and to the west. He pulled down on the steering toggle in his right hand, curving the right airfoil downward. The increased resistance pivoted his canopy in that direction. Scott picked out the smoothest spot and prepared for touchdown.

After the continuous drone of the twin Lycomings, the bliss of total quiet was something to be savored. The only sound was the whistle of the wind past his face and an occasional creaking of the harness and straps. Compared to the pandemonium of the day, this moment was nothing if not surreal. Would that he could have relished this instant in time—hanging motionless in space as his own gravitational force drew the earth up to meet him—but the dream was over as quickly as it had come.

At twenty miles per hour, the earth loomed large as Scott approached his landing site. Strewn with rock everywhere he looked, the ground below him was much rougher than he had remembered. He had driven the family here two years earlier to spend a few days exploring, but he had not looked at it with a skydiver's eye. To his left, he saw a patch of grass. He pulled on the left toggle and turned. Sensing that he was too high, he made a series of quick S turns, dropping altitude while continuously visualizing his landing zone. From a thousand feet, it had seemed like he was barely moving, but as he neared the surface, his speed seemed too great to hit such a small opening in the rocks.

Concentrate. Full flaps. Pull hard. Two-point landing. Scott talked himself through the landing sequence, long atrophied from disuse. As he pulled, the rear corners of the airfoil curved downward, trapping hundreds of cubic feet of air and becoming twin air brakes. He slowed to ten miles an hour, then five. If he pulled too soon, he could stall; too late and he would overshoot or land hard. Out of practice, he pulled too soon.

The chute hung on the air too hard—too long. Momentum carried his body forward, swinging him out under the shrouds like an oversized pendulum, then swung him back just as he touched the ground. He landed softly enough, but he was on his heels and rocking backward. The breeze caught the chute and pulled it behind him. Scott was falling, pulling hand over hand on the right control lines. Frantically gathering cord with both hands, forcing his airfoil to collapse and spill its air, he tried to keep his balance. He was too late.

Scott fell hard onto the rock-jutted surface. Rolling out to absorb the momentum along the entire side of his body, Scott was nearly out of trouble when he felt intense pain in his right elbow. He tried to ignore the pain while he finished dumping his chute, but he could feel the blood running down his arm as he collapsed his canopy and regained his feet. He looked around and only up close appreciated just how rocky this plateau was. *Thank God it wasn't my head.*

Scott shed his harness and stretched. He inhaled the first relaxed breath he had taken in hours and gazed at the magnificent landscape around him. The feeling of being followed, hounded, and shot at was now replaced with a feeling of unbounded scope and latitude. He was free to go where he wanted and do what he wanted—free as long as he did it on foot. Ultimate freedom also meant freedom from society and all that society afforded.

The blood trickling down his arm brought him back to the realities of the moment. He needed a bandage. He had no absorbent material other than what was on his body, and that he could ill afford to waste. Nonabsorbent as it was, nylon would have to do.

He pulled the bag from inside of his jogging suit and laid it on the grass. He was surprised at how soft and moist the grass seemed. By August, the grass here would normally be brown and brittle, but the massive storm had given this bit of earth a share of its precious few inches of annual rainfall. Native grasses, the essential cornerstone of the food chain that allowed the first animals to roam dry ground, were among the most resilient plants in the world; they had absorbed the precious water and reclaimed their hold on life.

Scott emptied the contents carefully onto the ground. Using the small knife, he cut an oversize bandage from the parachute and wrapped it several times around his elbow. Making three six-inch cuts in the loose end created four ties, which he wrapped in alternate directions and tied with one-handed surgeon's knots.

Spreading the parachute, he surveyed just how much he wanted to carry. He could afford no dead weight. The harness was first to go. Next, he cut a large rectangle of cloth from one of the corners, saving as many grommets and shrouds as possible. Then he cut off the rest of the chute cords and stowed them in the middle of the rectangle. *You can never have too much rope.* Tolkien understood.

Setting two bottles of water and a granola bar to the side, he placed most of his possessions into the middle of the rectangle with the rope, taking a mental inventory as he did so: *Six bottles of water, one breakfast bar, nine small pieces of candy, one pencil, one wool stocking cap, three WAC charts, and one GPS with weak batteries.* Scott folded the nylon until it was the size of a small backpack, keeping the attached ropes to the outside. He tied two pieces of rope around the pack to bind it neatly together then arranged four ropes to each side of the package and tied them off as shoulder straps. One strap would have afforded strength enough, but one strap would have cut into his shoulders. His design spread the weight over a larger surface area, the key to preventing painful blisters.

From the remaining nylon, Scott cut a six-by-ten-foot rectangle. One slit in the center, just large enough for his head, transformed it into a lightweight poncho. Finally, he cut a kerchief-sized piece and wedged it into his right pant pocket, insuring that the knife, his most valuable possession next to his shoes and the water, would not fall out accidentally. He cut a second piece to protect the lighter and the flashlight in his left pocket. Satisfied, he rolled a rock from its foundation, stuffed the remainder of the parachute into the depression, and let the rock fall into place.

Taking the granola bar and a bottle of water to a large rock, Scott was finally able to sit and enjoy his first meal of the day. Breakfast at 6:00 p.m. *Must be an intern again*, he said to himself as he relished the succulent apple-and-cinnamon main course, accompanied by the purest white the maître d' had to offer. Having licked the last crumb from the wrapper, he slipped it under a rock. Fatigued as he was, he knew there was no time for rest. He needed to put miles between himself and his would-be captors. He stuffed a full water bottle and the empty one into the last fold of the homemade backpack, using the poncho to wedge them into this pocket, and then strapped it on. Making one last sweep to be sure there was no obvious record of his visit, he turned and set off at a brisk pace.

Given the irregularity of the terrain, Scott knew that a power walk would be safer than a jog. One misplaced step, one sprained ligament, and he was as good as dead. As grandpa said, "The steady drip fills the pail."

He headed toward the ridge. Once there, he could better survey the lay of the land and decide on his next tack. *Breathe smoothly. Don't pant. Relax on the exhale. Don't clench your fists. Waste no energy.* The first hour passed, and still he had not gained the ridge.

Keep moving. Ignore the fatigue. Remember how tired you were of sitting in that plane. Keep the momentum. The next stage will set in. Then you won't feel the ache. You will only feel the motion.

Another quarter of an hour passed. Now the ridge looked promising, steadily uphill, steepening toward the summit. *Steady motion.*

He knew he had slowed down. Able to make four miles an hour on flat ground with his long stride, three in rougher terrain, he was now down to one and feeling the need for rest and water. *Not until you…make the ridge… Haven't earned it… Keep moving… They won't quit… Neither can you…* His legs pumped in time to his thoughts. *Your life…depends on it… Rachael's future…depends on it… Chad and Stephanie…depend on it…*

These thoughts renewed his energy. A new surge of adrenaline filled his arteries, carrying fresh blood and oxygen to his legs.

Saw his face…can identify…the one… That voice…must not forget…that voice… What did…they say…? How did…they say it…? Replay it… Replay it.

Anger fueled determination as he replayed the conversation again and again. His breathing fell in line with their words: *When President Brady…is finally dead… When King is president…everything will move…forward as planned…doesn't need to know…so ambitious…bold road…promised Molina…assured…military… President Brady… Antichrist…password clear…homecoming marshal…parade in September.*

What does that mean? he asked himself as he surged up the slope, fatigue forgotten, catecholamines countering lactic acid, the ridge just minutes away. Anger and hatred were two fuels he had suppressed his entire life. Now he let them burn, carrying him over the rocks at a clip reserved for younger men. Before they were spent, he had claimed the saddle, cresting the ridge and watching the next valley open below him.

He surveyed the terrain. Immediately oriented, Scott eyed his next objective. With barely time to catch his breath, he set off downslope. Intending to rest and drink when he gained the ridge, he instead let the twin fuels propel him on the downslope. With gravity at his heels, he was back to a four-mile-per-hour pace. It would not be this easy for a long time, nor would he always have the advantage of daylight. He must maximize each advantage. Downhill while tired, uphill when fresh. This time at least. Mostly it would be downhill when tired, uphill when tired.

From the high ground, he had glimpsed the winding dirt road that was his first objective. Reaching it before dark would be tantamount to adding half a day to his head start in case they figured out his ruse. *Go… Pump… Breathe… Pump… Go… Pump… Breathe… Pump… Flow… Pump… Breathe… Pump… Flow… Flow… Flow… Flow…*

Scott hit his groove, and it felt good. He moved his feet; gravity did the rest. By the time he reached the dry wash at the bottom, he felt rested for the next climb. He started up the slope, slowing to preserve his energy. And his water. He estimated the temperature at eighty degrees. If he pushed too hard, he would lose too much water. He paced himself, knowing that he must match his need for speed with his need for stamina. He could not have both. Life is a continuum of tradeoffs.

Nearing the summit as dusk settled over the valley, he could clearly see portions of the road winding between the hills to the north. He surprised himself that he had claimed this ridge without a break, without a drink. But he would need to drink soon. *Halfway up the next ridge, I'll take a break. By then I can find the road in the dark. I can't miss it now.* He powered down the next slope.

His thoughts surged in time to his breathing. *Keep the…adrenaline moving… Don't stop yet… It's getting dark…then danger…of injury… Injury means…death out here… You have…your whole life… to rest… Embrace the pain… Pain is proof…that you're alive… Cherish the pain…use the pain… Pain gives energy… Pain is life…life is pain.*

His elbow had swollen since his botched landing. The throbbing kept time with his steps. The warmth of fresh blood periodically seeped beneath the bandage, and Scott knew that, over the next forty-eight hours, the swelling and stiffness would grow worse.

His pace had slackened, but these thoughts became prods. He lumbered up the steepening slope, each breath labored, his mouth parchment. He eyed his rest stop. *Don't give in early, or the next time it will be easier.* He willed himself up the last of the hillside. *You've done much steeper. Remember the Sawtooths. Easy compared to those. Keep moving.*

A last surge of energy filled his bloodstream and carried him up to the grassy area in a determined push as dusk surrounded the rocks. He shed the pack, took off his top, and sprawled on the ground. Scott resisted the temptation to drink immediately. Thirsty people gulped, drinking more than they needed and often earning a gut ache in the bargain. He must conserve, so he let his body rest and cool first. He would feel less thirsty in a few minutes. *Discipline.*

As the Sierras claimed the sun, the air cooled. Scott savored it for ten full minutes, letting his oxygen debt abate as he breathed the clean mountain air. Finally cooled, he retrieved his second water bottle.

Knowing that multiple small sips were more efficient than one large gulp, Scott wet his entire oral cavity, saturating the dryness before swallowing each aliquot. He could easily drink three bottles; he satisfied himself with a half. *Pace yourself. You'll appreciate it more later.*

He needed to cool more efficiently, so now he folded his jacket lengthwise, placed it across his shoulders like a padded yoke, and donned his pack. Invigorated, he made good time up the remaining slope. The light was nearly spent, but cresting the ridge, he could see the outlines of the terrain ahead. Scott fought the temptation to jog down this last leg, reminding himself that one false step could be his last.

The sunset faded from indigo pink to dark lavender, a palette of purples at the edges of the blackening sky. It was easy to forget that he was running for his life. When the southwestern sky was filled with dust, the colors tended toward reds, but the storm had washed the air, scrubbing it clean and leaving crisp hues of a spectrum not often seen by the casual visitor. As he descended toward the road, he enjoyed it while he could, even though it was the exclamation point on the loss of light.

Scott had to make his way down this last drainage using night vision and his sense of feel. Darkness removed the eyes as the prime sensors, placing pressure sense and balance in the forefront. His years in the mountains now served him well. *Steady down. Don't be impatient. Each step counts. The full moon will be up soon.* He should have

174

kissed Rachael goodbye under that moon instead of leaving as he did. *What a fool I am.*

He avoided rocks, not by looking straight down at the ground, but by looking several feet in front, letting his now nearly useless cones focus ahead while his peripheral retina, packed with rods, picked out the black and gray obstructions. Prey animals had developed superb peripheral vision—few cones but masses of rods populating their retinas for motion detection and nocturnal survival—most at the cost of color vision. Predators had more cones, concentrated centrally for hunting. Man, the ultimate predator, had both.

Scott used his motion sensors to detect now a rock moving toward his left foot, now a hole approaching his right. Standing still, the peripheral rods were less useful, having been adapted over the millennia to warn of motion, of attack. Motion being relative, Scott's eyes now picked out the rocks gliding toward his feet. He wound his way down the slope, making time despite the darkness.

A mile and a half later, he was at the valley floor, the dirt road he had espied from the air unfurling before him like a golden freeway. Now he could make real time. He walked for a few hundred yards, stretching, and when he felt relaxed, loose and ready, he broke into a slow jog. After the frustrations of the day, he let his emotions fuel his feet. Although walking would have been safer, Scott knew his new enemies would not be fooled forever. He must travel beyond their perimeter. How big that perimeter turned out to be was the unknown upon which his plan hinged.

He felt the frustration of creeping one mile per hour melt away as his pace quickened to three then four. The road, smooth by mountain standards, was rutted and rocky. With the whole night ahead of him, this would be a good pace. Scott found a new groove and settled comfortably within. Only after the first half hour did he allow himself to stop on a high point and catch his breath while he took a few sips of the precious liquid. He caught his wind, felt his legs relax, and set off again.

Eighteen hours into this day from hell, his instinct for survival propelled body and psyche. This level of intensity was something he had not felt for years. His energy level was akin to working on a crash victim in the ER late into the night. Fatigue was forgotten trying to save a life. However, this feeling, with his own life at stake, was at an intensity level he had not experienced since his short stint in the Army. Adrenaline was adrenaline, but fear was something more. Fear commanded a unique realm in the brain. It accelerated the energy an entire quantum. Some people were incapacitated by fear; others were able to use it.

They picked the wrong guy to shoot at. Another hour passed, another short break, a few precious sips of water. *Must make it last.* Fifteen minutes later, he was at the junction. The easy part was behind him. He left the valley road and started up the steep, rutted jeep trail. *Shortcut.*

The full moon was magnificent, its fiery orange rising giving way to the yellow-white of full ascent. Scott spent the rest of the night slowly claiming the summit beckoned by the jeep trail. It wasn't the roughness that was the challenge; it was the pitch. Having left the valley floor at the two-thousand-foot mark, he now felt the strain of over a mile of vertical ascent. At least he was climbing to cooler air, the temperature dropping approximately four degrees per thousand feet of elevation. By the time he finally crested the last major ridge, the temperature was a very comfortable fifty-five degrees. Each degree conserved water, but he couldn't stay up here for long. As long as he had the protection of the night, he needed to keep moving. The ache in his legs was felt more deeply with every step now, his progress slowed to less than a half mile per hour as he encountered occasional Pinyon Pine mixed with the more common junipers, which inhabited the upper elevations of these mountains.

Thought of by many as arid wasteland, the mountain southwest was a macrocosm of thermoclines and biomes. The sparse vegetation of the valley floors gradually gave way to the mountain zone flora, made richer by the increased rainfall and the cooler temperatures. In fact, it routinely snowed in this biome in the winter, while just a few thousand feet below the plants never experienced a crystal of ice and tasted only a rare drop of water. Scott hoped that he would come across one of the infrequent mountain springs that fed a tiny but rich riparian flora but doubted that he would be so lucky. In daylight, the water-rimming plants stood out as a dark-green oasis against the brown background, desert plants having developed lighter coloring to better reflect the intense sun. Moving at night, he could assume no replenishment of water. Conservation was key. As Scott claimed the last ridge, the next and largest valley opened to inspection in the ghostly light. Finally, he could rest.

Selecting a flat rocky shelf, he shed his burden. Breathing deeply, he sat and studied the terrain. The drainage immediately offered was precipitous, a dangerous descent, but half a click to the left was a gentler incline, more forgiving in the moonlight. He took a prolonged rest and drank then started toward that couloir.

Skirting between the junipers, he came across a large specimen of the less common Pinyon Pine. Scattered on the ground at his feet he recognized the gnarled shape of the Pinyon cones, once a staple of the natives who inhabited these regions in centuries past. The natives inhabited the warmer valleys in the winter and moved into the mountains to escape the summer heat. Their campfires would release the oil-rich nuts from the cones that usually matured in September. Scott knew the cones on the ground this August night were crops from previous years, but the heavier ones would still have food value.

He picked up a solid cone and placed it on a flat rock then smashed it with a second rock. Pine nuts flew. He picked one up and tested it. It was dry, but after chewing for only a few seconds, he could taste the oil—heavenly flavor to a hungry man. He chewed until he had extracted what oil and carbohydrate he could, then he spit out the pulp. He could ill afford the water it would require for digestion. He put two dozen pine nuts in his pocket then set off again.

One half mile later, he was looking down the drainage he had studied from the trailhead. Although not as precipitous as the first, this drainage was rough in its own right. *The grass is always greener.* Looking to the sky, Scott could see the night was waning. A hint of light betrayed the sun's intentions in the east. He recalled his Egyptian mythology. Soon Ra would begin his journey, driving Thoth, the moon god, into the realm of the dead once again. He started down as quickly as he dared.

The descent steepened immediately as the canyon walls narrowed. With little vegetation to hold back the infrequent rains, flash floods over the last ten thousand years had washed the sidewalls clean, flinging tiny stones and man-sized boulders down the mountain with equal disdain. Now skirting an outcropping, now holding back to avoid slipping down smooth rock, Scott's progress was slow.

A thousand feet down, Scott reached a steep incline of smooth rock that had been washed clean of debris. The footing was solid, but it was washed clean for a reason. The steepness of the grade and the solidness of the rock made it impossible for anything to hold when a rain came. Too steep to walk down for fear of pitching, he quickly sat and used a five-point descent, utilizing as much surface area as possible to contact the rocky floor. He was over halfway down when he sensed the pitch steepening again. With twenty feet to go, he realized there was no way he could hold on and no way to turn back. He only had two options—slide or slide.

Bend your knees. Absorb the blow. Don't pitch forward. Don't break your arms. He slid, gaining speed foot by foot. Instinct forced him onto his back, increasing surface friction, when his bandaged right elbow caught a small swell of rock and sent pain shooting up his arm. The pain distracted his attention. Although momentary, the distraction was enough that he pitched on impact and his body sprawled across the rocky debris at the bottom.

Pain flooded his senses as a hundred points of rock greeted his flesh, thankfully not enough to cut, but enough to scrape and bruise. He lay face down on the gravelly surface, gulping air. "I'm getting too old for this."

Scott lay for several seconds, resting before he pulled himself up. At least he had kept his face off the rocks. Had he cracked his skull, he might never be seen again until the white of his vulture-picked bones caught a climber's eye some distant day.

The growing light in the east pushed him downward. The canyon mellowed for a few hundred feet, but that came to an end too soon as the gulley again presented a solid rock base that jutted out slightly before it fell precipitously, this drop much steeper than the last.

Exhausted, Scott almost welcomed the obstruction. The fatigue, the thirst, the hunger, the pain—all were taking their toll. He found a smooth spot and slumped to the ground. Insidiously, his guard was coming down; he was tempted to lie here and sleep. It would be so easy—just curl up and let go. But as quickly as he recognized the temptation, he willed it away. Sleeping here would expose him to sight from an airplane or helicopter, his dark jogging suit easily espied against the pale rock, but worse, it would expose him to the sun, and that would mean certain death. He had been tempted to sleep on the ridge in the cooler mountain air in the shade of a tree, but he had discarded that comfort for the sake of utilizing every minute possible. He couldn't quit now.

Slipping off the backpack, Scott undid the binding ties and unrolled the nylon. Retrieving the rope, he began tying the ends together. After three decades of practice, his hands, though tired, flew about their work. Using surgical square knots, two throws to tie and two for insurance, each strand was deftly connected to the last until he had over two hundred feet of rope—not one he would want to challenge with a vertical fall, but one with plenty of strength for his needs.

"No beeners," he said aloud as he took a few sips of water and reconstructed his pack. Without carabiners, he would have trouble retrieving his rope after a descent. Tied off, a rope must be left behind; slid though a carabiner and doubled over at the halfway point, it can be pulled through the smooth surface, the carabiner left behind as an offering to the mountain gods as the price of passage.

On the canyon wall, Scott spied a tiny juniper growing from a crevice five feet higher than where its siblings had been washed away years before. Resilient creatures, the trees of the southwest amazed with their ability to cling to life on wind-swept walls with little rain and no soil, roots reaching deep into a crack, drawing moisture from the soul of the mountain. Scott tested it. Three inches at the base, it was strong enough to support his weight. As it exited the rock, it curved skyward, stretching for sunlight. It was in this bend that Scott looped his rope, pulling it through and testing its travel.

Not great, but good enough.

With equal ends of the rope, he walked to the precipice and lowered the doubled strands in quick spurts, feeling the rope drop and sensing the weight increase with each feed. An unbroken gain in weight would mean the rope was still dangling. Scott breathed a sigh of relief as he sensed the rope hitting the valley floor below.

Donning his pack, he grabbed the rope strands in both hands and turned himself around for a backward descent. Normally he would have leather gloves for this maneuver, but that luxury would not soon be available. *Don't burn your hands. Don't let it get away from you,* he tutored himself as he let his body fall slowly backward, his feet still on the leading edge of the rock.

Novice climbers had a difficult time getting the proper mechanics of a rappel because of their instinct to hug the rock. Only by letting himself out away from the rock could Scott use his feet. Straight up, the body's entire weight was dangling on the hand grip, a recipe for disaster. By leaning well out, gravity pulled his body back toward the rock, and his feet accepted a portion of his weight.

With a good descender and smooth rope, Scott could have been down in seconds. Today, he moved both feet and then lowered himself hand over hand very carefully. *No room for error.* Any fall over twenty feet would likely end in death. He was dangling a hundred feet above solid rock. The fatigue he had been feeling now concentrated in his hands. With each step backward, he felt his hands tiring. With each release and replacement of the hands, he felt the grip refusing to tighten as firmly as the one previous.

Concentrate. You're over halfway down. His arms began trembling, a climber's worst warning. *Two thirds. Don't rush. Steady motion. Ten feet. Five.* He looked behind him. Large rocks were strewn among the smaller ones, and Scott picked out the best spot, swung his feet down, and landed firmly, his hands quivering from fatigue.

He took several deep breaths and then began retrieving his rope. Each knot caught on the little tree, but a firm flick of the wrist sent a serpentine wave up the rope, breaking each knot free in its turn. Scott coiled the rope, secured the ends, and slipped it over his head and left arm, keeping it at the ready.

Again, he started down, the freshening dawn making it easier to pick his way between the rocks but bringing the danger of detection as well. It was time to find shelter. Looking up, he realized how much progress he had made since leaving the ridge. It hadn't seemed like much, but descending always surprised compared to ascending. Now he could begin to see detail in the valley. He could just make out the smaller canyons across the large valley, and soon he would have enough light to fix a route.

Scott hiked to the bottom of this stretch, scrambled down an easy pitch of boulders, skirted a large washout on the left, scrambled down a second boulder jam, and finally saw it ahead to his right—another steep feeder gully coming into this canyon, its vertical walls allowing limited exposure to the sky. He made his way to its mouth, the weight of the day's burden suddenly lightened by the promise of rest. Striding into the opening, he found that it would do nicely. It wound to and fro, closing up quickly and offering several spots to remain hidden from the direct rays of the sun.

At the third turn in the gulley, he found a smooth south wall that had been undercut by flash floods for thousands of years, making a slight but critical overhang that faced north. In the northern hemisphere, the sun coursed to the south, and Scott would use this fact to protect himself.

He doffed his pack, grabbed a bottle of water and the breakfast bar, and walked back to the mouth of the gulley. Sitting on a rock, he rested his muscles and slowly enjoyed the water along with a few pine nuts, followed by the energy-packed bar. He ate slowly, savoring each morsel as he surveyed the landscape in the widening dawn. It would be a tough go, but he could do it. He was out of food, except for nine pieces of precious candy and a handful of pine nuts. He was down to five bottles of water, and he would drink at least one of those before he set out again, if not two. That depended on his urine output, which was already becoming very concentrated. His name would not be added to the ranks of those unknowing souls who had died hoarding their water in their canteens instead of in their bodies.

Returning to his sheltered overhang, he unfolded the pack and arranged the nylon sheeting and the poncho into a thin bed under the little overhang. Next, he stripped off his jacket and pants and spread these on top. He removed the scraps of fabric from his pockets and put them inside the stocking cap to use as a makeshift pillow. Finally, he crawled into his bed.

He wedged his torso firmly against the rock, then his legs and arms. Now he would have to sleep. He didn't know if he could, given the circumstances, but his body needed it. The temperature was 90 degrees Fahrenheit and would climb steadily for the next eight hours. He didn't know how long he could take it, but what he did know was that he had to stay out of the sun, or he would bake like the rocks a few feet from his face. Exposed all day, surface temperatures on rocks in this area had been measured slightly above the two-hundred-degree mark. Scott snuggled into the crevice that opened to the north, hidden from the sun. If he stayed tucked in this position, he could avoid the direct rays. His bones would rebel in less than an hour, but he would deal with that later. For now, he needed rest.

How had he come to this? How had he arrived at this juncture from his perfectly safe life, now seemingly an eternity from here? And how did the president of the United States come to be in the predicament he was in?

Suddenly, movement in the gulley floor startled him. He craned his eyes, and just within his peripheral vision, he caught the unmistakable shape of a rattler slithering down the rock toward him. He wasn't frightened. He knew he could lie perfectly still, and it would pass by, unalarmed. Still, his hand reached down and retrieved his knife, opening the blade deftly with a flick of his thumbnail. Slowly hefting a large rock in his left hand as it passed, he brought it down on the snake's back just behind its head, pinning it to the earth as he severed its head. It wasn't that he was afraid of the snake; he just knew he needed protein. He quickly skinned and filleted the still-writhing reptile, then draped the pieces carefully across a south-facing rock. By nightfall, it would be baked to perfection.

He wedged himself firmly against the rock and felt a wave of dream-sleep pass through him as he closed his eyes and slipped almost immediately into deep REM.

Chapter 26

Scrubbing Data

L ieutenant Colonel Floyd Curtis was still standing with the phone against his ear, his eyes glued to the map wall. He stood, frozen, for several seconds before Block realized something was wrong. He looked at him quizzically. "Sir?"

"The son of a bitch gave us the slip." The phone fell away from his ear in slow motion. "The son of a bitch gave us the slip. Again!" he said as he slammed the phone into its cradle.

"Sir?"

"Gentlemen, we have a new game on our hands," he said as he regained his composure, the disbelief sobering. "A whole new game. There is no body in that airplane. They are looking for a second plane, but part of the N number is legible, and it matches our missing plane from Leesburg. We have a jumper."

"Holy crap," Captain Turner said. "Just when we thought this was over."

"I wonder how long ago?" added Block.

"That is exactly the right question, Block. How long ago?" echoed Curtis. "Just how big of a head start does he have on us? We've been sitting on our thumbs for the better part of twenty-four hours while he's been going who knows where and in what. If he

183

made it to a road, if he found a vehicle, he could be almost anywhere in the western half of the United States or Mexico by now."

"Well then, this is over," Wainright said. "We don't have a prayer of finding him now."

"Nothing is ever over until it's over," Curtis countered. "He could have broken his leg. He could be lost, who knows? But one thing is for certain, and that is the fact that he is in some of the roughest, most God-forsaken wasteland known to man. No one is going to move very fast out there, especially a middle-aged doctor—if Piquard from Idaho is actually who this guy is—and especially not in the heat of August. He is not going far unless he gets to a road and garners a vehicle. We just have to figure out where he jumped, surround the area, and let no man, woman, or child out of the area until ID'd. We may still have a chance. There's always a chance as long as you're breathing."

"Sorry, Colonel, you're right."

"Now what's the first thing we need, Wainright?" Curtis stared him down as he forced him to think on his feet. It was not meant maliciously, and all his men knew it. They were all subject to this type of open-book exam from time to time, and they all knew that it made them think. It was a training exercise. They always learned something when class was in session and the colonel was teaching.

"More troops, sir." Wainright was forceful, certain of his answer. "We surround him, sir."

"And *where* are you going to put more troops?"

"In a large perimeter, sir."

"And where is the center of that perimeter?"

Suddenly, Wainright saw the weakness of his position, and the force of his voice faded as his body language spoke for him. "I guess I don't know, exactly, sir."

"So what do we need first? Anyone?"

"Information! Sir!" Six voices hollered in unison, each one trying to be the first with the Curtis mantra.

"And where can we get more information? Immediately?"

Now the room did go quiet for a few seconds, each man wracking his brain. It was Dugan who spoke first.

"The sentry, sir. Their radar is so strong, I have heard that they can tell if a man is carrying a gun or not."

"Jesus, Lord! Do you men mean to tell me that you are going to let an army grunt outsmart Air Force and Navy brains? Holy shit, what is this world coming to?" he said with his best Southern basic-training sergeant's voice, a little smile crossing his lips. In this room, there was always an intellectual race for his approval, and a left-handed compliment was often all they received as a reward. He turned back to Dugan.

"You have the right answer, but not exactly for the right reason. Their radar is good, but not that good. They never gave us a heads up in real time, did they? So I am going to call Tinker and find out. Intelligence will defeat brute strength nine times out of ten."

The men relaxed as he dropped the forced crescendo, but the lesson would never be forgotten by any of them, least of all Dugan and Wainright. A good teacher leaves his mark without inflicting marks.

"Kesselhoff, get me Tinker again, and get me someone who knows their radar."

Curtis had barely returned with a fresh cup when Kesselhoff motioned to his phone bank. "Line 2, sir, Colonel Alvine at Tinker."

"Good evening, Colonel Alvine," he said, smiling. "They make you work late, too, I see."

"Yeah, you know how it is. You sign that form every time you re-up that says, 'I will have no life of my own.' What can I do for you today? Don't tell me you need my E-3 again?"

"Not exactly, just as much information out of her as possible. You do spool the feeds and keep them for analysis, I hope."

"Of course, what's up?"

"They found the plane right where you said we would, but the body count came out to exactly zero."

"Aha! I see the problem."

"Now, the million-dollar question is whether or not you can find where he jumped by reworking the tapes. Obviously, your men saw nothing yesterday, or they would have reported it, so do you think you can help me?"

185

"I can't promise anything, but we'll sure try. We can scrub the data using different filters for data reduction for small objects. We filter out small soft objects like birds. If we didn't, the screen would be too full of targets. Normal mode is to pick up larger targets, and they must be metallic to reflect radar well. If we change filters, we might be able to see a man and a chute, but I can't promise. That's a hit-and-miss proposition even when we know we have skydivers in the area. Their radar fingerprint is too soft. We won't see the parachute at all, but we might pick up the body, especially if he has some metal on him."

"I'd appreciate any help you can give me, and I need it yesterday. This guy has a day's head start on us."

"I understand, Curtis. I'll get my people cracking on it ASAP, but don't stay up all night, waiting for my call. They were airborne for several hours. It will take some time to scrub that much data."

"I will be right here, but may I make a suggestion? The flight path was extremely deliberate up until the last fifty to one hundred miles, wasn't it? I think the explosion yesterday morning put out his radios. If it fried his whole panel, he wouldn't have autopilot either. At first, we thought he was becoming a little erratic because he was injured. Suppose he had been hand flying all day? Then after he jumped, that long, lazy turning descent could have been because she was flying herself. So how about having your men concentrate on that segment first? If they come up empty, they can always go back and look at the earlier stuff."

"Makes perfect sense. I'll get them moving. Talk to you later."

"Thanks, Wes." Curtis hit the receiver button then immediately made another call.

"Collins, here."

"General Collins, this is Curtis at Homeland. I'm afraid I need your brains and your connections again. Our mystery airplane is empty… Yes, empty… Yes… He jumped. I have Tinker scrubbing the AWACS data to try to find out where, but, sir, he's had a whole day to move. We need a much larger perimeter, and we need a much larger contingent. We need every man you can find, and we need them dropped in. That's the only way we can set up a perimeter quickly enough."

"I see," Collins said.

"I want to use the men we have at China Lake to establish an immediate line along the Sierra's to the west. No one can locate this Piquard, so let's assume it's him. He had been heading west all day, and he has a brother in Bakersfield, so he'll most likely keep heading west. That will be a start. Of course, if he's commandeered a vehicle, he could be long gone, but we have to try, Nest Pas?"

"Agreed, let's roll the boys out west. Is the weather clear enough to make a drop?"

"It's been clearing all day—just a few clouds around the higher peaks. They can jump before dark."

"Let's do it. I'll be right down, Floyd."

"I'll call General Kidner, and let him know what we are up to. Thanks, General."

They rang off, but Curtis didn't bother to set his phone down. He dialed Ernie Knoll's cell phone.

"Knoll, here."

"Ernie, this is Floyd Curtis at Homeland again. We need some roads blocked. Lots of roads."

Saturday, 11:15 p.m. EDT, Camp David

First Lady Janet Brady had been trying to explain the situation to Jeremy and David, trying to slowly soften the blow. The boys had taken the news fairly well. They were confused by the politics, but they would not believe, could not believe, that Scott was dead until it was confirmed. They saw no urgency to pronounce him dead. Their father was the president of the United States, but Scott Piquard was their hero. They had never seen him without an answer to whatever problem faced them on the mountain or in the river. They would need proof and told their mother as much.

Suddenly, the ringing of a telephone jarred the serene quiet of Camp David. Janet answered warily then stopped short and turned to the boys, tears already glistening in her eyes. "It's Dad. Scott's alive!"

Chapter 27

Dropping the Net

Sunday, 5:00 a.m. EDT, Homeland Security Command Center

As General Pat Collins reentered the command center, Floyd Curtis was on the telephone again. "That's what they said, Ernie. They have his jump zone narrowed to within a few miles. After scrubbing the data, they now confirm that they saw a radar echo just sixteen miles northeast of Highway 136. That's the valley between the Inyo Mountains and the Panamint Range, and that correlates with where he appeared to be having trouble. That was where he began losing altitude and getting erratic. Importantly, the suspected landing zone is only a few miles from an improved dirt road that could take him north or south, and south takes him directly to California Highway 190. By now, he could be going west on 136 or east or west on 190. North is very unlikely, as that is about a forty-mile trail that only off-roaders use. Our men will circle that entire basin, but your people need to intercept any and all human traffic along the Big Pine Road that intersects with its northern end. You have the full backing of the Department of Homeland Security. We do not have another hour to spare, Ernie. And remind your teams that it is critical that we take him alive. I'll call you as soon as I know something." Curtis cradled the telephone, massaging his ear. He turned to General Collins and grinned. "We may have him boxed in. The AWACS boys are certain they have his egress point. 36-5 North, 117-35 West. Of course, that information is now over thirty hours old," he added, the grin fading from his lips, "but we are a lot closer than we were a few hours ago."

"That's a nice understatement," the general interjected. "A few hours ago, we thought he was dead."

"General, I need to talk to you privately," Curtis said quietly as he cocked his head in the direction of his office. He started back as General Collins followed.

Collins liked Curtis. He admired his intelligence and his dedication, and although he outranked him, he definitely looked upon him as an equal. And the big plus for Collins was that he was enjoying himself immensely. There was that adrenaline-pumping something about a major operation that kindled his fire. It was like chess but with consequences. As Curtis closed the door behind him, the general's interest was piqued. "What's on your mind, Floyd?"

"General, I have been sitting on some intelligence, and it's driving me crazy. I've never been one of those secretive types. I like my cards all out on the table. Everyone knows where I stand. That's why I'm down here and not over at Langley. I need to share this with you. I cannot tell you the source, but it is A-1 rated. It will come out soon enough."

"Let's hear it!"

"If this guy is Scott Piquard—and we are virtually certain of that now—then we have some interesting permutations. He went to grade school and high school with the president of the United States, he served in the United States Army with the president of these United States, and he left Idaho two days ago on a flight plan to Leesburg in a twin-engine Piper, call sign November-6-8-7-*Whiskey Mike*, the same as the one on the mountain in California, give or take a little paint."

"Whew!" Collins exhaled. "What else?"

"I talked with General Nearman to confirm some data. They all saw the video of the perp in the tunnels, but Brady never said a word."

"Maybe they haven't seen each other in years. Maybe he didn't recognize him." Collins was going through all the machinations that Floyd had struggled through earlier.

"Exactly my thoughts, until FBI agent Ernie Knoll called me back a little while ago. His man in Idaho located Piquard's new office nurse and got her talking. Apparently, she had not been totally intimidated by our mystery Air Force man. She said that the good doctor and the president were not only friends but that Brady had called Piquard on Wednesday, and he cancelled appointments and left for Washington on Thursday. And the Bureau can't find a motel or hotel reservation anywhere in a fifty-mile radius in his name. So where was he?"

"Holy shit!"

"Exactly. What you do with this is up to you, but for the time being, I'm going to do my job and let the spooks do theirs. At least now I think I know why the president is so adamant that this guy is brought in upright and breathing."

Collins sat on the edge of the desk and tried to understand what he had just heard. Finally, Curtis interrupted his thoughts. "I trust my team, but you are the only one I have shared this with so far."

"Understood."

They walked back into the command center. "On my way over here, I was on the phone with Fort Bragg, home of the Eighty-Second Airborne," Collins said. "I just depleted one of their brigades, and they are not very happy with me. Fort Bragg has our only stateside airborne force, and they are spread very thin due to the mobilization on the Mexican border. I just pulled rank and ordered their paratroopers to be ready to jump at first light in California.

"If this was day number one, even knowing exactly where ground zero is located, we would still have to cover over 600 square miles of territory, assuming he was on foot and in top military condition. A 25-by-25-mile grid is 625 square miles. It is day two, so we now have over 2,500 square miles of land to cover, assuming same. As the colonel said earlier, our man may have acquired a vehicle by now, which would leave us totally unable to contain him. In that case, the city, county, state, and federal officers that our FBI friends are activating for Operation Roadblock are our only hope short of a hot tip.

"Now, let's assume that it is Piquard from Idaho. He is an older family doctor who, statistically will be, as you said, well-fed, out of shape, and thick in the middle," Collins continued as he looked first at Curtis' slightly protruding belly, and then his own. I'd give him 10 to 20 miles a day on flat ground, 8 to 15 on rough ground, less in the mountains. What do you think?"

"I would agree," Curtis replied. "He's been steadily heading west. He's got a brother in Bakersfield, and fugitives overwhelmingly seek out family for help. Ernie Knoll has that covered. Two teams are following the brother, there is a wiretap on his landline, and they have an NSA technician listening in on his cell."

"Okay," Collins asked, musing, "where else do we place our resources? I just had Hill Air Force Base release two AC130 Specter gunships. Have you seen the night vision capabilities on those babies? With 50-millimeter, computer-guided cannon on board, they were taking out roadside bombers in Iraq from two miles away in the middle of the night. The guys on the ground were dead before the sound reached them."

"Yes, sir," Curtis replied with unfeigned awe. "I saw the videos."

"The Eighty-Second will be ready to jump at dawn," Collins continued.

"Understood," Curtis interjected. "We need a drop plan by dawn. I have my own ideas, but since you are the senior officer, I'll let you make the call." Curtis was smiling slightly, both men knowing that it was the junior officer's way of saying, "If it's the wrong call, I don't get the blame." He drew something on a piece of paper, folded it once, and cupped it in his hand.

General Collins laughed and said, "Thanks, Floyd. You shouldn't be so generous." He picked up a laser pointer and addressed the entire room. "We now know, at least with some certainty, that our man jumped about here," he explained, pointing to the southern end of the Saline Valley, "sixteen miles northeast of California Highway 136 and due north of Highway 190." He punctuated his statement with a swirl of red light over the highways. "And we assume that he is heading west, but assumptions have killed more soldiers than bullets." He turned back to the map. "At dawn, we will drop nearly 800 men on the eastern slope of the Sierra Nevada foothills. If he has made it past that line already, it could only be with the help of a vehicle. West of there, every road and jeep trail now has or soon will have a roadblock, and it would take him days to climb *over* the Sierras, even with climbing gear. Our reinforcements from the Eighty-Second Airborne will be turning in from the northwest, and we will start our second perimeter here," he said, pointing to the northern portion of the Saline Valley, "and extend it in an arc west and south, then back to the east down here."

Collins paused, studied the faces in the room, and continued, "Now, this is where it would be easy to make another assumption. It would be tempting to think he would not go east. Only a fool would go into the desert in August. But if he made it to a road and made good time, he could conceivably make it past this perimeter, especially if our AWACS friends are off by a few miles. So we will lay down our eastern perimeter here, along the eastern edge of the Panamint Plateau, and we will save a few men for one last turn back to the south, here, at the western foothills of the Amargosa Range, just east of Highways 190 and 267. These men will be spread thin, but by dropping two men every three miles, we leave only a 1.5-mile gap, right or left, for each team. They will have night vision capabilities, and they will own the high ground. We will need to provide them with extra water since they will be on the eastern edge of the desert.

"I have also requisitioned a thousand marines from Camp Pendleton in California, and the local guard unit will truck them in once they land. We can use these highways to run water and rations up and down the eastern perimeter. The rest of the troops will have drops made, and they will have the advantage of cooler temperatures in the mountains. I will be setting up an ad hoc division headquarters to coordinate this joint operation, right here"—he motioned with his pointer—"at Panamint Springs."

Collins seemed satisfied with his plan, as did everyone in the room. Curtis winked and handed him his drawing. His perimeter was essentially identical to the one Collins had plotted. "With nearly four thousand men in a double perimeter, two Specter gunships with night vision optics, and Landsat prowling overhead, there will be no place for our boy to go. Lastly, leaving like he did on the run, he probably is not provisioned, so he has about three days to get out of there into our waiting arms. And if he gets lost and blunders into Death Valley—on foot in August—well then, the buzzards and the coyotes can help themselves after the desert is through with him."

Sunday, 5:30 a.m. EDT, Washington, DC

"Do we have *anyone* on those deployments?" The general was stalking back and forth, his anger as palpable as the damp night air.

"Two from the contingent that deployed last night, and three in the group that will jump in the morning. I also have a new man on one of the Specters. He can relay information that could prove timely. Other than that, we are spread too thin. There are not that many of us, sir. I am deploying some very reliable men to the major intersection checkpoints, but it will be pure chance if he crosses our path."

"They have their orders?"

"Absolutely, sir. There is no room for compromise."

"Then let's get it done. I don't care what it takes. Kill him."

"And if he gets away?"

"We're making plans for that contingency. Operation Facelift is underway. Misinformation is prepared, and a 'secret dossier' of his double life is being assembled. We've decided to leave the family alone for now, but there may need to be an accident later. I have my own man on that. For the present, I want them to look like the innocent, unsuspecting, long-suffering victims of a traitor. It isn't hard. The public loves to wallow in filth. We'll give them what they want."

Chapter 28

The Mouth of Hell

Saturday, 8:30 p.m. PDT, Panamint Mountains

While the search for data had been boiling in Washington, Scott Piquard had spent an interminable day sleeping on hot rocks. Distantly, Scott could remember one other time nearly as bad. He had endured the heat then, but at least the ground had been soft. Which was worse? Trying to sleep in this heat or lying on Paleozoic rock carpeted with gravel? He was too miserable to decide.

The first few hours had afforded sound sleep as fatigue overshadowed discomfort, but by midmorning, he had awakened, and getting back to sleep had proven problematic. The temperature was over one hundred and would not crest until midafternoon. The only plus was that he was over four thousand feet above the valley floor. Down there, the temperature would reach one-eighteen. At least he was making urine; he emptied his bladder and noted the dark concentration.

Experimenting with changes of position had revealed few options. The sliver of shade that afforded him his protection, his tiny million-dollar slice of real estate, had minute by minute crept toward his wall. At dawn, he thought he had plenty of room. By ten, he wasn't so sure. By eleven he had his head almost painfully wedged into the apex of his protective crevice and was curled into a contorted position, folding his body carefully into the available shade. By noon he was tucked against the rock with only inches of safety between his skin and the ultraviolet spectrum. He'd remembered to set his watch back three hours from its Eastern Time setting, but his watch showed daylight savings time, not real time. He had to wedge even tighter for another hour before the sun began its westward descent from apogee.

By 3:00 p.m., the heat had peaked, the longer shadows on his bed purchased dearly by the rise in temperature. He was sweating more than he hoped, and the heat would continue to draw water out of his body by the minute. "Why couldn't this have happened in May?" he said aloud.

Sleep had been fitful during the afternoon, dreams haunting the recesses of his temporal lobes. Tired though he was when dusk finally settled, he was relieved. He needed movement. The entire depth of his body ached. As the shadows lengthened across the valley floor below him, he dressed, the heat still an omnipresent factor despite the late hour. Sucking slowly, he enjoyed a piece of candy and drank another bottle of water as he prepared for the night. It had been seven hours, and he still had no urge to void. Better to carry the water in his body than in a bottle. He packed the snake jerky and slung the pack over his shoulders.

Walking to the edge of the next drop, he studied the terrain below him. He needed to memorize his landmarks and finish the descent while he still had some light, but he could move out into the open only after dark—and not just to avoid detection. How many people had died out here in the daylight, the sun desiccating them as they wandered, confused and disoriented? Heat was a factor, but direct sun was the deciding factor. Moving at night and lying up in the daytime was the only way out of this, and once the moon was up, he would have little trouble navigating.

Scott knew he must risk moving down the remainder of this canyon in the gray light of evening; he needed light to negotiate the climbs that remained. As he pondered, he realized how quiet it was— he heard no search planes yet.

In the distance, he could see the ribbon of pavement he had espied from the ridge at dawn, an occasional pair of headlights winding their way into the coming night confirming the highway's course. He had pushed himself hard the night before. The run had nearly killed him, but he had made nearly twenty miles at elevation, and now he would get payback as the highway looked to be no more than ten miles away as the crow flew. Of course, how the crow flew was not how the foot fell, but he was now confident he could make his objective before dawn.

Scott looked down and surveyed the first drop. He could make the first scramble without rope, but he could not see the second drop well. After that, the huge alluvial fan at the bottom would be easy. He started down carefully. *No falls now. You've made it this far.*

All day Friday, he had struggled with his plan. He had guessed and second-guessed himself, flying west instead of northwest toward home. They had resources beyond his imagination. He knew he was a dead man unless he came up with an escape plan. He needed an imaginative, if risky, move, and this had been his answer.

Pondering his decision took him back to his college days and a lesson he had learned, elementary yet elegant. Scott had won the fencing championship with a simple maneuver within a maneuver. "With your long arms, I want to show you a move," his instructor had said as she took him aside, "that you should be able to use effectively." And he had. In the championship match, the score was tied, two-two, match point. He had used the move only a couple of times during the tournament; overusing a feint trained the opponents, and without surprise, it was no longer a feint. As the final point began, Scott retreated, feigning trouble with his footing until he was nearly out of bounds. Sensing victory, his opponent attacked. As the attacker readied his thrust, Scott stopped suddenly, his riposte so subtle as to be nearly invisible, a feint within a feint. Leaning slightly forward with his arm fully extended, Scott's foil was level with his opponent's chest. The attacker lunged, but before his shorter arm could carry the foil to Scott, his lunge propelled his own chest onto the tip of Scott's foil. He never realized what was happening until he felt the point drive into his chest and felt victory slip away. He had "killed" himself, hoist by his own petard.

His new opponents would have thousands of men. They would have roadblocks. They would have airplanes. They would have satellites. They would have night vision lenses. What chance could he muster against all that? The only chance he could think of. They would have thousands of eyes, but that would do them little good if they were looking elsewhere. So he had decided to risk his life to save it. He would run to the one place they would be least likely to look. A feint within a feint. So down he went, not into the west, where they were preparing to drop thousands of men, but to the east, into Death Valley.

The rock here was steep, but its very steepness allowed the falling rocks and flash floods of the last million years to tumble on past. A gentler slope, like the one he had slid from the night before, became polished by flowing slurry. The pitch here still had enough jaggedness to afford grip. Taking his time, he made sure of his footing. He could not rely on help from the rope; there was nowhere to fasten it. The climb down went easily enough, although he again noticed the throbbing in his elbow as he strained his limbs. In minutes, he had descended over three hundred feet. Here the canyon bottom again flattened, the rock scrubbed smooth by erosive forces over the millennia. This stretch of canyon reminded him of Mosaic Canyon to the south. A family vacation had brought them here two years previous. They had hiked the marble-floored canyon that had formed when late pre-Cambrian dolomite and other carbonate rocks were buried under intense pressure and metamorphosed into marble, multiple rock types cemented together in a mosaic construct.

The memories from that trip were the nucleus of his escape plan. Without prior knowledge, he would never have attempted this. Lacking understanding of the valley, he might have attempted a shorter, southern route, but map knowledge alone was deceiving. Although more narrow, the southern valley was much steeper and far rougher. The southern end of Death Valley was the lowest point in North America. Badwater Basin, still sinking as the eastern tectonic plate slid under the plate to the west, resided 282 feet below sea level.

Although there was water pooled there, the name given it by the early visitors bespoke its lack of potability. The mountains of the southern valley were extreme in their vertical rise. One of the youngest formations on this continent, the tectonic plates had been crashing past one another at a severe angle for the past three million years. Although erosion had washed debris into the base of the valley at an astonishing rate—three thousand feet per million years—the mountains to the west were still being pushed upward, and now stood over eleven thousand feet above sea level at Telescope Peak. The total fault shift was over twenty thousand feet, a veritable sprint by the geologic stopwatch.

In this depression lay the remnants of an ancient lake decorated with horse and mastodon fossils. With climate change, the lake evaporated. The drying lake bottom concentrated dissolved salts into an increasingly smaller area, finally leaving the salt dried out in large flats that reached unbearable temperatures in the noonday sun. Caught there at midmorning, lost travelers had died before nightfall.

The northern valley, still deadly in its own right, was gentle by comparison. Wider and flatter, it hosted some of the largest alluvial fans in the world. Millions of years of erosion, driven by flash floods containing billions of tons of rock, gravel, and sand slurry known as alluvium, filled the bottom of each canyon slope with a constantly expanding mound of debris that fanned out as it exited the canyon and lost velocity. The alluvium was deposited at the base of each canyon like an inverted Japanese fan.

The northern valley also hosted isolated areas of beautiful sand dunes formed by the incessant desert winds blowing eroded particles off the mountains onto the valley floor. With no egress, the eolian particles were blown until they came to isolated wind pockets contained by the superstructure and were deposited in acres of sand dunes that were forever being reshaped by the winds. Although the first thought many people had of Death Valley was mile upon mile of sand dunes, they were quite small and isolated. The story of Death Valley was the story of rock.

Scott traversed the flattened portion of this canyon. Then, near the next fall, he found a small gift from the heavens. In the solid-rock floor along the eroded wall, he found a small depression that had filled with water when the rains came sluicing down out of the mountains two days before. Protected from the sun, it had not yet evaporated, and a quart of water sat in the rocky bowl. These pockets of water were lifelines for birds, insects, and other animals like the zebra-tailed lizard, several of which he had sent scurrying up the walls as if they had suction cups on their feet.

Quickly unbundling his pack, Scott took out two empty water bottles and a piece of nylon. Making a funnel-shaped nylon filter in the top of the first bottle, he began transferring water into the bottle using the bottle cap as a scoop. He would pour in a tiny amount of water and let it filter through the cloth, but it was painstakingly slow. He was short on resources. He needed tools. Specifically, he needed a cup. He looked over his tiny cache of resources.

Oh, the things we take for granted, he said to himself as he contemplated taking the flashlight apart. Suddenly, the solution struck him. In the wilderness, any commodity could become a tool. He fished into his pocket and found the discarded wrapper from his last breakfast bar. Waterproof for preserving the food, it served well as a ladle. He finished the chore quickly. "There are no hard jobs, just the wrong tools," his brother had taught him many years ago. Scratching an *X* on the lids of these bottles, he marked them for last use, lest they be contaminated.

Scott made good time for the next half hour, descending over a thousand feet as he carefully climbed down rough rock and gravel scree until finally he came to the drop-off he had been studying from above. It was a dangerous pitch, but at least now he could see the bottom. A thousand-pound boulder would serve as a rope holder, but he would be forced to leave the rope behind.

The light was fading as he looped one end of the rope around the bottom of the rock and secured it with five square knots. He tested the pull. It was solid. Down he went, both hands on the rope and both feet climbing from jagged outcropping to jagged outcropping. In the failing light, he was having trouble making out footholds, and suddenly there were none as the wall gave way to a sheer drop. The throbbing in his right elbow began afresh as his weight shifted to his hands. This time, the throbbing did not stop. He dangled from the rope as his feet scratched for holds.

Scott kicked himself out from the wall, and as he pendulummed back, he pulled his knees up to his chest. Catching his soles on the wall, he leaned back at a forty-five-degree angle. Now, approximately half of his weight was transferred to his feet, relieving the strain on his hands noticeably. Scott quickly rappelled twenty feet, where he once again found rough and sloping rock. He descended further until he could stand upright and rest his hands. His hands burned, and his elbow throbbed continuously. He could feel wetness inside the bandage and knew he had stretched the wound open again. Starting down, he traveled only thirty feet when his hand stopped against the warning knot. He was out of rope.

In the dying light, he could see the talus below him, but he had thirty-five feet of deadly incline between himself and safety. Scott shinnied to his right, where he could make out a tiny ledge. He sat on the small outcropping of rock and buried his head in his hands. Was he done? Had they won? Now he would have to depend on his fingers and feet—and in near darkness no less.

A wave of depression washed over him as his earlier optimism vanished. *I can't do this. I'm too old. I don't have the strength any more. Stupid plan! Why didn't I just give myself up?* The faint ringing in his ears and the ghostly face of the airport manager reminded Scott that he had tried to do just that.

"Quit feeling sorry for yourself. Use your anger," he said aloud as he peered into the darkness. Fifteen feet below, he saw a small shelf with several rough outcroppings leading to it. The wall appeared to have enough handholds to allow a free descent, and the shelf would allow a resting place. A thirty-five-foot fall would be deadly, but the shorter fall might be survived. *Break each impossible job into several possible jobs.* He took a deep breath and rolled onto his stomach.

Gripping solid rock with both hands, he lowered his body and reached with his right foot, over, down, over, down until finally he felt the first small outcropping with his toes. His fingers had started to tremble, and the relief he felt was genuine as his foot accepted the bulk of his weight. He had gained nearly seven feet. Repositioning his hands, he peered into the dim light and could make out his next objective. This one would be easier, lying only six feet below him and a little to the right. Two quick moves and he was on the ledge, but as he looked at his new environment, he did not like the view.

The wall of the remaining pitch was too smooth. To the east, a descending ledge offered sanctuary, but below that, there was no protection. From the end of that ledge, he could lower himself another eight feet and drop, but the rocks below the easy route contained several huge boulders and offered no landing zone. One bad move there—a wedged foot or a crushed ankle—would make him wish he had been shot in Clay Center. He turned to the west, back toward the mountain.

There was no ledge toward the canyon's crevice. There wasn't even a crack to wedge his left hand into, let alone the hoped-for chimney, a crack large enough to wedge his body into. All he had were about a dozen small irregularities in the wall to call handholds. At least the base was filled with smaller talus gravel and sand, the larger rocks having bounced away and down.

Scott removed his pack and dropped it to the ground. Reaching down with his left foot, he found the first toehold and gingerly transferred his weight. He reached with his left hand and grabbed a small knob. Now he must trust himself. He had seen climbers freeze, unable to relinquish their safety point. The longer they hesitated, the more precarious their position became. The best climbers were relaxed and limber. Scott had been somewhere in between, but that was years ago.

Transferring his weight, he was forced to find the spot for his right foot blindly. He had seen it, but now his angle of sight was altered. He swung his leg down, hugging the rock with his body, his cheek against the wall. His foot played blind man's bluff with the rock. His fatigue showed as his left leg began to quiver. Still he searched with his toes, finding nothing but smooth rock. As the quiver built, Scott could feel his heel pumping up and down as the fatigue reached the danger point. Five, maybe ten seconds, and he would fall. He tried to transfer more weight to his fingertips, but each time he tried, he felt them begin to slip. He bent lower still, and just when he thought his leg could take no more, he found the small irregularity in the rock. It seemed made for his toes. He transferred his weight and let his body rest momentarily. Then finding a good handhold, he was again able to look down. His two maneuvers, amateurish as they were, had transformed his twenty-foot drop into fifteen. He was nearly there, but where to put his other foot? The only place he could see was out of reach unless he first moved his right hand, and there was precious little that this rock was giving him for free. The tiniest little jut offered a two-finger hold, and although he did not feel he had the strength, he had to try. It was that or jump. He moved his fingers onto the lip and dropped his left foot quickly down but failed to find purchase as his right leg began to quiver. Each time he thought he had found the spot, his toes planted but could not grip. Again, he craned to look, finally seeing the toehold just below the unusable bulge his blind foot had been pawing. He found purchase, but almost as soon as he planted his weight, his leg began to shake. He had to hurry.

He transferred his hands and reached down with his right foot. Nothing. He craned his neck and looked. The spot he had hoped for was out of reach, and his legs had reached their limit. The shaking became violent as his bent leg began to fail. As his weight shifted to his fingers, they began to slide on the smooth rock. Scott felt the inevitable coming, so he turned his head, looked for the smoothest landing space possible, and launched his body as his fingertips failed completely. He crashed into the corner of the wall, letting the slanted stone break his fall as he slid the remaining twelve feet to the valley floor. He caught himself on his toes, banged his forehead on the wall, and plopped to his butt in front of a lizard, which watched him quizzically as if to say, "What was so hard about that?" He lay back and rested, not bothering to find a smoother spot.

After several minutes, the incessant throbbing in his elbow forced action. He sat up on the gravel and leaned against the inner wall as darkness crept across the eerie shadows in the valley. Retrieving a piece of candy and a bottle of water, he enjoyed his reward while he let his muscles expel their lactic acid load. After twenty minutes, his legs felt rested. Although he had done well getting this most dangerous descent behind him, he had made no lateral progress.

As the moon began to rise over the Grapevine Mountains, he could see his next objective, and it was many miles away.

Time to move.

Scott was standing at the apex of one of the largest alluvial fans in the world. He peered into the moonlight and picked out his likely path. Across the valley floor, he could see a pair of headlights winding down the road below the Grapevine Mountains in the Amargosa Range. Was that a military vehicle? Were they even now watching him with their night vision equipment? Was he deluding himself to think he could pull this off?

The top of the fan rested 2,600 feet above sea level. He still had a long descent before him, but it was a much gentler slope. The footing was rough and rocky, but compared to what he had just negotiated, this was but a hike. He felt his pace quicken as he grew accustomed to the footing, here more large rock, there more packed alluvium ribboned with gullies cut by flash floods.

Down he went, gravity at his back, unlike the nearly constant uphill struggle of the night before. Scott pushed himself. One hour passed quickly, then two, and before he knew it, the slope had flattened. He could sense the floor of the Valley of Death beneath his feet.

Had he chosen a slightly more southern route, he would have been slowed by Salt Creek, a prehistoric lake remnant five times saltier than seawater, home to the unique Salt Creek pupfish. Unpalatable, the salty water could only have served to cool his body, not slake his thirst.

Soon, he was crossing Death Valley Wash and easily making the two miles to the highway. Paved road would be heavenly by comparison. Tempting though it was, he declined the easy road.

That is precisely where they will be looking. Instead, Scott crossed the road and headed into the mountains to the east.

To his south was Titus Canyon, with its semi-improved road. He avoided that for the same reasons. He had chosen a straighter path for his escape route, up and over the Grapevines. He had six hours to make ten miles, uphill, but far more forgiving than the Panamint Mountains at his back. If he failed to attain the elevations of the Amargosa Range by dawn, he would bake in the exposed lower elevations of the valley. With less than two inches of rain reaching the valley floor per year, the plant life is sparse and specialized.

Flat and barren, the lower elevations and valley floor were devoid of shade offerings, and on long summer days, the ground temperatures could slow-cook a stew. There was no room for error. Even the modest elevations above would not afford much relief—they barely reached six thousand feet—but that twenty-five-degree temperature drop could be the buffer between life and dehydration. On he pushed, gravity slapping at his thighs with every step.

The previous night's fatigue had been challenging enough, but he'd taken little rest, less water, and virtually no food for forty-eight hours. The toll was beginning to tell. The slope was not as steep, but it was relentless, and the heat had not subsided as much as he could have wished. Two miles due east, he spied the opening to Red Wall Canyon, where he had hiked with his family. In the daylight two years ago, he had appreciated the colorful rock formations, but now the moonlight offered only variations of gray.

After an hour, his thighs cried for relief. He gave them none. After two hours, his lungs burned in protest, and his mouth developed the blood taste every distance runner knew. Finally, past the foothills and a mile inside the canyon itself, he came to the dry falls and knew he must rest. Unslinging his pack, he retrieved a bottle of water and took a few precious sips. Only two bottles of purified water remained, and two of unpurified. Those he would drink only if necessary, the risk of dysentery real enough to make Scott hold them in abeyance.

Looking back to the west, he was simultaneously surprised and pleased with his gain in elevation. If he could safely negotiate the dry fall, he knew he could do the rest. He finished the bottle of water while his legs reclaimed their strength, and then began anew. He ascended steadily, hands and feet in constant contact with the smooth rock, like a crab. He worked his way back and forth in the moonlight, scrambling here, climbing there, until the crest of the fall was reached. He stood erect and looked back over the valley. In his weariness, it seemed he had hardly moved, but now he looked down and saw another pair of headlights on the road, and their ant-like meanderings told him he had made good distance. He turned and pushed uphill again, forcing movement. Before long, he reached the first ridge.

Looking to the east in the gray moonlight, he could see Mount Palmer. At 6,710 feet, it was the tallest peak between himself and his next objective, and the most likely place to find the two things he would require at dawn—shade and cool air.

Leaving this first ridge, he lunged down the hill too fast. His momentum began to get away from him, and just as he was reining it in, his foot, weighted now with the beast of exhaustion, caught a rock and spilled him forward. Instinctively he flung him arms forward to break his fall, and as he went down, he felt the now-familiar pain deep in his right elbow as it was wrenched into forced flexion. Again, he felt the warmth of fresh blood inside the bandage. Again, the feelings of despair exaggerated by exhaustion played with his mind. Could he not sleep here for a couple of hours and be refreshed? Would a little time-out be that bad? He had done so much. What could it hurt?

He struggled with the questions, but his rational self forced them into submission. Should he oversleep, he would be exposed at sunrise. He must get up. He had to keep going. No matter how painful, it would only be worse if he waited.

Dragging himself off the ground, he started down the slope, correcting his pace. Down and up and down again he pushed. Each breath came harder. His lungs burned, and his tongue stuck to his lips. The blood taste had been with him continuously for two hours. The first gray light of dawn silhouetted the eastern horizon as Scott reached the final ascent. His dead legs were not quick to the will of his brain. Still he pushed. Sweat coated his skin as he lost far more water than he had consumed. The occasional episodes of dizziness became more frequent; increasingly he thought he would fall. On he pushed. Dawn was freshening on the eastern ridge ahead. Time was his enemy. Finally, against the brightening skyline, he could see the first juniper and, beyond that, the first Pinyon Pine, scrawny and stunted, holding on for dear life against all odds.

Like me.

Somehow, he had managed to beat the sun. He pulled himself up the hill, deeper into the cluster of trees, and collapsed on the ground against a large pine. His lungs sucked the fresh air, burning with each exchange. Scott breathed deeply for several minutes until his panting was replaced by more measured respirations. His air hunger satisfied, he retrieved his sixth bottle of water and some dried snake jerky. The taste was quite pleasant. Nothing complimented a meal like true hunger. Finally, he treated himself to two pieces of hard tack—dessert in the desert.

Finished, Scott walked to the north side of the mountain and found a ledge shrouded by trees. Questions gnawed at him while he made his bed. Was his plan good enough? Should he have stayed on the road and waved down a car? He propped a few broken branches against the bank, forming a crude lean-to to break up his silhouette. As he settled himself for sleep, he couldn't know that roadblocks were being readied at every junction of every highway within a two-hundred-mile radius. His instinct had been the correct one. Staying off the roads had been key.

Folding himself for sleep, his thoughts turned to Rachael as his arm instinctively reached for an empty hold. God, he missed her. If he lived, he would never take her for granted again. If he lived. Had he been awake even a few minutes longer, he might have heard the drone of the airplanes dropping paratroopers along the perimeter meant to contain him, but as the aircraft began their dawn run, Scott drifted into unconsciousness.

Chapter 29

White House Strategy

"When can we come back? I don't like it out here when you're not here." Janet Brady was not happy being shuttled out of harm's way. She was most comfortable by Gary's side, talking with him, involved. Her steady presence had endeared her to the public, her intelligence, grace, and beauty doing nothing to hurt his image. "Tomorrow?"

"Maybe. Probably. It will depend on the situation. I am feeling guilty enough right now, Janet. I don't need you playing that card, okay?" The tempo and the emotion were building in Brady's voice, signs that she knew all too well.

"Why guilty?"

"Because you are married to a true horse's ass!"

"Honey, what's the matter?" She could hear the crack in his voice.

"Janet, when I knew that it was Scott in the tunnels, I could have spoken up right away, vouched for him, led the investigation a different direction, but I didn't know what was going on. I needed time to think, and I needed to see what others were thinking. When the missile was fired, his plane lost altitude so fast that it went off radar. We were sure he was dead at that point until his plane showed up on radar a few miles to the west. Still I didn't speak up. When he landed in Kansas, someone tried to kill him again. Obviously, we both know that Scott didn't kill that airport manager—that bullet was meant for him. Still I didn't speak up. When his plane went down on Mount Whitney, I swear a part of me died, but I said nothing. Now we know he bailed out somewhere over eastern California, where there are thousands of soldiers closing in on him, and still I have said nothing. If I can find out who wants him dead, then I might have my first clue, but in order to do that, I have to continue doing what I have been doing. And that is why I am an ass. The person I owe my life to, the only person besides you that I can depend on to be at my side no matter what, my best friend in the world… what am I doing with him? I'm using him for bait." Now the tears did come. Despite the years in politics and despite his battle-hardened life, he cried.

Janet could hear the tears, but she didn't say a word for several minutes while she let him release the emotion and the guilt that had been building for days. However, when he was done, she did what she had always done. She offered a different perspective. "So how many troops do they have trying to corner our fugitive from justice?"

"About four thousand on the ground—plus AWACS and gunships and FBI and hundreds of local roadblocks. Why?"

"Let's see. He's given them the slip three times and dodged one missile, one bullet, and one mountain. Now they have to chase Scott Piquard out in the wilderness on foot? Only four thousand? I'd feel sorry for the soldiers."

It took a moment to sink in, but as usual, Janet was right. Scott was now in his element. Gary had watched him stalk a deer to within fifteen yards, only to let it go. "Not big enough to waste an arrow."

"You do your job. Scott will do his."

"I love you, Janet. Just a couple of years to go. Just a couple of years until we get our life back." He hung up and walked to the door.

Todd Pederson was waiting outside. Todd was anxious on a normal day, but today he was more than animated. He started pelting the president with messages the minute the door opened.

"The front commanders have been calling. They want to crush this thing before it gets any farther north. Commander Matt Karber has been calling hourly, and now he is here, waiting. He didn't buy the Camp David story. I doubt he will leave until he has your ear. President Ambrosio and President Molina are waiting by their phones for your call. They are very anxious to talk to their very good friend since the futures of Mexico and Nicaragua are tied so intimately to the future of the North Americans. The newspeople are all over me. I said I'd get back to them. La Fortuna and Reforma are decrying our lack of loyalty. Another day in paradise, sir."

"Get both presidents on the hotline and show Matt in. I'll see what he has to say before I call the chiefs."

Pederson disappeared and almost as quickly reappeared with Matt Karber in tow. Matt was tired and looked it. "Good morning, Matt. What's on your mind?"

"Good morning, Mr. President. May I speak freely, sir?"

"Absolutely, Matt. You know me better than that."

"Sir, if I may be so bold as to appear to be giving you unsolicited advice, we need to release our troops to move while the South Americans are still concentrated. It is unanimous among the intel people that they will withdraw the second we apply pressure. They already have what they want—a huge win against a war of aggression on their own soil along with a new international respect."

Brady looked at his adviser, thinking to himself, *Come on, Matt, what is really on your mind? You have made your position perfectly clear all week. You haven't waited up half the night to tell me this.* "What else?"

"This situation out west, sir—it's getting out of hand. The assassin has been giving us the slip left and right. He must be getting intel from somewhere. Sir, we need to release a full regiment from the Texas staging area and get this guy surrounded, and we need to do it now. We do not have enough men for the terrain we have to cover. And we need permission to fire if we make contact again. We don't have to shoot to kill, but we may need to shoot to slow him down."

The first to ask for blood, Brady said to himself. *Matt Karber? I never would have suspected it.* "I can't do that, Matt. There is more to this than meets the eye, and I want very badly to talk to this guy. As for the request for more men, I can't see the need. He's only one man, and they probably have him surrounded already. Besides, everyone has been telling me we need more troops on the border, so why would I want to pull men from there?"

"Only because they are mobilized and ready to move instantly, sir. We need coverage on Operation Whitney immediately. Replacements can be flown into Texas in two days. There will be no negative impact on our ability to act in the south."

"Operation Whitney has more than enough resources allocated. Good God, there must be over five thousand soldiers and support personnel on that fiasco alone. For one man! At that ratio, we would need a billion men to stop the South Americans."

"Sir, we cannot afford to lose him. What if he tries again? We need to use all force possible to bring him in or bring him down."

"Is there any news on the missing pilot from Idaho?" Brady asked, fishing.

"Not really, sir. There is very little information on him. He apparently was in the army and served in some covert operations in South America. The FBI has found little. There is nothing on him in their files, but they said you should remember the guy. He grew up in your hometown." Now Karber was the one fishing.

"What was that name again?"

"Piquard. First name Scott. Family doctor. Ring any bells?"

"Not sure. Maybe it will come to me. Thanks for your honesty, Matt."

"Thank you, sir. I appreciate you giving me this time."

Karber saluted and strode from the room, hat under his arm. Brady's eyes followed him. *So Matt is asking for blood. Mr. Conservative himself. Interesting.*

Todd Pederson entered the room as the commander exited, their steps nearly choreographed. Fellow staffers swore Todd had a third ear for the president's buzzer. "Ambrosio in Mexico and Molina in Nicaragua on the hot line, sir."

"And as soon as I'm off the line with them, I want Lon Winslow from the Joint Chiefs on the closed circuit. Tell him to have the latest position maps ready."

"Yes, sir." Pederson left as Brady picked up the line.

"Buenos días, Senores, este el Presidente Brady. ¿Cómo están ustedes?" Brady prided himself on his Spanish, and he used an interpreter only when protocol demanded it.

"Buenos días, Presidente Brady. ¿Cómo está?" Molina asked politely.

"¿Hola, cómo está?" Ambrosio chimed almost as quickly.

The conversation lasted less than three minutes. Brady let them know he was doing them a huge favor—one he did not particularly want to do since they had not listened to his advice earlier, but one he would do to preserve stability in the region. He also told them, with no pause to let them counter, that if they used the break in the action to regroup and try to regain ground, he would withdraw support immediately.

"But, Señor Brady, America promises us support, and then when the time for action comes, she is not there. Is this how we treat our friends?"

"When did I promise you military support?"

"Come now, we are grown men. We know that some promises cannot be made openly, but your men can make promises to our men and so forth, and it is understood in the world of politics what is meant. Pray, how could we have been so mistaken, Señor Presidente?" Molina's English was better than Brady's Spanish.

"I have suspected for some time that someone within our structure was making promises they were unable to fulfill. Now I need to know who those people are, or even my earlier offer of help may go unfulfilled."

"Surely you cannot expect me to know which subordinate of which subordinate talked to which subordinate of which subordinate? But be assured, it was very clear that if we took on the Satan of South America, we would not have to do it on our own. Your country promised us the help we would need to finish this job. Do not let this become another Bay of Pigs, I beg you. Millions may die if you do not lend us your full support. It is not too late. We have effectively drawn them out into the open. All you need to do is finish them off."

President Gary Brady smiled wanly as he witnessed one of the most incredible examples of Truth-Speak in his entire career. He had just heard a humiliating military defeat described as a brilliant tactic. The human animal never ceased to amaze him. Suddenly, a thought jolted him. *What if they were promised just that support at just that time and just that location? Their losses had been limited so far because they had retreated before it became an all-out slaughter. Maybe their timing was off due to my failure to die on time?* The chill that ran down his spine caused a physical shiver. *Maybe their plan was brilliant.*

"I will be talking with my advisers shortly. I will call you again. Good day, gentlemen."

Chapter 30

Sunday Night Fever

Sunday, 9:00 p.m. PDT, Amargosa Desert

As Gary Brady finished his phone calls and enjoyed a fresh cup of coffee that Sunday, Scott Piquard had been sleeping and sweating in his bed of rock and dirt. The north-facing ledge afforded him protection from the sun, and Scott spent most of the day unconscious to the world. The few biting insects that called this home had their fill, but he was too fatigued to know. The pain in his hips and shoulders aroused him periodically; he would roll, reposition, and be asleep in seconds. It was late afternoon before he was once more aware of his surroundings.

As red evening blended to gray twilight, the birds came to life. Scott lay, now more awake than asleep, his mind struggling with the one question he could not answer: *Am I far enough east?*

From his flight charts, he calculated that he had covered seventeen miles the first night and twenty-two the second. The distance seemed daunting, but it was the terrain, not the distance, that was the prime challenge. *It's not that far when you spread it out over several hours*, he told himself. *Some people run 26 miles and 385 yards in less than three hours.*

And some of them drop dead immediately afterward, his left brain countered, recalling the fate of Phidippides, the Athenian message runner who had delivered the news of the victory at Marathon. Historical documents showed him running not just one long trek that day, but three huge treks, totaling 306 miles in the previous two weeks. Some accounts have him running the Athens to Sparta run, 140 miles one way, in 36 hours. Scott's progress was meager by comparison, but he still felt like dying as he tried to move. His joints, muscles, tendons, and ligaments seemed frozen together. Every part of his body ached, rebelling with pain when he attempted movement.

It wasn't until he rolled clumsily onto his right side that he became fully aware of the pain in his elbow. As elbow met rock, the pain shot up his arm. Earlier, the pain was intermittent, but now it began throbbing with each heartbeat. Heat was palpable in the flesh surrounding the cut. A silent army of bacteria was marching, and they were hungry. Scott sat for a moment, allowing time for the pain to ebb as he listened for sounds of man. The quiet of nature was all he heard.

He popped a piece of the hardtack candy into his mouth. The sweetness was divine, and the stimulation caused salivation, which, though only temporary, abated the intense feeling of thirst. He would finish the candy tonight, using the calories instead of carrying them any farther. He had only one pint of bottled water and two of questionable purity to take him to his next stop, still eighteen long miles as the crow flies.

Can you do it, old man? A subconscious despair building inside of his head would allow no answer.

Scott was anxious to move, but he could not move without the full cover of darkness. By now, they surely would have found his airplane and realized they had been duped. Additionally, he no longer had steep mountain ravines to obscure his shape. He was about to enter open desert, two-foot sage bush and scraggly juniper plants the only silhouettes in the sandy terrain. So instead of setting out, he continued to limber and stretch, straining his ears for signs of would-be captors.

As he stretched, he noticed the tree downslope. Was that a Utah juniper with the edible late-summer fruit? Not likely, this far west, but it could be a California juniper, also bearing sweet, edible fruit.

Either one could provide precious liquid. Most likely, though, it was the ubiquitous Rocky Mountain juniper with its bitter, resin-filled fruit. Although edible, it is likely to cause gastric irritation rather than solace from hunger. He walked to it and took one of the small bluish fruits and broke the skin with his incisors. The bitter contrast from the candy caused him to spit it out immediately. Rocky Mountain juniper. Given time, he could have prepared it as a tea, but time and water were commodities he could not spare.

Still stretching as the darkness grew, he chewed on a few Pinyon nuts intermixed with bites of rattlesnake meat. The taste, albeit bland, was not displeasing. At least it was calming the hunger pains. He allowed himself the last of his fresh water and repacked his gear, putting the few remaining pieces of candy and the last piece of snake jerky into his pocket for easy retrieval.

With full darkness finally surrounding him, Scott put on his pack, lighter by the day, and started down the ridge that separated Death Valley from the Amargosa Desert. There were dirt roads to his north and to his south, but one more time, he took the road less traveled. He wondered if there were eyes on him even now, not knowing that two soldiers were sitting on the opposite face of Mount Palmer, straining their binoculars to the west as he started down the east slope and out into the desert of the Amargosa, the lights of Beatty beckoning in the distance beyond the Nevada border.

Starting down, Scott stumbled slightly. He caught his fall but sensed that his legs were not responding normally. His thighs were heavy, his feet leaden. His response time was slow, and he knew that he was in danger of falling if he tried to push himself.

At the five-thousand-foot level, the ground began to flatten toward the rolling terrain of the high desert, but already the dryness of his mouth and throat were crying for relief. What was it going to be like in four hours—or eight? Despite the hour, the desert air was still warm.

I haven't done that much work, he told himself. *I shouldn't feel this hot*. He slowed his pace to allow cooling. When he failed to cool, he slowed still further, knowing that overheating could kill him as surely as bullets.

After two miles, he felt no better, and after four, he knew he needed water. He slipped off his pack and sat on the sandy ground. He took a swig of the cached rainwater and held it in his parched mouth. He forced himself not to swallow immediately, but instead let it saturate his tissues, allowing only trickles to escape down his greedy throat. He sipped slowly. It tasted too good to judge purity. He finished the bottle.

Another hour had passed when he came to a washout with a two-foot drop into a narrow gulley. Scott used the break in rhythm to sit on the ledge and shed his pack. *I shouldn't be this tired*, he told himself. *It's early, and it has been all downhill so far. Cowboy up!*

Then, out of nowhere, Scott felt the cooling breeze he had hoped for the last two days. When he was holed up in the heat of the day, praying for a breeze, there was none to be had. Now he felt it again. He held up his hand but could not sense the direction. He licked his finger with his dry tongue and held it into the air. Still he could feel no wind. It had been unmistakable, the coolness. Was he imagining this?

Now he felt it again. This time it was colder, and it shook his shoulders as it traversed his back and coursed up into his neck. He turned his body to feel the breeze in his face but was met only with the still air of the Amargosa. *I know there was a wind that time. The senses don't lie.*

Except on occasion, he countered with the other half of his brain. The ongoing conversation was never fully quiet. *Like a mirage. Or when you are going crazy.*

Scott picked up a handful of sand and let it sift through his fingers, watching as it fell directly to the ground. There was no variation from the perpendicular as the next wave of cold wind hit him. Again it struck his back, despite the fact that he had just turned 180 degrees. He was slow to realize—slow to admit—what was happening. He wanted to lie down and sleep, curl up against the cold wind at his back, but a voice in the background was screaming with a muffled voice, *Keep moving, Scott. Keep moving now, or you will die!*

Despite the growing sense of otherness in his body, his medical training broke through the haze. He checked his pulse: 140. He seldom reached 130, even when running. *Tachycardia—unexplained heating and chilling, weakness, fatigability, slowed concentration.* The doctor inside his brain was screaming at him, but he was slow to hear. Finally, a single word broke through the fog. *Sepsis!*

He looked to the east. Just above the horizon, he could make out the faint glow of lights against the sky, and his heart sank at the distance. He might outsmart their radar specialists. He might outfly their jet jockeys. He might outhike their soldiers. But he couldn't outrun the simple staphylococcus. Alas. Was this his fate? Was he to die here, confused and delirious as the infection took over his body? Then a lifetime of problem-solving took over.

Retrieving an empty water bottle from his pack, he emptied his bladder into it. The small volume, amber color, and concentrated odor told him that his free-water debt was building. He was becoming more and more dehydrated, which magnifies the effects of infection. He needed water. A recurring fallacy was that it was better to drink your own urine than to die of dehydration. Scott had once heard a nurse tell a patient, "It's sterile, so it's better than dying." He had quickly disabused them both of that notion. It might be sterile, but it was still concentrated waste. The body dispelled it for a reason. Drinking urine put the concentrated salt and waste back into the body. Only "free water"—water that was not bound to salts and was less concentrated than your blood—could save your life. Continued concentration of salts and toxins led to cellular weakness, then cellular malfunction, confusion, disorientation, heat prostration, and finally, death. However, because it was sterile, he had another plan for it.

The odor from his elbow was forcing him into uncharted waters. As he removed the bandage, the unmistakable smell of staphylococcal purulence wafted upward, insulting his olfactory nerves. The wound needed draining and irrigating, and he had but one sterile commodity with which to irrigate it—his own urine.

With an abscess, drainage was everything. He pulled up his sleeve and tore at the wound, pulling as hard as he could despite the shrill pain that shot up his arm. He felt a ripping sensation as he dug his fingernails into the flesh, but it would not yield. He pulled out his knife and gritted his teeth as he sliced open the jagged skin. A gush of hot liquid coated his arm as the pus spilled onto the sand, the smell obscene. Scott clawed at the wound repeatedly until he had it opened, the abscess emptying its contents onto the desert floor. How many students had he taught? How many times had he preached to them that the treatment of choice for infection was drainage? How could he nearly have missed it?

He dug his index finger into the wound and tore at the sulcus. The pain rippled up his arm, but again he was rewarded with a small gush of pus. He forced his fingernail into the crease between healthy tissue and foul, and the pain coursed up his arm, bypassing the shoulder and slamming directly into his brain. There was no time for morning conference here, no time for anesthesia or comfort; there was only time for do or die.

As he tore at his flesh, he began to feel solid, healthy tissue. His finger bored into the sulcus of the wound until it was down to viable flesh. Fresh blood dripped onto the ground as the last waves of pain washed through him. Taking a piece of nylon, he wiped out the hollow. When the bleeding finally stopped, he poured urine into the wound in small aliquots, stopping between irrigations to wipe with the nylon. Scott did not wrap the elbow, but left it open to the air. Bacteria, like humans, did poorly when dehydrated. Lastly, he scrubbed his hands with sand repeatedly until they were as clean and dry as he could make them.

The pain had been good. He felt awake again. Scott drank the remaining bottle of brackish water. *Dirty is a relative word*, he thought as he tasted the cooling liquid. *Mineral laden* seemed much more appropriate.

The last two miles had been traveled in a fog. Had he stayed to the east, or had he wandered? Scott climbed to the next small hill above the ravine. The lights of Beatty were still squarely in front of him. He had stayed true, but he had to force himself to keep moving as a voice inside his brain told him that a little nap might rekindle his energy. He concentrated on every step. He moved one foot and then the other. No matter how tired he was, no matter how much sense it made to rest, no matter how convincing that voice was, he could not listen to its siren call. He reminded himself that only movement mattered. If he failed to make Beatty by dawn, he would die. He took a dozen steps.

Can move better if rested.

Can die faster if stopped.

On he argued, right brain with left, as on he plodded, right foot then left. Step by step he argued with himself, fighting second by second the impulse to lay himself under a sage brush and sleep for an hour—a half hour…fifteen minutes…one minute—of rest. Seconds turned into minutes, and he was still on his feet. He sucked the last of the candy, forcing saliva from his desiccated glands. Minutes turned into an hour, and he was still walking. On he plunged. Another hour passed grudgingly. Another mile passed, then another. The desert floor softened as rocky foothills turned to sandy flats with sparse plant life.

Now he began to chide himself for not steering toward the water source at Stovepipe Wells. *I should have gone southeast. I should have taken the sure thing. I will die in the desert, a stupid victim of a stupid plan.* The fever had driven too much water from his pores, insensible loss that escalated with each degree of core temperature.

He climbed the next small hill, the climbs thankfully easier as the topography flattened. Cresting, he looked east. In his mind, he knew he had come some distance, but to his eye, in the darkness of the middle of the night, he sensed that he had made no ground. Despair crept to the edge of his consciousness. *Move! Do not let your senses dictate to your cognition. Move your foot.*

To his left, he saw a bare patch of sand, a cove devoid of cacti and sage and rock, the softest spot he could ever remember seeing, beckoning him to lie down. *Move! Do not think of comfort. Think of Stephanie. Think of Chad.*

He moved one foot, then the other. Motion became monotony. Monotony became routine. Miles passed. The lights of Beatty still shone in the distance, and in Scott's mind, lights equaled water. But still so far.

Then off to his left, he saw a light—dim but there. It was only a little out of the way. What was it? A mirage? *Stay east*, he told himself, but suddenly a memory surfaced in his frontal lobe. *We were here.*

He walked toward the tiny light. One part of him said to go to the light; another said to go to Beatty, the only sure thing in his world right now. But what was that in the foreground? Was he seeing spirits? His eyes saw figures that looked like white-robed ghosts. Suddenly, he remembered. *We* were *here. Rachael loved the outdoor art gallery. Stephanie adored the bottle house. I know where I am.* His feet carried him north. There was nothing there except a ghost town, but a light shone a thousand yards from where he stood, and the thought of water shone through all his caution. *It's not a mirage. I know where I am.*

He felt his pace quicken despite his wanness. Soon, only a hundred yards separated him from the white ghost-like figures of the *Last Supper* and other sculptures in the Goldwell Open Air Museum. He skirted the museum and steered for the ghost town. On the southern edge of Rhyolite, Scott could see the faint glow from the travel trailer where the retired couple lived as they hosted tourists at the house built with mortar and liquor bottles.

Once a boomtown that boasted a brief population explosion of ten thousand during the gold rush of 1904, Rhyolite's population by 1922 was down to one. In 1905, Tom Kelly built his famous house with over thirty thousand bottles, not hard to find in a city full of miners and gamblers and the fifty-plus saloons that served them. With water costing as much as $5 a barrel, beer was almost cheap by comparison.

As he approached, the one memory he was searching for escaped him. Did they have a dog? Was all his stealth and hard work about to be ruined by one simple watchdog barking alarm in the middle of the night? He was almost certain that he remembered a dog, but was it friendly or foul? Would it lick his hand or go for his neck? And did he have the strength to subdue it if it did? In a recess of his brain, he thought he saw a longhaired black dog that was accustomed to strangers, bored with the comings and goings of humans, keeping to the shade rather than venturing out in the sun for a sniff. However, the cool night was different. Was this his time to roam?

Scott's pace slowed as he neared the little trailer, its lone light bulb casting a beam across the sandy parking space. As if on cue, the black dog emerged from the shadows. As the dog crossed the open ground between them, Scott fished in his pocket for the last piece of snake meat as a canine growl became audible deep in the beast's throat. Scott squatted low in a position of nondominance, the peace offering dangling from his outstretched fingers. Still wary, the dog lowered his head and extended his neck, his ears back. He sniffed once. The growl was gone. He took another step and sniffed again. Another step. Now he was practically touching the meat with his nose, and sensing no danger, he took it. In true canine fashion, he chomped twice and gulped it down, then asked for more with his sad eyes. Scott reached and scratched behind its ear as the dog turned his head to accommodate the friendly hand, the perennial itch soothed.

"Sorry, pooch, but that's all I have," he said as he scratched the other ear. He petted the dog once more and then stood. Scanning the couple's water tank, he saw that a pipe went directly from the tank on the four-wheeled trailer into the coupling on the side of the travel trailer. Trying to get water directly from the tank would make too much noise, but sharing a drink with his new friend could be done quietly. The dog's water bucket sat under the north side of the trailer, hidden from the sun. To Scott, it was a find worth more than all the gold that had been taken out of Rhyolite. Bending under the edge of the trailer, he quietly lifted the bucket.

Beggars and choosers, he reminded himself as he lifted the filthy bucket to his lips. When had water tasted so good? What king had been served finer liqueur from a golden chalice? When, since the dawn of man, had anything tasted so good? Probably never. Dog saliva and all.

Scott could almost feel his fever wane as he drank. Dehydration accelerated the effects of sepsis, and fever caused massive evaporation from the skin in an attempt to cool the body, a vicious cycle that ended in death before the days of intravenous fluids. Scott sat for a long while, finishing what was in the pail.

Still weak with hunger, he saw the small bowl with a few pellets of dog food gracing the bottom. They looked too appealing. *The brain sets priorities we are not even aware of,* he acknowledged as he scooped up the meager contents. Placing the utensils back in their exact positions, Scott set off to the east, the protein-laden doggy bits crunching between his teeth. The dog accompanied him the first few hundred yards but soon tired and turned to home. Scott continued on, munching on bits of the dried food. Little did he care what part of what animal it came from. It was food. *Protein, fat, and carbohydrate in a tasteful balance*, he said to himself as he crested the next hill and saw the lights of Beatty inching closer. From the Bullfrog Hills, the ground fell away nearly continuously to the bright lights of the little casinos.

The hiking was easy now, and he loped down the open terrain. Paralleling Highway 374, he angled north of the town to avoid the junction with 95. North of town, Scott found a washout that told of those rare times that rain did grace this area. Shunned by other hikers, it was precisely what Scott was looking for. He followed the low-lying ravine down into town. Staying to backyards and alleyways, he made his way toward the center of the city, where the all-night glow of casino lights beckoned with their hollow promises.

In a secluded backyard, he searched the foundation of the house until he found the garden hose. He turned the knob just an inch, avoiding the hissing sound that might awaken a homeowner, and waited impatiently for the liquid gold to trickle into his mouth. Never again would he take for granted the beauty and purity of water. He drank until he could drink no more.

Near the alley, he found a shed with several pieces of old lumber propped against the wall, forming a perfect lean-to. He slipped on his jacket and cap, crawled into his new shelter, and was fast asleep before the Monday dawn painted the skies to the east.

Chapter 31

Drills

Rachael Piquard barely slept. Through the haze of her fatigue, she thought she heard a car idling. She parted the curtain a fraction of an inch. The streetlight silhouetted two figures in a dark sedan as it cruised by, too slowly. *Why are they here? Did Gary send them?* she asked herself. She went back to bed, only to lie awake, wondering at every sound before she fell into a restless sleep. Idaho was not supposed to be like this.

Six thirty came much too soon. She slipped down the hallway to make sure Chad was awake. He had told her to sleep in. "Don't worry, Mom, I'll be up. It's first day." But she knew how teenagers could sleep through a minor nuclear explosion, lost in that unconsciousness that came with innocence and growing bodies.

She saw the light glowing under his door. She tapped lightly and cracked the door. "Can I get you anything? Oatmeal or hot chocolate?"

"No thanks. I'm just going to have some milk. Coach will run us hard to see who's in shape, and I don't want a gut ache. Some of the guys are going to be blowing beets. Not me."

"I'll get it."

"Go back to sleep, Mom. I can get it."

223

"That's okay. I can't sleep anyway." As she spoke, the realization of why she couldn't sleep struck them both.

"No word from Dad?" He asked the question, already knowing the answer.

"No."

Chad saw the quiver in her lips. "Don't worry. He'll be home today."

Rachael turned back toward the kitchen so he could not see the tear on her cheek. *The child is father to the man*, she said to herself, recalling Wordsworth.

"I'll set the things out," she said, wishing like every mother that he would let her do more for him. *Oh, how much simpler it was when they were babies.* She would love to go back and relish those years, savor their dependence and their unconditional love. *We never know what we have until we look back.* And that thought spilled another tear. She walked to the bay window and looked to the mountains. Why had she been so selfish? Why hadn't she supported Scott more, spent more time with him? Why hadn't she gone camping with him more? Why had she let him take the kids and go without her, pleading she was too busy? *Too busy? Cleaning the kitchen floor and washing clothes? What a sad trade.*

Chad came bounding down the stairs and into the kitchen, his stockinged feet sliding to a stop on the tiles as he dropped his gym bag and gulped a large glass of milk. Then he slipped on his shoes and dashed out the door. Jumping into his old pickup, he was halfway out the driveway before she could say goodbye—before she could say she loved him.

"Don't get hurt," she said through the screen door as she watched him pull away. "Please don't get hurt." Rachael liked football, but she worried every time he played, just like she held her breath and nearly closed her eyes every time Stephanie stretched for a hurdle. Such was a mother's lot. Another tear glistened down her reddened cheek.

As she turned and closed the door behind her, an engine came to life a block away, and a dark sedan accelerated down the street behind the pickup truck.

This one will be easy to follow, Renner thought to himself as he pulled behind the old Chevy with the chrome trim and new paint job. The chrome exhaust stacks coursing up the sides of the cab would make this one easy to spot. *My god, does everyone out here drive pickups, Jeeps, or Suburbans?* he asked himself. To Renner, the transplanted city boy, a Jeep was anything that was high profile and had four-wheel drive. He was accustomed to the shiny black Suburbans, impeccably cleaned and waxed, that the various agencies used in DC. Out here, they were caked with dust and mud, windshields half brown and half wiper-smeared. The concept of actually using a four-wheeler for four-wheeling hadn't sunk in for Renner.

As Renner followed the '56 Chevy to the practice field and slipped past unnoticed, a forty-power Zeiss spotting scope was trained on the activity from the side of the foothills. The $10,000 scope was perched on a mound, positioned such that one swivel on the tripod revealed the practice field, and another afforded a view of the expensive house with the huge backyard bordering the creek on the edge of town. He had slept part of the night, but not before watching the four-door sedan arrive and park near the house. Satisfied that the kid was where he should be, the shadow behind the spotting scope turned back toward the house and trained the zoom on the second-story bathroom window and watched the robe slip from the shoulders of the beauty standing in front of the shower.

Bet she works out. Wonder if she'd like to work out on this? he said to himself as he readjusted the swelling in his pants. *But the daughter, those perfect legs.* Intent oozed from the mountain. *After the old man and the kid are dead, I can take whatever I want.*

*****

As the evil on the mountain brewed its dark thoughts, forty teenage boys roared up the terraced hillside and onto the practice field with thoughts of domination of their own. Eight and one the previous year, the Bulldogs had seven returning starters and an undefeated season was not out of the question. The boys had been dreaming about it all summer, the seniors taking it seriously enough to run and hit the weights. Of these, Chad Piquard and Rob Allen were the natural leaders and team captains. They led the team through their calisthenics. When they were finished, the head coach blew his whistle, and when coach blew his whistle, all talk stopped, unless some poor freshman didn't understand the rules and felt like running laps.

"Listen up. Line up on the fifty, sprint to the goal line, walk back to the fifty, and start again. Let's see how well you can cover turf. On your marks. Get set. Go!"

Cleated feet pounded the ground as the mass of teenage testosterone raced down the field. Chad had been running with Stephanie all summer. His strength was good, and his endurance was great, but try as he might, he could still see Rob a half step ahead as they crossed the line. That was how it had always been as long as he could remember. Nearly as tall as his dad at 6 feet, 2 inches, Chad was 1 inch taller but 40 pounds heavier than his lithe friend. At 160 pounds dripping wet, the transplanted Nebraskan could accelerate instantly, turn on a dime, or throw on the run—and throw well. His completion percentage the previous season set a new school record, thanks largely to the huge soft hands on his tight end. But his tight end cursed under his breath every time Rob beat him.

They lined up again. Again, they pounded down the turf. Again, Rob crossed a half step in front. And again. And again. "Shit." He said it aloud as he gasped for breath, but after seven sprints, Rob was too winded to talk.

One last time, they lined up. One last time, they pounded down the turf. But this time, the starts were slower. The slow summer months had softened most of the legs. But to Chad there were not forty runners. There never had been. There were only two. He thrust his knees forward, remembering what his dad had said about running: "Everyone concentrates on the push-off, but you can't push off until your leg comes forward. Thrust the knee forward faster. That's half the battle."

One last time he had a chance to be number one. Thrust and plant. Push and lift. Now the summer workouts were paying off. He was stride for stride with Rob. Now strength and stamina matched speed and agility. Rob was quick, but he didn't have the endurance of his muscular friend. After seven and a half wind sprints, stamina overtook raw speed. Chad could sense himself pulling ahead. He could sense the victory as he crossed the line a half stride ahead. The world was watching, and he had just won gold.

Chad thought he was the only one who battled with these thoughts. He was too young to realize that good coaches recognize the effort and the drive in the committed ones. In their eyes, he had always been number one in that category. When games were on the line, when everyone was dying in the fourth quarter, they could always count on him to come through. They had seen too many talented players leave it on the bench because they never worked to develop what God had given them.

Chad had already taken several deep breaths and was regaining his wind when the last 280-pound tackle lumbered across the line, ready to drop.

"Jesus, you two, slow down. You make us look bad."

"Sorry, Tom. But it's fourth and fifteen, end of the fourth, and we're down five," Chad answered.

"Shit. It's always fourth and fifteen to you, Piquard," he gasped.

"Water break!" the head coach shouted.

As they walked off the field, two freshmen players fell in behind Chad. "Someday, I'm gonna be just like him," one whispered to his buddy.

"You're too dumb to be like him," his friend retorted, hitting him on the arm. "The only way you're ever getting a four-point is by adding up four ones."

The other freshmen laughed at the joke, but they all felt the same way. If they could just be like Chad Piquard or Rob Allen, every girl in the school would want to go out with them. Generations changed. Nothing changed.

There was no contact on first-day practice, and after running and blocking drills, they broke into units and worked on plays. By 8:15, the boys were dragging. They were almost done for the morning but would return at 6:00 p.m. for the second session of two-a-days.

"Piquard!" Coach was hollering from the sidelines. "Phone call."

Chad jogged to the sideline where the vice principal was standing next to the head coach. Phone calls were unheard of during practices. "Some guy from the FBI wants to talk to you. Is something wrong?"

"No. Everything's fine."

"Go to the office," he said. "Practice is almost over anyway." Coach watched him jog to the building as he turned to the vice principal. "Something's wrong."

*****

As the boys finished their drills, the munitions inventory at Fort Lee was reported correct, and the lockdown was lifted. As the gates swung open, a black Mustang convertible slipped through the checkpoint and sped away, three days late for an important meeting.

Chapter 32

Breakfast in Beatty

Monday, 8:00 a.m. PDT, Beatty, Nevada

Scott's biologic alarm clock rarely let him down. It was something he had inherited from his father, this ability to awaken when needed. Only three hours had passed, and he was far from rested. It would be better to stay to the night, but there were things to be done that required timing. Scott dragged himself from under the lean-to.

"Get off my property, you filthy bum." An elderly woman was standing at her screen door, broom in hand. "Get off my property, or I'll call the police."

Scott backed away, bowing in submission. "I'm sorry, ma'am. I just need a little food. I'd be glad to work for it. I lost my wallet, and I don't have a penny on me."

"That's what they all say after they've gambled away their kids' food money. Now get!"

Convinced that she meant it, Scott backed away, still bowing slightly and looking at her feet. His posture of submission was already mollifying her. As soon as he was clear of her property, she went back to her sweeping, forgetting the incident nearly as quickly as it had occurred. Pathetic, homeless bums in Nevada were not a rare sight.

Scott strolled down to West Main Street, cars and people bustling to start the new week. He smoothed his hair as best he could as he started down the sidewalk, the smells from the local cafés beckoning. Here he could smell coffee, there bacon and warm maple syrup. It was painful to smell the foods and not partake.

Passing the small cafés, he sought the anonymity of the larger casinos. Spying the largest one, he crossed the street and walked past it slowly, memorizing its layout. When he did enter that building, he wanted to look like he knew what he was doing and where he was going. Seeing what he wanted, he walked down the street for another block and then reversed direction. Entering the casino, he immediately turned and made his way to the men's room. Looking in the mirror, he saw that it was worse than he thought. No wonder she had called him a dirty bum.

Scott stripped off his jacket and T-shirt. After drinking his fill, he submerged his head under the warm running water and scrubbed vigorously. Turning attention to his elbow, he pulled back on the flap of the wound and irrigated it copiously with clean water. The heat had abated somewhat since he had drained it, but the redness and tenderness were far from gone. At least the stench was gone.

It seemed a year since feeling the luxury of warm running water. He tarried at the sink, indulging himself. Finally, he rinsed and used paper towels to dry his head and body. Raking back his hair with his nails, Scott was able to get it looking somewhat presentable. Next, he took damp paper towels and whisked off his pants and top. Dressed, he was ready to try his luck at gambling—this time for food.

Scott walked to a bank of slot machines and feigned interest in the game one of the customers was playing. He stood watching—not the machine, but everything around it. He memorized the floor plan and continued loitering, ambling around the casino until he saw a condiment tray near the open end of the buffet line. He nonchalantly walked past the counter and pocketed a handful of ketchup packages. Making his way back to the men's room, Scott slipped into a stall, tore off the end of one packet, and sucked out the contents. He didn't know ketchup could taste so good. He quickly polished off the nine remaining packets.

Five ounces of food. It's a start.

Drifting back to the buffet area, he toyed with the slot machines next to the empty waiting line as if playing. A few minutes later, opportunity knocked. As the waitress turned back to the kitchen, a tall gentleman stood up from his table and headed for the check-out counter. Scott smoothly covered the distance and took his seat. There wasn't much, but it was food. He quickly finished off a nearly empty salad bowl and then gulped down a tiny amount of soup that sat cold in the center of the table. From the plate, he picked up the unfinished pieces of chicken and picked them clean, then salted the pile of chicken skin on the edge of the plate, and ate them like jerky. After chasing that with a partial cola in which the ice had melted, he reached for the bread left on its plate. Scott began to open a packet of jelly when the waitress started his way. She looked at him and stopped short, the wrinkle on her forehead obvious.

"Did you forget my coffee?"

"I'm sorry, sir. I didn't hear you." As she looked around again, Scott decided not to push his luck. "Where is the men's room, miss?"

"Right over there." She pointed toward the back of the room. "And there is another one out near the entrance," she added with a perplexed look.

She disappeared into the kitchen and returned shortly with a large Styrofoam cup of coffee and a bowl filled with packets of half-and-half. As soon as she turned away, Scott stuffed the cream packets into his jacket along with the sugar packets from the table setting, put the remaining jelly and bread in the opposite pocket, picked up his pack and his cup of coffee, and headed for the back restroom. As he neared the restroom, he checked over his shoulder then darted through an "Employees Only" doorway. Finding himself in a hallway outside the kitchen, he quickly walked to the rear exit and out into the alley.

His heart was pounding for fear of detection, but the boredom of their everyday life made the average kitchen employee oblivious to what was happening around them. He walked down the alley, sipping his coffee and munching on the bread. Scott looked at his watch. It was time.

Entering the lobby of the adjacent casino, he walked to the phone booth. He dialed a number using the prefix for a credit card call. The operator came on the line for assistance. "Credit card call," he said politely.

"Card number, please."

He gave her the clinic's credit card number, then dialed a second number when he had a dial tone. He knew his home phone would be bugged by now, but had they thought of this? Thankfully, he had a memory for numbers.

Monday, 8:30 a.m. PDT, Granger, Idaho

Chad Piquard kicked off his spikes and walked into the school. He hurried down the hallway to the office, the words "FBI" hammering in his ears, tears licking at his eyes. The secretary smiled sadly and pointed to a phone in the corner. Each step closer to that telephone brought deeper dread. He did not want to pick it up. Instinctively, Chad knew calls like this can only mean bad news, and now he feared that he was going to hear about a plane crash, a missing father, a shattered life. He wanted to let it blink, forever on hold, and live a lie if he must. He hesitated but knew he could not avoid it.

He reached and picked up the receiver. "Hello?"

"Look at the floor immediately. Do not look up. Do not let your emotions give you away. Keep looking at the floor. You are being followed and watched every second of the day. Don't try to talk right now. Just say, 'Yes, sir.'"

"Yes, sir," Chad answered, nearly choking on the words upon hearing his father's voice.

"If anyone asks, you tell them that someone from the FBI in Washington called, asking for the whereabouts of your father. You told him you didn't know. You have not seen him in several days. He kept asking you questions about his activities, but you didn't know what he had been doing or where he had gone. Got that so far?"

"Yes, sir."

"Are you alone?"

"No, sir."

The secretary heard the replies and went about her business. Scott knew someone would be listening to Chad's end of the conversation but had guessed correctly that the school phones were not tapped.

"I had to call you during practice. It was the only way I could get you without calling the house or your cell. They will be bugged, so don't use them! Someone is trying to kill Gary, and now they're trying to kill me. All I know is that it's military, and they have more resources than I do. Say 'No, sir' again."

"No, sir." Chad's emotions had settled, and his voice had stopped quivering.

"Now say, 'I don't know where he's been. He hasn't called in several days.'"

"I don't know where he's been. He hasn't called in several days."

"Now listen closely."

Chad lifted an eyebrow while he listened, scanning the room. Beyond the glass wall of the office, he could see a stranger in a dark suit looking his way. He interjected a "Yes, sir" and a "No, sir" occasionally, but otherwise he listened and concentrated. If ever he needed to get something right, it was today.

When they were finished, Chad politely said, "I'm sorry I couldn't have been more help, sir. I haven't heard from him in several days. Goodbye." He hung up the phone and headed for the locker room, his feet barely touching the floor.

Chapter 33

Coincidences

Monday, 9:00 a.m. EDT, Homeland Security Command Center

Lieutenant Colonel Floyd Curtis was accustomed to little sleep, but the four stolen hours had barely recharged his batteries. It had become a way of life. When he was younger, he had used alcohol to combat his native insomnia, but the heavy-headed feeling he always blamed on lack of sleep disappeared when he passed on the extra beverages. He eventually accepted the fact that he didn't need more than five or six hours. Instead, he learned to use the time productively.

Curtis had not seen the light of day since Friday, electing instead to live in the command center and stay close to the action. He disliked having to catch up on what happened while he was away and for once they had a real operation. He was on his third mug of coffee when General Pat Collins arrived.

"Good morning, General," Curtis said as he saluted. Collins waved off the salute, having told him three times in the last three days that it was not necessary, but Curtis was not about to treat a general officer in any way short of protocol in front of his men. That was an inoculum that did not need culturing.

"What's new?" Collins asked, accepting the cup of coffee Floyd handed him.

"Nothing, really," Curtis replied, lifting his cup to the general in a toast to the start of the day, "except that we think we have our man cornered in the Panamint Range here." Curtis pointed to an area on the map. "One of our troops saw definite movement with his night vision lens just before dawn, but whatever he saw was in the trees, and he only got a glimpse. He was pretty sure it was on two legs though. They have three platoons closing on the area."

"That's great, but what you're telling me is that someone saw something, but they don't really know if it was a crook or a coyote, right?"

"Correct. The regulars only have first generation goggles. Most of the officers have thirds now, but they can't afford to outfit everyone. The third-generation night vision headsets cost ten times as much."

Collins pounded his fist on the desktop. "Damn it, I've been harping about this crap for years. We could outfit a thirty-man platoon with high-quality NVGs for $150,000, the same amount of money it costs to fly some VIP to a golf date or a Thanksgiving dinner." Collins was known for his refusal to take VIP flights, always traveling by transport or commercial airliner to punctuate his convictions. "Now, instead of knowing exactly what we are chasing over in this corner of the world," he said, stabbing at the map, "we will spend that much in fuel costs alone, reconning and supporting those poor devils who are hiking out there in the heat. It never ends. We won't get our troops proper equipment because of cost. Then when we are in a bind, we'll spend ten times that amount trying to fix the mistake. God, I'm glad I'm close to retirement."

"Amen to that," Curtis echoed. "It's the same with intel. One key piece of information can completely change how you approach a situation or save you from approaching it at all, but we are still hampered with old radar, old jammers, old listening devices—you name it. 'For want of a nail!'"

"Amen."

"Anything new up top?" Curtis asked.

"Not really. There was one sad story on the radio, though, now that you mention it. An army captain was killed this morning—hit by a truck coming down a tight curve on a hill. The truck crossed the centerline and smacked his Mustang convertible into the trees. It was just a few miles from Fort Lee, where the spooks hang out. The sad thing about it is that the base was under lockdown all weekend. They had just finished their inventory, and the lockdown had barely been lifted. Poor schmuck. Five minutes either way and he would still be alive."

"Married? Kids?"

"No particulars yet."

They busied themselves for the next two hours reviewing the status of their western operation and personnel strength when Block handed off a call to Curtis. "It's that FBI guy Ernie Knoll again."

"Curtis here," he said as he picked up the handset. "Ernie?"

"Yeah, Knoll here, but I don't know if you are going to want to talk to me. I just got done chewing some very serious butt out in Idaho. It turns out that our man Klugiewicz, in Idaho, didn't do his homework quite well enough on Saturday. You are assuming that you are chasing a middle-aged doctor who is probably a little soft and thick around the middle from the good life. Well, you would be wrong. I've been on the phone with the chief of police, who was away for the weekend. This Piquard guy can do a 10K in under sixty minutes. He backpacks, bow-hunts, fishes, and camps. This guy is at home in the woods. I would advise you to expand your perimeter immediately."

"Actually, Ernie, we did a worst-case scenario and set up a perimeter based on what a young, healthy soldier can routinely do. Our borders are pretty wide, but I appreciate the heads-up. It will definitely affect our planning. Thanks."

The remainder of the day was painfully uneventful as the minutes dragged into hours. No news from any sector. Ideas continued to flit around in Floyd Curtis's head until, by evening, he could stand it no longer. After Collins departed for the night, he dialed the phone number of the police chief in Clay Center, Kansas.

"Good evening, Chief, this is Floyd Curtis from the Department of Homeland Security. I was just wondering if you have any autopsy findings on that airport victim yet? I know he was shot, but do you have any particulars?"

"No, sir. Not really. Just that the shot was clean, right through the heart, and like I told the officer from the base, it was a typical armor-piercing wound because the exit wound was almost identical in size to the entrance wound. Of course, the echoing thing we've all talked about—I assume you know about that?"

"Not exactly."

"Well, some of the platoon members thought the shot came from south of the airport, others thought it came from the east, others west—you know how mixed those reports get. It had to be the echoes off the hangars. Still, I can't figure why he killed him right out there on the tarmac. Why not back in the building, out of sight, where the sound wouldn't carry? Doesn't make a lot of sense."

"No, it doesn't. Look, I appreciate your time. This has been very helpful. Thank you again."

"No problem. We're here if you need us."

"Thank you very much, sir. Have a good evening." Curtis hung up and sat against his desk. *Why would a civilian be carrying armor-piercing rounds?* He called Block over to his side.

"Eddie, I need you to do some research for me. I need you to get me a list of all military men who have died in the past week—no, make that two weeks—how and where, along with their vital statistics, rank, position, job description, etc. There have been too many coincidences to suit this jaded old man."

Chapter 34

Teenagers

Monday, 11:00 a.m. PDT, Granger, Idaho

Rob Allen was just getting comfortable for a post-practice slumber when the "Bombs Away" ring on his cell phone shattered his reverie. Wishing he'd shut it off, he looked at the caller ID window and saw that it was Chad Piquard's cell. His friend had acted peculiarly that morning, and he wondered what was up.

"Yo!"

"Rob, I need a huge favor. I can't talk. Can you come over right away?"

"Sure. What's up?" he asked, now fully awake.

"I need you to bring your dad's pickup and come over and help me. I'm kinda in some trouble and have to get some stuff done by five, or I can't go to afternoon practice. Can I count on you?"

"You know it. What'd you do?"

"I screwed up. I'll tell you later. Just come over right now! And one more thing. Wear that red Cabela's chamois shirt that you wear camping and those cargo pants with all the pockets and your mountain boots. Okay?"

"Sure. But why?"

"Tell ya later. Please hurry. And don't tell *anyone* where you're going. Got that? This is really important, Rob."

"Sure. Give me ten."

"Thanks."

Rob dressed quickly and headed for the garage, wondering what his friend had done to get in trouble. *Piquard never gets in trouble—like never.*

Agent Klugiewicz sat in his car, bored. He hated stakeouts. Like any young man, he wanted action. He didn't know how many hours it was going to take this kid to mow the grass, but the backyard was huge, and he knew he was in for a long day of back and forth and back and forth. "Should have gone to dental school," his dad would say when he complained about his job, but for his part, Klugiewicz could not bear the thought of peering into halitotic mouths day after day.

He made a journal entry: "10:00 a.m. Piquard Jr. mowing lawn, blue jeans, Denver Broncos T-shirt, Broncos cap, sunglasses, hiking boots." As he finished the entry, he saw a rusty Dodge pickup taking the corner too fast and practically sliding into the Piquard driveway.

He added another journal entry: "Tall, thin Caucasian male, approximately eighteen, baggy cargo pants, red shirt, sunglasses, hiking boots." Klugiewicz picked up his binoculars. "And Nebraska Cornhusker cap."

He finished his entry as he watched the new arrival walk around the side of the house and talk with the Piquard kid. The two boys walked back to the driveway, and the Husker fan hopped into his pickup, pulled into the street, then backed into the garage. Klugiewicz had to use his binoculars again to see into the darkened aperture. He could see them loading something into the truck, something very long and thin, before they went into the house. Minutes later, the kid in the red cap reappeared in the garage and hopped back into his pickup, exiting as quickly as he had arrived, while the Piquard kid walked around to the back of the house and commenced his long day of mowing.

No wonder his legs are so strong, Klugiewicz thought to himself. *Rich doctor won't even buy a riding mower*. By then, the vehicle registration page was up on his laptop.

He made another journal entry: "Dodge pickup, rusty gray, registered to Robert Allen Sr., left Piquard house at 10:25 a.m., driven by teenage male, assumed Allen Jr. Pickup loaded with red kayak. Piquard resumes mowing."

Monday, 11:00 a.m. PDT, Beatty, Nevada

As the morning's activity was being recorded in Idaho, Doctor Scott Piquard, professor of medicine and successful private practitioner, pilfered his sixth dinner roll on his way past the buffet line of a fourth casino. His pockets were stuffed with butter and jelly packs, ketchup and sugar envelopes, crackers, and rolls. He toyed with the idea of ordering a full meal and making his escape, but the risk was not worth it. He would be content with the leftover piece of prime rib nonchalantly lifted from an abandoned plate. Starving people didn't care how they got their food. Etiquette was inversely proportionate to hunger.

The hunger pains fading, he searched for a place to rest in the city park. The miles that night would not be as demanding, but the stealth would more than make up for it. Making his way to a grassy area in the shade of a huge tree, he planned his evening's activities. He knew they would be watching; the only question was, *How many?*

Scott thought of the rocky beds of the previous nights as he lay himself down on the plush, manicured lawn. Within minutes, he was deep in a fitful sleep, but the late morning temperature was already over one hundred, and it was not long before he was yearning for the cool mountain air. The deep slumber he desired eluded him.

He tossed in the heat, struggling to sleep, but the conflict moving in the foreground could not be ignored. Nor the voices. Nor the gunfire. He rolled onto his belly and peered over the bushes. He could see several soldiers moving through the sparse foliage. Fire flashed from the gun barrels in bursts of three.

He grabbed Gary Brady's arm and pulled his friend's ear close to his own mouth. "We need to move. Over there, to our right and ahead a hundred yards, is a natural depression. Meet me there if we get separated."

"We can't go that way, Scott. We need to go south."

"They're searching south. They won't expect us to go north. We're outnumbered a hundred to one. Our only hope is to go where they're not looking. Now follow me," he said as he jerked Gary to his feet. He saw the last of them off to his left, and now he ran right and north, angling between the two platoons, bending low to cut his profile, the small plants whipping at their faces, unnoticed in the rush of fear and adrenalin. When they made it to the low ground, they crouched in the depression. "The ground slopes down to the east here. This drainage will take us back to the river bottom, but we can't use that. It will be sniped. Across the river is a grassy area. If we get past that before dawn, we can lie low and maybe make it back to our base."

"That'll take two days going that way."

"Three."

"Three?"

"Yeah. We can't move in the daylight, or we're dead, and moving at night will slow us down. Better late than dead."

"What about the others?"

"Don't know. I was cussing myself for getting separated, but that's the only reason we're still alive. I don't know where they came from, but I'll bet Kidder fell asleep on watch again."

"We don't have food for three days."

"All we really need is water. Maybe I can find some edibles to chew on while we're holed up."

"Sounds great," Gary replied sarcastically as he followed Scott northeast.

Scott had been right. Once they had outflanked the enemy, they could hear gunfire to their south, but ahead all they found was darkness and eerie quiet. Soon they were across the river, totally exposed for the only time that night, thankful for the constant overcast that covered the moon like a trusted ally. Their luck held. By morning, they were tucked into a thicket, several ounces of wild grain lying in Scott's helmet between them.

"You need to grind the kernels with your molars. If you swallow them whole, they swell up in your intestines and give you a gut ache."

"Where did you learn that?" Gary asked.

"I don't know. I read it somewhere. Archeologists have found millstones dating back thousands of years. The molars on many pre-historic skeletons were ground down to the jawline from eating raw grains. Now eat some and get some sleep. We need to be rested by nightfall." Somehow, they managed to sleep for several hours despite the heat. And somehow, they made it back to their company over the course of the next two nights, moving only in the dark. They had eluded the enemy until they were within sight of their camp on the dominant hill. Now, another real danger would begin. The hill was well fortified and had a strong perimeter, but it would be surrounded by enemy snipers who would control the flow through that perimeter. If they made it past the snipers, they still ran the risk of being shot by their own men. Penetration would require a night approach and absolute silence, but their men needed to know they were friend-lies. In between, in no man's land, they could be shot by either side.

They spent ten hours crawling silently through the lowest and toughest terrain, which left them alone and mostly hidden. It was not until they could actually see an American soldier that they came under fire. They were losing the cover of darkness and needed to hurry or they would be exposed. Morning light was filtering through the trees as they started their run, shouting, "GIs! Don't shoot!"

What made Scott look back he would never know. Instinct? Fear? As they began their sprint, he glanced back and caught move-ment in a tree fifty yards behind them. He pulled Gary down behind a large tree just as he felt the pain and heard the report. It was strange how the pain had come before the sound. An extra-quick sensation—more like heat than the painful sharpness he had expected—told him a bullet had torn hide from the back of his right thigh. Luckily it was tangential, missing the muscle before exiting.

"Sniper. The tree he's in has a V split about twenty feet up." He peered around his tree and threw a burst of fire into the tree. The sniper knew where Scott was, a key advantage, but the inexperienced tree climber made the mistake of letting off a too-quick shot, and in the half darkness of early morning, his own muzzle flash betrayed him. Scott showered the tree with the remainder of his clip and was rewarded with a distant thump.

Now it was Gary's turn to help Scott as they raced through the dawning light to safety. He grabbed his arm and pulled him along as they shouted up the hill, hoping that they had not spent their nights in the wild only to be welcomed home by a flurry of friendly bullets. They limped into camp and collapsed on the ground, exhausted.

The sweat poured from Scott's forehead as a uniformed officer kicked his shoe. It had been night. Now it was daylight. Or was it the other way around? In his confusion, he covered his face, fearing a blow to the head.

"What are you doing here?" the voice asked, jerking him back to the present.

"I don't know," Scott said as he squinted up into the glaring sun at the officer's face. Frantically, he looked around. The park bench and his homemade backpack oriented him.

"We don't allow vagrants in our town. Move along."

"I'm not a vagrant, sir. I just lost all my stuff. Someone stole it. My family is coming to get me. I won't be a problem, I promise."

"Just move along."

"Yes, sir. As soon as they get here, sir, but I have the right to use a public park, don't I?"

"I guess, but you better be gone by dark."

"Yes, sir," he answered politely as the police officer turned and walked away.

Scott sat up, happy that the dream came but rarely these days. He had never figured out why, but usually the dream ended with a bullet in the head instead of how it had really happened—Gary helping him limp into camp to the cheers of their mates, who had given them up for dead.

And he was grateful that he had awakened gradually instead of attacking the policeman. In his earlier years, he had been so proud of his self-control, so cocksure of his mastery of emotion, until the night he awakened with both hands on Rachael's throat, so certain he had seen the dark enemy uniform, so sure the gun had been in his face, so convinced the dream had been reality. But after that night, he often questioned where reality began and dream faded. And since that night, he cherished his wife more than ever as she calmly understood and wiped the sweat from his body and soothed him back to sleep, never questioning, never fearing, and never bringing it up again. Somehow, she understood what those teenage boys had gone through in those years in those foreign countries, so proud to enlist in the buddy system and serve their country and so disillusioned with war and killing upon their return that it was seldom mentioned again.

Scott changed positions to shield himself from the late afternoon sun and then slept fitfully for a few more hours. Unable to sleep as the evening light dimmed and wishing to avoid another confrontation with the local gendarmes, he readied himself for the night.

*****

As the evening light faded in Idaho, Agent Renner reviewed his notes. The Allen kid had returned with an empty pickup, and the Piquard boy had finally finished the mowing. The boys went to afternoon football practice and returned. The girl had come out and run wind sprints for nearly thirty minutes. The mother had not left the property.

He summarized his notes. "No activity of note."

Chapter 35

Booking a Flight

A s the cool canyon breeze flowed from the mountains, Scott ambled to the park restroom. He scrubbed his sweat-soaked body with cold water and drank the velvety liquid until his stomach ached. Then he filled his water bottles. Settling the bottles in his pack, he turned reluctantly toward the sink; he was beginning to anticipate the pain. Clenching his jaw, he tore at his elbow until the wound opened again, the electric pain shooting up his arm. As the bleeding tapered, he irrigated it with the cool water. There was less drainage this time, but the heat and the redness were holding their own.

Returning to the park bench, Scott retrieved a dinner roll from his pocket. Caressing the top with grape jelly, he ate it slowly, enjoying each morsel and licking the packet clean. After four courses of bread and jelly, he enjoyed his vegetable entrée by opening a dozen packets of ketchup and sucking the little envelopes dry. With the sun well below the western horizon, Scott checked his flight map and started out once more. This night, however, he was not heading east.

Scott left the city to the south and traveled a mile before turning west. Shortly, he came to the road that was his first landmark. He crawled into the ditch on the east side of the county road and peered over the pavement to the west. The rising moon was at his back, and in the distance, he could see his target—a faint solitary silhouette in the moonlight.

On hands and knees across the road, through the opposite ditch, and into the sandy field beyond, Scott made his way silently. If anyone was looking this way with night vision goggles, he could only hope they would see an animal on all fours and make a bad assumption. Once in the field, he dropped to a belly crawl and moved slowly, feeling for cacti before each move. He had all night—no need to get hasty now. Several hours later, he was one hundred yards from the entrance to the Beatty airport, and here he moved even more deliberately. He sidled from yucca to sage, ever watchful for movement. No light shone from the lone airport building, and he had only seen one person moving around the tarmac at intervals.

By 4:00 a.m., he was nearly to the perimeter fence when he heard a vehicle approaching from town. It was a dark van, the type used by several of the military services. It pulled into the airport entrance and parked alongside an identical vehicle. Dome lights flashed against two silhouettes, and two voices could be heard faintly across the open ground. Soon a door opened and slammed, an engine started, and the second vehicle roared out of the gate. Scott was close enough now to see a lone silhouette against the moonglow.

Perfect. A double guard could have proven impossible, but could he pull this off? Could he overpower a young soldier? He knew he could not do it with sheer muscle power, but age brought its own advantages. Fifty feet of blacktop separated them. By keeping himself in line with the van and the lights of Beatty, the glare of the city lights would constrict pupils looking his way. Quietly, he closed the distance.

Thirty feet from the van, Scott peered into the darkness as he detected a scratching sound. The sound was immediately revealed when a cigarette lighter exploded to life in the dark night. Two quick puffs and the lighter died, leaving the glow of a cigarette at the front of the van as his new focal point.

Scott fairly rejoiced in the discovery. *A smoker.*

Night vision equipment was nearly useless if the user was smoking a cigarette. The intensity of the light obliterated all background signals, and when users stopped to smoke, they took the equipment off. Scott now had three minutes to move. On hands and knees, he crawled silently to the back of the van. He had nearly discarded the article he now retrieved from his pocket, but growing up on the edge of wilderness, he had learned that anything concrete was a commodity. Cupping a small piece of rope in his left palm along with the smooth, oblong object, Scott inched to his feet. Holding his small knife in his right hand, he rapidly shook his left hand.

*****

Private First Class Elton Benjamin Franklin was contemplating the moon this beautiful summer night as he took a drag on his cigarette. Like so many others, he started smoking in basic training but promised himself that he would quit as soon as he was out. His mother didn't know he smoked. She would thrash him if she knew.

Mrs. Franklin had raised her sons for better things than she had gotten from life, like the deadbeat husband who drank up what meager earnings he did make in the fish houses where only the poorest of the poor blacks worked. He died young from cirrhosis of the liver, leaving her to raise the three boys on what she could make from cleaning rooms at the local hotel. But she made the boys study hard every evening, made them use proper grammar as best she could, taught them manners and respect, and set their sights on a college education when they were very young. It was not a distant thought that they were to go to college; it was an expected part of their life, and the only way she could see to make that happen was through the GI Bill. Her boys were not going to clean fish in southern Louisiana the rest of their lives. Thus, on their eighteenth birthday, she had personally marched each of the boys into the recruiter. She made sure they signed the right forms and made sure they got the signing bonus and the good student bonus and whatever other bonus she could wheedle out of the poor soldier behind the desk. By the time she was done with the recruiter, he was ready to pay her just to leave.

PFC Franklin was looking up at the moon as he dropped his cigarette butt on the ground, mulling over a poem he was writing about the moon's eternal allure for man. He wrote every night and intended to have a respectable portfolio by the time he started college. He would not let his mother down, and he would continue to send her a part of every army paycheck he received, even though he now had a wife and little girl of his own to support. It was a promise he made himself one night when he was a freshman in high school and had awakened to a strange sound coming from the kitchen. Elton had slipped out of bed and tiptoed down the hallway. He could smell the potato-and-vegetable stew simmering on the back burner, a pot large enough to feed the four of them for several days. It was that night that he saw the food stamps on the corner of the table, and the sight had shocked him. Until that night, he did not know that his family needed them. He was always so proud that they were not on welfare like most of the neighborhood. He hadn't known that his mother was embarrassed to use the stamps but resorted to them rather than watch the boys go to bed hungry. Thus, she did her shopping late at night, after they were asleep, trudging home with sacks of food, glancing warily into the shadows. Nor would she buy the pricy, ready-to-eat items that her welfare friends bought. She purchased bulk commodities that stretched each dollar four times further.

Elton stared at the table where he heard his mother sob as she worried over the pile of bills on her "desk." She was making the monthly stacks of the ones she could pay and the ones she couldn't pay, then restacking them in piles for those who would get a five-dollar check this month and those who would get more. As he grew older, he came to realize that it was a painful monthly ritual, but no matter how hard times got, she would not give up. She would never ditch a bill, even if it meant paying five dollars a month for years. The Franklin boys had learned integrity not from a book or a lecture but by living with it every day of their lives.

PFC Franklin was just crushing out the spark from the end of the butt when he heard the noise. At first it was faint, and he couldn't be sure, but the second time it was unmistakable. It was just around the back of the van. "Rattlesnake!" he whispered to himself as he snapped on his night vision goggles and grabbed his rifle. He couldn't help it. It was a guy thing, as natural as water running downhill.

Night vision equipment was excellent for spotting, but it was not good for close work as peripheral vision was almost nonexistent. It was this fact that Scott Piquard counted on as he shook the rattles one last time. Franklin's head was down, expecting to see a snake. When Scott saw the first boot come into view, he flicked the piece of rope and the rattles a few feet in front of the advancing soldier, riveting his adversary's attention on the snake-like movement in front of him. Before the soldier had a chance to focus, Scott took one step and snap-kicked, planting his foot at the junction of the right calf and the top of the boot. He leaned his weight into the kick, knowing that he would only have one chance. He either won or lost tonight; there could be no draw. His weight carried forward as he heard the man scream and felt the fibula snap. The soldier crashed to his left, the rifle clattering in front of him, and he was frantically trying to figure out what was happening when he felt the knife at his throat.

"Don't move, or I'll finish the job," Scott said as he pressed the tip firmly against the jugular under Franklin's jaw.

Franklin could feel the sharpness, and the irony flashed through his mind that it would be a knife that would take his life after managing to avoid that fate in the slums all those years.

"I won't. I promise."

Scott took the man's service pistol from its holster and the Kershaw knife from its black Kydex sheath, then pocketed his own puny weapon.

"Who are you?" Franklin asked.

"Special ops," Scott lied, his game improving.

The lie had its desired effect on the soldier, his eyes growing larger, his stare riveted on Scott. "What do you want? Why did you attack me?"

"Because you would have taken one look at how I'm dressed and either shot me or held me for your superiors, neither of which scenarios is acceptable at this time. The president of the United States is under threat of assassination from within the military, and I am the only honest soldier who knows about it. You make number two, but I don't know if you are honest—yet."

Scott set the pistol and knife several feet away before walking behind Franklin and grabbing him under the arms. Pulling him against the tire of the van so he could sit upright, Scott bent over his leg and examined it briefly. "It's a clean break. It's not through the skin. It should heal fine if you live six weeks. But there's the real problem. Can I let you live and take the risk of black ops finding out that special ops is in on their little secret? Or do I just kill you now and eliminate my risk?"

"Oh Lord. Please don't kill me. I never did anything to you. I'm honest. I've always done my duty. Please! I don't want to die. I don't need to die."

"Maybe. Maybe not. But I only have a short time to make this decision. I need to be hundreds of miles away from here before dawn. I have to get word to President Brady, but certain people will kill me if they see me in Washington. They have already tried three times."

Scott bent and took Franklin's wallet from his pocket, flipping it open. In the front was a picture of a young lady holding an adorable baby girl, the child obviously the daughter of the gorgeous woman, both sharing the same light eyes contrasted against the same perfect chocolate skin.

"So is this your family?"

"Yeah. She's my only kid. Kind of an accident, but a beautiful accident. We were going to wait until we had a little more saved up, but I wouldn't trade her for any amount of money."

Scott finished looking through the wallet and threw it back onto Franklin's lap. "So what do I do with you?" he said quietly, almost to himself.

"Who are you anyway?" Franklin's pain had subsided somewhat, and he was more relaxed.

"My name is General Michael Green, personal attaché to the president and first lady, Rangers' Special Ops Unit out of Fort Benning."

"You don't talk like you're from Georgia."

"I'm not."

"Then where are you really from?"

"Here and there, everywhere and nowhere. Sometimes I don't even exist, like tonight." Scott turned his head and looked at the six aircraft on the tarmac, all the while keeping Franklin in his field of vision. "I need to requisition one of these aircraft. And my need is such that it must remain a secret for at least a day or two. Thus, I have three choices. I can take you with me and expect you to slow me down or try to kill me when you have an opening. That option is unacceptable to me.

"I can kill you and dump your body in a lake, making it look like you went AWOL and making your little girl grow up thinking her daddy was a coward. That option is unacceptable to you and something I don't want to live with.

"Or I can leave you here and make you promise not to tell anyone what happened and hope the plane is not missed for a day or two. By then, you're off to sick bay for a cast and R & R."

Franklin's eyes widened as he clutched his wallet to his chest, a motion not lost on the doctor—the doctor who could in no possible scenario make option number two come to pass but whose very life might hang on his ability to convince this boy otherwise.

"Man, you don't need to kill me. I won't say a word. I swear on my mother's honor."

"The president has been targeted. Every time I try to warn him, someone tries to kill me. I have been shot at, I have had an airplane shot out from under me, an innocent man is lying in a morgue in Kansas with a bullet meant for me, and an entire battalion is looking for me in the Sierra Nevada Mountains. I haven't had squat to eat in four days other than the rattlesnake whose tail I just compromised you with. I need to get a message to DC, and I don't have anyone I can trust. The people behind this are senior military. I overheard their plot to have Brady shot and then shoot the shooter—turn on their own man to cover their tracks. I've got more important things to do than to worry about a private first class who can't even guard the smallest damn airport in the country."

"Can I help?" Franklin asked. "I mean, is there any way to help the president and still follow orders?"

Scott had correctly sized up the young soldier. Impugning his ability hurt his pride even as he looked death in the face. This was exactly the opening Scott had been hoping for. If you forced a man, he'd rebel; if you let him volunteer, he'd strive to succeed.

"What can you do? You're lying there with a busted leg, disarmed by an old fart three times your age, and you have no authority or rank that can help me."

"I don't know, but how do I know if you are telling me the truth?"

Scott looked down at him and thought to himself, *Now he's getting defensive, using logic. Good.* Aloud he said, "Do you think I could make this up on the spur on the moment? And why? If I was the bad guy, you would already be dead, soldier."

The look on Franklin's face told Scott that he had scored an ace with that volley. "As your senior officer, I could order you to remain quiet, but you wouldn't. As soon as they started grilling you, you would realize that you know them, and you don't know me, so you would tell them everything. You would become a team player. Exactly as you should. Exactly what they are counting on."

"What if I just played dumb? What if I said I knew nothing? I fell and broke my leg, headed for town, and never saw a thing. I go to sick bay, and nobody knows differently."

"Won't work. The minute they find out that a plane has gone missing at the same time you just happen to acquire a broken leg, red flags are going to pop up all over the place. Where is your unit?"

"We're mobile. Two of us are assigned to Beatty for this recon job. My partner is at a motel, getting some sleep. We relieve each other every twelve hours."

"Where's your medical unit? Where are you going to get X-rays and a cast?"

"I don't know. I'll wait for orders, I guess."

"You could become my aide-de-camp."

"How?"

"I would write you an order to get X-rays and a cast in town and then take medical leave for two weeks to keep the leg elevated. You would immediately leave the area and be incognito for two weeks.

You would not use your cell phone. They can ping that. You would talk to no one from your unit except your replacement. You will have written orders from me to cover your ass. You cannot go to your home. They will be looking for you. In two weeks, this will all be over, one way or the other. Brady or I will be dead, or the perpetrators will be identified. I am the only one who knows what they look like, and I didn't get a very good look. But there is one voice I will recognize—if I can keep myself alive."

"I'll do what I can," Franklin said.

"How do I know I can trust you?"

"Because I said I would. I am a man of my word."

"Your mother teach you that?"

"Yes, sir. She says it doesn't matter how much money we have because when we go to our grave, the only thing we have left is our honor. Our integrity is the one thing nobody can take. We have to lose that all by ourselves."

"You have a smart mother."

Scott gathered up Franklin's things, then walked over, and handed him the rifle, knife, and pistol. The test of his life was on. He had spent the last thirty years studying people, and now he would find out if he could judge character or not. He backed away ten feet and sat on the ground powwow style.

"Now, let's see what your mother taught you. I am unarmed. There are thousands of soldiers out there looking for me. They have been told that I am the assassin. That explains why every time I turn around, I get shot at. You can be a hero and shoot me right now. You can claim the prize."

Scott could see the gears turning inside of the surprised soldier's head. He held the weapons and looked, somewhat stunned, at his prey. Franklin picked up the pistol and pointed it at Scott's chest. "What happens if I just wound you and turn you over to my commanding officer? I get a promotion, and they can figure it all out later. Mission accomplished."

"There are thousands of soldiers looking for me. Let them accomplish the mission. They won't miss you. But our team is tiny, and the president's life hinges on your actions. You make very little difference if I'm wrong. You make a huge difference if I'm right. Why would I go to all this trouble to contrive such a complicated lie? If I was lying, I would have just killed you and been halfway to Texas already. I need your help, and I don't want your death on my conscience."

Franklin's doubt was palpable. No longer under threat of death, he held all the cards. He was operating on logic now, not fear. Franklin didn't realize it, but Scott had already won. "And if I don't believe you?"

"Then when the flags are at half-mast next week, you can tell your wife and your mother all about how you were a hero and how you shot an unarmed man who trusted you after you swore on your mother's honor. And when your daughter is old enough to understand, you can take her to Arlington and show her Brady's grave and tell her how you got your promotion. Or you can get your leg fixed and go straight to Washington and deliver a message for me. I can't go there, or they will kill me. But if Brady doesn't get that message, we fail."

"How do I do that?"

"You go directly to the White House security office and tell them that you have a message for Todd Pederson. He is Mr. Brady's chief of staff. You will never get in to see the president, but if you are in full dress uniform, they should at least give Pederson the message. Don't take no for an answer. He can take it from there. And if they won't let you talk to him, ask for Sam Davies at the Secret Service office. He knows me, and he's close to Brady. He can deliver the message."

"How do I get to Washington?"

"Don't tell me you don't have a credit card?"

"Sure, I've got one."

"Then rent a car, get to Vegas, and take the first flight you can get. You don't have time to drive. The army will reimburse you later, and if they don't, I will repay you myself—if I'm still alive."

"What do I tell them here? Who broke my leg?"

"You did. You were climbing up on that shed to get a better look around, and your foot slipped." Scott pointed at the radio on his belt. "Throw me that radio."

Franklin tossed it to him. Scott walked over to the side of the small airport building and threw the radio hard against the ground, pieces flying in every direction. He walked back to Franklin. "You couldn't call for help because your radio shattered when you fell. If someone notices a plane went missing while you were gone, you have no knowledge of it. The time gap covers your tracks. Can I count on you?"

"Yes, sir, General Green."

"You give Pederson the message and make sure he repeats the exact same words to the president. Brady will understand the message."

"And what is the message?"

"It's simple. Only one line. You can't forget a one-liner, can you?"

"No, sir, I hope not."

"Say, 'The eagle's nest is empty, but there is still one alive in the Bat Cave.' Got it?"

"That's it?"

"Repeat it."

"The eagle's nest is empty, but there is still one alive in the Bat Cave."

"That's it. You just make sure Brady gets the message. He'll understand. We're both counting on you. Now get yourself to town. I'll tell your mother she raised you right."

Scott quickly wrote Franklin's new "orders" on a piece of the young man's writing paper, authorizing him to have the leg casted by a civilian doctor in Beatty and two weeks of sick leave. Then he saluted Franklin smartly and walked to the Maule M-4 parked at the end of the row of airplanes.

The door was locked, so he used his Swiss Army knife screwdriver blade to pry at the small luggage door, finally forcing it open. He unfastened the tie-downs and took off his pack, inched snakelike into the back of the aircraft, crawled over the seat, and unlocked the door. Crawling out again, he secured the luggage door and retrieved his pack. He checked the wing tanks, ensuring they were full, sumped them both, and then climbed into the pilot's seat. Reaching up under the dash, Scott located the wires directly behind the key-hole, pulled as hard as he could, and was rewarded with a handful of different-colored wires. He was not a mechanic, but he reasoned that if high-school dropouts could hot-wire a vehicle in fifteen seconds, he should be able to figure this one out for himself.

Holding the little flashlight in his teeth, Scott directed the beam onto the bundle of wires and started the process of trial and error. On the third try, he got a spark, and the engine groaned momentarily. A few more tries and he isolated the two magneto wires, the ground wire, and the wire to the starter motor. He twisted the first group together and held the starter wire to them, feeling the annoying tingle of a twenty-four-volt aircraft battery going up his arm as the engine cranked several times but did not fire.

"Prime it," he reprimanded himself, his usual start-up sequence obviously not the norm tonight. He primed six times and was rewarded with ignition on the third revolution. Quickly dropping the starter wire to disengage the grinding Bendix, Scott secured the wires with several tight twists. He could only pray they would stay together.

Dawn was freshening as Scott taxied to the runway in the little tail dragger, performed a run-up, spread out his maps, and plugged the GPS into the cigarette lighter. Preflight completed, he pushed in full throttle and took off to the south with just enough early morning light to enable him to navigate visually. He needed to stay low to avoid radar, so taking off in the dark had not been an option. He turned southeast, hoping that Private First Class Elton Benjamin Franklin would not let him down.

Franklin crawled to the driver's door of the van, hoisted himself up onto his good leg, and watched the little speck disappear toward Las Vegas. He loaded his gear and crawled inside. He looked at his watch: 4:25 a.m.

"I wonder what's in Texas."

Tuesday, 2:00 a.m. PDT, Granger, Idaho

Rachael Piquard curled in her recliner and looked through the window at the same coursing moon that had captured Private Franklin's imagination six hundred miles to the south. Sleep eluded her. She took another sip of Merlot. It was an expensive bottle she was keeping for a special occasion, and tonight was as special as they came. Despite their protestations, the teenagers finally went to bed around midnight, they, too, alive with renewed energy. She held her glass aloft, toasting the moon through her large picture window and toasting her husband somewhere out there. Alive!

The news Chad brought home from football practice that morning had been almost too much to contain, but they followed Scott's instructions exactly. When Rob Allen arrived with his father's old pickup, the boys quickly exchanged clothes and loaded the truck. Rachael made the boys sandwiches as Chad packed several items into a small backpack. While Chad made his run, she stood guard as Rob mowed the backyard, all the while hoping that the size difference between the boys would not be noticed from a distance. She was ready to run interference if anyone approached.

Twice she fixed Rob a large iced tea and carried it out to the deck, hollering "Chad!" loudly several times to get his attention over the drone of the mower, insuring that anyone listening heard the name as well. Rob played his role perfectly, Chad's cap drawn down over his sunglasses, face hidden. The entire mission was accomplished in time for afternoon practice. That evening, Rachael insisted on Rob's spending the night—as much to contain his excitement as to fix him a huge steak for his complicity.

Now, she sat alone in the darkness. A chill rippled through her body as she realized how close she had come to losing Scott. She threw a blanket over her legs and watched the moon course through the sky, reminiscing.

Rachael could still remember the exact day and time she had met Scott Piquard. It was winter, near the end of the semester, and she had been sitting in philosophy class, watching the snowfall through the window. She was listening to a brash young student arguing with the professor about a point of logic and the subsequent ramifications if that point was invalidated. She had never forgotten the moment.

Most undergraduates, herself included, were afraid to question their professors, let alone enter into a full-fledged argument with them. The entire class was stone quiet as student and teacher went to and fro. When the student made his final point, the teacher replied, "Well, that's not the way the experts see it."

He had turned back toward his desk to resume his lecture when the tall student had dropped the bomb. "I can't believe you just said that." The room went dead as the professor froze. "You just used the argument of authority to prove you were right. That's the oldest and worst argument there is. It is essentially circular and therefore of no value."

The professor spun around, smiling. "And can you give me an example of what you are talking about?"

The student stopped short, and Rachael thought he was defeated. But then he said, "Freud."

The professor grinned. "Explain."

"You tell me I am suffering from complex X. I counter that I am not. You say that Freud said it was so and therefore it is. That type of argument leaves no room for how screwed up Freud himself was. Because he was a famous pioneer, no one was willing to argue that he might have been wrong for fear of being wrong themselves or at least perceived as wrong by their colleagues. Claiming that something is right by citing an authority brings you back to the question. It doesn't prove you are right. It recalls Galileo and the Middle Ages and the control the church had on people's minds. They were trying so hard to improve how they climbed the ladder that they never questioned whether the ladder was against the right wall."

The professor smiled. "Excellent, Mr. Piquard. Most excellent."

That was the precise moment in the earth's revolution that Rachael had decided that she was going to meet this tall handsome firebrand. Beautiful as she was, she never lacked for attention, but somehow her suitors invariably turned out to be good-looking jocks or model types, their IQs trending marginally higher than their ages.

When the bell rang, Rachael fought her way past the throng of students pressing through the doors, but when she finally gained the hallway, he was nowhere to be seen. She always sat in the back of the classrooms, out of harm's way. He, she noticed, always sat up front. Later he would explain that he never wanted to miss a word; he was paying his own way through school, and he wanted to get every penny's worth. Just when she thought she had lost him, she saw a head above the crowd rounding the corner.

She was nearly out of breath, and her words were weak as she came up behind him. "That was gutsy," she said for lack of anything more original. She didn't know what else to say. She was afraid to say anything, but she was more afraid that if she didn't say something, the moment might not present itself again.

As Scott turned toward the voice, he missed a step as he saw the beautiful smile, the silky skin, the thin figure capped by the long brown hair cascading over her shoulders. The subtle scent of her perfume would carry with him for years.

"Pardon me?"

"I just thought that was a great interchange, although I thought it was a bit risky," she replied. Her words felt lame, and she looked down at the floor. Like most girls her age, she did not realize that her blush and her coquettish demeanor made her even more attractive to the unsuspecting male of the species.

"Why risky?" he retorted, suddenly defensive.

"What if you were wrong?"

"But I wasn't."

"But what if you were and didn't realize it?"

"How could you listen to the argument and think that?"

"Sorry. It's just the way it struck me. You don't have to argue with me too."

"Sorry. It's just that there are some things that… Hey, I was just going to grab a cup of coffee. How about you?"

"Yeah, me too," she lied. She needed to be at econ in ten minutes, but laissez-faire, Adam Smith, and Milton Friedman would be there for years. This one might not.

"Turns out he was," she said out loud as she smiled. "Thank God, he was."

Chapter 36

Flight Number 4

Tuesday, 6:00 a.m. PDT, Nevada airspace

C ompared to what Scott was accustomed to flying, the Maule M-4 handled like a precision toy. Each flick of his wrist translated to movement in the airframe. This was real flying, dodging power lines and radio towers, rising up fifty feet to clear a hill, or rocking the wings to slip between two trees.

Having traveled far enough to be invisible to Franklin, Scott was beyond the small cluster of six-thousand-footers southeast of Beatty. Climbing with the terrain, he applied left rudder and rolled into a forty-five-degree bank. Anyone watching from Beatty would have seen a small airplane leaving on a course for Texas. If Franklin did not remain on the team, they could scour Texas. He rolled out of his turn and headed north.

Compared to the roar of his twin, the small Continental engine purred quietly as he hugged the valley floor, descending to the Amargosa River bottom. Creech Air Force Base was well behind him. At this altitude, he doubted that their radar operators would have a hint of his existence. Had they known he was there, they could launch a drone that he would have no hope of shaking. Originally named Indian Springs Auxiliary Air Field after the nearby Nevada community, Creech Air Base houses the Unmanned Air Vehicle

Battle Lab, and the boys down there would love nothing more than to have a live exercise to replace their usual games. Scott was in no mood to be their toy today.

Cutting across the river, Scott steered up the Sarcobatus Flat toward Lida Junction thirty-five miles to the northwest. Crossing the tiny unpaved strip at Lida Junction, he climbed into the mountains to the north. Had he stayed to the low ground, he would have crossed the Tonopah military test range and its precision radar units. Across the ridge, he descended into the valley once more and slipped northeast, up the Big Smoky Valley. Less than three hours into his flight, he could discern the nine-thousand-foot peaks of Mount Tenabo just to the right of his course.

Now in more open desert, he was soon in sight of the four-lane ribbon that marked the Salt Lake-to-Reno corridor. Crossing I-80 in an isolated stretch between Battle Mountain and Elko, he angled well east to avoid Mountain Home Air Force Base. His choice of the Maule was perfect since it carried a generous fuel load and was STOL designed, short takeoff and landing, for mountain flying. Within another half hour, he could see the mountains of Idaho ahead. Skirting populated areas, Scott coaxed the airplane further north into the seclusion of the Sawtooth Wilderness and beyond. North he went until he was nearly where they were looking for him but exactly where they would never look for him. By midmorning, he had his objective in sight as he cleared the final pass, skimming the bottoms of the low-lying clouds that hovered in these high places. By some stroke of luck, he was nearing home.

Chapter 37

Update

Tuesday, 6:00 a.m. EDT, Homeland Security Command Center

Lieutenant Colonel Floyd Curtis was deep in thought when Wainright interrupted him. "Line 2, sir. It's Ernie Knoll from the FBI."

"Hello, Ernie. Did you get the pictures?" Curtis asked.

"Perfect match. I am dying to talk to the wife, but we have a top-level hold on any contact with her, and that came from Director Meyer himself. Surveillance only! So far, there has only been activity as usual at the Piquard home. Very few phone calls—none important. Piquard is the person we are chasing, all right. But, Floyd, I don't know if we are chasing the right person. I've been doing some more research. Got a minute?"

"I've got all week, Ernie," Curtis replied sardonically as he sat down and propped his feet on the desk. He grabbed his mug, took a sip, and added, "Actually, I've got all month. Shoot!"

"Well, this Piquard is an interesting guy. Supports everything in town—scouts, church, sports—you name it. Hard worker, high income, all that. But there is no question that he is, or was, a personal friend of Brady's. Their kids are friends, their wives are friends, and they spend time together periodically. So I think I know where this block on his file originated. And I also know why he had no hotel

262

reservation in DC. I found out through a friend at Secret Service that he is on a list at the White House as having checked in last week with a trace of explosives of some type on his baggage. He was clean otherwise, and they let him in on the order of the president, but his name was tagged with a 'level one' alert."

"Very interesting. *Very* interesting. Why didn't we know any of this sooner?"

"I'm guessing the same reason that his file was locked. Someone is slowing down our access to information, and whoever it is has the ear of the director. I'll give you three guesses, and the first two don't count."

"Brady, Brady, or Brady?"

"That's the way I read it."

"That explains why the president issued the 'no deadly force' order so early," Curtis added. "Our job is to assume the worst and sort it out later. So let's assume this guy has gone over the edge and had some explosives somewhere. Can he still use them? And what else do you know that I can pass along to my soldiers in the field. How do my men catch him? What are his weak points?"

"Good question, Floyd, but you aren't going to like the answer."

"Great!"

"Piquard's great-great-great-great-grandfather emigrated from France in the eighteen hundreds and moved west, trapping and hunting, finally settling in the mountains of Idaho. He married a young Indian girl and had a couple of kids. He never moved back to civilization, although his kids eventually did. But the families always stayed in or near the mountains and knew their way around them—which brings us to Dr. Scott Piquard.

"One thing I found interesting is that he can afford a lake cottage or a mountain cabin but doesn't do it. Instead, he heads up into the mountains with sixty pounds on his back, family in tow. They will live out there for a week or two with what they can carry on their backs."

"Christ, just what our guys will want to hear. This weekend gig is turning into a real pain in the ass. Our guys are running out of water, it's a hundred and fifteen in the shade, and the only things they have seen moving are a coyote and a lizard. We've already had to pull four men into sick bay from heat exhaustion. I'm guessing that this guy is dead by now if he's been out there for four days with no water."

"Floyd, how do you know he has no water? And how do you know he's even still in your containment perimeter? I think you had better entertain the possibility that he got up into those mountains west of there and knows how to hold out. If he got to elevations where he can find water or snow, he could hole up for weeks."

"You're probably right, Ernie. General Collins and I have already extended our western line, but that doesn't mean he can't sneak through. That country is rougher than hell, and we do not have enough men to cover that much ground."

"Floyd, I know you want to catch him very badly, but think about what I said earlier. Who is it that we really need to catch? Let's not lose sight of the overall picture just because we have one target. The more I learn about this guy, the more I think we may have the wrong person."

"Then why the 'level one'? Why was he in the secure tunnels? Why were the shots fired in the first place? Why in the hell is he running? And if he's innocent, why would he kill the guy in Kansas?"

"I don't know. But if he was in the White House and wanted to kill Brady, why bother going down to the tunnels? The dead man in Kansas bothers me the most, but too many pieces don't fit. And when that happens, I begin looking for a different puzzle." Knoll paused and waited for Curtis to respond, but there was total silence on the other end. "You still there, Floyd?"

"Yeah, I'm here," Curtis responded distantly. "Ernie, I've got to go finish something. I'll call you later. Thanks again. You're doing a great job. Bye."

"Wainright, where's Block?" Curtis hollered across the control room.

"He's still up in the library, sir."

"Get him on the line for me." The furrows in Curtis's brow threatened to leave permanent creases in his skin.

A few seconds later, Wainright handed him the phone. "Block is on, sir."

"Block, what have you got for me? Anything interesting?"

"Hello, Colonel. I'm afraid this is kind of slow going. The access sites for this information are spread all over the place, but I've been pulling them together. Boy, you wouldn't think so many soldiers die of accidental deaths, but they do. Copters crash—everybody knows that—but the number of auto accidents really staggered me."

"It's the age group. They just can't slow down. That's why insurance rates are so high until you hit twenty-five or more. So what do you know?"

"Let me print the last couple of pages, and I'll be right down, Colonel."

"Thanks, Eddie."

Several minutes ticked by as Curtis sat and stared at his map wall, the indistinct thoughts milling in his head troubling him even more since Ernie's call. He worked things over and over in his mind, but nothing seemed to fit. Finally Block came into the room with several small stacks of paper from the library printer.

"Well, sir, here's what I know so far, but I can't promise that this information is exhaustive. There have been seven service deaths in the continental United States in the past two weeks. Of those, one was a fall from some scaffolding in Oregon," he said as he made little stacks of his notes. "One was a drowning in California, one is pending as a suicide in Maryland, one was a motorcycle crash, and the rest were car accidents."

"Okay, how about the ones that have any geographic connections to our mystery airplane, our mystery man, or anything remotely related to his travels?"

"It's pretty thin, sir, but the suicide was in Maryland, not far from DC. And it just occurred this weekend, so I put that in 'related', over here," he said, pointing to one of the piles of paper. "His bio and service information are in there. Everyone thought he was this ultra-Christian religious type, but the guy went whacko and was burning incense in some kind of Muslim shrine when he blew his brains out. Investigation is still ongoing."

"Odd."

"The guy from Fort Lee—the one General Collins was telling you about—was an Apache pilot, Captain Ray Lang. He was driving his Mustang convertible home from the base when a gravel truck smacked him into the trees. He was dead at the scene. No one else was injured. Poor guy! He has one of the most dangerous jobs in the service but buys the farm like that because some bozo can't handle a truck on a curve. Sad."

"No doubt. Wife and kids?"

"Single."

"What else?"

"The rest of them are too far away to be connected," Block said, pointing to the larger stack, "except for one." He picked up the top sheaf and held it out for Curtis. "You said the other day that there were very few coincidences, just lack of knowledge as to how they are interconnected. Well, sir, it seemed like a coincidence that this guy on the motorcycle was stationed at Fort Riley, Kansas. So I made some calls and found out another 'coincidence.'" Now Block was smiling and paused for effect.

"Come on! Spit it out, Block."

"Lieutenant Shane Larrington was on one of the choppers that surrounded the airplane at Clay Center, Kansas."

"No shit!" Curtis's eyes widened.

Now Block's smile faded. "But that's where the story ends, sir. He never made it to the airport. He stepped in a hole and was picked up later by his squad leader. He had to be carried back to the chopper, upset at not being in on the action. His ordnance count was complete, and he was seen in sickbay with a sprain—nothing broken—and given a couple of days of R & R. Then he took off on his Roadster this weekend, and they found him piled up in the river valley—took a curve too fast. Broke his neck. Dead at the scene."

"Okay…? Anything else?" Curtis asked.

"Nothing I could see, sir, but I printed them all up for you. Maybe you will see some connections I didn't."

"Superb work, Block."

"Thank you, sir. But it was your idea."

"A man can't operate in a vacuum, Eddie. It's men like you who make my job easier. Now go get some sleep. You look like you've been up all night."

"Yes, sir. Excuse me, sir, but I'm not totally sure that I see the connections."

"There may be none. But we can't know unless we look."

Block saluted and left as Curtis turned to the stacks of papers, picking up the one near the center. He read over Lang's profile and then dialed the number for Fort Lee. It took a few minutes and two transfers before he heard the voice on the other end of the line.

"Goodale here. What can I do for you?"

"Hello, General Goodale, this is Lieutenant Colonel Floyd Curtis at the Homeland Security command center. If you have just a minute, I would like to ask you a question about Friday."

"What do you need to know, Colonel?"

"I was just curious as to whether Captain Ray Lang was airborne Friday morning."

"Yes, as a matter of fact, he was. We were running sims, and he was up north of here. Why do you ask?"

"Oh, nothing really. Just piecing together a memo my CO wanted done today. Are you sure Lang wasn't deployed to the west, sir?"

"Quite sure. You're interested in that missile launch, I'm sure. So am I. But as I reported, our ordnance inventoried perfectly."

"Right. Well, thank you anyway, General. By the way, will there be an investigation on Lang's death or an autopsy on the body?"

"There is always an investigation, and the autopsy is already done. Blood alcohol was zero-point-zero, and the urine screen was negative for common drugs, but the final drug analyses will take a few days. Looks like a typical bad-luck deal."

"Who was driving the truck?"

"Just a local hauler with a wife and three kids scraping out a living."

"Anything odd about him or the situation?"

"Nothing at all."

"And Lang—was he a good officer?"

"Very."

"Nothing peculiar there either?"

"Not a thing. He was a good man. Born-again Christian. Committed. It will be hard to replace him."

"Thank you so much for your time, General. We do appreciate it."

"Good day, Colonel."

Curtis hung up, wishing he had more particulars, but his curiosity about one thing at least was satisfied. Lang was an Apache pilot. Apaches could fire Sparrows. Lang had been flying the day the missile was fired. Now Lang was dead. Probably a coincidence, but he wouldn't sleep well until it was run to ground. He read the second report before dialing the next number.

"Fort Riley."

Curtis introduced himself and asked to speak to the major. There was a series of clicks and pauses while the call process somehow made its way through the post. Soon a deep male voice answered, "Major Syverson here. How may I help you?"

"Hello again, Major." Curtis made small talk for a minute, his tone absolving Syverson of any guilt for losing their prey the Friday before, and then he got to the point. "Major Syverson, what can you tell me about the Larrington chap who died this weekend?"

"Nothing out of the ordinary if that's what you mean. Very committed. Never had a discipline mark on his record. Strong church man. Perfect young officer."

"Major, I understand he was out on the choppers that surrounded our rogue pilot last Friday. Could you tell me more about that?"

Syverson told Curtis what he knew up to the time of the motorcycle crash. "Nothing out of the ordinary, I would say," he summed up.

"Just one more thing, Major. Where was Larrington deployed that day? Where was he from the hangar when he hurt his leg?"

"Due south. I debriefed the pilot who picked him up, and he said he had to swing south to get him because he couldn't walk."

"And what direction was the airplane parked?"

"What possible difference does that make?" Syverson asked, now a slightly perturbed tone insinuating itself into his question.

"Oh, probably none, but I have to prepare a memo for my CO. He's a stickler for detail, and I don't want my butt chewed, so I've learned to dot all the *i*'s and cross all the *t*'s. Sorry to be a pain."

"That's all right. Just hold on. I'll have to call Captain Norton. Don't hang up. I'm just putting you on hold." While Curtis held, he turned to Kesselhoff. "Hey, Flyboy, where's the door on a Piper Navajo?"

"Back left, sir."

"Thought so. Thanks."

Minutes later, Syverson was back on the line. "Curtis, Norton said the plane was facing west on the ramp. Can you tell me what this is about?"

"Probably nothing, Major. Thanks. I'll call you if I find anything else."

Curtis then quickly dialed the Clay Center Sheriff's office. "Good day, Sheriff, have you found the bullet that killed the airport worker yet?"

"No luck so far, sir. We looked over the entire tarmac but found nothing. Actually, we gave up on any hope of finding it."

"Sheriff, I need you to get all the metal detectors you can round up and begin searching every square inch of the field north of the airport, starting at the north edge of the tarmac from where the plane was parked by the gas pumps."

"Why is that, sir?" the sheriff asked.

"Just a hunch, Sheriff. Just a hunch." Floyd's eyes were closed as he visualized the layout at Clay Center, a chilling premonition unnerving him.

Chapter 38

New Orders

General Peter Wilson, smartly dressed in his Air Force class A uniform, entered the small Chinese restaurant and ordered noodles with smoked duck and snow peas. Neither the owner nor his wife spoke English; ordering was accomplished by pointing at the picture menu on the wall next to the cash register. He paid for his order and took a seat in the back of the little restaurant, facing the door.

Minutes later, Admiral Art Zemlica entered the restaurant, ordered, and took a seat at the adjacent table, facing the back of the room. In the cramped seating of the tiny restaurant, they were nearly face-to-face.

"We have launched Operation Icarus. I have ordered all elite teams to Idaho," Wilson said, just loud enough for Zemlica to hear. "Icarus must be stopped, or our entire operation, years of work and planning, could be ruined."

"What makes you think you will find him in Idaho? You can't find him anywhere else," Zemlica said, the exasperation in his voice obvious.

"New information."

"Pray tell."

"According to satellite pictures I received this morning, there is an airplane missing in Beatty, Nevada. There were six parked there at dark last night. There were five at this morning's pass."

"It wasn't guarded?" Zemlica asked incredulously.

"Yes, it was. The guard on duty broke his leg in a fall, and there was a gap, a couple of hours, between his leaving and his replacement showing up."

"Convenient."

"Too convenient."

"Where is this soldier now?"

"Not sure—probably right here. He told his replacement that he had a handwritten note from some general to get his leg fixed and then take two weeks medical. He rented a car in Beatty using a credit card. Next contact is a credit card transaction at the Las Vegas airport, purchasing a ticket to Reagan National. We are crosschecking but haven't found anything else yet. His name is on this napkin." He slid a napkin to the corner of his table. "See if your man can find any information on his whereabouts. Red says he has it covered, but I have Al working on it too," Wilson added, a hint of sarcasm finding its way into his tone.

"So you think Icarus stole an airplane and is heading toward Idaho? Anything on radar."

"Not a blip. This Icarus can fly, I'll give him that."

"This Icarus can also make some serious tracks. How did he get to Beatty? He didn't have time to build wings."

"No clue. Must have hopped a truck or something. He couldn't have run clear across Death Valley with no provisions. Oh! One more thing. A team of Service agents showed up at his house. Now we have both them and the Bureau to deal with. I've sent our best shots. If he shows himself within a thousand yards, he's dead."

"Yeah, just like in Kansas," Zemlica said, his stab of sarcasm less disguised. "This time let's shoot the right man, or we're all going to burn."

"There's more," Wilson said. "Our man on live sat is tracking a small plane dead-heading toward Granger, Idaho, from the Beatty area. What are the odds? It has to be him. I have a chopper with six men ready to pounce the minute he lands. There's no way he can get away now. This gig is over," he added with a smug grin.

"Have them plant five hundred grams of C-5 on the body. By the way, who else has this intel?" Zemlica asked as he finished his noodles.

"No one yet. I had our man log the photos in an incorrect folder, which should buy us twelve to twenty-four hours, but it's just a matter of time."

"We need to find this missing soldier from Beatty and see if he knows anything. I want to talk to him before he meets with an untimely accident."

"That makes two of us. Have your men crosscheck all bus, airline, and rental car reservations. He's black, five-ten, one-eighty, and has a cast on his right leg. He should be easy to spot. If he's found, extract the information, and then have him disappear. He won't be missed. He's AWOL anyway."

"For the Brotherhood!"

"For the Lord!"

Chapter 39

Provisions

T he outline of the pass leading into the final valley was barely discernible below the low-lying clouds, but there was ample room for the little tail dragger as Scott skimmed the flat undersurface of the clouds and kept the winding dirt road in sight off his left wing. The Maule floated across the Payette Wilderness for another fifteen minutes, the skies steadily bluing. Clearing the massive swell of land that formed the southern wall of this deep canyon, Scott could finally see the main course of the Salmon River glinting in the sun. The whitewater churned and boiled over the rocky obstructions that had tried for centuries to slow the raging river, always in vain.

The airplane glided effortlessly above the ribbon of blue-white water, its 425-mile course the longest free-flowing river within a single state in the Lower 48. Attempts to dam it, to "tame" it, thankfully were halted by foresighted men like Senator Frank Church, in whose memory a large wilderness area was named. The US Army Corps of Engineers had managed to kill most of the rivers in the country by the time Scott was grown, and one of the main reasons he returned here after medical school, despite more lucrative offers in larger cities, was the natural rawness of the wilderness that was too-fast disappearing. When distant colleagues asked why he would want to live

273

"out there," he no longer bothered to rationalize his choice. As he explained to Chad and Stephanie, "If they have to ask the question, they won't understand the answer."

The dam builders had lobbied aggressively, claiming that another hydroelectric plant would improve the quality of life in central Idaho. "It's a wasteland, unusable except by the animals," they claimed. They were willing to ruin one of the most pristine areas on the continent for a pittance of electrical power. Scott argued that preserving this wilderness was at least as important as protecting the oil in the Middle East so overweight people would not have to walk an extra block. Furthermore, he argued, saving the wilderness was actually free. "Do nothing, and it will take care of itself. No concrete to haul in, no campsites to build, no nature trails to pave so that tourists could drive $200,000 mobile homes in for the experience of roughing it." But as he grew older, he grew tired of the arguments. At a party one evening, a dim soul had accused him of being a member of "the forces working against progress and economic development." He had simply smiled and walked away. Time, like wilderness, is too precious to waste.

Now Scott could see the small grassy plateau high above the river, one of the only places in the area flat enough to land a small airplane and still be near a road. "I hope Chad made it without being followed." He throttled down and banked into a hard turn, approaching upslope. Dropping full flaps when his airspeed slowed to white line, he glided down in almost total silence to the welcome grass below. The plane floated upslope until the wheels gently kissed the grassy ridge. Scott added power to drive the plane to the top of the clearing. Swinging sharply sideways between two clumps of trees, he leaned the mixture, killing the engine. Climbing out and stretching, Scott felt the indescribable relief of being back home.

Unloading his meager belongings, he blocked the wheels with large rocks and collected several large branches and propped them against the aircraft, breaking up its silhouette. He grabbed his gear and headed for the steep shelf bordering the river a thousand feet below and carefully descended a narrow game trail leading to the valley floor.

His legs were stiff, and he slid and sidestepped down and down, nearly falling several times, the footing precarious in the loose dirt.

Reaching the river's edge, he started downstream, searching for his target. In less than a half mile, by a thick clump of Ponderosa Pine hugging the water's edge just beyond the dead-end road, he saw a glint of color. Chad had done his job perfectly. It was so well hidden that he nearly missed it. The flash of red told him his kayak had made it to the river one last time this season. The branches that held the camouflage netting in place were tossed aside, but he folded the netting and stuffed it behind the seat. He would discard no commodity, regardless of how flimsy or useless it might look. All morning, he had marveled at how easy it had been to distract Franklin using the rattles from the snake and how hard it might have been without that one tiny asset.

Scott removed the life jacket, helmet, spray skirt, and the two halves of the break-down paddle from the oval cockpit of the kayak. This exposed a small river bag that held riches worth more than their weight in gold. Scott greedily opened the bag and extracted a large round of elk salami and a small brick of cheddar, saving the deer jerky and candy bars for later.

But real joy touched his soul when he saw, tucked under the knee braces at the front edge of the cockpit, Chad's finishing touch. He bent in and retrieved the six-pack of Pepsi with a note that said, "We love you, Dad!"

For the first time in this ordeal, he could not hold back the tears. Scott cried in the realization of what he had, what so many people only dreamed of having. Many people never got the chance to experience the gift of a truly loving family. Even if he were meant to die out here, he could die happy in that knowledge.

The tears dried as he finished unpacking the small day bag with clean woolen socks, waterproof paddling jacket, fleece shirt and pants. Sitting on a boulder, he took a bite of the salami. Chateaubriand never tasted this good. Scott fairly gulped a bottle of soda as he ate half of the salami and cheese. With a full stomach, a short nap was tempting, but time was wasting. Despite having been on the go all night and half the day, despite the utter fatigue washing over him, he needed to hit the water. The clockwork had turned. In their youth, he and two friends had attempted to run a calm stretch of river by moonlight, the beauty and uniqueness of the experience too tempting, but a small set of rapids negotiated in darkness had nearly cost them their lives. The desert's dangers had posed their greatest threat in the sunlight, but if he did not respect it, this river would kill him as impersonally as the Death Valley sun.

The day was warm, and he decided to save the clean clothes for later. The ones he had on could certainly use a little water. Scott packed his gear behind the seat with the climbing equipment Chad had cached there, donned the helmet and spray skirt, and cinched the Velcro on the paddling gloves. Chad had thought of everything; Scott did not need blisters added to his collection of infirmities.

Putting both hands on the cockpit rim, he swung both feet down and into the narrow space then sealed the spray skirt around the rim. Pushing off with his hands, Scott grasped his paddle and took one power stroke. The swift current pulled him downriver to the west, toward home but not to home, as the boiling water drowned out the *whump*, *whump*, *whump* of chopper blades heading for the grassy ridge above.

The swiftly moving river afforded little time for reflection. Fickle and ever changing, she demanded too much attention. He paddled just enough to keep centered and out of the rocks, letting the river do the work. Here a red-tailed hawk soared on currents, searching for movement below. There a kingfisher hovered and dove and was rewarded with a small fish that would sustain him for a day. Food was life. On the cycle went.

A splash at the water's edge gave notice that Scott had intruded on a beaver's privacy. More often heard than seen, they sought the safety of the deep when travelers passed too close. The decrescendo laughing call of a canyon wren echoed from the shady side of the wall above him, the little brown-and-white bird preferring the cooler side in summer and the mud houses of the ubiquitous cliff swallows dotted the steep canyon walls. He might spot a golden eagle today, but the baldies would not return until late fall to take up their winter homes.

The current gained force as the canyon walls narrowed further, forcing the water tighter and deeper as they conspired to form

Ruby Rapids. With nowhere to go but through and down, the water increased its speed to obey the laws that governed all. A few gentle roller-coaster waves brought his boat to the entry of the rapids. Eyeing the inverted V of raised water that signaled the center of the water's flow, Scott paddled his kayak directly into the tongue. A lifting, surging sensation of exhilaration passed through him as the front of the boat became airborne and then fell into the trough below. White water churned around and over the prow as he sliced through the small haystack wave below. A wall of cold water slammed into his face as he crashed through the second large wave on the down surge. He rocked momentarily, but a quick stroke on the weak side corrected his tilt, centering him once again in the swirling current. He paddled hard, pulling the boat forward with powerful strokes. Much like a bicycle, a kayak maintains its upright position better with momentum. His arms felt strong despite his fatigue, and he pulled the boat through the small set of rapids quickly, exiting the class three stretch a hundred yards downstream into a wide area where the river once again returned to her placid, lulling, deceitful self. She would rock him gently for a spell and then try once again to separate him from his boat. And on the cycle went.

Beyond Ruby Rapids, several miles of calm, unobstructed river moved placidly with the lower flow of late summer. It was time to paddle. Meandering at four miles an hour, the river would carry a raft twenty or thirty miles in a long day, but a kayaker could double that with a steady stroke. Scott settled in, setting the balls of his feet firmly against the foot pedals and leaning into his strokes. Reminding himself that the weak-side hand was just as important as the drawing hand, he pulled with one arm while pushing the opposite blade through the air with the up hand. The kayak stroke was not like the constant draw, draw, draw of the canoeist's paddle. Finishing a proper stroke with the double-bladed paddle left his arms in perfect position for the next stroke.

In less than an hour, he covered the six miles to Riggins, and once again, the danger of detection lurked. He hugged river right as he followed her hard bend to the north. Here she accepted the contribution of the Little Salmon from the south and quickened her pace. As the town floated into view, he feared watchers on the banks, but all he saw were the dark, empty eyes of the abandoned lumber mill, looking upstream.

Several teenagers were gamboling in the class III rapids below town, their odd-shaped little play boats with the flat noses specifically designed to dive under the water for endos and other maneuvers. Kayaking had come a long way since his first round-bottomed, torpedo-shaped homebuilt of forty years ago. That old boat was just as content upside down as right side up, but it had definitely forced him to hone his technique.

He greeted the boaters with a quick "Yo!" as he negotiated the rapids and proceeded due north. In minutes, he was beyond the city. Houses were plentiful along this section of river, as were boaters. He kept his head down and paddled. Another mile brought him to Race Creek, and below this, a string of rapids that could be tricky at low water. He played it safe in the gentle water near the edge, paddled for a few miles, and soon he was turning west around Big Foot Island, the only island on the Salmon River permanent enough to hold an official USGS name.

At last, after five days of hell and high water, he espied his destination. Looking like just another mountain to the uninitiated, the familiar silhouette, just a few miles from his house, flooded his mind with memories of days long past. He pulled river right and came ashore, dragging his boat into the trees at the bottom of the cliffs and emptying its contents completely, then turning it upside down, and covering it with netting and branches. Walking back to the river, Scott kicked off his shoes and plunged into the water for a much-needed bath.

Scott treated himself to dry socks then repacked the small daypack Chad had left—a real pack with straps so luxuriously padded that the rope burns on his shoulders barely noticed the weight. Slipping into the climbing harness, he hung the gear sling under his right arm and the climbing rope over his head and under his left arm. Peering about to make sure there were no prying eyes, he started up the talus slope toward the sheer drop of the mountain's face, hoping he could make this climb solo. He recalled Kierkegaard. "It is not the road that is hard, but that hardship is the road."

Chapter 40

Messages

White House chief of staff Todd Pederson had struggled through the long day and was preparing for the evening briefing, so he was nonplussed when the visitor's entrance guard called and asked him to come down. "Some soldier insists that he has to talk to you or President Brady and no one else. He will not give us the message, and he refuses to leave. He says some general told him specifically to talk only to Brady or you and that it's a matter of life or death."

"I'm too busy for this crap. I'll send my aide, Patrick."

Patrick strode down the long hallway, the treasury building greeting him in gloomy shadows from the east side of the White House, the sun no longer brightening its ornate capstones. The visitor's entrance should have been closed, but the soldiers at the door had been reluctant to turn away one of their own. Patrick walked into the small security office nestled behind the metal detectors and the heavily armed soldiers that now protected every entrance to every major government building in the district.

"Who wanted to talk to Pederson?" he asked, but the answer was obvious. Three armed soldiers and one Secret Service agent were standing, facing a nervous young soldier seated across from them, the cast on his right leg protruding from his pant leg. The soldier snapped to attention when Patrick entered the room.

"Good evening," the Secret Service agent said. "I'm sorry to bother you, but this man will give me no information and insists that he will talk only to Pederson or the president himself. We ran a security check on him, and he is supposed to be at his post in the Nevada desert. His company sergeant has him listed as 'absent without leave' since early this morning. He claims to have an order from some general sending him here, but he won't even show me that." The agent turned and glared directly into the soldier's face. "I'm about ready to arrest him for being AWOL and have him thrown in jail until he starts cooperating."

"What's your story, son?" Patrick asked gently, his interest piqued by the words "Nevada desert."

"Good evening, sir. Are you Mr. Todd Pederson, White House chief of staff?"

"No. I am his chief aide and am here under his direct orders."

"May I see some identification, please?"

The ranking officer took a threatening step toward the brash young man, but Patrick was simultaneously amused and impressed with his composure. "Normally, the person being questioned does not ask for ID. It's usually the other way around," he said as he showed him his card.

"Just following orders, sir. The general said to make sure."

"And your name is…?"

"Private First Class Elton Benjamin Franklin," he said, standing alert and saluting formally.

"So what can I do for you?"

Franklin looked around at the others in the room. "Alone, please, sir. My orders explicitly said *alone*."

The captain of the guard stepped in front of Franklin. "I have had enough, soldier." But Patrick interrupted him.

"That's okay. Give us a minute," Patrick said and jerked his head toward the door. The men left the room and closed the door.

"Now, what is going on, Private? I am all ears, believe me."

"There is a plot on President Brady's life. This general from special ops overheard it, so they are trying to kill him too. He instructed me to come directly here to warn the president." Franklin reached into his inner pocket and extracted a sheet of his crumpled writing paper and handed it to Patrick. "He said they would never let me in to see the president, so he told me to ask for Mr. Pederson and he would take care of the rest."

Patrick read the scrawled orders, but the signature was illegible. "And you believe he was absolutely serious?"

"Serious enough to break my leg, sir."

"He did that?" Patrick asked, pointing at the cast.

"Yes, sir. I screwed up. He tricked me. It happened so fast I was on the ground before I even knew he was there. He could have killed me if he wanted to. He knows his stuff, that's for sure. I guess that's why he's special ops."

"Okay. Tell me the whole story."

When Franklin was finished, Patrick escorted him to his office, instructing a guard to wait outside. "Coffee?" he asked as he led Franklin to a comfortable chair.

"I would love some, sir. I've been traveling all day. The general said I was not to rest until I delivered the message."

Patrick poured him a cup from the warmer and then excused himself, leaving the door open so the guard could see inside. "Wait here until I get back. I'm late for a meeting. Help yourself to the coffee. I'll send some sandwiches down. Excellent work, Franklin," he said as he left. The guard, seconds earlier feeling far superior to the detainee, looked in at him and felt the tables turn on a word.

Patrick hurried late to the meeting and slipped a pile of papers under Brady's elbow. The meeting had started, and naval commander Matt Karber was briefing the room on the developments in Panama. "As you can see on this satellite photo, the Southern Coalition troops have halted due to our shelling, but they are not pulling back. They are playing chicken with us. A few strafing runs along this line, here," he said, shining a red streak back and forth across the Columbian border, "would show them we are not just here for target practice."

Several chuckles broke the tension in the room filled with military personnel tired of the waiting and itching for a fight. One voice from the back of the room was heard above the murmuring. "Let's blow the hell out of them. How many times do we get a bunch of drug lords all packed into one place like this?" A wave of approval spread through the room until Brady spoke.

"If you can find me one drug lord in that front line, I'll buy you a new Hummer. They are safe in their mountain homes, financing the sixteen-year-old kids who are carrying their 'war of liberation' to the enemies of the north. Don't fool yourselves, gentlemen. When was the last time you saw a general in the front lines?" The murmuring stopped, and the meeting ended quietly. The president was leaving for his last briefing when Patrick gently touched his arm. "Yes?"

"There is something I think you need to hear, sir."

"Okay...?" The impatience was obvious in Brady's voice.

"Not here, sir. Privately."

Brady turned his head quizzically at Patrick, but he knew his instincts and followed him to his office. As they entered the office, Private First Class Elton Benjamin Franklin was sipping his coffee. When Franklin saw who was entering the room, he jumped to attention so quickly that coffee sloshed onto the floor. He snapped off a salute and stared at the ceiling, too nervous to look his commander in chief in the eye.

Brady returned the salute with his own trademark greeting—half salute, half wave, half pointing into the future. "At ease."

Patrick took the cup from the soldier. "Tell him exactly what you told me."

Franklin repeated his story precisely, but his body refused to stand at ease. He remained at attention as he let the story unfold. When he was finished, Patrick asked the first question. "So why didn't you shoot him, wound him, capture, and hold him—do the job you were stationed there for?"

"I couldn't help but trust this man, you know? He seemed more concerned about me than about himself. He looked like death warmed over, and yet he examined my leg and made sure I was in a comfortable position, told me it was a clean break and would heal okay. He could have killed me a hundred times, sir. Instead, he handed me back all of my weapons and just sat there, waiting for me to make my decision. If he was just interested in escaping, I would have been dead in two seconds. If he wasn't telling the truth, then I'll never trust another person until the day I die."

Brady nodded. "Describe him one more time."

"Six-two or three, thin, short brown hair. But he looked pretty rough, sir. He hadn't shaved in days, and his clothes were filthy. He kinda smelled of BO. And he wasn't in uniform. He was just wearing a dark jogging suit and had this odd, homemade pack he had some things in. But he was in good shape—like a runner, you know?"

Brady stood there, looking at the soldier. It was either the absolute truth or the most perfect lie he had ever heard. "And what were those exact words again?"

"The eagle's nest is empty, but there is still one alive in the Bat Cave."

Brady shook his head as he looked long into the face of the young soldier, but he could see no deceit. "Wait here. I have one more meeting, and I need to think about what you just told me."

Brady had gone to the meeting and was returning to his office, contemplating the evening's turns, when a page met him in the hallway. "Mr. President, your son Jeremy is on your personal line, and he says it's very important."

President Gary Brady was not usually perturbed when his sons called him at work—in fact, it was usually a pleasant distraction—but as he walked to his telephone, he recalled his explicit instructions to his family. He did not want their calls to be traced, so they were to stay at Camp David and remain incommunicado. Therefore, it was with a little more than passing irritation that he picked up the phone. "Yes, Jeremy, what is it?"

"Hi, Dad. Sorry, but I had to call. It couldn't wait."

"What couldn't wait?"

"Chad Piquard has been trying to call but he didn't know where to call and when he finally got the operators, they just relayed him to somebody in public affairs who thought he was a weirdo and he didn't want to give them too much information because he didn't want anyone else to know what he was saying so he kept trying to call me and David and we weren't answering and he was going crazy and finally I turned my phone on and saw thirteen missed calls from Idaho and called him back and…"

"Jeremy! Slow down. Take a breath. Now, what did he want?"

"I'm supposed to give you a message, but it's kinda weird. He said Scott called him and said you would understand."

"Scott called?" The excitement in his voice pitched instantly. "When?"

"This morning, while he was at football practice—told him never to use the house phone, it would be bugged—so he called the school and since then Chad has been borrowing his friends' cell phones trying to get ahold of us. Scott said someone has been trying to kill him and he's been on the run and there's a dead guy in Kansas and a rocket took out his radios and he had to bail out and live in the desert with no water and snakes and run all night and almost starved to death…"

"Slow down, Jeremy. Slow down and take another breath."

"Chad said to tell you this right away. It couldn't wait."

"You did the right thing, Jeremy. What is the message?" he asked, the anticipation building exponentially.

"You are supposed to meet him at the bat cave. I don't know what that means, but he said to tell you those words exactly. He said you would know. Is everything all right, Dad?"

Brady stood relaxed and relieved. "Yes, Jeremy, everything is all right. Everything is very all right. Thank you so much." He hung up and punched the intercom.

"Patrick, bring that soldier in here at once."

Patrick turned to Franklin and said, "Come with me!"

Franklin followed without questioning, but when they arrived by the back entrance to the Oval Office, he was again speechless.

Brady reached into a desk drawer and retrieved a Christmas card. "Do you recognize anyone in this picture?" He thrust the card in front of the soldier's face.

"Yes, sir!" Franklin said without hesitation. "That's him! That's General Green."

"Patrick, mobilize *Air Force One*. I am going to Idaho after morning conference. Thank you very much, Corporal Franklin."

"Excuse me, sir, but it's Private Franklin," Patrick corrected.

"Son, I recognize talent when I see it, and if I say it's Corporal Franklin, then by God it's *Corporal* Franklin."

Chapter 41

The Bat Cave

E vening was waning as cold as the desert had been hot. Scott chose to climb in his wet clothes, knowing that the arduous ascent would work up a significant lather and also knowing that wet clothing dried faster on the body. He was saving his dry clothes for sleeping, but as the sun disappeared behind the western face, he began to have second thoughts. Evening temperatures dropped quickly in the northern mountain air, and he could feel the chill seep into his marrow despite his caloric burn. Ascending more slowly than anticipated, he realized that his climbing skills were atrophied with disuse, as were the muscles that in his earlier years would have propelled him up this face in half the time. He had scrambled over a half mile of fallen scree and game trails before reaching the face. Once on the face, he used his protection wisely, using enough to stay safe, yet holding some in reserve lest he'd run out short of the ledge. The gear sling was nearly empty—he was out of hexentric nuts and had only two cams and one piton left—but the shelf was not far above him now and, just a few feet from that, protection for the night.

Climbing solo was a different game; Scott did not have the luxury of a cleanup climber. One by one his eccentrically shaped metal wedges with their small cables were left behind, a tiny dotted record of his ascent. As small as they were, it was hard to believe that, wedged into cracks in the rocks, these few ounces of hardened alloy and braided cable could hold over a thousand pounds of weight. He was looking at a tiny crack in the dark igneous rock that provided the only spot to place a piece of protective hardware. And he needed protective hardware. His legs were starting their warning quiver, and that meant danger.

He looked at his remaining equipment. There it was—the perfect piece of pro for this spot. Decades ago, he would have used a piton here, but the popularity of climbing had encouraged companies to put out stronger and more innovative equipment that was softer on the environment. He unclipped the ZeroCam from the gear sling and wedged it tightly into the crack, a crack so small that his index finger would not fit inside. This was another thing Chad had taught him. Scott hadn't even heard of ZeroCams a few years ago. Attaching the carabiner and clipping in the rope, Scott stretched for the next foothold. A few more moves and he would have the ledge. He put his weight on the foothold and reached for an outcropping with his right hand, but just as his fingers touched it, his right foot became airborne.

Every climber dreads it, but climb long enough and it is inevitable. A piece of rock would sit passively in one place for sixty million years and would feel solid when tested, but when you trusted it, it would break off just to see if it could kill you to relieve its boredom. And basalt was worse than most.

His left hand had a good grip, but it was not strong enough to restrain the instant acceleration. Scott fell. Luckily, he was only two feet above his last protection, which would have meant a four-foot fall if someone was belaying him. Solo, however, he fell several feet before his slack pulled tight. To compound the jerking insult to his back, he scraped hard against the rock as he pendulummed across the face.

When will this be over? was all he could think as he regained the rock and scrambled to the left instead of the right, finding niches he had missed in the faltering light. Four quick moves and he was just below the ledge. Weathered and dull from exposure, left by a climber in years past, a piton was imbedded just below the ledge. Testing it, he found it solid, but he could not trust his life to it. Near it, he saw a second tiny crack, and here he drove in his last piton with firm blows of the tiny climber's hammer. Clipping carabiners into both pitons, he passed his rope through and scrambled up the last five feet of face. Level at last, he saw that he only had about two feet of ledge along the underside of the ancient overhang. A large breakaway had narrowed the ledge—one of the reasons schoolboys no longer frequented the area like they had fifty years ago. A fall here meant certain death, and few boys would trade that and the long trek from town for the safety of a virtual mountain climb in the comfort of their oversized couches. He looked at the ledge that had seemed large when he was a child.

How did we ever survive? However, back then, television was a novelty, the term *video game* had not been coined, and youngsters had to actually do things.

Inching along the ledge, he let his rope glide through the carabiners attached to both pitons. The cave would be just above him, directly above the overhang. The ledge was precarious, and nothing looked the same. The sage had been right about going home.

Scott crouched under the last of the overhang as he took a few steps to the right. A simple move up and to his left, and he was at the mouth of the cave. He crawled inside and sat, resting his exhausted legs as he stripped off his gear. The temptation to sleep was overwhelming, but he could not give in quite yet. There were still twenty minutes of precious twilight. Shed of his extraneous weight, Scott left the cave and made his way along the trail to the right, the safer access route from above. This led to the gully above where vegetation became more plentiful, and as he walked, he gathered deadfall until his arms could carry no more. Depositing his load at the cave, he repeated the cycle four times before full darkness.

Taking out his pocket flashlight, he shined it around the cave. It seemed so tiny now, so huge then. Half a dozen bats hung by their locking talons at the back of the cave. When they were kids, they had not known that bats served as a huge reservoir for the rabies virus.

They had somehow lived through their ignorance, but rabid or not, tonight he would have to coexist with his little friends. Soon they would leave for their night of hunting. He would not bother them, and they would not bother him.

Changing into the fleece clothing, Scott felt the warm comfort of the soft material, but August nights in the mountains get very cool, and he wanted fire.

The fire-building secret that Scott had learned over the years—the thing most novices did not have the patience for—was to prepare an adequate pile of tiny toothpick and matchstick-size twigs, and to light the fire only after an eight- to ten-inch nest of these was built, adding finger-size kindling twigs above these in an A-frame arrangement. Novices took a small handful of too-large twigs and placed wrist-sized pieces of firewood on these, expecting them to catch. Each piece he used was devoid of bark, dry when touched against his lips, and snapped crisply instead of bending.

Holding the tiny flashlight in his teeth, Scott built his nest of kindling around his tinder, a large piece of flight map wadded tightly in the center of the nest, leaving an opening just large enough to fit his lighter inside. Flicking his lighter once, the flame jumped into the paper, consuming its fuel and spreading the heat quickly into the delicate pieces of wood above. In seconds, the fire was crackling, the heat and smoke shooing the bats out for their nightly food gathering.

Sitting back, he took a few minutes to relax, enjoying the heat and the mesmerizing light. This cave, demystified in grade school by the two adventurers, had become a familiar haunt to them. But as maturity exacted its demands, their magical bat cave, named for its nocturnal inhabitants as well as the Dark Knight of their comic books, lost its allure, neglected and forgotten like Puff.

The end of the natural concavity changed texture and diameter noticeably where some forgotten miner had deepened the recess in hopes of finding his millions. This stretch of river had seen brisk activity after the discovery of gold in 1860 and another surge during the Great Depression of the 1930s, but the small yields of very fine "flour gold" in this region did not support continued mining.

Scott fed the fire steadily, leaning progressively larger pieces of wood against the burning teepee as the bed of coals glowed red in the darkness. He cut a thin slice of salami and carefully laid it across a forked branch. Then he held it at the edge of the fire, letting the flames lick at the meat, slowly browning one side and then the other. When it was sizzling, he opened a bottle of Pepsi and sat back to enjoy his first hot meal in days.

For a second course, he added a thin piece of cheese, holding it above the lambent flames until the cheese threatened to run. The tastes took him back to a simpler time, a time when Spam fried in the rusty skillet with the broken handle had been their explorer's staple, a meal that could be appreciated only by the very hungry or the very poor. The one thing that could have improved on this repast would have been a piece of bread and a teaspoon of mustard, but unabashed luxury would have to wait.

Full darkness was an hour gone, and the full stomach was making him sleepy. Scott stoked the fire, but ever paranoid, ever prepared, he slipped back into his climbing harness and clipped in the rope. Curling into a semicircle around the fire, the white-hot coals massaging his face, Scott drifted into a dreamless sleep.

Chapter 42

An Unplanned Trip

"Sir, this is not a good idea. Please, Mr. President, let me send a team of men to bring him back here. I *cannot* allow this." Greg Stroud was beside himself, standing in what he recognized as a classic lose-lose position. If he let the president go and something happened, Stroud's career was over, his legacy draped in crepe; if he confronted the president any more forcefully, his career might also be over.

"I am going to Idaho, Greg. Have *Marine One* on the pad at dawn and have *Air Force One* ready. We will hold our scheduled briefings, conference with the chiefs, talk to the senators, and then we will leave. Tell *no one* where we are going—in fact, tell no one we are even going. Security is that much easier. No press. No releases. Double my contingent if you need to, but I am going. No one else can find the place."

Todd Pederson, Secret Service chief Greg Stroud, Navy commander Matt Karber, Air Force general Curt Nearman, and Marine general Anthony Shaffer were standing in the room with the president. Elton Benjamin Franklin, unsure of his rank at the present time, was standing dumbfounded at the back of the room.

291

"Where in Idaho are you going, Mr. President?" asked Curt Nearman.

"I will tell the pilot that in the morning."

"I'm sorry, but that won't work. We have to file flight plans and plan fuel burn, and *Air Force One* can't just land any place. There needs to be enough runway for our safety margin, and people need to meet you there. Please, sir."

"Lewiston, Boise, or Mountain Home Air Base would serve my needs, in that order."

"Then I would have to insist on Mountain Home for security reasons," Stroud said, and Nearman concurred immediately.

"Who is this person you need to see?" Nearman asked, his misgivings obvious.

"Someone I must talk to, in person and alone," Brady said, glancing at Franklin.

"That is out of the question," Karber said, too loudly. "Your life is in danger, and you are venturing out into the middle of nowhere to meet with who knows what kind of person. What if he's the one that wants to kill you?"

"The man I am going to see is the last person on this planet I would fear."

"How can you know? We don't know whom to trust right now."

"Because the man I am going to see is the man you saw on those video tapes, and he is the best friend—probably the only *true* friend—I have."

Karber's look carried the shock of revelation. "You have known this for days and have withheld that information? You have purposely slowed our investigation."

"This man would take a bullet for me, so drop the subject!" Brady ordered.

"Forgive my incredulity, sir, but how could you possibly know that?"

Brady walked up to Karber until they were practically nose to nose, his face red and the vein in his forehead starting to bulge. He locked eyes and said, "Because he already has!"

Chapter 43

Maneuvers

T he flower-shaped mauve phone in the back office rang once and went silent. Exactly sixty seconds later, it rang again. It was answered on the first ring.

"Brian's Flowers. How may we help you today?"

"Do you have any gold and pink chrysanthemums?"

"No, sir. We only deal in purple chrysanthemums during this phase of the moon."

"What phase is that?"

"What phase do you want it to be?"

"Blue moon phase."

"How can I help you?"

"We need every available man moved to Idaho. Immediately! Saturate Granger and the surrounding area. Dr. Scott Piquard. Shoot on sight!"

"Understood. Do you want me to move the teams in the desert?"

"Everyone! And make sure Booker is ready to grab the daughter in case we need leverage."

"How did he get through? There were over five thousand men out there."

"How do I know? He's like a damn ghost. I just know that if he is not dead in the next twenty-four hours, all of our work is wasted."

"Do you want me to destroy the files?"

"Not yet, but be prepared. Have your backup disks close, and have the acid bath ready. Don't try to reformat. The ghost images can be rejuvenated too easily."

"Yes, yes, I know that. Actually, I've been thinking a little fire would be convenient as well. I just need to know if and when I need to get out of the flower business. I have been converting assets to gold coin and can move quickly."

"I envy you. I am not that invisible."

"Win big, lose big."

"Are the properties in Buenos Aires clear?"

"Paid in full."

"Has funding been a problem?"

"Hardly. Task Force 131 is so well funded it was easy to divert a few million to our little band. As long as we are fighting terrorists, no one is really looking."

"I'll be calling."

"Don't leave me hanging. If I don't hear from you every twelve hours, I am closing shop."

"Understood."

"For the Brigade."

"For the Brotherhood."

"For the Lord," both voices said in unison as the line went dead.

Chapter 44

Ballistics

Lieutenant Colonel Floyd Curtis had not slept well, and the early morning call from Ernie Knoll found him partially awake, restless.

"Hello," he said groggily.

"Floyd, Ernie Knoll here. Sorry to wake you, but what's going on in Idaho?"

"I got a little ditty during the night, but I didn't want to wake you up. Why?"

"A friend at Andrews told me that *Air Force One* is being readied for a flight to Mountain Home Air Base."

"Why Mountain Home? That's quite a distance from Granger," Curtis said.

"Security for one thing, I would guess, and the strip at Granger is too small for *Air Force One*."

"Did you get more backup in Granger?"

"We've got agents on every damn street corner and still nothing. What did you get?"

"There is a little airport at Beatty, Nevada, which is a fair poke from Mount Whitney, believe me. Monday night's sat pics showed six aircraft parked there. Tuesday night's showed five."

295

"Do you think it's related?" Knoll asked.

"Not only do we have to assume it is, there is another tidbit. The army private who was guarding the Beatty airport was using a shed for spotting. He fell off and broke his leg. The place was unguarded for a few hours."

The only response on Knoll's end of the line was a long decrescendo whistle as he digested the implications.

"And to top it all off, this PFC is missing, last seen at a doctor's office in Beatty, getting a cast on his leg, then dropping out of sight. His sergeant has no idea where he is. His relief man talked to him briefly. He said he had a note from some general, giving him two weeks' sick leave. No one knows of any general officer in that vicinity. What are the odds?"

"A million to one?" Ernie said, more statement than question.

"Less," Curtis said emphatically.

"What the hell is going on, Floyd? Is there something you're not telling me, or are you just as confused as I am?"

"More so, I think. There is more to this Piquard than meets the eye. Do you suppose he is still active, only deep?"

"Now, that is an interesting thought. Very interesting."

"I've been mulling it over ever since you said his file was locked from up top. Think it over, Ernie. See if it changes your approach. Call me back in a few hours."

"Okay. Talk to you later."

Curtis was still on his cot, but he knew there was no way he was getting back to sleep now. He showered and was making his way to the coffeepot when a call was patched through to him. "This is the Clay Center Sheriff's Office," a pleasant female voice said. "The sheriff would like to talk to you."

"Good morning, Sheriff. Curtis here. You have something for me?"

"Yes, I do, son. One of my men found a bullet straight north of the tarmac. Its energy was spent, and it had barely penetrated the sod."

"Ballistics?"

"It's a full-metal jacket, just like the coroner predicted. But it's got some strange markings on it. Analysis will take another day or two, but under the microscope, it's scored with what looks like aluminum streaks."

"Interesting," Curtis said as he looked at his maps.

"How did you know where to have us look, Colonel?"

"Lucky guess, Sheriff. Thank you, sir. Thank you very much. Look, I'll talk to you later, but right now I have another call."

Curtis clicked a button for an open line and dialed Ernie Knoll again.

"Knoll here."

"Piquard did not fire that shot! I'll bet my career on it."

"Pray tell."

Curtis quickly reviewed the new findings for him and then asked, "Ernie, can I get you to do me a favor?"

"What do you need?"

"Can you drive out to the Fort Lee area and interview that gravel-truck driver who collided with the Apache pilot? That's bothering me to no end. I think we're missing something up there."

"Sure. The usual? Check his bank accounts for influxes of cash, anything out of the ordinary, land transfers, cash purchases. Anything else?"

"I don't know, Ernie. Something's wrong, but I just don't know what."

Chapter 45

Hot Tea

D awn came late inside a cave inside a mountain inside a canyon, but despite his anticipation of sleeping late, Scott's throbbing hip bones, sore shoulders, and aching muscles would not allow it. Squirming in his half sleep, Scott could not find a comfortable position, and as consciousness triumphed, he surrendered the battle and dragged himself to the mouth of the cave. The dawn was unfolding as it only could in the northern mountains, lush with green and the colors of life. Not that the infinite reds and browns of the southern desert lacked their unique beauty, but for year-round vibrancy, he loved the northern Rockies.

Scott stretched and limbered as he carried two loads of deadfall to the fire and stoked it, the coals from the night still glowing red under the insulating coat of ashes. When it was kindling, he placed several small stones on a flat rock inside the edge of the flames. Climbing the path once again, he gathered several bearberry leaves, ignoring the plant's bland red fruit. By the time he returned, the tiny stones were scalding hot. A bottle of water had warmed near the fire all night, and into this he crumbled several of the yellow-edged leaves. Carefully picking up his boiling stones with a pair of homemade chopsticks and blowing off the ashes, he dropped the stones into the water, each sizzling its way quickly to the bottom. Wrapping the bottle in his jacket, he let it steep for several minutes. Before long, he had a pint of hot tea with which to enjoy the sunrise.

Bearberry, or kinnikinnick, was often used as a tobacco substitute by the Indians and the early mountain men, but Scott preferred its tea, which can settle an upset stomach or provide warm relief from the cold. He sat and dangled his legs over the lip of the cave, looking across the canyon to the southwest as one of the wonders of the world peered back at him. Most of the people who came here left without knowing that they had just visited a Pacific Island chain.

Two hundred million years ago, the Seven Devils Mountains were part of a chain of volcanic islands named the Wallowa Terrane originating in the Pacific Ocean near the modern-day Aleutian Islands. Slipping and sliding with its tectonic plate over the molten lava below, this chain came crashing into North America at the astonishing speed of several centimeters per year. The collision forced many of the rocks into an almost vertical position along the suture line, forcing the rivers into their northward courses here. These ancient rocks, much older than the infant volcanic rocks formed only fifteen million years ago, contained the same mollusk shells in limestone beds that the Pacific chains house. The younger contrasting lava flows formed columns that could be seen from the river, demarcating the old from the new.

Sipping his tea, Scott mused how transient he or any human was compared to the big picture of this earth, this universe. The speed with which a single life came and went was like a fraction of a blink in geological time, yet men lived their entire lives thinking that the earth belonged to them. Perhaps ignorance would be more blissful. He thought of the higher-paying positions he had turned down, the offers to go to Washington and rub shoulders with the power brokers of this country, and he knew—looking out on this vast, beautiful, awful wilderness—that he had made the right choice. In DC, he would have been just one in a million clambering for the spotlight. But here, in the Idaho backcountry, he had made a difference in many lives. And when his thoughts turned to Rachael, his heart ached with a throbbing he could not bear much longer. When would he see her? So close to home but unable to go home.

And what if Gary did not come? What if neither message reached him? Should Scott go home? Should Scott go to a newspaper office? Would they guard that like they had in DC? Maybe the best alternative was to go to a radio station. They did not have the lag time of a newspaper, and a radio station in an anonymous town would not be watched. He would hole up and regain his strength until his food ran out in two or three days. If no contact was made by then, he would walk out to Highway 95, hitch a ride south to Riggins or McCall, and let the final hand be played. As he turned back to the fire, the ironic thought crossed his mind that if time passed any slower, the Seven Devils Mountains would crash into his doorstep.

Chapter 46

Air Force One West

Morning briefings often moved slowly, but this day, they seemed interminable. The people in the room could sense the president's impatience, but when *Marine One* could be heard whumping down on the White House lawn, everyone knew they must pick up their pace. When Brady whirled his pen in vertical circles like a turning wheel, faster and faster, they knew it was time to speed up or risk being cut off in midsentence, and rarely had the pen been this frantic.

"So that about does it, I would say," Brady intoned as the last briefing ended. "The strafing runs in Panama have succeeded, the northern advance has halted, and the panic in the south is soothed for a day or two. Our troops on the border are well poised to stop a panic run on the border from Texas to the Pacific. We have enough men down there to start a small country, and the dollar is up another tick.

"Now, about tomorrow's agenda. I am needed out west for an emergency meeting. We can teleconference if I am not back in time, but basically everything should be static, barring any major changes on the border."

The room was abuzz, but he shook off all questions about his sudden departure. It was a technique that had worked for him from the start of his administration. Most president's felt the need to answer why they weren't answering, but from day one, Brady simply shook his head left then right—like a pitcher shaking off a pitch—and went on to the next question. Like well-disciplined children, his cabinet and his press corps knew it did no good to pursue a subject after that.

Greg Stroud followed him up the stairs. "I am the only person Scott Piquard will trust," he told Stroud, not for the first time. "I used my best friend for bait, and it yielded no prey. Now I must go bring him in."

"And if something happens?"

"Do whatever you would have done if I had been killed last Friday."

Brady grabbed his overnight bag as Stroud tried to wrestle it away. Stroud felt that a head of state should not carry his own bag; Brady felt that no man was above a little hard work. The Washington crowd had wrestled with the concept of a poor country boy still acting like a country boy, the very thing that had won him a first term and a landslide second. Unknown to him, it was exactly this inability to rise to nobility that had earned him the enmity of those who would have an empire.

Brady won the wrestling match and hustled down the stairs. Sam Davies stood next to the door, sunglasses on, freshly shaven, and impeccably dressed in a new suit. "I thought you were due for some time off, Sam? You have been here almost continuously since last Thursday."

"So have you, Mr. President."

"Well, that's my job."

"And this is mine, sir. Last Friday, you asked me to see this through, and I intend to do just that."

Brady put his hand on Sam's shoulder and smiled. "Thanks, Sam."

The ride to Andrews went quickly, and as they entered the base control zone, they could see the silhouette of *Air Force One*, tail number 28000 (Air Force designation VC-25A), waiting on the tarmac below the control tower. Just south of the tower sat an identical Boeing 747, tail number 29000, fully equipped in case of equipment malfunction on the primary. Nearby stood the 757-200, designated N80001, *Air Force Two*, along with its identical backup, for the vice president's use.

Brady greeted several of the people whose life revolved around making sure that the Flying White House was ready to go twenty-four hours a day. Although most trips were planned, these people were tasked with readiness for the unthinkable. In time of war, particularly nuclear war, the president might need to go airborne and move halfway around the globe. These aircraft were the most sophisticated in the world, with more electronic gadgetry packed inside the 231 feet and 10 inches of space than some third world countries owned. With the president on board, they were capable of running the country from the air.

Brady hustled up the steps and greeted the pilot, who would fly left seat today. "Put some juice to her, Colonel. I've got miles to go and promises to keep."

Capable of 525 knots or 603 miles per hour rated speed, the airplane could actually reach a cruise speed of at least 630 miles per hour. The colonel, however, kept it at a prudent 500 knots. To attain the privilege of flying this craft, a pilot needed a minimum of 2,000 hours and must have a flawless record. With a perfect record to date, *Air Force One* was considered the safest aircraft in the world.

Within its 4,000 square feet of floor space, *Air Force One* contained 87 telephone lines, 28 of which were encrypted. One of these was used to place a promised call to the Pakistani ambassador. The conversation went as Brady had expected, and he was sincere when he said that he was fighting for more aid but that Congress was strapped. It was Brady's reputation for honesty that calmed the ambassador's worries and allowed them to part on a positive note.

By the time he hung up, they were over Ohio, and by the time he finished his list of calls, he felt the slowing of the craft and the downward angle signaling their descent into Mountain Home Air Force Base. After landing and paying his respects to the base commander, Brady was anxious to keep moving. His detail was taking ground transportation from here, a fact that had not made the president very happy, but he acquiesced when he realized that the time change added three hours to his day. A nap would serve him well.

His detail chief had been extremely unhappy about not being able to sweep the area prior to their arrival, and it was only now that Brady told them where they were going. More tired than he realized, Brady slept soundly for nearly two hours, and the ride north seemed short. Dusk was settling on the mountain roads, and they were still a few miles from Granger when Brady directed the driver onto a dirt road to the west. Murmurs of protestation arose immediately, but a stern look halted all discussion. The armored limousine turned onto the dirt road leading toward the rim of the Salmon River Canyon.

Sam Davies looked quizzically at Brady.

"Don't worry, Sam. This is probably the safest place in the country for me right now." Brady looked out into the waning light, memories of days long past flooding his stream of consciousness, days when he and Scott would pack eight peanut butter sandwiches and seal them in plastic wrap, fill their dented Army-surplus canteens with water, throw in a couple of candy bars if they were rich that week, and head out on their bikes for an overnighter. Usually it was just the two of them, most of the other kids unwilling to make the several-mile trip or unwilling to miss that many meals; just as often, they were unable to wrest permission from their parents to go out into the mountains, alone and isolated. Those were days when boys went out on their own and were actually on their own, days when a boy became a man not by having another birthday but by fending for himself.

Brady pointed up to the west. "See that peak of the mountain where it looks like the Leaning Tower of Pisa, Sam? That's where we discovered the eagle's nest when we were kids. We watched year after year as those majestic birds used the huge nest in the gnarled tree that sat on the cornice of the nearly impassable ledge. We never got too close so we didn't frighten them away, but as the years went by, the eagles came less often. DDT was being sprayed on crops, washed into rivers, and taken up by fish, the main diet of bald eagles. It softened their shells and killed their offspring before they could hatch. Scott's grandfather warned people about pollution and overpopulation long before others had the words in their lexicon, but people just made fun of 'Mountain Man Piquard.' But how right he had been. Two hundred years ago, there were 75,000 nesting pairs in the Lower 48, but by 1965, only about 450 pairs could be found, which finally led to the Endangered Species Act of 1973."

Brady's mind floated, and the scenery changed. It was fall, and they were stalking a grouse with their pellet guns. He made a perfect stalk and a perfect shot, dropping the bird with a single shot to the head. They cleaned it and took it back to the cave. Adding nothing fancier than potatoes, carrots, salt and pepper, and a few ground petals of sage and chickweed, they brewed a simple stew. For young Gary Brady, it was a formative moment. Nothing augmented a meal like a daylong appetite, but the fact that he killed the game and made the meal from scratch satisfied his pride more than his stomach. It was one of those bell-weather days in his formative years, a day when he realized that he did not need others to do things for him, a day when he realized that no matter how bad things got, he could survive. And from that day on, he had been a different person. Independence did that.

The line of vehicles proceeded along the dusty, winding road until it became nothing more than a trail, and they could drive no further as the feeder canyon dropped precipitously toward the rim of the Salmon River Canyon, nothing visible but a steep foot trail. Brady said that he would walk the rest of the way alone, at which point Davies began to protest.

"Save it, Sam. I've been through this with Stroud. You can escort me partway, but if my friend is down there, I am going to talk to him alone."

"Understood," Davies answered. "After you, Mr. President."

The ground sloped rapidly as they descended toward the canyon's edge. Brady was sure-footed on the narrowing trail, and in minutes, they came to a long, narrow trail that wound down steeply and seemed to drop into the thin night air. Brady turned to him and said, "I'll take it from here, Sam. Come only if I call you. There is a little ledge to the right, and it leads to a cave. If he's not there, I'll be back in ten minutes."

"I don't like it, sir."

"I only need a few minutes to talk with him, and then I'll bring him out with me."

"Yes, sir, but I still don't like it." Sam posted himself at the top of the footpath and watched as Brady easily negotiated the trail. He would have felt better if bright sun was illuminating the path for his boss.

Gary Brady was alone perhaps once a month since taking office. The ever-present guards and politicos and phone-carrying aids had become such a part of his life that he barely noticed them anymore. But now, standing on the precipice of the second deepest canyon on the continent—second only to the Snake River Canyon and a fifth of a mile deeper than the Grand Canyon—he was exhilarated by the panorama as well as the sense of isolation.

He stepped to the ledge and called loudly, "To the Bat Cave!" The childhood phrase, so long forgotten, flooded his brain with memories.

From the cave, he heard the voice he had expected never to hear again: "To the bat cave!"

He sidled along the ledge until he was at the mouth, but he was unprepared for the sight that awaited him. Why he hadn't thought about it was a mystery to him, but for some reason, he expected to see the same Scott Piquard that he had talked with the Thursday before, an upper-middle-class, refined gentleman with that air of intelligence that set him apart from a crowd. The filthy man with the week's growth of graying beard and the unmistakable smell of body odor was barely recognizable inside the cave, his climbing harness on, a rope dangling from a carabiner for a quick escape, standing alone in his sartorial splendor. A dirt-stained hand reached out to help Brady up the last reach, and as he stepped into the mouth of the cave, Gary grabbed and hugged him.

"You look terrible, Scott! Are you okay?"

"Never been healthier. I've burned off more unneeded fat this week than I thought possible. But you, my friend, you are a sight for sore eyes. I didn't know if I would ever see you alive again. Someone wants you dead very badly, and they are very, very powerful people. They've barely missed killing me four times, and all week I feared you were already dead. I had no way of knowing if you would get my messages, and I did not have a next step. What I do know is that we can't trust anyone. They have some kind of network that allows them to reach across ten states at the drop of a hat. They were waiting for me in Kansas. I thought my little feint at Manhattan would buy me enough time to talk to the local authorities, but they were already there, and but for that poor airport attendant, I would have been dead too."

"You are officially charged with the murder of that man, by the way."

"Gunshot wound through the chest. Pierced my plane too. I had to patch it with duct tape to pressurize. I was not carrying a gun, but I cannot prove either of those statements. I'm sure that *Whiskey Mike* is now a pile of scrap, and a tiny bullet hole could never be found."

"So exactly what happened down in the tunnels last week? I have played that over and over in my mind until it is driving me crazy."

"I heard voices in a utility room. It was dark in that hallway, and it seemed strange, so I inched closer to hear better when I heard your name used. They were going to kill you that day. High-ranking officers. They had a shooter that looked like a senior officer, and they were going to shoot the shooter to cover their tracks. Before I could get out, the lights came back on, and they saw me. That's when the shooting began, and I've been dodging bullets ever since. And not only bullets. What the hell did they use on me in West Virginia? It knocked out all my instruments, screwed up my controls, and my ears still haven't quit ringing."

"Proximity armed Sparrow. We thought you were dead for sure."

"It was closer than you will ever know."

They shared information for nearly a half hour, and then Brady said, "Let's go up to the vehicles. Some fresh coffee and real food would be good for you."

"Who is up there?"

"Several Service agents and my military escort. It won't get any safer, Scott."

"They were all military men in the tunnels. Which ones are you going to trust?"

The question caused Gary to pause, and in the silence, they heard footsteps coming along the rock.

"I told you to come alone."

"It's probably just Sam Davies. He's the one that picked you up at the airport. I left him at the top of the trail, but I've been gone longer than I expected."

The crunching sound got closer, and as it neared the mouth of the cave, they could see in the dim light a tall, thin soldier edging around the last corner, using one hand to steady himself, the other carrying a briefcase that was handcuffed to his left wrist.

"Who are you, and what do you want?" Brady asked.

Scott turned to Gary. "You don't know him?" he whispered, panicking.

"Major James Richards, United States Air Force, special communications branch, sir. Trouble in Central America, sir. I have an urgent message from the general," he said, lifting the briefcase slightly.

"What is the message?"

"I do not have that knowledge, sir. I am to call the general when I am ready." With that, the major took out his sat phone and dialed a number. It rang once, and he spoke quickly. "Hello, General. I will have the telex set up in thirty seconds. Would you like to talk to the president first?"

The major looked blankly at his phone as it went dead and said, "That's odd. He said he would have to call back."

"Which general?" Brady asked, but Scott was already pushing Gary toward the opening of the cave.

"He said you would know," Richards said.

*****

Sam Davies had been beside himself since Major Richards had bypassed his authority with a top-secret order, but that thought was obliterated as a blinding flash lit the night sky, followed by an ear-shattering roar thundering up and down the canyon. Davies raced down the trail to the sound of thousands of pounds of rock hitting the earth below the face of the mountain, but he already knew that no one could have survived that explosion.

Chapter 47

Without a Trace

Wednesday, 9:00 p.m. PDT, Salmon River Valley, Idaho

The terror that Sam Davies lived with, dreamed about, had sworn his life to prevent was now engulfing his brain in the totality of the destruction he saw. The huge cloud of stone dust was choking the air as he scrambled to the base of the trail. He reached the drop-off and looked at what was left of the ledge. The near part of it had been dislodged along with the overhang that had formed the unique shape of the mouth of the cave. What had been an easy walk along a narrow ledge now became a dangerous sidestep. Even though he knew no one could have survived that blast, he had to try to reach the cave. Fresh debris slowed his progress as he kicked away loose rock. The cloud of finely-powdered stone took several minutes to clear. The only sounds were the men coming down the trail behind him and the gradually fading sound of rocks settling into the sites where they would rest for the next ten thousand years.

Sam kicked the last piece of rubble away and looked into the cave. The dust plume was heavy inside the cavity. He could see nothing. He shined his penlight inside but could discern no detail. Securing a handhold, he pulled himself into the opening. Swinging the light back and forth, he searched the cave but found nothing until a glinting scrap of metal caught his light.

"Wait there for now," he hollered at the men starting along the ledge. There were no bodies, but he saw a piece of chromed steel chain. The picture of the officer with the briefcase handcuffed to his wrist flashed through his head. *Piquard did not do this*, he told himself, and the realization was numbing.

"No one comes in here until an intel team arrives to do a proper investigation." Sam climbed out and carefully picked his way along the ledge to the base of the trail. "Send a crew to town and get several hundred feet of climbing rope and a box of flashlights and get back here as quickly as possible. Anyone who was in that cave is now down on that scree slope." Four men were dispatched to town for climbing equipment while Sam conferred with the others. "We need to call Washington."

"I agree," said the colonel in charge of the detachment.

"Why did I let him go down there?" Davies said aloud. "Why did I let him talk me into it?"

"The man can be stubborn," one of the agents consoled. "He gave you a direct order. We all heard it. This was not your fault."

"I had one job, and I failed."

Several soldiers tried climbing down, but the face was too sheer, and they aborted as quickly as they started. Two soldiers followed the rim south, but they could see no good routes down in the thickening darkness. Over an hour crept by before the men returned from town with ropes and lights. Once the search party was safely down, they organized a grid search, but after an hour of searching, they had found nothing.

"We're looking in the wrong place," Davies said loudly. "We are looking *under* the cave, where someone would fall. The bodies would have been blown out God knows how far, and they could be hundreds of feet below us. Let's extend our search out and down." With that, the men began fanning out down the steep slopes. It was another half hour before the first soldier announced grimly that he had found a bloody piece of bone. "Looks like a piece of skull," he hollered into the night air.

"Don't touch anything," Sam hollered back. "Just mark the spot. We will need DNA analysis on everything." He remembered the gruesome scene at the Pentagon in 2001. The scene tonight in the eerie darkness brought back a flood of memories, none good.

Chapter 48

President King

Thursday, 1:00 a.m. EDT, Washington, DC

Marshall King sat on the faux balcony of the vice-presidential home. Unable to sleep, he was enjoying a glass of Giuliana Foresi's Elba Rosso when the emergency telephone rang. The taste of the wine and the lingering aroma of the Italian dinner would be forever blended with the memories of that long night.

"King here."

"Mr. Vice President, this is Chief Justice Charles White. There is compelling evidence to believe that President Brady is dead. Your presence at the Oval Office is required immediately. An escort will pick you up. There will be a temporary swearing-in until we have further confirmation. Mrs. Brady is being flown over from Camp David, and you should bring your wife as a witness."

King was in a state of bewildered shock and confusion as he hung up the phone. He had spent the entirety of his adult life grooming for political influence and power, hoping that someday he would go down in history with the select few who had succeeded to the most powerful position in the world. That the tragedy of one man should lead to the dreams of another left him both confused and excited. Sadness for his running mate was too quickly overtaken by the rush he felt. The guilt he should have felt was too quickly rationalized away as part of the job.

He awakened his wife. "The president is dead. We need to go to the White House immediately." He took comfort in the fact that at least *her* look of horror was genuine.

The military escort arrived within minutes of the phone call, and he and his wife were quickly shuttled to the private entrance, where they were met by Chief Justice White, Todd Pederson, and a cadre of officials who were politely deferential to the man who could suddenly alter their political futures.

The United States of America had the longest history in the world of orderly succession to office in a free society. The country had not been without a leader at the helm for more than a few hours in over two and a quarter centuries. The much longer lineage of kings and queens in England, Spain, and France was the never-ending story of intrigue, deception, and murder within families for the ultimate aphrodisiac—power. After a review of the facts, the chief justice administered the temporary oath of office.

The long night sped toward dawn as meeting after meeting was hastily arranged. Mrs. King consoled Janet Brady and the boys as best she could, but she knew they needed their privacy, and she returned to the vice-presidential quarters. Marshall King, however, had no need of sleep, and he met with cabinet members and other officials through the night. The intoxication of sitting in the Oval Office prevented sleep, and he used his time well. By dawn, he had confirmed the loyalty of those he would need to make a smooth transition and assure reelection. Only after the last meeting wrapped up did he notice one last man standing patiently outside in the hall. He had seen him earlier, but assumed he was there for the meetings. After he noticed his lingering presence, patiently waiting all night for a minute of the new president's time, he invited him inside.

"What can I do for you, General?"

"We have a unique situation in Central America, Mr. President. In a few more days, we will lose our opportunity. How would you like to go down in history with Washington, Jefferson, and Roosevelt as one of the most brilliant and forward-seeing presidents of all time?" The words had been chosen carefully, and their effect was immediate and profound.

Chapter 49

The Son Is Father to the Man

Thursday, 6:00 a.m. PDT, Granger, Idaho

Rachael Piquard was inconsolable. Neither Chad nor Stephanie slept. They spent the night trying to comfort each other. Janet Brady called, telling Rachael what little she knew, and promised to come to Idaho with the boys within forty-eight hours. Details were sketchy, and no identifiable bodies had yet been found. The outlook seemed more and more grim as the night wore on.

All networks were broadcasting details of the swearing-in of the vice president and the orderly transfer of power, if only contingent, and leaks about the "secret double life of the dangerous doctor from Idaho" were emerging less than twelve hours after the explosion. The Piquard family kept the television on in hopes that some positive news would come, but the night passed with newscasters repeating the same lines ad infinitum in their perpetual challenge to fill airtime. As the new man of the family watched the charade, he realized why his father watched so little television. The hollowness of the chatter and the uselessness of 95 percent of the material were all too evident, even to a teenage boy who, with a single thrust, now had a stake in that news.

Chad was dressing for football practice, determined to treat this as a temporary setback, when the announcer told the world, "The

Piquard family is believed to be awake inside this home, but we have seen no activity as yet this morning. This is the home of the suspected assassin, Dr. Scott Piquard." In three seconds, Chad's emotion went from astonishment to shock to anger as he heard the words and saw his home on the screen of his own television set, the rising sun illuminating the house as a camera played the shot for the world to see. He grabbed his gym bag and started for the door, anger roiling his face.

"You are not going out there, Chad. You need to stay home today," his mother was saying, but he could not filter it through his outrage. He continued toward the door. "Chad!" she shouted. "Stop right now!"

The sharpness in her tone broke through his barrier, and he stopped short of the door. "I *am* going to practice, Mother."

"You need to stay home today."

"Mom, I need to go. Dad always says that life goes on, no matter what we do. He sees people die all the time and says that the circle remains unbroken. He would be the first to tell me to go to practice. I need to go and run and hit something right now. Besides, he's not dead. They didn't get him last week, and they didn't get him last night. Why do you think they can't find his body? Or Gary's? Don't you think they could at least find four shoes? He's smarter than all of them, and you know it. He's alive, and I'm going out there as if nothing has changed."

Rachael looked up into her son's face. "So much like your father," she said as she shook her head. "Go ahead. Go to practice. Be strong, like he would be. Show the world that you are not ashamed to be a Piquard." She started sobbing again as she hugged him. "I can't do it, but you can."

The week had been too much for her, and the hope of the last three days had been crushed with the latest news. She was certain that whoever had tried to kill Scott all week, whoever had tried to assassinate the president of the United States, had now finished both jobs. And she could endure no more of the highs and the lows of hope and despair, the not knowing, the wishing, and the praying. She felt beaten. There was no way she could go out in public, yet there was a mother's pride in the seventeen-year-old man standing next to the door, ready to face the world in his father's place. If the men were dead, there was one thing that this family knew: Scott Piquard had tried to save the president's life, not take it. And with that knowledge, they would go on.

She reached and opened the door for him. "Don't hurt anyone, okay? Sometimes you don't know your own strength." She kissed him on the cheek as the door opened, and hundreds of flashes caught the picture, the newspeople as addicted to emotion as their viewers.

Chad started toward his pickup amidst the flashing cameras but was stunned by the total disregard the reporters showed. The street was filled with reporters, and more were arriving by the minute. They had stayed to the street until the door opened, but like a mob in the heat of a lynching, they rushed across the grass the instant the first reporter made a move toward Chad. Chad pushed through them on his way to his pickup, not offering a word. He reached his truck and pushed his way around to the left side, but one reporter would not get out of his face. He continued to thrust a microphone into Chad's face and pelt him with obnoxious questions, but he went too far when he pushed his body between Chad and the truck and accidentally hit him in the mouth as he thrust the microphone into his face.

Chad pushed against the puny reporter so that he was pinned against the vehicle. At five-foot seven and one-fifty, the newsman was dwarfed by the tight end, and the proximity of their touching bodies accentuated the difference in size as Chad looked straight down into the face craned completely back on its spindly neck. Chad's first impulse was to smash his face in, and no one could have blamed him after the microphone had struck him.

But Chad's second impulse was something his father had taught him: "The true measure of strength is not having to use it." He remembered the words now and spoke softly to the little man. "You don't know my father." He climbed into the pickup and backed out of the driveway.

The picture of the mother kissing the son goodbye, with that quote in 36-bold, was uplinked and circling the globe before his taillights were out of sight.

Atop the mound on the mountain's slope, another message was downloaded to a black sat phone as the soldier peered through the spotting scope, hoping for an open curtain on the daughter's bathroom. "Damn!" was his only response as he read the message, which read, "Mission cancelled. Return immediately." He took one last look into the scope and began packing. "I'll be back for my reward when this is over, little girl."

Chapter 50

Night Swim

Scott Piquard was living the inertial dream. He was trying so hard to move, but everything was happening in slow motion. What he wanted to happen in seconds seemed to take minutes, yet he was in motion even before he had seen the puzzled look on Gary Brady's face. He was fingering the carabiner dangling from his harness even as he heard the president echo his own question: "Which general?" Scott pushed Brady toward the mouth of the cave as he fumbled frantically to clip the carabiner to the president's leather belt. *Oh god, I waited too long,* he said to himself as he heard a muffled ring at the same instant he felt the snap of the clip and pushed Brady off balance.

"What the hell…?" Gary Brady was saying as Scott pushed him out of the cave and into the blank space of the night. The only thought Brady could grasp as he fell was that his friend had indeed gone crazy and was now pushing him to his death on the rocks below. His mind raced and whirled, groping to understand as his feet searched for the safety of the rocky ledge, and as a thousand thoughts raced through his mind, the night air was shattered with a flash of light and a deafening roar. He felt pain in his ears as he fell, then felt the blast of heat just above as he tumbled through the night air. Hoping to understand before he died, his mind toggled with his body as he felt a sudden jerk and instantly understood. He could feel Scott's legs enveloping him as Scott struggled with something in his hands. Pain shot through Gary's back as he was snapped backward against his leather belt, something stronger than Scott's legs binding them. More pain greeted him as they swung and tumbled against the stone face but miraculously not impacting the rocks below. Then once again he felt himself in a downward spiral as Scott fed rope through his descender, depositing them roughly but quickly on the shelf below. He was lying on his side at the bottom of the mountain face before he realized what had happened.

"Don't say a word," Scott whispered as he quickly unclipped them and retrieved his rope through the carabiners above. Rock rained down around them, but most of it landed well beyond the penumbra that protected them, the momentum of the blast catapulting most of the rock well down the slope. "Don't make a sound. Best they think us dead," Scott whispered as he looped his rope and pulled Brady down the game trail. By the time the echoes of cascading rock receded into the valley, they were into the concealing brush. The plume of dust hung heavy in the air and obstructed their view of the ridge just as it obscured them from above, and before the dust settled, they had reached the valley floor.

The game trail they descended led to a wall where the river cut under the mountain, and here Scott pulled the kayak from the brush. "Do you want to paddle or swim? We need to be far away from here before dawn."

"I'm too out of practice," Brady countered. "Maybe we should wait for dawn—wait for reinforcements?"

"Which reinforcements are you going to trust this time, Gary? Don't you realize how close that was? How high up they have infiltrated? They are able to send a man to his death to deliver a C-5 briefcase, special delivery, right under everyone's nose. It's obviously someone who is trusted. The American people will not accept a military coup, but they will accept a new president if the old one is assassinated. These guys are smart, they are organized, and they go very deep. I have had all week to think about nothing else except staying alive, and this much I know: I trust no one except you and me. If we wait here, the next headlines will read, 'President killed in freak helicopter accident.' No! We're getting the hell out of here. We need to be twenty-five or fifty miles downriver by morning, and we have to take everything with us. There must be no trace that we were down here."

"Then you paddle. I'd be swimming within minutes anyway."

"I'll drag you a tow line. You take the life jacket, and I'll pull you along as best I can. You can swim until we get to Demon's Drop, then you can walk around, and I'll meet you below. You could probably swim Demon too, but I don't know how rocky it is this late in the season. There are a lot of campers this time of year, so eventually we'll get lucky and be able to make a midnight requisition for a second boat. Then we can make some serious time."

Scott cut a fifteen-foot piece of climbing rope and tied it to the rear handle of the kayak with a triple surgeon's knot but reminded Gary there could be no knots in the free end. "They could get fouled between two rocks and founder the boat. You'll have to hold on as best you can, but don't wrap it around your arm. You need to let go in an emergency. We're better off separated in an emergency anyway, or we'll endanger each other. If we get separated, meet at the top of the next set of rapids no matter how small they are, river right if possible. Got it?"

"Got it."

Scott finished packing the boat and slid it down to the water's edge. "Ready?"

"What happens if you need a life jacket? What if you spill?"

"I have the boat's flotation. Remember the time I swam the waterfall at Lunch Counter? I trapped air in the boat and kept her upside down. And if I get in real trouble, you'll just have to save my sorry ass."

"Well, it's about my turn."

"Let's get moving." Scott slid into the cockpit and secured his spray skirt as Gary slid into the cool water. "Thank God this didn't happen in May."

Water temperatures in the lower Salmon in late August were usually quite comfortable, in the seventy-degree range, but Gary had worked up a sweat churning down the hill, and the coolness of the water struck him immediately. It was only a few minutes before the excess heat from the scramble was gone.

Brady tried kicking as Scott pulled him into the current but soon realized that he could do little to keep up with a kayak. Brady could feel the rope pull on his arms, and he streamlined his body to torpedo through the water as best he could. His primary job now was to make Scott's easier.

Fifteen minutes later, the roar of the first rapids was building as they strained their eyes for the center of the chute above the first drop. The long series of large easy waves made for an exhilarating ride. Gary shot the rapids in white-water position—sitting, knees bent, and feet forward in case he rammed a rock—but the float was clean. They made good time through the flat stretch, and as the roar of the next rapids began its crescendo, they pulled together to talk.

"It's only a class II, but the left side is smoother," Scott said above the rumble. He could tell that his friend was getting chilled after thirty minutes in the night water.

"I'll take your word for it. I haven't seen this stretch in years."

"Let go. I'll meet you at the bottom," Scott hollered to Gary. He sensed the acceleration as his sea brake released.

The class II run was easy in daylight, but in the darkness, Scott's timing was delayed; and a curling wave struck the side of the boat, tipping him dangerously to the right. A high brace with a feathering finish brought his boat upright after the dangerous tip, and a back-stroke on the left centered him again. Just as he thought he was safe, Gary floated through and instinctively grabbed at the boat, tipping him again. He braced again, but Gary's body was in the way, and Scott could not complete the stroke. The boat began to roll, and just as he thought he was going for a swim, Gary pushed up on the boat, forcing himself under water and righting Scott once again. Seconds later, they were through the rift and into calm water below. "Thanks for the help. I thought I was going under."

"My fault. I was too close. I shouldn't have grabbed the boat."

"No harm, no foul. We still have a couple of miles to go. Can you make it, or do you need to rest and warm up?"

"Let's keep moving. I'm okay for now."

Holding river right, they could see there were no campers at either of the next two campsites. Gary would have to swim the next several rapids—fun at high water but tricky and dangerous at low water as the holes and rocks become exposed. Around the next large turn to the left, they could hear the roar of Green Canyon Rapids.

"You swim along the edge and try to walk around if you can. The center is full of rocks. If you have to swim, stay right on the third one, or it will sweep you into the wall." Scott centered his boat, bumping and grinding rocks down the middle, but he misjudged the curl at Wright-Way Drop and slammed against the left wall. He had nearly corrected when a reflected wave, unseen in the darkness, flipped him.

The total darkness was disorienting. He closed his eyes and bent fully forward until his chest was on the front of his cockpit. Reaching up along the right side of his boat, he made sure his paddle was parallel with the water and began his sweep.

Don't lift your head too soon, he told himself. *You always lift your head too soon.*

He swept firmly out to the side and back, the goal being to turn the boat with the hips while leaving the head and arms in the water until the very end of the roll. As he had done too many times, Scott pulled his head up prematurely. He took a gulp of air and sank back under the surface.

Too soon! Too soon! Concentrate!

This time, he kept his head down and swept until he could feel his hips righting the boat as his back contacted the stern of the cockpit. Finishing the sweep, he was in the correct position, lying on the back of the kayak as he completed his stroke. He quickly regained orientation and paddled through the bottom. The water was gentle below, and he waited until he saw Gary making his way safely across the rocks at river right.

"I nearly had to swim there, and my shoulder is not going to take another one of those. I'm going to walk Demon's Drop with you. There's a big hole in the middle, and in the darkness, I don't know if I can miss it. If I don't, I'm dead."

"Understood. We could use a break anyway."

Although Demon was still a half mile away, they could hear the roar of her voice. Always dangerous, she has a changing personality, depending on the flow, and she often bested more proficient kayakers. In the darkness, portaging was the only safe thing to do. They pulled ashore and grabbed the handles of the boat, picking their way along the rocks. Gary was cold, and Scott was wet from the spray skirt up. The night air felt warm by comparison, and at the lower end, they took a few minutes to rest. Scott retrieved his last bottle of water, and they shared it slowly. They could drink the river water if necessary, as they did when they were young, but Giardia was always a danger now that sheep and men had overpopulated the country; and having diarrhea for the next two weeks was not an option.

"This is the only bottle I have. I lost everything else at the cave. We can fill it at Pine Bar put-in, but we have no food."

"That's okay. I had a snack on the way up here." Gary was starting to feel hungry, but one look at his gaunt friend in the pale moonlight quieted his pangs.

Rested, they took to the water once more. The two miles to Pine Bar went quickly. They hugged the right bank as they approached and could make out the shapes of a few vehicles near the dead-end road. They pulled ashore well above the rapids. The campsite was dark and quiet, the three small tents silent save for a few intermittent snores. Stealthily making their way through the brush, they came to the first vehicle with a kayak on top. They unstrapped it silently. Gary spotted paddles leaning against a tree and slid quietly around a tent and expropriated one. Scott filled his water bottle and was eager to quit the site, but he waited while Gary continued to search around the camp. Finally, Brady stopped and held a spray skirt, life jacket, and helmet aloft triumphantly.

Making off with their booty, they were gone into the night while the unsuspecting campers slept; their trip would be ruined, but they would be alive. Scott hoped that he and Gary would be able to say the same.

As they geared up, Gary shivered. "I wish I could have found some fleece."

Scott pointed at Brady's suit. "Is that wool?"

"Yes."

"Then take off your underwear and your shirt, anything cotton, and put the wool back on. Let the wool work for you."

"Good idea," Gary said. Cotton was the worst thing to wear on the river, although when they were young, it was all they had until they discovered the wool clothing at the army surplus store in Boise.

They snapped on their spray skirts and pushed into the water, making quickly for the middle of the river to set up for the class III rapids below. It was with a grim bit of mirth that Brady absolved Scott with an absolute and total presidential pardon for bypassing the permit station at the kiosk and continuing downstream without the one thing the state of Idaho and the BLM insist on—a piece of paper. Each year, poorly prepared boaters kill themselves or require rescuing, causing river rats to quip, "You can embark with all the stupid you want, but don't forget your permit."

Scott led, picking his way through the rock garden that at high water was an exhilarating run but at low water was tricky at best. He ran it cleanly and spun his boat to watch for Gary, who had back-paddled to stay clear of Scott's run. Gary was out of practice, and it didn't help that he only had two hundred yards to warm up before being forced to run a low-water class III. He took the first three waves and turns without incident but misjudged the next hole and slid into it instead of around.

The nose of the kayak slammed into the rock below. He was certain he was going under when the water picked him up and deposited him nearly on top of the rock. Novices leaned away from rocks, an instinctive move, but that tipped the boat into the oncoming water, and it was quickly pushed down and under. Brady leaned into the rock, placing his right paddle blade on the top for a second while the boat floated up and around, then used a power stroke to push around the hole below the rock. As quickly as he had entered the rapids, he shot out the bottom, adrenaline pumping.

He pulled alongside Scott and pumped his fist in the air. "Yessssss! I did it!"

"I thought you were done for there. Nice job."

"Let's go. I'm ready to kick some ass," Brady said triumphantly. The rush was pumping him up for the all-night run. Their speed was now fairly blistering compared to earlier, and they were soon bumping through the aptly named Rock Creek Rapids just above Rice Creek Bridge. These rapids would prevent a powerboat search from above; kayaks could barely clear the hidden rocks at this flow. They cruised past the abandoned gold-mining site at American Bar, and around the next bend, the crude road played out. There would be no road access for the next twenty-five miles—exactly what they wanted.

Time flew as they cruised downriver, the names of the playful rapids mostly escaping them, named as they were after early settlers or their nearby creeks, but as the river made the big horseshoe bend and turned west again, it was impossible to forget the name of the next set. Bunghole Rapids had humbled many a boater in the steep drops that formed in late summer. Labeled a class II, it was universally proclaimed a class III by anyone who took it upside down. They both ran it cleanly, stroking hard and maintaining momentum to carry them through the splashing rollers.

Three miles on, Scott pulled river right and insisted on portaging Half and Half Rapids. "I don't think I can run her. I'm getting tired."

"No arguments here," Gary said as he pulled alongside in the large eddy above the difficult class III. "Half the time you make it, and half the time you don't." Wedging their paddles into the cockpits, they grabbed the handles of both boats and made quick work of the portage.

The night wore on. Portaging Snow Hole Rapids, one of the few class IVs on this stretch of river, they continued into Snow Hole Canyon and, past midnight, were on the Oxbow. This five-mile loop marks the northernmost reach of the Salmon. Here the mountains force her back to the south where her destiny intertwines with that of the Snake. The moon was now on their left as it reached apogee, and its glow revealed a tent at Maloney Creek.

Scott pulled alongside Gary. "It's time for a midnight raid," he whispered. "I'm starved."

"You think we should risk it?"

"Stay in your boat and hold mine. If I have to make a run for it, you have the boats positioned for an instant takeoff. It won't matter if they see my face in the dark, but we can't let them see yours, so take off if I get in trouble and wait for me downriver."

"I don't know. I don't think this is such a good idea."

"I don't care anymore. I've been running and lying and stealing for what seems like a month now, and our friends over there truly want to help their fellow boaters—they just haven't been given the opportunity yet. I'm here to aid them in that quest." Scott jumped out of his boat and made his way quietly into the camp.

River runners appreciated how the roar of the river soothed them to sleep, drowning out the noises of the night. Scott was banking on that now as he moved smoothly along the shore, the white noise of the rapids covering his sound. Slipping into the camp, he found a collapsible cooler. Unzipping it quietly, he was rewarded with a smoked chicken still in its wrapper. Two beers and two bottles of water complemented his larder. Arguments in camp the following day would incriminate the head packer, but they had plenty and would be no worse for wear.

Scott bounded back to his boat. He didn't bother with his spray skirt but pushed away immediately, leading Gary a mile downriver before speaking. "We have a meal and a nightcap, but we have a few more miles before we take our break." The Oxbow turned south, and the waves seemed magnified as the moon glinted off the boiling waters of China Rapids. Named after the Chinese gold miners who drowned when their wooden boat capsized a century earlier, she demanded respect.

"We need to portage here. This baby does an S curve that is tricky enough in daylight."

"So what's our plan? Or are we just running?" Gary's voice showed his fatigue.

"It's formulating. I'll tell you about it over chicken dinner. Let's make this portage and put a few more miles behind us. That will make tomorrow's run easier." They made quick dispatch of the portage and started south. "We'll get some sleep above Slide. I don't even want to run that baby in the daylight—forget in the dark—and you can't portage unless you want to waste half a day dragging your gear over the boulders. We'll have to run her and pray, but not until we are rested and have the advantage of daylight."

"I can't do Slide, Scott. Don't try to bullshit me."

"We also can't portage her—it takes hours—so just blast through the centerline and avoid the left. It may be a five in June, but this is August, and we can make it. Frogg calls it a 'nothing' below four thousand, and it must be close to that now." They both respected and feared Slide Rapids, the most dangerous rapid in the narrow Blue Canyon area. Even at their youthful best, they had difficulty with Slide at medium flows and had never attempted her in the spring.

The night was waning when they finally reached Wapshilla Rapids, only four miles above Slide. It had been years since Gary had seen Wapshilla. While only a class II run, the tricky right turn just before the exit sometimes fooled even seasoned boaters. Amidst the fatigue and the darkness, Gary failed to react in time, crashing into the lower wave at an angle. He was upside down before he knew what hit him. He tried to roll—once, twice, three times—but each time he surfaced, he only had time for a quick breath before going under once again. Out of air and out of energy, he bailed. Performing a quick upside-down somersault, he exited the kayak. Never for a moment losing his grasp on the boat or his paddle, a dead man's mistake if ever there was one, he kicked to shore.

"Damn! I nearly made the entire run. I almost had it."

"Hey, you did great for being out of practice—and in the dark no less. Not many people could have done this in the dark. You haven't lost it yet, stud."

"My knee took a whack. Hurts like hell," he said as he took a seat on the nearest rock. He pulled up his pant leg and, despite the darkness, could see a trickle of blood coursing down the leg.

"There is a road that empties into Wapshilla Creek, and we don't want to be near any roads. It's about four miles to Slide. You good to go?"

"If you can, I can," Brady said with verve he didn't feel.

Forty-five minutes later, they were pulling their boats into the brush above the dangerous run that would be on their minds for the next several hours. After stowing the boats between large bushes, tied so an errant wind could not whisk them into the water as an offering to the river gods, they unloaded their gear.

"Help me gather some firewood, and we'll get you dried and warm."

"You're going to risk a fire?"

"Why not? There are dozens of fires in this river valley every night. We'll just be one of the crowd. Let's get some wood."

Ten minutes later, they had a respectable pile, and Scott set to work, cracking hundreds of tiny pieces of toothpick and match-size twigs before he shaped the larger kindling around it; there was no paper to catch quickly tonight. Gary huddled in his wet clothes. "Still insist on the single-match challenge? Perfect or else?"

"I don't know what you're talking about."

"Right."

Scott flicked the lighter and held it under the nest of twigs. Slowly, a piece smaller than a toothpick began to glow, then flamed, sending its heat to the ones above it as the lower tinder began to kindle, passing the heat efficiently up the neatly arranged wood. Gary huddled near the building flames as Scott fed more kindling. Scott's fleece was nearly dry by the time the wood was collected, and Gary's wool was starting to warm near the flames.

"So where do we stand?" Scott inquired as he tore the chicken and handed half across the fire.

Gary popped the tabs on the beers and handed one across as he took the mouth-watering chicken. "I don't have a clue."

"Who was Major Richards?"

"I don't have a clue."

"You've never seen him before?"

"I don't think so, but I see so many."

"Then he's not from Washington?"

"I don't know. He definitely wasn't on *Air Force One* with me."

"He acted surprised—probably thought he was doing his job. The phone was the trigger."

"Yeah! I heard it just as you pushed me. Actually, I thought you had lost your mind until that blast wiped out my eardrums. My ears are still ringing."

"Same here."

"What made you suspect Richards?"

"It wasn't just Richards," Scott said, feeding more wood onto the fire and taking another bite. "I suspect everyone. The second I saw the look on your face, the second I realized you were not expecting him, I thought we were totally screwed."

"What in the hell made you keep your harness and rope on?"

"Every time I've turned around the last few days, someone's tried to kill me. I may be slow, but I'm not that slow."

"So tell me again about the tunnels." The fire was working its magic on Gary. As his clothing dried, his spirits recovered.

Scott recounted the story as best he could. "Their uniforms were definitely Army, Navy, and Air Force, high ranking, so this is not a simple plot from one branch. And the ease with which they followed me, the rocket, someone waiting for me in Kansas—it's all too chilling. Then this Idaho connection, and so quickly…" Scott added as he recounted everything he could remember. "They used the name Al, but no other names were mentioned. The only out-of-place thing I remember was this reference to someone's kid being royalty this fall for homecoming. It was strange, like 'Let's kill the president and take over Central America, then watch my son in the homecoming parade.' But then, these are not normal people we are talking about."

They picked the bones and babied their beers. Finally, Brady asked the question that had been ignored all night. "So do you have a plan?"

"Here's the only thing I could come up with on the run," Scott said as he lay on the last of the wood. He explained his plan. "Let's just hope he's home," he said as he finished. "But even if this part works, whom can *you* trust back there?"

"I don't know," Gary said as he snuggled around his side of the fire. His curled figure claimed half the heat, while Scott's vied for the other half. "I just don't know."

Chapter 51

Reramp

Lieutenant Colonel Floyd Curtis was dumbstruck as the reports flowed in. More than dumbstruck, he was devastated. He had not left the building in nearly a week. He showered and worked out and sent his uniforms for laundering, but his commitment to a project was so total that he could not take time off in a crisis.

When asked, he replied, "Soldiers in a war zone don't get time off."

His close friends thought he was overdue for promotion based on commitment alone. But this day he felt like he had failed and failed miserably. He felt so helpless sitting in this fortified bunker, safe from the dangers out there. Try as he might to track and find Piquard, he had failed. At one point, he was convinced that they were after the wrong man, but after the events of the past few hours, he didn't know what to think. What bothered him most was his inability to help his commander in chief when he needed him most. He dialed a number.

"Collins here."

"Good morning, General. You've heard the news? Yes. Terrible. Absolutely terrible. But I am not giving up just yet. I think we need to move all the men in the desert. I also think that we need to get ten thousand men to Idaho as quickly as we can. So far, they have only found a few pieces of bone and flesh and cloth and parts of two shoes. Until we have three bodies with DNA confirmation, I am operating under the premise that Brady is alive. If he is alive but injured, then the faster we work, the better his chances. I say we pull out all the stops and reramp our operation."

"I'll be right in, Curtis. Give me a half hour."

Twenty-five minutes later, General Pat Collins strode into the command center in a fresh uniform, ready for the day's work. They began calling around the country, mobilizing units and aircraft for another lift. The pieces were stringing together when the bright-red phone rang. No one was ready for what happened next.

"Joint chiefs hotline for you, General," Block said to Collins.

"General Collins here."

The other soldiers in the command center watched in silence as they saw his face turn ashen. He listened quietly, but when he tried to ask questions, he was cut off. His face sagging in defeat, he said "Yes, sir" and hung up.

"The acting president of the United States has clear and indisputable evidence that Scott Piquard was a double agent working for the Colombians, and he has issued a statement that the assassination of President Brady will not go unpunished." He turned to the entire room and spoke. "Gentlemen, we are at war."

Collins turned to Curtis. "Well? How's that for a reramp? I believe that was the word you used."

Curtis slumped against his desk, his face in shock. "How did they get that kind of intel? Why didn't we hear about it? Whom are we attacking? Who are our allies?"

"Who knows anymore? For now, I am ordered elsewhere. It's been very good working with you." He shook Curtis's hand and saluted him smartly in front of his men. "Carry on, gentlemen," he said and strode from the room.

A feeling of emptiness, of hollowness overwhelmed Curtis. He turned the command over to his relief and walked slowly from the room, beaten. He held such hopes the Friday before, but a clean victory not only eluded him—it had escalated into this. He threw his things into his duffel and withdrew from the arena. He had earned a few days off, and the first order of business was a Crown double and some much-needed sleep. The bright light hurt his eyes as he squinted against a sun he had not seen in days. He put on his sunglasses and dragged his feet to his car. As he started his Malibu and turned on the air, a thought struck him. There was one bit of unfinished business.

He dialed Ernie's Knoll's number. "Curtis, here. Did you ever find anything out about that gravel-truck driver?"

"I don't know what you got me into here, Floyd, but I've been up all night, talking to his widow."

"Widow?"

"That's right! Gunshot wound to the head. Coroner labeled it a suicide already. Case closed! His wife said he wasn't handling that army captain's death very well, but she never thought he was suicidal. Things had been tough financially for several years, but he had just come into some very lucrative cash contracts when the accident happened. They found him the night before last, sitting in his pickup with a bullet hole in his head."

"Jesus! Another dead end. Ernie, everyone we've wanted to talk to has been turning up dead."

"Well, let me add a little something else that might help you sleep at night. I went to the morgue to have a look for myself. The bullet entered behind the right ear and exited the left forehead just above the left eye."

"Okay? What does that mean to me?" Curtis asked, puzzled. "I'm not a forensic pathologist."

"Oh, probably nothing—unless you do a little basic homework."

Curtis tried to picture the scene. "Okay! You have my interest."

"Floyd, the guy was left-handed."

"Holy shit!"

"Holy shit is right," Knoll echoed. "What the hell is going on?"

Chapter 52

Downstream

As Curtis and Knoll shared info in Washington, Scott was stirring at half past dawn in Idaho. He sensed a tremor, as if he had been shaking, and his clothing was damp. The fire was but a few warm embers, and he went to collect kindling. His elbow was pulsating, and he could feel the heat of infection licking at the tissues in his arm. He arranged the kindling as Gary roused. Pulling up his sleeve, he saw the swelling and the redness of the skin. He walked to the river's edge, and once more he gritted his teeth and pulled at the flesh, the searing pain shooting too familiarly up his arm. He drained the pus, washing out the abscess as he knelt over the water and let the swoon pass. He washed his hands several times before returning to the fire, which Gary had now rekindled.

Unbeknownst to them, Gary Brady was no longer officially considered the president of the United States. In fact, he was not officially alive. As reporters dogged the Brady and Piquard families, as soldiers combed the mountainside below the cave for body parts, and as troops moved rapidly into Panama with lightning strikes, Gary Brady and Scott Piquard warmed their hands by the crackling fire and enjoyed fresh-brewed bearberry tea. They had been unwillingly transported to a simpler time, when fire, food, water, and shelter

335

commanded 95 percent of a person's day. The concept that the major pursuit of a man's life should be directed toward entertainment could never have crossed the minds of their forefathers.

Scott hid his pain as he walked uphill toward a feeder creek to collect fresh water. Walking into a depression where the creek filled a small erosion, Scott happened upon a tiny microcosm where pooled water allowed plant growth to flourish above the cleansing forces of the flood line. Here he found several low-growing bunchberry plants laden with their scarlet fruit, ripe in the late summer sun. Nearby, at the outlet of the drainage, several dozen cattail plants flourished in the clear water.

Scott called to Gary, placing him in charge of harvesting the berries, while he bent over the cattails and groped in the shallow water along the buried rootstock, retrieving the horn-shaped cones, or corms, but leaving some for regeneration, as Grandpa Piquard had taught him. He gently washed the large pile of corms in the trickling water and filled his pockets. By then, Brady had his pockets flush with berries, and they returned to their fire.

Ripe bunchberries were nearly tasteless, but the men knew they were getting sustenance as they chewed the pulp down and spit out the seeds. Although the seeds have food value, if eaten in quantity, they can cause colic—this they remembered from their youth. Some lessons need but one session.

They saved the more flavorful corms for last. These were tasty eaten fresh—akin to a crunchy, bland cucumber—or cooked like a potato or ground into flour. They recognized the cattail as one of the most versatile of plants. They grew to respect and appreciate it under the tutelage of the old wise man before his death.

"Are you sure we should risk this?" Gary asked as he doused the fire and buried the ashes deep in the sand. He was still tenuous about Slide Rapids.

Scott stood and pointed theatrically downriver. "The undiscovered country from whose bourn no traveler returns, puzzles the will, and makes us rather bear those ills we have than fly to others that we know not of…"

"Screw you *and* Shakespeare."

"Let's scout her out," Scott said in his most optimistic tone as he picked his way south along the rocks. On the canyon walls above, the high-voltage power line crossed the gorge above the massive landslide that pinched the river and forced all the might of the river through the dangerously narrow and rocky gap. At high water, this was a class V, sometimes a VI—runnable only by an extreme expert.

"We can do it at this flow." Scott looked down on the rolling white water. "That hole," he said, pointing, "can eat an eighteen-foot raft, so be sure you stay wide there. There's a reflector off the wall about a hundred feet below there, so stay away from the wall. Watch those whirlpools. They will suck you under with no warning. And don't try to roll too many times. It's too turbulent. If you don't make it on the first try, you probably won't on the second or third either. You've done it at higher flows. You can do it again."

"I was twenty years younger when I did it before. Small point, I realize," Brady said with a sarcastic grin.

Over his shoulder, Scott hollered, "Swimmer buys!" And with the challenge tendered, he headed to his boat.

Gary slipped into a back eddy and watched Scott disappear into the first trough before he pushed off. From the advantage of the scouting point on the mountainside, the waves had looked smaller, but as Scott's head disappeared completely, Gary's apprehension grew. The waves were larger than he thought. He gave Scott a head start, then paddled in his wake.

He saw the red helmet reappear as Scott crested the next wave and crashed into the haystack below. Scott's body was totally engulfed in the wave, not even his helmet showing. Gary could just make out his paddle held high to prevent catching a blade and just as quickly saw him emerge safely into the triple roller coaster below. Paddling hard to the right, he missed the big hole and continued down into the narrows below. Just when Gary thought Scott would run it clean, he saw the boat swing hard right and plow into a roller sideways. In an instant, Scott was upside down and struggling to roll. Miraculously he rolled up on the first try, but he came up near the wall, and another wave took him over again. Gary thought he could see his head pop up a couple of times, but he was caught in a whirlpool and spun 360 degrees. Gary paddled hard toward his friend as he saw his head go down into the center of the vortex. As he power-stroked, he saw Scott emerge from under the boat, paddle in one hand, cockpit rim in the other. But he was still spinning, trapped in the whirlpool.

Gary came alongside, offering the rear handle of his boat for Scott as a towrope. Scott grabbed it, and Gary pulled as hard as he could, but all he could feel was the churning water of the whirlpool pulling him backward and down. He pulled harder and made a foot of progress. Then suddenly he felt Scott's body pull free of the sucking vortex, but as they crashed into the next wave, Gary's boat was hit by a reflector and was instantly upside down. He tried to roll, but his paddle collided with Scott's helmet, and he couldn't complete the sweep. Out of breath, Gary bailed. He came up for air, gripping paddle and cockpit, just as Scott's kayak swirled and knocked him under the water as boat and body washed over the top of him. Their arms, trained by long practice never to let go of the cockpit rim, tangled with one another as they fought swirling wave after swirling wave, slamming against each other and the boats like an outdated pinball game. When Gary thought he could hold on no longer, they were suddenly spit out of the bottom of the rapids, coughing and gasping for air. He saw Scott just a few feet away.

"Nice save!" Scott hollered.

"We made it!" Gary hollered back. And that made them both smile.

They kicked to shore and drained their boats. "We are only three or four miles from the confluence now, and if we can run Eye of the Needle without getting hurt, we're home free. Let's boogie." With that, Scott turned downstream and shot across the eddy line, Brady quick on his heels.

Soon they were looking down on the quick, turbulent run of Eye of the Needle. Their confidence was up. Scott crashed through the middle, dropped into the trough, and shot cleanly out the bottom, shouting "Yee-haw!" in triumph. Paddling hard for several strokes, Brady built momentum and shot through almost too hard, the front of his kayak going airborne off the top of the big wave and then crashing into the one below, sending a wave of exhilaration through the young-again boy.

He pounded through the last two waves, screaming at the top of his lungs. "That was awesome! God, it's good to feel alive again."

"I'll race you to the confluence. It's only a half mile."

"You're on."

They paddled hard in a playful race, both knowing they needed stamina today, not speed. Reaching the confluence with the Snake River in a dead heat, they entered the fast-flowing central channel and began their day's work. Paddling for endurance, the play-quality class II rapids of this stretch were welcomed as speed makers, no thought given to scouting or portaging now.

"We have about forty-five miles to cover. We should still have enough daylight to climb out and find Clint. Let's just hope he's there."

"Amen," Brady replied as they leaned into their foot braces and paddled smoothly and long, Gary's old rhythm emerging from the disuse atrophy to which he had so long subjected it.

Scott's elbow throbbed with each stroke, but he said nothing to worry his partner. Instead, he used the pain as a reminder that he was alive, and it steeled his resolve. *Only in death are we pain free.*

By noon, they were well downstream and stopped for a break. They each drank their only bottle of water and stretched their cramped muscles. Rested, they took to the water, the steady swish of their paddles the only sound breaking the serenity of the canyon, blue sky and soaring birds above, salmon and trout below. Occasionally, they overtook a group of floaters and waved hello from a distance as Gary kept his face down, but this portion of the Snake was much less frequented than the tumultuous upper stretch of Hells Canyon, and they mostly paddled in quiet isolation.

"We need to stay wide right of Heller Bar takeout just around this corner," Scott said twenty miles below the confluence when he saw the waters of the Grande Ronde sluicing in from the left. "If there are any river cops trying to pull people over, I'll holler something in German while you keep far right and keep moving." But rounding the turn, they saw Heller Bar was empty this weekday afternoon. No one from the search group had thought to look this far downstream, their assumptions dooming their conclusions.

The only man who was beginning to understand how Scott Piquard's mind worked was home sleeping in his own bed for the first time in a week. Floyd Curtis would have doubled the perimeter of the search, but after a week in the subterranean fortress, he had gone home, beaten.

The two men plowed on, fatigue now a long-familiar companion, their mind-set putting it not in a recess but accepting it, embracing it. Hour after hour, they stroked the slowly moving waters, pushing the river behind them as the sun slid west of the Blue Mountains of Oregon. On they paddled, their strokes flowing as smoothly as the water; they had become one with the river as their energy merged with that of the surging water below them, carrying them finally to the bluffs below Lewiston. Exhausted and parched, they climbed from their kayaks.

As Scott stood, a wave of nausea and lightheadedness again shook him, and for a brief second, he thought he would fall. His body felt like it was on fire, but he said nothing. "We need to walk out here. The airport is on the southwest edge of town, but we need to circle north to get to the hangars. I hope Clint is working late today."

"He's done well for himself," Gary said. "When he found flying, he found his passion. He was the best center I had—hardly ever muffed a snap—and he could block well for his size."

"Well, let's see if he can run interference for you one more time," Scott said, "but first we need to swamp my boat."

"Why?"

"My name is written behind the cockpit, and I am sure that name is all over the news these days. We'll leave your boat here—maybe someone will return it to its owner—but we need to scuttle mine unless you want to leave a calling card."

"I'll buy you a new one."

"Screw the boat. Buy me a plane."

"If we live through this, it will be brand new, my friend. *Brand new.*"

Scott tossed his unmarked paddle, helmet, and lifejacket into the bushes. Putting a dozen large rocks inside his boat, he turned it on its side and filled it with water, coaxing it upright and pushing it into deeper water as the last of the air escaped.

"Let's go," he said, not bothering to look back. "The airport is only a couple of miles from here."

Lewiston, Idaho and Clarkston, Washington are built on opposite sides of the Snake River, where the Clearwater contributes its waters to the Snake on its trek to the Columbia River Valley. The cities' namesakes were the great explorers who set out on a mission whose scope could only be held in awe even by today's standards. When one considered the equipment they had and the total lack of foreknowledge with which they embarked, words failed.

Lewis and Clark dubbed the upper Salmon River the River of No Return, for they knew that once they entered it, they could never turn back. They had skirted the deepest part of it and worked their way down the Clearwater drainage. But they eventually were forced to run portions of the Columbia farther downstream that were equally no-return propositions, paddling heavy, cumbersome, dugout canoes. As they camped on October 10, 1805, at the beautiful site where these cities would eventually bear their names, Clark had written in his journal, "All the party have greatly the advantage of me," for they could buy dogs from the Nez Perce and "greatly relished" the fresh meat, which he could barely stomach. Finally, on the fourteenth, he shot some ducks and, for the first time in three weeks, had "a good dinner" of blue-wing teal.

Someone among the first whites to come to the Snake River area mistakenly named the locals the "Snake" Indians because of a misunderstanding about their sign language. Living largely off hunting and the prodigious salmon runs before the white man dammed the rivers and cut off their life-giving flow, a single man could harvest a hundred salmon in one day during the run, a ton of fish to dry and smoke for the lean winter months. When the early whites tried to communicate and ask their name, the natives made a slithering, wavy motion back and forth with their hand, and the whites mistook it for a snake crawling, hence the name. The natives were trying to tell them that they lived by the river where the salmon ran. And so went much of history, truth so delicately relative.

By the time Scott and Gary reached the hangars, the last shreds of daylight were filtering between the buildings. Scott had visited Clint Warren periodically at his crop-spraying business and knew where his hangars were located, but the buildings were dark, and the hopes of quickly finding their old classmate vanished. Scott left Gary in the shadows and walked to the FBO. Most airports had a local phone so pilots could call for fuel in the middle of the night, and Scott located it in the entryway. He looked up Clint's number.

On the third ring, a familiar voice answered. "Warren's."

"Mr. Warren, this is Agent Caruthers from the FBI. I need to talk to you about something of the utmost urgency, and it is imperative that you talk to no one, not even your wife, about this phone call. Please come to your hangar immediately and *tell no one* where you are going. The United States government needs your help."

There was a long pause while Clint Warren digested what he had just heard. On a normal day, he would have suspected a prank by a friend, but the newscasts had hardly veered from speculation on the assassination long enough to report a few local stories, and Clint was still as numbed by the possibility of one friend's death as he was by the possibility that it had been caused by the other.

"I'll be right there."

Minutes ticked like hours before the two men saw headlights approaching and the security gate opening. They stayed to the shadows until the pickup stopped next to the hangar of the Warren Spraying Service. Clint stepped out, but seeing no one, he unlocked the door to the hangar. That was when Gary spoke.

"Green 47, Green 47, right guard pulls, on two."

"Jesus Christ," Clint said as he jumped.

"No. Just call me Gary." Brady walked into the glow of the yard light, and the two came together in a hug that could break bones. Scott followed close behind, and Clint noticed him flinch as he hugged him as well. "God, it's good to see you two. The news stories are crazy with speculation." Then he hugged them both again and ushered them inside the hangar. "Can I get you anything? You guys look like shit."

"Anything wet," Scott answered as he plopped down on the old couch.

Clint threw them two bottles of water and followed up with chips, jerky, and Mountain Dew. No self-respecting spray pilot ever had a hangar office without the finest luxuries: a forty-year-old couch, a thirty-year-old refrigerator, and a twenty-year-old television on a finely dusted cement floor carpeted with ten years of flying magazines. The men assuaged their hunger before anyone spoke again.

Finally, Clint could stand the silence no longer. "Okay! Tell me."

"We need you to get some clothes, all the bandages and tape you can find, a disposable razor, all your credit cards, and all the cash you can muster in an hour. And then we want you to fly us to DC. Please tell me you still have the Saratoga."

"Why not just call someone and tell them where you are?"

"Because they keep trying to kill us," Brady intoned. "Now that they think we're dead, we have some room to maneuver. Here's the plan." Brady laid out their plan, but as he finished, Clint noticed the sweat on Scott's face and saw the ashen color.

Warren reached over and touched Scott's forehead. "Christ, man, you're burning up. What's the matter?"

"War wound," he replied, pulling up his sleeve and exposing the pus-filled bursa. They could see the red streak snaking up his arm into the axilla. The constant paddling and dirty river water had done their damage.

"That's blood poisoning," Clint said.

"Help me to the sink," Scott said, his voice more weary than it had been. At the sink, he repeated the tearing procedure, and the pus again oozed out. The long days of paddling had swelled the limb more than ever. "Do you have any hemostats or forceps, Clint? It needs better drainage."

"I've got that old pair you gave me for fish hooks, but they're not very clean."

"It's too late for clean."

Clint retrieved the slightly rusty hemostats, and Scott showed him how to insert them deeply, still closed, into the wound and then quickly open them wide, pulling the sides of the wound apart to effect drainage. Clint performed the maneuver once. Pus shot into the sink, and Scott nearly fainted from the pain. Gary grabbed a chair for him to sit on while he draped his arm across the sink.

"Do it again," Scott ordered. "Deeper."

"Are you sure?"

"Do it!"

Clint inserted the hemostat deeper and could feel flesh tear across bone as Scott's head rolled and he forced down reflex vomit.

"Again."

"Jesus, Scott, let's get you to a hospital."

"Again!"

Again and again Clint performed the procedure along the length of the wound. Again and again Scott reeled, but did not pass out. Sweat poured from his body. Finally, the entire wound was opened, and he let the water soothe his arm.

"What am I going to tell my wife?" Clint asked.

"Tell her that you got a high-paying charter to San Diego," Gary said. "Invite her to go with you but tell her that you must leave immediately."

"She won't leave on such short notice."

"Exactly why you should invite her. She won't suspect anything if you offer to take her along."

"Okay. I'll be back as soon as I can."

Clint headed to town. In under an hour, he was back with $300 in cash, all his credit cards, and several changes of clean clothes, as well as a shopping bag full of bandages and tape. He also brought what medications he could find in his medicine cabinet, and in this random collection, Scott espied a partial bottle of Augmentin that Clint had started for an infection but did not finish once he began improving. Scott took a loading dose of the antibiotic and put the rest in his pocket. After squirting antibacterial cream into the opening, they dressed the elbow.

Clint performed his preflight while Gary loaded the cargo, and soon they were taxiing to the active. "November-Eight-Four-Three-Two-Bravo taxiing for departure," Clint called to the tower. He opened an instrument flight plan to San Diego, but the Saratoga was airborne less than fifteen minutes when Clint called Salt Lake Center and cancelled IFR, discontinuing their radar tracking. Dropping to minimum VFR altitude, he turned toward Virginia as ten thousand soldiers descended on Idaho to find them.

Chapter 53

Rout

cting President Marshall King was in the Oval Office, but he was no longer standing in front of the desk. He was saddened by the shocking news, but events swirled around him with such rapidity that he was forced to move with them or risk being left behind, and he had trained his whole life not to be left behind. There were appropriate times to mourn. Now it was time to run his country. He sat at the desk, basking in the praise being lavished upon him. Like so many men of average intelligence who lack the gift of introspection, he actually believed what he was hearing because he had waited so long to hear it.

"This is the most amazing and meteoric victory that any nation has ever witnessed." The words stroked him like warm olive oil. "The Northern Alliance wishes you to know how much their citizens want to bestow upon you the title of El General." The flush of adoration was intoxicating. The philosophical reasons his predecessor had cited for keeping the country out of the war were smothered entirely in the adulation. "But the Northern Alliance owes you no more than the people of the United States of America when they speak of the pride that you have restored to their country. 'Supreme commander of the entire North American forces' is what people are saying in the streets." The general and the commander were the only ones present, but to King, it could have been the entire nation offering their praise.

"Thank you, but without your guidance, I could never have navigated such treacherous waters." Two days into his presidency, King found himself in control of powers he could only dream of the week before. The southern armies, previously advancing against unsophisticated and poorly organized battalions in full retreat, had broken ranks in their rout and exposed themselves horribly, only to be mercilessly crushed by the attack from the Norteamericanos. The deadly blows of the combined Air Force and Navy air strikes made a clear path for the ground forces airlifted into the southern isthmus and the northern arm of Colombia. Amphibious landings at Golfo de Uraba and Golfo de Cupica well south of the battle lines had cut off their retreat, the bulk of the southern forces were trapped and paralyzed, and the northern forces were claiming real estate mile after mile. News broadcasts had embraced King as a brilliant strategist, and the urgency of the search for the old president had already begun to fade with the need for new ink.

"You had this so perfectly planned that I cannot take the credit. The ships were in position. The aircraft were mobilized. The troops were amassed and ready to move. I did nothing." He stammered his humble protests. He knew they must be said. But he also knew that had it been a catastrophe, he would have had to accept the blame.

"Mr. President, you are too modest. You alone had the foresight and the courage to take action. Bold times require bold leaders."

The words were like caresses from a mistress. "You are too kind. It is to all our men and women in uniform that I owe my thanks."

"They will appreciate that, Mr. President, as will the joint chiefs. By the way, you do understand that Admiral Winslow may be stepping down as chairman, don't you?" the general said in muted understatement, new intrigues already astir in the new administration. "He was very loyal to President Brady, but…" And what was left unsaid was far more important than what was said.

"I think I expected that, and although I would be terribly saddened at such a turn, I think I know who could fill those shoes perfectly," King said in an equally understated tone.

"Also, sir, the leaders of the United Nations of Central America wish to meet with you as soon as possible to offer their thanks and to begin planning for this new era in the Americas. Quite frankly, sir, they want their picture taken with El General. One minute they were ready to flee for their lives, and the next, they are heroes in their own countries. You have no idea how powerful that makes your bargaining position, but it is imperative that you move quickly. Memories are short, but we have some ideas on what we think is the best military outline for the region. If you wait until this is over, you will lose the power hand just as America did at the end of World War II when Stalin was already an entrenched victor in the east and no longer needed us."

King was not a military man, and he relished the advice. When your broker showed you winners, you kept buying.

Chapter 54

Backup

Clint Warren slipped the Piper Saratoga through the smooth night air, the visibility "severe clear" after the cleansing storms. Scott had taken the copilot's seat for takeoff, but once safely airborne, he took a second dose of antibiotics, climbed in back, reclined his seat, and sank into a deep sleep. During the long night, Clint landed to refuel, and hundreds of miles from home and with a new set of controllers, he had filed a flight plan to Fredericksburg, Virginia, using the "Angel Flight" call sign of the volunteer pilots around the nation who donated their time and aircraft to help the disadvantaged sick travel to medical appointments. Meanwhile, Gary joined him in front and used Clint's iPhone to try to arrange the next step in their hastily constructed plan. Cell service two miles up in the middle of nowhere was nonexistent most of the time, and it was a painstaking process.

Unable to trust anyone from the military side of this convoluted equation, they decided that the Bureau and the Secret Service were their safest allies. The problem was that Gary Brady, president of the United States, had no way to contact them. He hadn't made his own calls in years, and if he did, it was with speed dial on his cell phone to call Janet or the boys. He didn't even have *their* numbers committed to memory thanks to the electronics age. But he did hold one card; he knew that Sam Davies lived on the Maryland side, relatively close to the capital, as he had heard Sam comment on how short his commute was. Years ago, this might have taken several calls to directory service, but with a smart phone and WhitePages.com, he was whittling away at the list. There were dozens of "Davis" listings but only a few "Davies," and of these, there were only a few with the first name of Sam or Samuel. He hit several dead ends, but on the fifth call, a sweet, sleepy voice answered, "Davies."

"Hello, is Sam home?"

"One minute, please," she said.

Seconds later, a deep elder voice responded, "Hello."

Gary knew immediately it was not the Sam Davies he was looking for, but he was on the edge of desperate. "Excuse me, I was looking for Sam Davies, but I know by your voice that I have the wrong number."

"You might be looking for my son, Sam Junior."

Brady's face lit up as he gave Clint a thumbs-up. "Possibly. Can you give me his phone number?"

"May I ask who is calling?"

Brady did not hesitate. He had been expecting this question. "My name is Clint. Clint Warren. We trained together, and he made me promise to look him up if I was in the area, but I lost his number. I'm sorry about the early hour, but my business is quite pressing."

"Are you Service?"

"I'm sorry, sir, but I am not allowed to answer that question." It was the perfect response.

"Of course. I'll give you his home and his cell, but he might not answer with everything that has happened."

"Believe me, I understand better than you can imagine," Gary said. He jotted down the numbers and read them back twice. Then he thanked Mr. Davies again.

"Bingo!" he said as he high-fived Clint. He took a deep breath and dialed the number on the notepad. "Please be home," he contemplated aloud as the phone rang once, twice, three times. After five rings, he was getting discouraged, but on the sixth ring, it was answered.

"Hello."

Brady recognized the voice immediately. His pulse quickened. "Sam, I need your help."

The statement was simple and direct, but Sam Davies would remember it as the seminal moment of his life. There was no mistaking the voice or the implied command. For the past three days, his life had been in shambles, a hollow shell barely resembling its former, meaningful construct. The lasting legacy of his career was already being written. The president of the United States had died on his watch, literally under his nose, and he had done nothing to stop it. He was questioned for hour upon hour and finally sent home on extended leave of duty. He was asked to remain close to home—a polite euphemism for house arrest—while investigators pieced together how a Secret Service agent let the president walk into a bomb.

Sam had tried to posit his theory that the bomb was in the military attaché's top-secret briefcase. He disclosed his discussions with the president in the command center and instead argued that the seared hand bones found at the back of the cave near the piece of handcuff showed that the handcuff was probably at the epicenter of the explosion, but no one was buying his story with the DNA still pending. He shared the president's theory that it was a military operation and that Piquard happened into it accidentally. He argued that the major likely had no idea what was in the briefcase, believing instead that he was carrying top-secret papers of state. They had listened and then asked him the same questions again, then again, wearing him down, looking for that first lapse in consistency, but it never came. When the blame game starts in Washington, the fallout ends careers, and Sam knew that his was worse than over; his was more like a cancer that would gnaw slowly. And now, magically, as he was slipping into a living hell, a hand was being offered to pull him back from the abyss.

Sam straightened his back and stood at attention. "What do you need me to do, sir?"

"Arm yourself, and meet us at the Fredericksburg Shannon Airport at dawn. We are still several hours away, so you have time to help with some other arrangements. We need to activate the Bureau and the Service tonight. We need a contingent of people ready at dawn to go to all the major buildings, including the Pentagon, and seal them. I don't want to just show up. I want to freeze all activity, put a lock on all computers and communications systems before anyone can go deep. We'll need manpower to do that. Director Meyer lives due south of the capitol. Find his address and stop there on your way to Fredericksburg. Have the director give you the name and number of the FBI liaison working this case. He will be up to speed, so if he is available, have him meet us at the airport as well. Then have Director Meyer go to his office and wait. I'll call him as soon as we land. In the meantime, he is to activate as many agents as he can—only those with high-level clearance—and have them ready for immediate deployment. Lastly, call Greg Stroud and have him do the same."

"I doubt that Mr. Stroud will listen to anything I have to say, sir. They have been grilling me nonstop and haven't believed a word yet."

"Tell Stroud that Operation Artist's Pallet has been activated. He'll understand."

"Yes, sir."

"Hurry, Sam. I'm counting on you!"

"Thank you, Mr. President."

Brady slumped back in the Saratoga and took a deep breath. "Well, that's a start. There is one other person I can trust. Todd Pederson has been with me almost from the start of my political career. His cell phone will have phone numbers of anyone we need to contact, and that will make things happen faster once we pounce." He found Pederson's number and dialed as soon as they had service again.

Friday, 4:15 a.m. EDT, Washington, DC

Sam Davies had barely slept in three days, but now he worked with a renewed energy that made him feel twenty again. Director

Meyer was nonplussed when he was first awakened, then astounded at the story to which he was treated. He gave Sam Ernie Knoll's cell number, then dressed, and headed to the Hoover Building to await further instructions. Greg Stroud was dubious until he heard the words *artist's pallet*. Only a handful of people knew that contingency code. He dressed and drove to H Street.

Driving south, Sam dialed the number Meyer had given him. A sleep-deprived voice answered on the second ring, "Knoll, here."

"Hello, Agent Knoll. This is Sam Davies from the Secret Service. The president of the United States has asked me to request your assistance in a matter of the gravest importance. Can we count on your help?"

"Of course," Knoll answered without hesitation. "President King has my sworn oath of loyalty."

"That's nice, but it is President Brady who is asking for your help tonight."

The silence was palpable. It took the quick-thinking Ernie Knoll many long seconds to sift through what he had just heard. "Go ahead. I'm all ears!"

Sam filled him in. "And if you know another agent who is close by and totally trustworthy, bring them along. We need to protect the president, but without a huge motorcade tipping off his whereabouts."

"I'll meet you at the Fredericksburg airport. How will I recognize you?"

"I'm six-two, two hundred, black hair. Ask if there is a taco stand nearby. I'll answer that there is one exactly nine-point-eight meters per second squared north of here."

"Nice. Got it. See you in a couple hours."

Ernie Knoll only had to think for one second before he knew whom to call. He had called Lieutenant Colonel Floyd Curtis so many times the past few days he knew his cell number by heart. Curtis answered on the first ring. "Floyd, Ernie here. You are not going to believe this one. I promised you I would share intel, and I have intel with a capital *I*. Where are you now?"

"At home, in Reston."

"Perfect. Can you be rolling quickly?"

"Immediately."

"Dress in civvies and meet me at Stafford. There is a huge parking lot just off the 95, a block west on Courthouse Road. Meet me in the southwest corner, and make sure you're packing."

Friday, 5:30 a.m. EDT, Fredericksburg, Virginia

The Fredericksburg airport was nearly deserted in the awakening blue-gray light. Ernie Knoll and Floyd Curtis drove down Circle Drive past the rotating beacon and pulled into the parking lot outside the tiny FBO. They saw a young man carrying some ropes to a hangar, and a lineman was towing an airplane out to the tarmac. A lone man was standing on the sidewalk.

Ernie walked up and offered his hand. "I'm Ernie Knoll, and this is Floyd Curtis from Homeland. You're six-two and two hundred and the only one here. I'm guessing you also know where I could find a taco stand?"

"Yes, exactly nine-point-eight meters per second squared north of here." He laughed. "I'm Sam Davies, Secret Service. Who knew it would be this quiet at this hour? But better safe than sorry." They shook hands, and Sam led them into the little office. Security at small airports is virtually nonexistent, and they continued out onto the tarmac and stood under the tiny awning over the door. They shared information as they strained their eyes to the west.

"What are they flying?" Ernie asked.

"Just a light single is all I know," Sam replied and then turned to Floyd Curtis. "I know Ernie is with the Bureau, but what is your position?"

"Lieutenant colonel, US Army, communications and intelligence, attached to the Homeland Security command center."

Sam was startled by the reply. "Ernie, may I have a word in private?"

He led Ernie down the tarmac in front of the hangar. "President Brady said this is military based. He said only Bureau, Service, or

Homeland—but no military. I guess I didn't make that clear, but Curtis is both. How do you know you can trust him?"

"He's worked harder than anyone on this. He slept at the command center almost all week. Why would he do that if he wasn't dedicated?"

"To have inside information?"

"Possible, but I doubt it. He was so shook when he thought Brady was dead. He felt defeated. You could feel it in his voice."

"Okay! But you brought him—you watch him. Anything even the slightest out of line, and you take him down. Got it? I didn't come this far to have things go south now."

"He has to have the highest clearance to work in the command center."

"Yeah? Whoever is behind this has the highest clearance also. They waltzed a bomb right up to the president of the United States. I fucked up once. I'm not doing it again! You just keep him in sight at all times."

"Done! But when I called him, I didn't tell him anything on the phone except where to meet me. And we have been together since then, so he could not have called anyone."

"Good. Sound strategy. Sorry if I got a little testy, but it's been a hell of a week. Let's get back."

As they walked back toward Curtis, the overhead speaker monitoring local air traffic came to life under the cornice of the building. "Shannon Traffic, Angel Flight Three-Two-Bravo, fifteen west, landing Fredericksburg, runway six."

"I hope that's our plane," Davies said. "This waiting is killing me."

Friday, 6:45 a.m. EDT, Fredericksburg airspace

Thirty miles out, Clint Warren had received clearance to Shannon Airport. Well outside of the Washington Air Defense Identification Zone, the Shannon airport was small, isolated, and open to standard flights, perfect for their needs. He turned to Gary.

"Scott is burning up back there. He is drenched in sweat. We need to get him to a hospital."

"You heard him. He's so damn stubborn. He won't go until I'm inside the White House."

Gary crawled in back and shook Scott awake. "Time for dress rehearsal."

Scott clawed his way out of unconsciousness. He pulled off his drenched shirt and took a dose of antibiotics, followed by the milk and sandwiches Clint had packed. "Good," Scott mumbled, "better than snake." He was hungry, always a good sign in a sick patient.

When they finished eating, they unpacked the bandages Clint had brought. Anyone at the airport would recognize Gary Brady's face, but not after Scott was done with the Angel Flight "burn victim." He expertly dressed Gary's head and left arm, adding a mixture of mayonnaise tinged with ketchup, the ooze lending the too-new bandages an authentic patina. With the little remaining gauze, he made a quick wrap around his own forehead and right eye, the gauze and the week-old beard offering a much different guise from the face in the news.

As they finished, Clint keyed his mic. "Dulles Approach, Angel Flight Three-Two-Bravo, Shannon airport in sight."

"Angel Flight Three-Two-Bravo, cleared for the visual, runway six, Shannon. Frequency change approved. Cancellation and down time this frequency."

"Dulles Approach, Three-Two-Bravo cancelling IFR."

"Cancellation received. Squawk one-two-zero-zero."

"Three-Two-Bravo, squawking VFR."

As Clint went through his final landing checklist, Gary Brady gazed out over the hills that had seen so many Union soldiers slaughtered in the futile three-day frontal assault on the rebel army's hilltop embattlements. When Gary first read about the battle, he marveled at the arrogant insistence with which General Burnside repeatedly forced his men up the steep hills instead of using a flanking move. After three days of carnage, Burnside was relieved of his position, but it was too late. The Union lost so many men they were forced to withdraw across the Rappahannock. The panoptic view took him back to another time, another war, and so many other wasted lives.

As Scott put the finishing touches on the bandages, Clint turned onto final approach, lowered the gear, and greased the landing. The smooth-flying Saratoga was much more forgiving than the huge chemical haulers he usually flew. He taxied to the tie-down area, then he noticed three men walking toward the Saratoga.

He called to Gary. "Recognize them?"

"Yes. That's Sam Davies. We're good to go."

Three disheveled, unshaven, and exhausted men climbed out of the Saratoga, and the three others went from happy to concerned when they saw the condition of their boss. Bruised and lacerated from head to toe, he looked more like a homeless vagrant than a commander in chief.

Sam was the first to speak. "Welcome home, Mr. President."

"Thank you, Sam. This is Scott Piquard and our mutual friend Clint Warren."

"This is Ernie Knoll, FBI liaison on this operation, and this is Lt. Colonel Floyd Curtis, one of the chief operations officers at the Homeland Security command center. He has been working this case from the start."

"Dr. Piquard, we meet at last," Curtis said as they all shook hands. "A pleasure to meet the man who did whatever you did out west to avoid our traps. I really must hear the whole story someday."

"I assure you it was a little bit of doing the unexpected and a whole lot of luck," Scott answered as he noted the earpieces and lapel microphones on the three men. Gary and Scott had both started a bit at the introduction of a lieutenant colonel.

"I have read your dossier from top to bottom, Doctor," Ernie Knoll added as they started across the south tarmac toward the hangar office, "and Floyd and I had suspected that there was more to this than some rogue gunman out to get the president. There have been too many deaths too conveniently timed."

As they walked inside, Brady noticed the morning paper sitting on the desk. "Damn! They've done it anyway!" The words exploded from his mouth as he saw the headline: ROUT IN CENTRAL AMERICA.

A huge picture layout showed US forces rolling across southern Panama, with jubilant locals waving tiny American flags handed out by the GIs. In the top-right corner was a picture of President King greeting the ambassadors from Panama, Nicaragua, and Costa Rica. He stared at the paper, speechless.

"King's popularity is soaring," Sam said. "Everyone loves a winner. People who didn't have the time of day for him last week can't wait to get close to him this week." It was said with a hint of sarcasm. Sam had been around long enough to know the power game. It was part of the law of this particular jungle. "We already have over two hundred KIAs."

"That's two hundred mothers and fathers that someone has to talk to," Brady echoed, looking at Scott and recalling their conversation from the night before fate struck.

"That's not all, sir," Floyd Curtis added. "The military leaders, with King's full approval, are emptying our staging camps along the border and pouring troops into Mexico, Guatemala, Honduras, and even Belize. The people there are so panicked that they are welcoming us with open arms. We already have firm control of northern Colombia across both sides of the isthmus. Our troops have the bulk of the Southern Coalition armies trapped. It's more than a rout, sir. It's a slaughter, and there is no sign of a letup. It appears a few of our generals are going to make an example out of the trapped Colombians. There was a rumor, unsubstantiated, that over a thousand men tried to surrender and were bombed into oblivion. We don't know if there were any survivors, but as I said, it's unsubstantiated."

Brady slumped, a defeated look on his face. "We're too late."

"Sir, they were moving at dawn the day after the cave explosion. This was orchestrated in advance. King may not have been in on it, but he isn't turning a deaf ear."

The room was silent as the news sunk in, but finally Ernie Knoll broke the silence. "My guess is that you did not call for a huge motorcade because you wanted to show up unannounced and because you don't know whom to trust?"

"Exactly."

"Then it's just us. We have a Suburban and a sedan. How about Floyd and Clint leading in the sedan and we four following in the Suburban? Any traffic problems or accidents, and they run interference for us."

"Sounds good," Brady said. "Stroud and Meyer need to have as many agents and Capitol Police as possible ready to move. I need to call them now. I want all major buildings sealed so that desks and computers can be checked. We don't know what we are looking for, but one key clue could open a lot of doors."

"You expecting anyone else?" Floyd Curtis called from near the north door. "There is a Hummer pulling up with four or five men inside."

"Quick! Into the hangar, everyone!" Sam barked.

Floyd stepped into the rest room in the corner of the office, leaving the door ajar an inch, as the others slipped through a door that opened into a small hangar. The hangar was dark, with only a small window in a back door letting in a gray light through the grimy pane. They closed their door and locked it.

Curtis whispered into his microphone, "The first two that got out are high-ranking military. I didn't get a look at the others. What's going on?"

"No idea!" Ernie replied, but he already had his Glock out, as did Sam. Ernie leaned against the doorframe and peeked through the small window into the office. "Five officers—four army, one navy." He narrated the action for the others. Ernie gripped his Glock 22. Often mistaken for a .22 caliber because of its model number, the .40 caliber felt solid in his hand. He did not know what was coming down, but whatever it was, he was more content to watch it through his gunsights. He trusted people only as far as he could shoot.

Knoll's words were like ice in Gary Brady's chest. He stayed in the shadows but could see through the small window. He did not recognize the army men, but Naval Commander Matt Karber had angered Brady earlier in the week with his hawkish views and insistent demands. The man next to him, an army major, had the solid build of a professional soldier, not a spare ounce of fat on his frame.

Karber's voice spoke from outside the door. "You can come out now, sir. We have been tracking your progress all night. A data search of pilots within a three-hundred-mile radius of Granger showed that Clint Warren was your classmate. When his plane took off for a late-night flight, the rest was easy. Mr. Warren was kind enough to use his credit card for fuel, so our man at the NSA simply mapped your movement east. We were going to let you come in quietly, but there has been a terrible accident. The first lady and the boys have been injured, and we need to move this timetable up. We need to get you to the hospital."

Any other plea might have been ignored, but Gary Brady had been worried about his family all week. The urgency in Matt Karber's voice erased any doubts Brady might have had. He unlocked and opened the door.

Ernie Knoll, the consummate skeptic, muttered "Oh, shit!" under his breath, then whispered something softly into his mouthpiece.

He brought his pistol into position and edged catlike to his left. Unlike poorly done television drama, he did not make a loud chambering noise with his gun to betray his position. A man who carried a gun with intent to use it had a round already chambered, affording him a full clip. Nor did his Glock 22 make a telltale click when the safety was released. As his finger touched the trigger, an ambidextrous safety lever set into the trigger released with an ounce of pressure—not exactly child safe, but then, it was not designed for children.

Ernie Knoll whispered into his mouthpiece. "Five targets, all armed. Four in view. Fifth male out of sight, presumed by office door."

Curtis had his weapon drawn and was now wishing that he had upgraded to the newer Glock, like Knoll and the boys at the agency. The extra rounds could make the difference between success and failure, but his job relied on brainpower, not gunpowder. He had grown lax despite every tenet of training, and now his failure could have group consequences.

"For want of a nail," he muttered to himself as he secured his grip on the older-model 9 mm.

Matt Karber was in front, and just behind him stood a massively built soldier wearing the insignia of the Army Rangers, the name Lynde clearly stitched on his nametag. His countenance was the unsettling one. Never smiling, too serious, Brady sensed that he was all business.

"What happened to my family?" Brady pressed. "Are they okay?"

"They were leaving for Idaho, sir," Karber said. "They were just entering the beltway toward Andrews when a drunk driver hit them. They are pretty banged up. The first lady has a fractured rib, and Jeremy has a broken leg. He is in a lot of pain. They want you there, sir."

"Thanks, Matt. How do we get there?"

"We will drive you there, sir. There are just the three of you, and there is room for your pilot friend."

"Very well, let's go."

"What about the plan, Mr. President? Shouldn't we go to the White House first?" The voice came from behind Brady.

"This must be the infamous Dr. Piquard," the Army Ranger said. "You are a hard man to find, Doctor. You should have stayed home. You have a nice family. I've been watching them."

His subtle smile was almost imperceptible, but Scott's blood heated at the implied threat, and he took Brady by the elbow, pulling him back into the hangar a step. "Let's follow through with the plan, Gary," he whispered. "We need lockdown as soon as possible. If they *are* in the hospital, then there is nothing we can do now that we can't do later. Trust no one."

Gary shook his head in agreement. "Gentlemen, we have a complication. We appreciate your help but would prefer that you simply escort us to the White House. We have our own transportation and need to use it for security reasons. After that, we can proceed to the hospital."

"That is not going to work," Major Lynde said. "We have a pressing timetable." He turned back to Karber. "Matt, I need to borrow this for a minute." He reached for Karber's sidearm. "Doctor

Piquard might feel safer with a gun in his hands." He pulled Karber's weapon before Karber could reply and held it toward Scott with his left hand. "You are a hunter, Doctor. Would you feel more safe if you were armed?" Without waiting for a reply, he deftly drew his own pistol with his right hand and fired a single shot.

Matt Karber stood with a blank expression. He briefly sensed something was wrong but was having trouble grasping the fact that part of his brain was on the wall above the desk as he crumpled to the floor. "Nice guy," Lynde said. "He was handy, but he wasn't one of us."

Just then, Floyd Curtis spoke, his pistol barrel peeking through the small opening at Lynde's head. "Drop your weapon!"

Instantly, and with the coolness that came from battle experience, the major raised Karber's weapon and aimed it squarely at Brady's head in the same instant that he brought the pistol in his right hand up under his left arm and aimed it at the bathroom door. "Who's in there?"

"Lieutenant Colonel Floyd Curtis, US Army, Homeland Security. Now drop your weapon or you will have a bullet in your left eye."

"I've heard good things about you, Curtis. You can be one of us. We need people like you. We are on the verge of turning this country around, and you can join us. You can be on the winning side. And a general's star is yours if you do."

"Don't listen," Brady said. "They'll kill you the minute they get the chance."

"You would already be dead if I wanted you dead, Curtis. But I want to give you a chance to join us. Brady is out. King is in. There is nothing you can do about that now. Look how easily we tracked them. You are playing with the A Team now. They will find Karber's bullet in Mr. Brady and my bullet in the assassin's head. I'll get a promotion. You can either accept it and live, or you can die a needless death. Either way, this thing is over."

Curtis had thrown them off guard, but Lynde's stalling talk gave the soldiers behind Lynde a few extra seconds. They were slowly moving their hands toward their side arms, but knowing your enemy's strength is critical, and they did not know Davies and Knoll were behind the other door in the darkened hangar. Brady's back was blocking Knoll's view, but as the army captain closest to Lynde reached for his weapon, Ernie Knoll, known to his partners as a master of timing, simply said "Now!" into his lapel microphone.

Knoll's single shot caught the captain in the left eye, sending him reeling against the desk. Major Lynde, a seasoned battle combatant, heard the unexpected voice and fired both pistols even as his feet were moving. Curtis had hesitated only a fraction of a second, and his shot missed its mark as Lynde dove across the desk and landed in the corner, the desk momentarily shielding him. The fourth officer was bringing his pistol up to eye level just as Sam Davies's bullet entered his right cheek and sent him reeling to the opposite corner of the office.

Curtis did not hesitate a second time. He dropped to the floor and fired under the desk, hitting Lynde in the leg. Lynde fired a short burst under the desk, forcing Curtis back inside the restroom as wood splinters from the exploding doorjamb pierced his right hand and cheek.

Gary Brady had lurched backward at the first shot and pushed Scott back into the hangar, clearing the doorway for Sam and Ernie. They held their ground as the fifth officer opened the outer door to escape. Ernie's shot caught him in the chest but was not immediately fatal, and the captain turned and fired a burst of rounds into the open hangar door.

Ernie shot him three more times as he crumpled into the corner, his gun clattering to the floor from the limp hand. Ernie dropped to the ground and fired under the desk, hitting Lynde in the arm. Lynde fired back, but his angle was wrong. Twice wounded, he fired erratically. Ernie fired again, this time a little higher, and the drum-like thud told him the seasoned warrior was wearing a vest.

Desperate, Lynde lunged for the south door to escape onto the tarmac. Sam and Ernie both fired volleys, scoring hits, but Lynde was strong and running on adrenaline. He made it through the door as Ernie changed clips. Sam raced to the door and emptied his clip into

Lynde as he tried to round the corner, the last one severing his spine just above the vest and dropping him into a heap of twitching death.

"Clear here!" Sam called.

"Anyone in the vehicles?" Ernie hollered back as he crept along the wall to the window.

"I can't see anyone from here," Sam replied as he leaned over Lynde's body and peered around the corner. "My angle is bad."

"I don't see any movement," Ernie called out as Floyd joined him by the door, gun at the ready in his bloody hand.

Just then, the engine on the Humvee roared to life, and the driver slammed it into reverse and floored the gas pedal. Sam emptied his clip into the windshield, but the bullet-resistant glass held. Meanwhile, Ernie and Floyd raced through the north door.

"Tires! Shoot his tires!" Ernie hollered.

They sent a flurry of bullets into both front tires. Not equipped with combat tires, the Humvee's front tires blew out simultaneously. The driver threw the transmission into forward and started down the driveway on rims as Sam raced to the passenger's side and jumped onto the running board. He flung the door open, emptied his clip into the driver, and rolled into the grass as the vehicle careened into a parked car. Sam rolled onto his feet and ran to the other side of the vehicle as he dropped his clip and slammed a full one into the gun. He pulled the door open, put a double tap into the driver's head, then reached in, and shut off the engine.

"Clear here!" he hollered to the others.

"Clear here!" Ernie answered as Sam came around the vehicle and joined them on the sidewalk. They ran back to the office, guns up, and one by one made sure the soldiers were dead. Then they walked back into the hangar. Clint Warren, unarmed, was huddled in the corner behind a fifty-gallon drum of oil, his eyes wider than they had ever been.

Sam swept the hangar, but it was empty save for the Super Cub sitting in the middle. "Where's Brady?" he hollered at Clint.

Clint pointed a shaking hand at the open door in the back of the hangar. "They ran that way."

Chapter 55

Check

When Gary Brady retreated into the hangar, slamming into Scott, Scott had grabbed his sleeve and pulled him around the Super Cub and out the back door. Together they shot across the road and sprinted between the rows of hangars to the north. Dodging between rows, they were quickly out of the line of fire. They raced north as gunshots echoed off metal hangars. They did not know what the outcome of the firefight would be, but they knew their men were outnumbered, and they could not afford to wait. As they cleared the last row of hangars, they ran to the perimeter fence and were over it in seconds. Shannon Park Drive lay ahead, and as they ran to cross it into the trees ahead, a blue sedan pulled around the curve.

Todd Pederson was frantically waving his hand. "Get in, quick! Let's get the hell out of here," he added as they heard a last burst of gunfire. He turned left on Tidewater, then floored the sedan, and headed for the freeway entrance. "Sorry I didn't get here sooner, but now I'm glad I didn't. That Hummer pulled in just in front of me, so I waited to see what was going on. When the first shots were fired, I saw you run out the back of that hangar, and even with the bandages on your face, I knew it was you."

Both men had forgotten about the bandages in the melee and now took a second to unwrap their faces. "I don't know when I've been so happy to see your face, Todd!" Brady said as Pederson turned onto the Parkway and was soon merging with the northbound traffic on 95. The traffic was dense, and Pederson blended in with it.

"Safety over speed," he said as he matched his speed to the traffic in the right lane. "Don't need an accident now."

"It would fit with the events of this week," Brady said, allowing himself to relax for the first time in days. "Let me use your phone to call Stroud and Meyer. They are awaiting instructions."

Pederson reached into his jacket pocket then stopped short. "Crap! I left in such a rush. I was syncing my contact list. It's still plugged into my computer!"

"You've got to be kidding. If anything can go wrong, it has," Brady said in exasperation. "Now what? How can we contact them?"

"I know where there's a pay phone right on our way. I can call the White House operator for their numbers. That will be faster than going to my apartment."

"Good idea."

The time flew by. Brady compared notes with Pederson while Scott struggled to stay awake in the back seat. His role in this was now over, and his adrenaline level was waning rapidly. He could feel his temperature rising and had opened his sweat suit to cool. Suddenly, a light went on in his head.

"Gary. The *homecoming* comment I heard in the tunnels. It's been bugging me. Maybe it wasn't literal. Maybe it's a code, like Operation Homecoming."

"Operation Homecoming was a Vietnam program for returning vets."

"Exactly. Perfect cover. Anyone who happens across it wouldn't give it another thought."

"Okay. Let's keep that in mind."

Soon they were merging with traffic joining the 395 into city center, and as they neared the river, Pederson merged into Highway 1 traffic, then took the first exit onto Main Avenue Southwest, and pulled into the small parking lot by the Washington Marina.

"It's right over here," he said as he pulled up to a copse of trees and shut off the car. "Quickly, both of you, come with me." They got out and followed him down the walkway, no foot traffic to contend with at this early hour. "It's just behind these trees, by the water."

As they entered the trees, Pederson turned around briskly and said, "This is all the further we go." The snub-nosed revolver in his hand glinted in the sunlight.

"What the—Oh god! Not you, Todd!"

"You just wouldn't listen, would you? You brought this on yourself. If you'd been born again, this would not have been necessary. If you had done what needed to be done, the war would already be over, millions of lives saved for the glory of Jesus. We have a little mess to clean up at Fredericksburg, but that can all be blamed on the plot the good doctor cooked up."

"Todd! My god! Don't do this," Brady pleaded as Pederson cocked the revolver and took aim. A single shot rang out. Brady flinched but felt no pain. Pederson pitched face down, the force of a large caliber bullet driving his skull forward and splattering blood and gray matter on the ground in front of Brady.

They stood there dumbfounded as the six-foot six-inch general stepped out of the trees. "I was almost too late," Gus Taylor said as he walked up behind Pederson and kicked him to make sure he was dead.

"Gus! Still covering my back after all these years."

Brady started toward Taylor, but Scott caught his arm and spun him around. Scott's head was spinning in his fever and his confusion, but alarms were going off inside the chaos that was his brain. "Run to the White House, Gary. Run, and don't stop until you get there."

"Are you going mad, Scott? It's over."

"That's right. It is over," the deep, booming voice said behind them. "Poor Todd. But every war needs expendable foot soldiers."

"That voice. In the tunnels. He's a murderer. Run."

"We are all killers," Taylor said evenly. "We get paid to kill, and we are glorified when we kill especially well. People are too cowardly to do their own killing, so they gladly pay us to do their dirty work. Don't give me that crap, Piquard. You've been to war. You've pulled the trigger. We are all killers. The only real question is, which battle do we choose to fight?"

"But why this one, Gus?" Brady said. "What did I ever do to you?"

"What you didn't do is more to the point. You didn't take action when you should have. We had Central America in our grasp, but you wouldn't act. A few more days and the window of opportunity would have closed. Our Christian brothers were getting slaughtered, and you wouldn't help. Instead you sit and wring your hands and try to act so righteous while you spew your atheistic bullshit."

"I've never avowed atheism, and you know it."

"Agnostic, atheist—what's the difference? Either way, it's the Antichrist at work. Any blind fool can see that."

"A wink is as good as a nod to a blind man," Scott said as he inched closer to Brady.

"What the hell is that supposed to mean?"

"You wouldn't understand," Scott said, stalling as he positioned his feet. Lunging, he pushed Gary and hollered "Run!" just as Taylor fired. The shot meant for Brady took Scott in the back, collapsing his right lung. He collapsed onto the grass.

The push had given Brady momentum, and he sprinted north up the edge of the parking lot toward the Washington Mall. Taylor stepped out of the trees to get a clear shot, raising the gun in his practiced two-handed hold. The sights were converging between Brady's shoulder blades when Taylor heard a roar and saw a vehicle jump the curb at sixty miles an hour. It was the last thing he saw as the car slammed into his body and catapulted him into the trees.

President Gary Brady sprinted north, waiting for the shot that never came as Ernie Knoll and Sam Davies piled out of the car and ran to Scott's side. "Is he breathing?" Sam asked as Ernie knelt and rolled him onto his back. Scott inhaled then coughed bloody mist onto Ernie's arm. "He's alive, but barely. Let's get him in the car."

"I don't know," he answered as he looked at the crumpled vehicle drizzling coolant onto the ground. "I think I ruined the radiator when I smoked the big guy."

Sam lifted Scott and carried him to the road as Ernie sprinted into the middle of the road and flagged down the first car. "I need you to drive us to the George Washington University Hospital," Ernie said as the driver rolled down his window.

"I'm sorry, but I'm already late for work." The driver was explaining when he saw the muzzle of a Glock in his face.

"Maybe I forgot to say please?" Ernie said as he yanked the driver out of the car and took the wheel. Sam opened the back door and laid Scott gently inside, blood bubbling from his chest each time he coughed.

"How did you find us?" Scott whispered through the froth in his vocal cords.

"Ernie's a total skeptic. He put a homing pin on the hem of your jacket," Sam said as he gently cradled Scott's head in his lap and applied pressure to the wound.

Ernie laid rubber to the intersection and turned toward the hospital, praying they had time.

Friday, 8:30 a.m. EDT, White House

The guards at the White House entrance knew something big was stirring because Sam Davies had called Stroud on the drive north and told him to activate every man he could, but they were dumbstruck when a breathless Gary Brady came sprinting up the sidewalk.

"Welcome back, sir," the senior officer said as he saluted. "Mr. Stroud and Director Meyer are waiting outside the Oval Office."

Brady hustled down the hallway and saw Stroud and Meyer. "Who else knows?" Brady asked between gasps, his lungs burning.

"No one, sir! We didn't know what to tell them."

"Perfect!" Brady opened the door to the Oval Office. "Hello, Marshall! Mind if I come in?"

Marshall King's jaw dropped as far as was anatomically possible. He tried to cover his shock with a smile, but the smile played him false. King stepped out from behind the desk as Gary Brady took his position and began barking orders. Secret Service, FBI, Homeland, and Capitol Police personnel exploded into action throughout the area, sealing buildings and computers to all incoming and exiting traffic, while the joint chiefs did the same at the Pentagon. Over the next twenty-four hours, order began to rise out of chaos.

Chapter 56

Mate

Sixteen dozen arrests had been effected by dawn. Using *home-coming, parade, Brigade,* and *Brotherhood* as keywords, computer searches provided thousands of cross-linked communication patterns that centered on the four key conspirators. The phrase Scott heard in the tunnels—"Red will take care of it"—now made sense when connected to Taylor's code name, Red Sierra, and further cross-links unlocked ever more clues. General Wilson, Admiral Zemlica, and Brigadier General Al Carpenter were met at their front doors as they tried to disappear. Links to a general in Special Forces Task Force 131 were being teased out, but the covert nature of their work made identification difficult.

Using data mining, ghost images on erased drives would continue to indict people in the Brigade for many months, and the hidden date signatures would help spell out the flow of command. Many had gone to ground, but the deadly thrust had been parried. It would be years before anyone would dare speak, even surreptitiously, about the Brotherhood.

The war would be de-escalated diplomatically, the dates for troop withdrawal set. Nearly everyone south of the fifteenth parallel felt they had garnered the best deal they could, considering the alternatives. Marshall King's presidency would go down as the shortest in history, and the *death toll per minute*, a term coined specifically for his hours at the helm, would hopefully never be matched. King would serve out his vice presidency distanced, like a leper on an island, an example for those whose ambition might tempt them beyond judgment.

The Brady family had never left Camp David, and there had been no accident. Gary Brady's star had never shone brighter. His personal suffering and near death made him even more loved. A hero is best born in a crisis.

A floor of the surgical wing had been commandeered by the Secret Service, and Scott's care was directed by the chief of surgery and eight consultants, each a department chairman. Surgery went well, and blood loss proved tolerable.

A private jet had whisked the Piquard family to Washington while Scott was in surgery. Rachael left the children with the Bradys while she made the initial hospital visit. She needed to see him alone the first time. She had too much to tell him, so many ways to say she was sorry for not supporting his decisions, and was too worried how she would find him.

Rachael approached the room with a trepidation she had not felt since that day in the college hallway. What would his physical and mental condition be after all he had been through? She had so much to say, but when she turned into the doorway and saw him lying helpless—tubes coursing in and out of his body unnaturally, a smear of dried blood on the back of his left hand where an IV had swollen and been removed, pink foam bubbling from the tube draining the damaged lung—the sobbing began. She lurched back into the hallway, the wall her only support, and let the tears come, unable to stop them. When she had composed herself, she stepped into the doorway again, afraid to approach. Her husband, her lover, her best friend, lay panting for each breath, the oxygen tubing in his nose replacing the breathing tube used during surgery.

Scott heard her sobs and slowly opened his heavy lids. The joy he felt at the sight of her was all he had longed for the past week. How many times had he thought he might never see her again? He looked into her eyes and spoke in a raspy whisper before she had a chance to say anything. "I'm sorry. I'm sorry for putting you and the kids through this. I promise I will make it up to you, if you will just forgive me."

The simple statement only made Rachael's tears flow more heavily, and although she had so much to tell him, her voice would not work as she began sobbing and gulping for air. She sank to her knees and took his hand, her tears washing away the old blood. Scott weakly whispered, "Shhh." And nothing more needed to be said. Rachael had not left his side since.

Three days later, the infection was ebbing, and Scott's lung was holding air. The chest tube was being pulled as the chief of surgery commented on his condition. "Very little body fat, and your muscle tone is excellent. Your workouts definitely aided your recovery." Only later did he hear the full details of the previous week's workout schedule.

Janet Brady visited that afternoon with a purpose. "Rachael, I am taking you home with me. You're tired, and you haven't had a bath in three days. Don't fret. He won't be alone. There are visitors on their way up. It's going to be man talk for a couple of hours, and the kids are coming to meet the men who helped Scott and Gary."

Rachael kissed Scott goodbye and promised to hurry back. An hour later, the Secret Service escorted two groups of people up the elevators.

"Well, well, if it isn't the B Team," Scott said as Gary Brady came into the room, followed by Sam Davies, Floyd Curtis, Ernie Knoll, Clint Warren, and Corporal Elton Benjamin Franklin. After them came four teenagers.

"What do you mean B Team?" Clint said, feigning hurt feelings.

"Well, you heard that major. He said we were playing against the A Team, so we don't want that name."

"*B* for Brady or *B* for *best*?" Curtis asked.

They filled Scott in on the flurry of arrests and the army of reporters downstairs who couldn't wait to get a glimpse of the Hero of Hell Week. It was the first time Scott had seen Franklin since the night at the Nevada airstrip. "I am so sorry about your leg, but I only had one chance. My best friend was going to die if I failed. I hope it doesn't hurt too much."

"It's okay, except for a little throbbing at night. But when I lie awake, my mind is churning with ideas, so I get up and write some pretty good stuff. I've been brimming with ideas since this happened. Actually, I would have to say you did me a favor, Doctor Piquard."

Ernie Knoll turned to the president. "By the way, sir, it was you who sent that bird colonel to Idaho to slow down our investigation, wasn't it?"

Brady grinned slyly. "Just needed a little time." Then he turned to Floyd Curtis. "You helped save my life, and for that, I have put your name in for promotion to brigadier general. I have been assured it will be done in a few days once the committee hears how you stood your ground in the face of point-blank gunfire."

"Sir, I was just doing my job, but I am honored. Thank you. Now I have a question for Dr. Piquard," Curtis said, turning back toward the hospital bed. "Ernie and I have been trying to figure out your politics all week. One piece of evidence would tell us you were liberal, but the next would say you were conservative. You do free care for the poor and belong to several conservation groups, but you list yourself as a Republican, and most of the people in Idaho say you are definitely right of center. It sure confused us when we were trying to figure if you were the assassin or not. So which is it?"

"Ah, labels. When did liberals get the franchise on caring for the sick or saving our wilderness? Conservation. Conservative. Same root. Where's the question?"

A look of understanding crossed Curtis's face as he smiled and nodded.

They carried on the banter for nearly two hours before Scott showed signs of tiring, but the teenagers could not get enough. They wanted to know every move, every word, every step, and when the men were done, they wanted to hear it all again.

Finally, Brady interrupted. "We need to go so Scott can rest, but first, about that name," Brady said as he opened the large satchel his aide had been carrying. He pulled out seven mahogany plaques embossed with 24-carat gold and handed them out to the men. The large golden letters read, "The Magnificent Seven," followed by a presidential commendation for service and bravery. The presidential seal graced the lower plaque in solid gold.

He turned to Scott. "Your Presidential Medal of Freedom ceremony is being planned around that Redskins game I owe you and the kids. And the Magnificent Seven will all be there together so that these men can receive their Medals of Honor and Medals of Freedom as well." He turned to Clint Warren. "This time I'll take care of the charter."

"Dibs on right front," Clint said, a pilot to the end.

*****

Near quitting time, the dispatcher called to the man parking his cab for the night. "Hey, Aaron. Some guy wants to talk to you. Says to wait here. He has some money for you, and he's only a few blocks away." The other drivers began ribbing Aaron, knowing how he had been taken for a ride by a fast-talking guy and lost a full day's wages. The banter stopped when four motorcycles and two Suburbans escorted the sleekly polished black limousine into the garage, and their mouths dropped as the door opened.

"Are you Aaron?"

"Yes. Yes, sir. I'm me. I mean I'm him. I mean I'm Aaron."

"My friend said he owes you some money, and he never leaves his bills unpaid. He's still in the hospital, so I said I would take care of it. You helped save his life that day, and by trusting him, you helped save mine." He handed him a roll of $100 bills and shook his hand warmly.

As the entourage drove off, the garage was hushed, and a new respect hung over Aaron for the rest of his career. For the rest of his life, he would regale his grandchildren with stories of the day the president of the United States stopped by to pay a fare, and everyone knew that his real reward had nothing to do with money.

Epilogue

A few days spent recuperating at the White House was all Scott could handle. The kids were back in Idaho, and as his infection cleared, he was getting a serious case of cabin fever. He needed to get home. He and Rachael boarded *Air Force One*, accompanied by the first family.

The president of the United States would throw out the ball at Chad's first game. Greg Stroud was pulling his hair over security, but the mayor of Granger had told him not to worry. "Ninety percent of the people in the stands will be Idaho hunters. I can ask them all to bring a gun and help with security. There won't be a safer place for Mr. Brady than at that football field." It took Stroud a minute before he realized the mayor wasn't joking. He continued pulling his hair.

On Friday night, after Brady threw out the ceremonial ball, Chad caught seven passes, scored one touchdown, and had thirteen tackles in the Bulldogs' victory. Back at the house, the families visited and laughed and played pinochle as in years too long past.

Toward midnight, Scott was tiring. He was beginning to make his excuses toward his bed when the Brady boys cornered him.

"You said we could all do something together when this was over. When do we get to go? You promised."

"What did you have in mind?" Scott muttered, his eyes darting from one boy to the other.

"Either mountain climbing, white-water kayaking, or fishing."

Scott looked at Gary, wide-eyed, and Gary returned the glare. They turned to the boys and said in unison, "Fishing!"

About the Author

D r. Ken Bartholomew is a family physician, a graduate of the University of Utah College of Medicine. He has published scientific papers as well as full-length books. He coauthored a book on the role of computers in medicine in 1991, published a book on death with dignity in 1994, and a book on the aging brain in 2017. This is his first novel.

An associate professor of clinical medicine, Dr. B has taught medical students from the University of South Dakota for forty years, along with students in nursing, nurse practitioner, and physician assistant programs.

An accomplished climber, kayaker, diver, marksman, and archer, he has explored the wilderness in search of adventure. Staring a grizzly down at ten yards, or cutting his way out of a logjam while rafting the icy waters of the Alaska wilderness, taught him a new level of adrenaline rush. With over two thousand hours of flight time, he is also a seasoned instrument-rated pilot and has "dead stick" landed his airplane on a single-lane dirt trail after the engine blew.

Dr. B has taught outdoor survival skills for years, and his record for fire starting with flint and steel is eight seconds. He loves to teach the next generations that if you can survive in the wilderness, you can surely survive in a leather-upholstered society.

He lives in Fort Pierre, SD, with his wife, Twyla.

CPSIA information can be obtained
at www.ICGtesting.com
Printed in the USA
BVHW091823190123
656644BV00005B/44